THE VERY RICH HOURS OF COUNT VON STAUFFENBERG

THE VERY RICH HOURS OF COUNT VON STAUFFENBERG

PAUL WEST

The Overlook Press
Lewis Hollow Road
Woodstock, New York 12498

First published in 1989 by
The Overlook Press
Lewis Hollow Road
Woodstock, New York 12498

Library of Congress Cataloging-in-Publication Data
West, Paul, 1930-
    The very rich hours of Count von Stauffenberg / Paul West.
        p.   cm.
    Reprint. Originally published: New York: Harper & Row. c 1980.
    1. Schenck von Stauffenberg. Klaus Phillip. Graf. 1907-1944—
Fiction.   2. Hitler, Adolf. 1889-1945—Assisination attempt. 1944
(July 20)—Fiction.   3. World.War. 1939-1945—Fiction.   I. Title.
PR6073.E766V47   1989
8113'.54—dc20   89-8861   CIP

ISBN 0-87951-368-3 (Cloth)
ISBN 0-87951-418-3 (Paper)

Second Printing

CONTENTS

◆

IV

V

VI

VII

February 15, 1919

My dearest Countess,

Your letter extended even further your generous reception. The enclosed photograph increased my awareness of certain things, and I am grateful: now I understand the sorrow you mentioned in your last-but-one letter when you spoke "as the mother of three sons." At the same time I discern in the amiable group the overwhelming happiness with which you are blessed, having three beautiful and gifted boys, each of whom will develop in his own way in the years to come.

> —Rainer Maria Rilke to the Countess Caroline Schenk von Stauffenberg, mother of the Stauffenberg brothers

They resisted the enemies of their nation and gave their lives for the maintenance of the law of God.

> —Memorial Chapel, Lautlingen Cemetery

No one is safe against some idealist of an assassin who ruthlessly stakes his life for his purpose.

> —Adolf Hitler, *Table Talk 1941–1944*

It is like a wild-West novel. If one looks at these people . . . their level is really incredibly low. . . . At the trial all the people in the courtroom could see what little men all these people were. The assistant judges asked how such men could have become officers. Well, how could they? I had to take what was available, and tried to make the best of that material.

> —Adolf Hitler, August 31, 1944

The preparations made were utterly inadequate, the choice of personalities to fill the principal roles incomprehensible. . . . The assassin was completely deceived as to the effect of his bomb and behaved with more than foolhardiness. . . . If a man disagreed with Hitler, then it was his duty to tell him so whenever he had an opportunity to do so.

> —Colonel General Heinz Guderian, 1952

1

Tunisia

◆

Only kneelers find wild strawberries. Heads down over the grass, she and I knelt forward from squatting position, each with an old thermos cup in hand, and plucked nipples of red from the tiny downcurled stems. Overbalancing, we squashed more than we picked, and we giggled from cramp as we tried to stand, Nina with a smudged berry popped into the whistle of her lips, I rubbing finger on thumb to even out the vermilion stain. Looming above the spiders in the vetch and the sawtoothed strawberry leaves, we gathered enough in a couple of hours to make a jam, sealing with it into a tapered jar all the unspoken softness of that afternoon in 1933, three months before our marriage. We washed and stirred and boiled the crop ourselves, musing and almost whispering in the high-beamed clammy kitchen on the cook's day off.

And now, ten years later, I was writing to Nina from North Africa, newly arrived, as out of place as a transplant from the Moon, trying above all not to linger on the thought of wild strawberries, and all the other things I couldn't have within the arid diagram of life in the Afrika Korps. Keen-sweet, the tang of homemade jam came and went where my tongue touched my teeth, and made me long to kneel on the short coiled grass of home again, in Lautlingen or Bamberg, plucking and pinkfingered, dawdling to smile the smile of tacit love even as the children stampeded toward us crying, "Look at that!" A white sailplane floated over the trees, its varnish gleaming, an Ark aloft.

Then I snapped to, clenched my pen, and tried again, more briskly, as the desert sun began to fail.

"Dearest," I scrawled in right-hand lunges:

> This golden Hades is no place to be blowing one another to bits. It's a place to come and think, to be Job or St. Anthony, from which to view the stars while flat on your back in a dune or to study the molten vignettes in mirages. Tanks go lurching over the sand like some disintegrated conveyor belt still working, though its parts have lost contact with one another. The belt has a rhythm of its own. There is debris everywhere, stunted and uncannily chaste as if no hand has worked this field gun with its torn barrel, or that buckled-up motorcycle with its khaki sidecar ripped in half. What a mess! I've learned a new music, which is the solid churn of the Panzer, crunching sand with its perpetual-motion iron treads.

Yet, I thought, with all this to see, with an incessant oasis for either eye, I am brutally lonely; I did not know that life is mainly empty spaces, or that our lives in that respect are like the universe itself.

In Russia, whose summers I forgot, snow had muffled everything, but in the Tunisian desert sound came into its own, and the silence over the dunes was wholly unlike that over the snow. The silence blazed vacant and upward into the never-ending blue, whereas in Russia the sound seemed unable to lose itself and hugged you as you moved about.

I was glad to be in a place where the sun had not vanished into some abyss above you, but plastered you non-stop, made metal impossible to touch, perspiration blind you by day, and sudden chills wake you at night. The sturdiest of communication planes, the Fieseler Stork, became a familiar sight, always flying low, an aircraft a plumber might have dreamed up, not so much ungainly as littered with afterthoughts, so much so that it might have doubled as a tractor or a launch pier for a rocket. I saw men sleeping alongside a tank's treads and one man trimming another's hair with a safety razor while both stood on a blanket as if to protect the sand. Trousers aired on the barrels of tanks' 75-millimeter guns. Rubber-kneed soldiers floundered upward in sand dunes or crouched for cover alongside ammunition boxes stacked behind a wall. I took a stand-up bath with my feet in an enamel basin, using only two or three liters. Incongruous images found a permanent home in my brain, from naked soldiers gargling at a well, with clumps of untidy thornbush at their feet, to a dump for tires that looked like leftovers from some giant's game; from wounded tourniqueted soldiers huddled in a corner of a roofless house, with a black wooden cross behind them against the wall, to Italian tanks padded with sandbags to bolster their flimsy armor.

We used everything we found in this zone of the imported; nothing we needed grew there of its own accord, and you had an acute sense of being merely a figure against an overpowering ground. Interlopers, intruders, but, more than either, arbitrary aliens whose own customs became stranger day by day, almost as if there were no appropriate region to return to. You did not belong in the desert, but through some weird reversal of the converse you did not belong anywhere else either. You felt a denatured human, stuck in the middle of nowhere according to farfetched rules. A salute in the desert was a vain wave at the sun. A pair of heels clicked was the shuffle of a lizard against the sand. A command was a long-level horizontal echo that went out and out, ranging over the impacted flatness and ending only God knew where. Words themselves were the meagerest signs in that enveloping fug. You felt very much on the surface of a *planet*, one of whose wastelands we were plowing up to no visible end.

All the same, it took me only a few days to learn the ropes, adjust to the furious alternation of lull and combat. I saw how the 18-88 flak gun, used as an anti-tank weapon, had too high a silhouette and so had to be dug well in. Peering through the downward vision window of a Stork flying at no more than eighty kilometers an hour, I saw another aircraft flash past beneath us, to one side, four times as fast. The Messerschmitt seemed like a piece of the desert on the move. Its black patches corresponded to those immediately below it. Its fawn was that of the sand. I saw only the black cross, trimmed white, on the side of the fuselage, the erect silhouette of the fin, the blurred whir of the airscrew, a flash of canopy, a sprig of aerial. Then it was gone, a thing burst up from underground with debris from the desert on its top, homing fast.

How few of them there were in the early spring of 1943.

This one should have been above us, to protect, not skulking low, like some mechanical lizard.

"An *archeologist*," my pilot sneered. We had a single machine gun, pointed upward from the rear of the cabin, and three fifty-round magazines. "The falcon scoots back home to mother. And we're the sitting duck who protects his rear. They can keep their damned Messerschmitts anyway. That was one of the 109 Gustavs. You're always having to trim them. They only fly well on full power. And they're bastards to land. They swing around when you take off and the wing slots come open during tight turns. Funny, once you've taken off all right, you try not to think about landing, and once you're down you don't want to take the lousy thing up again. I flew 'em once. I suppose it shows! I smashed up three of those babies before they shipped me out." His voice had become louder with each word.

What could I say? All *this* plane was good for was looking down: the side windows were actually wider than the body. We were a wind chime on stilts. Was there, above us, like the force that controlled the ancient Greek gods, yet another Stork, not to help us out, but to observe our end? No one shot us down. I saw the front as it was on my map, from a few thousand meters, where it was cooler, for which I thanked God, and vowed not to go up again, not in one of *those* at least. *Storks* indeed!

Regrounded, to peppery heat and the taste of salt, I saw funnel-shaped clouds of smoke from burning tanks hang in the sky from day to day, creating unusual patterns of wedge and cone. Spatted and greenhouse-canopied Stuka dive-bombers took off from the roughest runways I had ever seen, pitted with scrub and shrapnellike stones, but they always lurched into the air at the very last like birds of prey with broken wings. I took soup in the open at a makeshift table, with the hottest of spoons. I became accustomed to the aroma of musk, which made men smell like laundry, but I never got accustomed to the way in which one's underclothing went from soaked to stiff, from stiff to bonily unabsorbent, and, when at last removed, made a faint tearing sound like adhesive bandage.

Far from the snow-wrapped atrocities in Russia and the lush greens of the Bamberg countryside, after a week I was an old hand, an old sweat, but after a month even more out of my element than when I began. In the desert, I found, what you learn has no lasting power. Desert warfare you can learn about, especially on the spot; but something subtractive in the atmosphere denudes you daily of what you think you have acquired. No doubt the famous Colonel Lawrence had written about this, in a book I never read. I knew only that in the desert you were always present at the hypothesis of your own absence, and your actually being there made hardly the slightest difference. After two months, I was (I flattered myself) more than competent as an operations staff officer, but my sense of self had dwindled steadily from the end of the first week, and each day that I wasn't intent upon some problem with a map and a wadi, a stalled tank and the new exigencies of tank warfare in hilly country, I sensed bits of me missing, as if a small cube of me that was there yesterday had fallen away. Dilapidation of the soul.

But browsers in the Divisional Records Office saw just a strong-enough face in photogravure that matched a strong-enough face in the flesh—seen in profile, anyway. The thick dark hair, already graying, tended to wave and would have done so had it not been clipped severely short, as befitted my trade. My solid underjowl was that of a man-about-town whose mildly convex nose suggested its use as a beak. My ears were small, a sure sign, as Lord Byron pointed out, of an aristocrat. My cheekbones seemed forced upward and outward by the tense clamp of my mouth, which, while remaining a level line, promised a haughty pout, or the start of one, as the lower lip moved always a fraction too far forward. The bottom of my philtrum bulged. My thickish eyebrows almost met. It was a face which, had I met it on a stranger, would have worried me as rather self-satisfied, with a touch of something unreliable running through it, a flash or cordial self-interest that wanted to be praised.

Perhaps discerning observers found clues in my face to the gentle disarray beneath: the man of parts whose pieces didn't quite fit together; but if they knew they never told.

Enough of me stayed put one moonless night when we were surrounded by British troops. It was hard to tell who was where, but the British seemed to know, or they thought they knew, firing non-stop into the darkness. I could tell from the flashes that we were encircled a good three hundred degrees, through another sixty of which we would have to withdraw and, once out of range, get back into the main line of retreat as best we could.

In my best British tones, learned from Professor Pfau in Hannover and for two weeks polished at the Royal Military College, Sandhurst, I called out, "I say, stop shooting, you chaps, for God's sake! We're in the direct line of your fire!" It worked, and in the velvet lull that followed we crept out through the gap, crouched low, each man touching the back of the one in front of him for bearings. Once we were some hundred meters away and no longer running into enemy positions, I shouted as loudly as I could, "O.K., chaps. Fire at will again!"

After a pause, they did, mainly perhaps to bolster their spirits; in fact, they were aiming at vacancy or, in view of how much they seemed to be moving around, one another. Half a kilometer away, we could still hear sporadic firing as the British wasted their ammunition, calling out to one another in a fashion I would have thought dangerous, considering how far in the desert a voice carried.

No doubt the British commander reported the whole thing as a successful action, although puzzled by reinforcements who had come and gone unknown. As for myself, I told that story several times, carefully unembellished, but dramatized at least as far as the British accent went, and each time I heard again the sounds of one September Saturday when I witnessed a game of cricket on the gigantic manicured lawn which was the Military College playing field. To me it seemed a game for the annihilation of time, for the genteelest imaginable dispersal of vigor into dreamy and haphazard stances to which the numbers that appeared on the scoreboard bore no more relation than psalms sung have to the awesome silence in the farthest reaches of the universe.

2

Carthage

◆

You never hear the one that gets you, but the one that gets you in a minor way—nicks an earlobe, lops a finger's tip—can be the loudest thing in a lifetime. I had become thin enough for some sand to get between my finger and the broad gold ring that bore the inscription *Finis Initium*—the end is the beginning, a fairly orthodox Christian sentiment. Kneeling, out of well-schooled prudence, I was moving the ring to and fro to unstick the grains, most of them a dun graphite in color. My open shirt allowed the small golden cross to swing forward from my chest on its simple chain, and I thought of Nina at home in Bamberg, with her parents and our children in the dredged-out greens of German winter's end. In the distance someone was unfurling a map like a piece of unwieldy laundry. Others were dismantling a trestle table. It was a drab little scene, with the humans mere silhouettes against the eye-blighting azure and the creamy scald of the desert itself: ideal for a bout of self-imposed misery, whether homesickness or just the longing for war to end so that we could all go frolic in the sea.

I suddenly felt overcome by the presence of emblems unnoticed for days. The cross was an heirloom from the Lerchenfeld family, my first gift from Nina, and it was this rather than the ring—dating from my first years of soldiering—that stirred my heart, made it muddy and thick. I fondled the ring, tapped the cross back against my chest, perhaps to clear my downward line of sight, slightly lost my footing, and swayed, with one knee poking upward as the other sagged back. There came a twinge of neuralgia in the upper knee, no more than a faint surprise followed by the wry thought that I was beginning to creak a bit even in this unhumid paradise, and then I heard a bang, more like a stifled thwack, followed at once by several others. All the silhouettes in the middle distance had vanished, as had the fluttering map and the folding table.

Utter windless silence over the camelthorn scrub.

Next a coughing moan forty yards away, coming level to me through a mirage.

Someone came running. Over there a man had been killed, in one of those puffs of smoke; another had been injured. I churned against the sand in order to get up, but I fell over, an odd taste of bile in my mouth as if I had licked a revolver barrel, and something in my kneecap felt bizarrely free.

"Colonel, you are bleeding" was all I heard.

"No, really? It couldn't possibly . . ." It could, though; something had cut through my knee and gone its erratic way, and I would have felt more pain if I had bumped the knee against a table leg.

"Clean wound," I heard as someone wasted good cognac on the scratch, "but deep enough." And the silly thought came to me, *Don't get sand in it*. Later, when I buttoned up my shirt, I privately added the gash in my American-style trousers to the cross and the ring. Another emblem. I had been spared to read a prayer over the dead man and to promise my commander, Freiherr von Broich, that from then on I would *use* the foxhole not far from the caravan. I had discovered one of the crucial ironies of desert warfare, and I told a new arrival:

"The desert, in certain lulls, tempts you into a special euphoria. And various delusions. Such as: Out of this unblemished sky no death can come. Sunbathe all day. Not so much as a snuffle at night. But it's quite otherwise. This is mortality's paradise, a picture postcard without mercy, a reminder of mankind's uncanny skill at converting bliss into horror, simply because—by some standards anyway—there's no horror there to begin with." He flinched. "And then we show our prowess by eradicating the horror in the most barbaric way imaginable. Sorry," I joshed. "End of sermon. There's work to do. The phone still rings. Even now a whim from Berlin is streaking toward us to cancel the one that arrived only ten minutes ago! What a rabble."

He laughed but in so subdued a manner that I looked at my knee, still oozing a little. "You can't expect people who have broken their spine once or twice," he recited with accusatory slyness, "to stand up straight when a new decision has to be made!"

"It has a familiar ring." Had he been talking to Nina?

"Claus von Stauffenberg, late in 1938," he said. "I must

have met a dozen men who quoted it." And he was off, with the most parabolical salute I had ever seen, something in which a wave, a *Heil*, and a traffic policeman's flourish mixed in ceremonious spiral. I was shamed, unable to spot one of my own wisecracks, of which there were few enough, if indeed it was one at all. Already I was old enough for one part of me to have forgotten the others, or at least no longer to have any bearing on them. Waiting, aloneness, celibacy: how I loathed them, and now some anonymous, no doubt ruddy-faced artilleryman beyond the horizon had sent a tooth-sized bit of poor-quality metal to peck my knee, to remind me that the war went on. I had left Germany, saying, "High time I got the hell out of *this* army!" I had opened my mouth wide on all kinds of inappropriate occasions. The war in the desert was as good as lost; exemplary as our retreat was, to the Tunis bridgehead away from an army *its* government had not abandoned, it was still a retreat. Helpless to do anything while with the ever-relocating headquarters, I was just as helpless among the blood-soaked dunes. Fuming with disappointment, I wrote an almost reckless letter to Zeitzler, Chief of the General Staff, who had stood up to his Führer all through the Stalingrad debacle. It required no answer, of course.

Yet even that wasn't enough. My knee healed, but my mind gnawed away. The days passed in a humiliating doldrum of salt-smelling men and machines hot enough to be fresh from the foundry. Then I heard that my sculptor friend, Frank Mehnert, had been killed in combat on Lake Ilmen: the second friend to go, the first having been the poet Wolfgang Hoffman, six months earlier, at Sevastopol. Life was withering in the pink, I told myself. Yet *I* was alive and eager. Amazed, I stroked my eyebrows, absently wondering why they had grown so bushy-bristly in the last year or two, and certain hairs self-announcingly long. With field glasses I raked the distance on all sides, thrilled to see that nothing moved in that sable blank except mirages waxing white above and below the horizon.

To whom did it matter that, some nights, when sleeplessness converted itself into the malaise I nicknamed "fluttery tummy," I let the tears form and pool upon my open eyes, even as meteors flashed into the atmosphere? I had a devastating sense that this was *my life* dribbling through my fingers like sand; a door closed, a friend died, a parent went on aging, and I was caught up in some preposterous charade that honored the family tradition while it gobbled up my future. Waking felt no better, with the dunes and wadis like smoothed-out drinking chocolate until the sun rose higher, revealing a deathscape from some other planet. It was easy to shed a tear, to call to mind the elegant although sometimes too poignant ruminations of the aviator Antoine de Saint-Exupéry (whose desert raptures I remembered well), but it was unspeakable to have to school myself in an old philosophy that said, Never mind how unpromising your moments are; they are *your* moments, they will not come again; therefore squeeze them—savor them, drain them, cram them—for all you are worth. *Notice, notice, notice.*

So I did, reluctantly, yet alert for the sake of being alert, an almost impersonal witness whose senses never quite spoke the language of his mind. Such a provisional existence made me ache; I had become the desert's thing, the war's thing, and (I told myself) Paperhanger Schicklgruber's too, whom I called "S'gruber" in my heart.

Then the entire front went up in flames. The Italians surrendered while Germans fought on and our own higher command began to quarrel among themselves, blaming the Italians. Air attacks poured upon us from all points of the compass, strafing everything in sight, so much so that the ground troops couldn't move. There was nothing to do but retreat northward by night, and I found myself moving toward Gafsa with all the tattered panoply of modern strategy: map cases, folding tables, dividers, protractors, files in steel boxes, and my own battered shaving things. In crumpled trousers and an Afrika Korps shirt, hastily wiping mud and glass splinters off my maps, I must have been an unimpressive figure in the divisional command post (a trailer) in the olive grove west of Sidi Mansour. Was this the free-reined intellectual who, with the fastidious, heavily educated von Broich, talked until midnight of literature, philosophy, and politics? I saw that question in the eyes of the recently arrived young lieutenant, Albrecht von Hagen, who quoted so slyly and listened so hard.

"What do you think," I asked him right out, "is the *point* of your being sent here to Tunis just now? If any!"

His answer was the epitome of unamused, civil candor. "To get myself taken prisoner, I suppose. I'm hardly going to reverse the direction of the war single-handed."

I laughed feebly. "That's about the size of it. We're lucky. That'll be the end of the war for us." Then I sent him on his way, having once again insisted, in my not quite military busy way, on meeting everyone, whatever his rank. I had never agreed with the clinical view which said, If you had to order men to their deaths, better not know them. I knew almost all of mine by name, which made me a sort of walking hotel register. *Hagen*, I made a mental note: a younger Broich?

Only seconds later we were being shelled, and, as soon as he entered the trailer, I stood and pointed out to Hagen the two foxholes not far from the window.

"If that starts up again," I told him, with a spry jollity I didn't feel, "*you* take the right-hand one, and I'll take the other." I could hardly give him my best attention, trying to explain to commanders under fire that they could neither expect reinforcements nor retreat. We had no reserves and we would have to hold the line until sunset if the Italians in the south were not to be swallowed up from behind. The phones buzzed non-stop.

"Yes, yes," I yelled into the mouthpiece, "I too have been face-down in the muck. I can hear infantry fire even as I'm talking. I'm sorry, but there's nothing we can do. Over. Out."

All the time, the absurdity of desert warfare hovered just be-

yond the fringe of my mind's eye: soldiers lost in a sandstorm
en route from a tent to the latrine, as if in echo of what had
happened on polar expeditions; games of football, played by
either side, ludicrously left uninterrupted by an ethic that respected the leather ball more than life itself; the eerie way in
which, on the sand, we seemed to be using the principles of naval warfare, with no towns or cities to get in our behemoth
way; the terrible sights to be found inside the inadequately armored British tanks; the sweet-sour stench of flies burning
after being collected in millions by soldiers in special clothing;
the charred driftwood littered about, which was in fact a pattern or trail of soldiers burned alive and then incinerated further by the sun for weeks, months, a year even. All this droned,
hummed, rat-tatted in my head, especially when I had had too
little sleep, and not even the belly-laugh memory of Rommel's
fake tanks, made of timber and painted canvas, lined up on
the dock, or the full-dress dinner party the British obliviously
staged when he entered Tobruk, could cheer me up. I was
tired of the constant search for an open flank to go round,
whose erotic sound reminded me of privileges I dared not remember lest I misread a name on a map or issue the wrong orders to some poor devil with his head down behind a dune already thick with lead.

The end of the 1943 Tunisian campaign was close at hand
and Broich agreed with me that I should be flown back to Italy
and thence home to Germany, where I might be of use. I was
fit, had lost weight, and so was slimmer and seemed even taller
than usual; a luxury-loving, renegade part of me longed for the
sea in the Gulf of Gabès, due east of Gafsa. Well, if not that,
then any sea. First, though, I had to do my own share in the so-
called withdrawal and delaying action. Since the Allies had
complete air superiority, a divisional commander and his chief
of staff did not travel in the same vehicle. I went first, to set up
the new command post, farther back, and Broich told me,
"Look out for aircraft. I'll follow in about an hour, once the

last battalion has come through." Off I went. It was April seventh, and much too clear to be moving about on the sand, with apocalyptically named aircraft, such as Lightnings and Thunderbolts, rasping over us in the lower sky.

I saw a slab of pale brown wafting over me as the plane made a low pass, then banked at no altitude at all, and came back firing right at my car in parallel multiple furrows that raced toward us and, instead of passing us by on either side, cut right through. Was it a mine as well, I dizzily wondered before a black sluice out of nowhere rolled down my face and I toppled after it into a clanking iron pan. At the main dressing station they amputated my right hand above the wrist, and the third and fourth fingers of my left hand. They also removed what was left of my left eye. My left ear was injured, as again was my left knee, although these were minor troubles by comparison. My driver had been killed outright.

For three days I lay in a coma, in traction, under those scalding azure skies. Then I was transferred to a hospital in Carthage, nearly dead and almost certain to be totally blind even if I survived. Back in the desert, Broich had tried to cross an open plain with only a wireless truck and two dispatch riders, and twenty fighters had attacked them. Yet they escaped to find, not far ahead, my own vehicle riddled with holes.

The pain had a roaring, sucking plunge that dwindled to a feather tickle, which then became a comb of needles stroked across my nerves. The empty eye tugged the length of my body at my knee, which vibrated in my wrist and in the thumb and two remaining fingers of my other hand. So much of what one is, after water, is raw meat, and I was never so conscious of the fact. It helped not at all to know that Leibnitz (my battle reading) had said that only God is completely without body, and that the births and deaths of natural bodies are not abrupt transitions but gradual changes. With a priest hovering to give me the last rites, I felt a new vigor invade but not displace the pain, like heat moving into mercury in a superfine tube, and, at death's door, I drew back the hand that made as if to knock and turned my spoiled face toward the thought: *me, now.*

(Scarcely audible)

3

An Hour Glass

◆

But that emphatic *me*, topped by the urgent *now*, was more of a problem than I'd thought: Who *was* I, and *when?* Born in Jettingen on November 15, 1907, I'd had a silky, aromatic, and gracious childhood deep in the bosom of an old Swabian family of devout Catholics, on my father's side at any rate. That was one way of putting it. I'd lacked for nothing except some form of intolerance to goad me to a fine edge. All along, I'd needed an *event*.

Swooning or wincing, I remembered my early days as I lay blind, with a high fever, in the military hospital, Carthage, right next to where the ancient Temple of Aesculapius had been, the Roman god of medicine and healing. I soared back to them from the pain, from the anesthesia itself, laxly telling myself, these are the last of the deaths a hero dies. I'd still been born in Bavaria, yes, and I was still the third son of Count Alfred Schenk von Stauffenberg, who descended from Hugo von Stophenburg, who showed up in a document dated August 21, 1262, which seemed almost as close as my boyhood itself, and I was also tiny Hugo waddling through the Middle Ages with a wet bottom even while my elders' lances clashed.

Then the sludge of delirium cleared and, in a half-lucid interval, barbed-wire sharp but incommunicable, I cared more about my father's having excelled at humdrum tasks around the family home than about his having supervised the abdication of the King and Queen of Württemberg in 1918. Again I saw him papering rooms, tinkering with the wires behind baseboards and partitions, and even with chisel, mallet, and tenon saw repairing the furniture. Not that he was all graciousness and charm, the affable amateur handyman with curls of wood shavings in his hair and a powder of sawdust over his smile; he could be genially sarcastic, even when he was outside in an old suit weeding the paths of the little spatula-shaped rough patios of the estate at Lautlingen, pampering his roses, pruning the fruit trees, and in spite of the austerity of Alpine seasons managing to grow artichokes. He could be almost uncouth, especially when he and his brothers conversed, which they did through a ritual series of clipped growls incomprehensible to an outsider. He called this "signaling," and it shocked my mother when she first heard it, very much conscious that she had been Caroline von Üxküll and was now trapped in some kind of bear garden. Yet her maiden name, Üxküll, had something of that same growling quality, between belch and a whispered command to an invisible wolfhound. Nor was I, in those days, better-behaved, and even afterward I often neglected to shave or have my hair cut, and I cared even less about wearing a uniform of exquisite fit. Understandably, then, I never much cared how other people looked either, and it took me years to develop a knack for inspection; if my men seemed unkempt and untidy, they seemed natural enough to me, and I found no fault. I was sloppy, and I fixed most of all on things of the mind.

That was my mother in me. Never quite in touch with court protocol or family mundanities, she lived in a world of Goethe and Shakespeare, quite often answering someone's questions as if she were speaking from within a play or a poem, and making an illustrious line (or even a speech) do duty for her in the world of everyday. As lady-in-waiting to the Queen, she remained diffident, always self-possessed in a starched sort of way, but mostly on edge, as if accustomed to a slightly different tribe of beings at a colossal distance from ours.

"I'm going to be an architect, Mutti," I told her, and she nodded, as she did when I resolved to devote my life to the cello, and the trios began, with Berthold on the piano and Alexander on the violin, the three of us making plaintively cumbersome sounds that veered between the lush and the strident. Even our pet spaniel joined in.

Eventually I gave up the cello, feeling that it was no use being a dabbler: to master an instrument one must give one's life to it, and no second thoughts. But such thoughts came each month, and I moved on, becoming more proficient at reading than at music, not a cellist but a book-ist, although my Latin was always a little weak compared with my English, which was understood even in London and at snobbish, plummy Sandhurst. After all, I had two brothers at Heidelberg to live up to.

Time began to swell: there in Carthage, under the spell of its resonant name and tortured by multiple wounds that had every right to finish me, I let my mind swarm. Like some root fertilized with blood I came back to life perspiring, then shivering, which reminded me of our days in the old castle called Stauffenberg, now a ruin, in which we had a spacious suite of rooms on the second floor.

How cool the summers were in that massive towered Renaissance hulk! How stark the winters, when, I think, our lips moved into conversation because they had twitched into a shiver. In the summers I learned how to scythe hay, and not only on level ground but also on the slopes. I had a favorite place, the "Felsentor," a prominent Alpine peak like a steeple amid the greenery of beech forests and the valleys below, in one of which the lazy old village nestled. Hiking for scores of miles, we fingered our region with our minds and senses, three brothers born into all kinds of responsibility, but most of all to the land and those who worked it. We even spoke the Swabian dialect and, after being away, began to speak it again as soon as we re-entered Swabia. Texture of earth: that's what thrilled me always, and the desert's texture came to me even as I lay blind, alternating twitch with rigid faint, like the fine-ground broken glass in my eyes. I played pieces for cello in reverse, repeatedly fell into the summit of the Felsentor, and heard my father hammering at the plywood partition that walled me up in the old family castle never to be seen again.

Yet more frivolous dreams came too, and by no means because I was feeling better. There was an initial slab of time in which, at an almost total bodily halt, I did vertigo mental solos, an aviator without a plane, sketchily remembering the year in which my brothers and I had become infatuated with the theater, not merely going non-stop to the old Royal (which had kept its name even after the Württemberg monarchy gave way to a republic), but also acting in plays, or bits of plays, in the drawing room at home. We lived, after all, in a palace that was a relic from a fabled era, and it seemed an ideal place for something theatrical. When we did Act Four of *Julius Caesar*, I played Lucius (a chance to play my cello as well) opposite Berthold's Caesar's Ghost and Alexander's Brutus. The overwrought Brutus asks Lucius to play something for him, but sees how sleepy the lad is and says, "I know young bloods look for a time of rest," to which Lucius responds, "I have slept, my lord, already." That line always brought a tear to my eyes; the boy was so willing, so game, so done-for. Three lines later he falls asleep, and he sleeps all through the apparition of Caesar's Ghost.

Years later, as I lay on my Carthaginian bed of pain, hovering between the living and the dead, Act One supplanted Act Four, and various garbled versions of lines from One and Five washed everything else from my head:

> O setting sun,
> That thunders, lightens, opens graves, and roars
> As doth the lion, thou dost sink tonight
> In his red blood, most like this dreadful night....

> O setting blood,
> That doth sink tonight in thundering red graves...

> O sun, the lion, red ...

Clank went the words in some gigantic metal tunnel in which the amplified sound of my racing pulse made a hectic counterpoint. I was dying, I knew. I was beyond pain, but some jumpy impetus kept going through me, and something as trivial as my constant throat infections took its place in the full concert of bodily harm. Stauffenberg was hoarse again. His too-light voice kept contradicting his vigorous, manly image. Cough, cough, my throat was always too narrow for something that lodged there like a bird in a gutter.

Most extraordinary of all, even as I felt the blood from my eyes pour over me again and two steel rods enter my ears in order to raise me to some kind of sitting position, I was in the middle of Christmas 1922, just after attaching holly and tinsel to the walls and windows of our drab little schoolroom. Silently the lights of the Christmas tree lit up. We read aloud the passage from the First Epistle to the Corinthians 13:2: " . . . and though I have all faith, so that I could remove mountains, and have not charity, I am nothing." Then we recited some poems of Hölderlin, joined hands, and sang with our teachers in a ring round the Christmas tree. It might have been a campfire in the Alps, into which we had slung our makeshift spears while ritually intoning lines of poetry or gibberish of our own invention. Life hummed with crackling joys and our parents awaited us with gifts fresh from Ali Baba's cave.

4

Loves

◆

Have I, I kept asking in my delirium (or hearing it asked on my behalf by some impossibly aloof understudy then present in Carthage), *had a life?* Is there going to be any more? Or was that it, so poorly remembered? A wraith of a life, at most.

There came no answer but the facts, as if I had been looking myself up, a ghost in the reference room. I read on, and on, and I soon began to believe that I had actually *been.* Two years after the twins Berthold and Alexander went to the Eberhard-Ludwig Gymnasium in the royal capital, Stuttgart, lonely Claus followed them, to learn Latin and read widely in poetry, philosophy, and classical history, It was indeed I of whom, at thirteen, and my brothers at fifteen, our mother sent a photograph to the poet Rainer Maria Rilke, who wrote back saying we were in many ways lads with a future. All lads have a future, but he was right beyond that commonplace, even if he was only being polite.

At seventeen, I moved into the circle of yet another poet, Stefan George, who had a profound influence on all three of us, catalyzing the lawyer in Berthold, the historian in Alexander, the patriot in me. In 1926, I became a military cadet after matriculating, and thus a part of the miniature army, 100,000-strong, permitted Germany by the humiliating Treaty of Versailles, and in particular the 17th (Bamberg) Cavalry Regiment, in which, after first serving in the ranks and then attending the infantry school in Dresden and the cavalry school in Hannover, I was commissioned as a second lieutenant on January 1, 1930. After that, I went on another course, this time devoted to regimental close support with gun platoons. Strangely enough, I emerged as a peacemaker of sorts, and I was much happier dealing with men than with things, which an architect would have had to do. Philosophy in action dealt with temperaments, not lumps of stone, and I felt this even more when promoted to full lieutenant on May 1, 1933.

On September 26th of the same year, I and my Nina married in Bamberg's historic St. Jakob Church, she in a tight headdress reminiscent of something worn by England's Elizabeth the First, I in gleaming cavalry boots, dress uniform, with a sword. Her face had an entranced givingness as we went down the ancient steps, her hand on mine.

Honeymooning in Rome, during the eleventh anniversary of Mussolini's fascism, we felt caught up in an opera, peering at domes and porticoes while the streets drummed with marching feet. It was a retreat from time into yet another time, from the regime of a mere beginner, S'gruber, to the regime of the rogue he copied. Feeling like truants, we behaved more openly than we would have at home; but no one saw *us*, hugging and embracing at a table on the Via Veneto, or dawdling by some pumice-colored broken bust dumped on its cheek down a side street. It was a time of noise: bands, cheers, speeches, loud-speaker vans, commemorative cannons, but, for us, also of hearty soups flavored with high-smelling cheese, mouths smeared with tomato sauce, soft white bread dipped in milky coffee, hands held on crumb-gritty tablecloths, glances held as if we were hypnotizing each other, and long warm nights of murmuring, mucous, intimate union, as if the next or the last day would never come, as if no one else existed, but only our taut or slumping bodies, lingering on the rose petals I'd put in the bed in a room full of the musky aroma peculiar to Italian cigarettes.

"This is *our* time," I insisted gently. "What we have now becomes—invulnerable. A birth of love."

"There's been a gestation, true enough," she said with a sly undertone. "Since 1931."

"What a wonderful woman you are—so spontaneous, ripe, responsive." However I put things, I sounded wrong.

She hummed at the ceiling. "*Words*, Claus. The best is in the nerves, which have a language all their own. But, if you insist, how much do you love me, then?"

"Grossly, grandly, humbly, purely. Words, as you say."

"Yes. The considerate body tells it best of all."

"And, after that," I said dreamily, "Haydn's C Major 'Cello Concerto." She paused, laughed, grew serious again, and lifted me against her as if I were cork.

Then we were back, our stay curtailed by S'gruber's currency restrictions. I felt three times the man (the youth?) I had been: amplified, tenderer, more alert to things I'd only given a passing glance. My life was filling up in a wholesome fashion. I was full of requited love, indeed brimming with it; I had moved backward into the old Bavarian aristocracy and forward into the future, which now included an advanced equitation course at Hannover, where I was obliged to ride four horses each day, two from the school and two of my own. With my father-in-law, Baron von Lerchenfeld, who had been consul-general in Shanghai, Warsaw, and Kovno, I bought a horse, Jagd, whom we chose as a foal at the stud farm and trained to meet the highest criteria for dressage. My life had begun to soar, to thrum, to bloom.

Working Jagd from day to day was a delight, and the finest register of our movements together—all that bunched muscle flexing and tapping with butterfly precision—brought me to the point of ecstasy. It felt almost illicit as, with a snort and a sudden concentration of raw energy upon a single point, we did what should have been impossible, crossing the frontiers between the species. Coaxing her was a new rhetoric, and managing to draw from her such prodigies of discipline as the piaffer (in which the horse trots in place with a high action of the legs) was an almost saintly avocation. Jagd's strict impetus was one of the virtues of Creation, akin in my thinking to the poise with which certain pilots land or the accuracy with which certain archers hit the bull's-eye. When she moved or halted, I sensed intricate and heavenly design, a potential in the matrix of created things, a potential always there and awaiting a horse and a rider to tap it. Dressage was articulate rhythm, embroidery done with an instrument of brute force, and I became expert at it because it always had this metaphysical side. Indeed, in 1935 I came top in my class in the subject, and in so doing beat several members of the team which eventually won the 1936 Olympics.

But that was merely a triumph on the scoreboard, whereas

the true magic of dressage had something in common with winning good from evil or, if not quite that, at least honing raw material into lustrous form. It was like owning a chunk of Creation's original masonry and being obliged to fashion out of it something that included strains of poetry, landscape, and fidgety trust. The horse's name meant "hunt," but I consecrated her—as I realized after a year or two—to equine architecture: I was building, or designing, with heaves and checks, with lunges and retreats, with blood and muscle and bone. Jagd was my Stonehenge, my Beethoven, my Rodin. In the privacy of my quarters, I would pretend I was the horse and, on all fours, attempt the most complex of the movements we did together. Ungainly and muscularly uncouth, I nonetheless began to understand what it was that Jagd had to do each time we went out to practice or to compete. I myself was not equal to such superfine tensions, and the spectacle of a tall cavalry officer, doing the piaffer on the buffed brown parquet of his room, with high-stepping leg motions, was something no horse would relish. Never mind: he who rode must also be the ridden, or there was no merging, no symmetry. Jagd was momentum, I her in-the-saddle architect. And, sometimes, when I was at my best, I was a little bit *her* momentum, as when she was so precariously perched that the merest part of her own force would have been too much, and I would move her back or forward with just a finger's weight, and we executed the maneuver perfectly, which a floating feather would have wrecked. Dressage became my catechism. There was always a perfection beyond the one achieved, and I regretted the time we had to spend with guns and tanks, or even on preparing for the English interpretership exams. Not that I was any intellectual dynamo, I who, in spite of private tutors at Lautlingen after my delicate health as a child had kept me from school, scored only acceptable grades as an external candidate in the matriculation papers: *Good* in French, history, and math, but only *Satisfactory* in the other subjects, and (shame, shame!) merely *Ade-*

quate in Latin. Yet I found the presence of a mind in my head increasingly exhilarating, never mind how ordinary the mind was.

I had done a dandy's quickstep into the army; but I had also moved into a much more pensive dimension as well, and in fact, on December 4, 1933, with my two brothers and eight friends, I was at the deathbed of Stefan George, in Minusio near Locarno. The Nazis had tried to claim him as their poet laureate, much to his perplexity and embarrassment, so, as his sixty-fifth birthday approached, he decided to get out of the way, lest the Party smear him with homage. Four days before his birthday, the twelfth of July, he left Bingen and made his way uneasily right into the lion's mouth: Berlin. From there he traveled to Wasserburg on Lake Constance, next to Heiden im Appenzell, and then to Minusio, his habitual winter resort, in September.

How many times, at café tables, with our strong coffee gone tepid in the wind that brought color to the cheeks and mysteriously fanned the mind's glowing coal, had we not seen the blue tinge of his facial skin? We had turned to him as if he were a sundial. His head was lordly, like an exquisite massif. His drab skin had no wrinkles, taut as it seemed. His face had many angles of bone. His shock of hair, brushed back, was black rather than gray. His hands were pale, those of a gesturing invalid, at odds with the resonant baritone of his voice. His long double-breasted frock coat had two clasps at the top, open to reveal a cravat of black velvet that overflowed the collar. On a ribbon that tethered a monocle or a watch, he wore a discreet gold toggle, and his elastic-sided shoes looked tight enough to have been sprayed on. He always seemed unapologetic for knowing almost everything. Youthful supermen, we spoke austerely with him about the antagonism of mind to soul and the need for a national leader to focus on. Far from the Nazis in his pajamas of indeterminate bluish hue, he was just as far from us, who had come to pay him tribute, receive whatever blessing

he had. His breath had a flavor of burnt paper. His eyes were
blank as fingernails, with dead-iris moons. And his hands hardly moved at all, seeming when they did to be stirred this way
and that by some unseen current.

Had it not been for that lost leader, that zealot of the lyrical
mind, would we have been such easy meat for the paperhanger, the dolt I called S'gruber? Maybe not. The death of
Stefan George in December 1933, six months after I had been
promoted to full lieutenant, removed not only a mentor and an
idol, but also a point to steer by: a lodestar. No longer would he
give us his cautionary look, yawn at the sheep-gray sky, then
read us half a dozen poems in which a bud erupted, a son
came home, ripe fruit thudded to earth, almond trees came at
once into blossom, and rigid air collapsed around a house.

"Snoring in the bowels of a mountain," George said, "the
absent leader bides his time." Then Schicklgruber came, im-
proving garbage heaps into cesspools, providing psychopaths
with a new bauble called the law. But all that was later, when
our eyes began to work again. With George gone, a certain poetic streak in us became homeless. Was that it? Even though
his poetry lived on? A genius died and a charlatan usurped the
role of god. I would better have reread the classics, studied
music more intensively, ridden a wider variety of horses, or
gone to New York to look at skyscrapers, than to have sucked
at the teat of Naziism. I was not so much duped as I was a
sleepwalker. Deep down I wanted a king, not a Führer, a
Franconian and Swabian court, not a Star Chamber of gangsters. Easy to say; impossible to know at the time.

Naively, I had never thought I would look down at the face
and body of my idol as he lay in state, somehow more consum-
mately himself in death. His eyes remained closed, but his face
had ignored the physical transit, as if braced to twitch into saying a new poem. A vibration that brimmed over ran from eyes
to cheeks, from them to his pursed lips, while his limbs had the

perfect discipline of the ski jumper's, trim with frozen poise in a supine float over peaks and crevasses unknown to the living. As I stared at him, I willed him to deploy his limbs again, ready to land on the hard-packed snow of his bed linen.

There it was! A shiver of preliminary tension in the jaw! I tried not to blink, and my eyes, as if glad of an excuse, began to water and pour, refracting his image a thousandfold until a mere effect of light restored to his lips the missing tinge of permanganate. Overwhelming mine, his eyes opened and aimed little farewell gazes about the room while I seemed to hear his lonely, abstract voice saying, *Each word is a little grave.* And, under that impetus, I recalled a meeting I had dreamed, when he held court in the upper floor of a house marooned in a flooded valley (a reservoir, a lake?) and I rowed across to one of the windows, saw the blue-and-white shutters open outward, swung by an invisible hand. In through the window I clambered to stand alongside him in a foot of water. When I looked out again, the boat had gone; and when I turned round, so had he, in loss prefigured.

My brothers came into the room and stationed themselves at his bed, but my reverie held on to me until I knew that Stefan George's life had been only a departure from an ampler condition to which he'd now returned: an interim, a didactic lull during which he had been our foster father. At once the figure on the bed tautened and dried and, without moving, withdrew from us by falling back into focus.

They all go, I thought, even gods who have come to life. Is there somewhere to go after them? Or do we all fan out toward different destinations, at the mercy of a body chemistry that adapts to life and death alike?

How curiously undone I was by his death. When he was alive, I had always fancied I could see his death mask in his talking face, but the face on the pillow was nothing like what I'd imagined, as if sculpted and tinctured by neither death nor life, but by some force arithmetical and aloof, which concentrated the sun's rays not to burn a hole in paper, or to freeze, but merely to halt them in a gray enervation I'd only seen in ferns. Looking at him, I for a moment saw all things as they would be after *I* was dead. Then I saw them as they were just then. There was no difference. We were all sleepwalkers. There was nothing to hand on.

Even so, the poet had designated Berthold his heir, while Goebbels, as wet nurse to the new Germany, had made slavish use of George's name in propaganda stunts. So it was not improper of us, in accordance with the Tessin custom, to stand watch, with our friends, day and night round the deathbed of the man who had invented our minds and made them work like waterfalls. I myself drew up the roster for our two-day watch. He had called us an elite, and now we paid elitist homage, in dark double-breasted suits.

Only a year later, well aware that I was in for a guttersnipe orgy of invective and filth, I was detailed with a friend to represent the regiment at a Nazi demonstration in Bamberg. It was Party Day, and the first speaker was Reichsleiter Schemm, followed by the Nuremberg Gauleiter, Julius Streicher, who, in front of several hundred undeveloped minds from the German Girl League, railed against Jews in such revoltingly scatological language that my brother officer and I got up and walked out down the center aisle. The massed eyes of the besotted faithful watched us go, bathing us in contempt, incredulity, and here and there a flush of awe.

On January 1, 1937, I made cavalry captain, and my ride-'em-cowboy signature sprawled a little more, and the right-angled triangle that nestled to the left of the downstroke in my final *g* sent out a feeler across the line, pushing the period, I fancied, eastward. I truncated my signature to a basic "Claus Graf Stauffenberg," dropping the "Schenk" as merely medieval, and initialing my books with a less than enigmatic (I hoped) "Gf St." Were these the emblems of someone who felt his presence in the world had become securer, more solid? Or

were they no more than trimmings, done by someone who had
felt secure and solid from the very first? Either way, they
brought with them a tremor of self, a sense of lustrous desola-
tion. I had moved, oh so antlike, from one square on life's grid
to another: budging, leaning, scarcely daring to hope that such
tiny steps led to a destiny not altogether routine. I should have
been jubilant. Perhaps I was; but something dismal—a needle-
point of bone-racked apprehension, a twinge—brought me almost to tears, and not just because I was going this way rather
than that, but because I was learning how to tremble as others,
less fortunate than I, trembled daylong and on, through prosaic nights, in lives that had only a thimble's width. I was still
growing up, inside a demeanor more crisp than the tiro skulking within, and I shivered.

Careful, I told myself, you aren't alone. Other lives wind
round you, cushioning you, but also limiting the chances you
can take. I was the father of two boys, one born in 1934, his
brother in 1936. Our ancient family was putting out shoots
again, but I saw nothing blood-curdling on the horizon. I
doted, with a tear, on my baby's crystal drool, on my toddler's
every lurch. Yet, in the smeared shimmer of each eye's iris, in
the thumbable satin pulp of each earlobe and each intricately
nailed finger, I saw a promotion bigger than that to captain of
cavalry: I had become the doting custodian of *lives*, of futures,
of emotions within me that were as new as the boys. With every caress came a pang. With each burble, or new word, came
an almost scalding recognition that these brand-new lives were
full of lively cells beyond control. I no longer had the sense, as
when crouching to pick wild strawberries with Nina, of being
two or three million years old, before any human had died.

I was nothing if not an ordinary man who had a headdress
bigger than others did: a title, and all that. I was, if anything,
less than ordinary: I hadn't followed my brothers to university,
I was no more competent than others who had slacker, poorer
years to come than I did. I lazed, I mooned, I maundered, I ho-

hummed, and above all I presumed. A man with a keener sense of career would have gone the cocksman's way, and left children to others, compiling a little black book of telephone numbers all the way from Stuttgart to Vienna, and so denying himself the tender daily complement of a mind that read *my* mind, a face without whose moss-soft angularity a day was not a day; an unfussing devotion that was like a glass of spring water borne toward me, brimful but never spilled, with a casual long-fingered ivory hand. *Love* was the word I said, and what kept me from being a popinjay, a rake; I tried to live up to God's reflected grandeur, and take such crumbs of it as came my way.

I knew that Nina, unlike my own mother, would never send a photograph of *her* sons to some poet, to voice the almost ineffable agony of motherhood. So much of what she did, and did not do, I took for granted. With what stately bravura her face matched her gait. How her deft yet emphatic motions with a fork harmonized with those she made when proffering a book or (with some new volume) making the spine crackle when opening it wide (this with a jocular smile of self-rebuke). Arm movements, like a flood with camber and an unfurling loop-like gesture during speech, came to me again and again, but less often, so far, than the look with which she received the semi-facetious tone I used when downright serious. Then she gazed at me with what seemed like averted penetration, both pitching the topic into the middle distance and piercing it there with slow-motion skill.

It was uncanny, then, to find my deepest thoughts returned to me inspected, searched to their very pith, without a word spoken. How many conversations we had thus, first my flippant-sounding voluntary, as if a playboy or a comedian were proposing to devise the Sermon on the Mount, followed by her tacit reading of all I said, all I implied, and all I never realized I had implied as well. An art? Of course. But it was also the most agile form of communion I had known: a mercury in the mind, a frisson in the stare. A slight commalike shift in the corner of her eye meant I had overdone it, but that she wouldn't argue the point. A sudden forward pressure in her lips indicated assent, but also her wish that I go it alone, not adding her support to my already foaming zeal. In three words, she was sage, attuned, and wistful.

Quite early in my career, I had to evolve some idiom for the strange staccato blurts of misery that piled up inside me. I was often away from home. I would, inevitably, be more and more away. Would I forever go forward with my head craned backward? Yearning? Worrying? Hoping? Would Nina become a series of compulsory vignettes as I rode, or tapped my pointer against an oilcloth map? One day she would help to bind the cook's hand, cut while grating cheese. Another day she would smooth the plumage of a pigeon that had collided with one of our high windows. I saw her inspect forks for verdigris and appraise the color gradations of the flowers potted along a whitewashed wall. She checked one of our ancient retainers as he made to polish the brass of the sundial's face.

"I don't want it to glare." Said with characteristic enactment as she averted her eyes from a disk brighter than the sun itself, then shut it out with her open palm patting something in mid-air.

Mundanities, these, but evocative of deeper things. When I was away, did she yearn for me to come back changed? Or intensified? Was she too busy to think about either? Or, just because I was away, did her onrolling thoughts overshoot, having nothing to intercept them, and take her into ranges of critical remorse she would never express? Each day, virtually, I enacted her misgivings, testing the advantages (we would never have a chance to tire of each other) against the snags (there would never be the joys of casual intimacy from sunny day to rainy day, from Tuesday to Monday). I envisioned a whole series of famine-fed reunions in which each was a novelty to the other and what was physical was drenched in mental craving.

Nine months after our marriage, she had baby Berthold to look after, and that much less energy for doubt. Two years later, she had Heimeran, our second son, who halved what was left of that energy. Would she eventually know me only in our children?

"I try to imagine what your life is like," she said. "I know you've told me, but I still can't quite figure it out. I understand Shanghai better—I know how it *sounds*. Or Warsaw." I stared at the white collar of her dress and blurred my eyes a little; her head lolled on a round white beach. "How it *smells*"—she laughed, stressing the verb as always. "What it *sounds* like."

"Two toddlers," I countered. "Always on your hands. . . ."

"Oh, I have *help*," she scoffed, with a ripple of warm levity. "They do sleep, as well. I think you think I'm Penelope, or somebody like that." Her index finger almost wagged at me.

"Oh, it's horses, and commotion, and non-stop orders, and polish. Heels clicking. The standard stuff, I'm afraid. The public image of the military life is pretty accurate."

"And lonely." She began nodding even before I answered.

"If you have time to think about it. It comes on strong whenever I write you a letter." At once I regretted saying so.

"Oh dear, then you perhaps shouldn't . . . " How youthful her distress made her seem. Her voice trailed away, but her lips remained parted, as if to tempt the right words in.

Wry exchanges slit my thoughts. Were they by letter or, something that became rarer as time went on, telephone? Or had I mingled the modes, hearing what I read and lingering syllable by syllable on the words as if they were elegant penmanship? It began mildly enough, the first exchange.

"I couldn't sleep last night. You were not here."

To which she replied, "Your sleeping habits have begun to change. You seem to sleep nowadays only for the sake of work." How blithely she assimilated even the worst of things.

I told her it was like being adrift on an ocean, aboard a raft, with one hand trailing in the emptiness below.

"Not altogether," she retorted. "Try doing what I do, and count in weeks not days." Later on, much later, she was able even to convert that argument into months, becoming expert in the elasticity of time.

It was hard, always, to complain to a paragon; you whine or mutter best to someone who is in much the same condition as yourself. Misery likes a twin, not a companion.

"Always among *men*," I wrote or said. "Surfeit of musk, belly laughter, and surreptitious allusions to another sex, like *voices off* in some ham-fisted play." It was her habit to take my metaphors or similes to heart, discuss them at length, then return them to me—soaped, brushed, polished—with an aroma on them from the household, as if they had been next to camphor, neatly stacked sheets redolent of soap, or imperceptibly dulling brass. What my metaphors meant, or the grand noise they evoked, she set quietly aside as something too private. So I'd start again, sending the same metaphors in different words, only to see her fend off the gist and work her usual wonder with the means.

For example: "I almost sleep better on a horse than in a solitary bed. What do you make of *that*?"

"Remember," said she, "the horse is a live creature utterly dependent on you. What if you fell off?"

But, I told myself without informing her, I have bad dreams, I sleep badly, I pitch into each day's work with everincreasing neurotic energy drummed up out of fatigue.

"A career takes me from home," I explained. "Most men seek out a career and develop a home from that."

"Your home will always be your home. An Englishman's home is always his castle. So why should not a German count's castle always be his home?"

That down-to-earth.

Another tack: I told her, "Work isn't enough—" (it must have been by telephone, I had a distinct sense of having been cut off short by her response).

"Women invented work; men invented love. Now who said that? A man or a woman? Or a cuckoo!" What a warm, ebullient voice.

Choking on the quotation, I laughed at her with tender mock resentment. "Damn it, I'm not just a soldier, a horseman, a dab at interpreting into English, an intimate of generals. I am a human lover." And I believed in the holiness of the mucous membranes. Skids to joy.

In the end, however, almost beyond words, swamped with paperwork and rumors of a new European war in the making, I bore my seed with me each leave and left it there, with an awful chill feeling of having reduced the abundance and the casual variety of intimate life to a chain of rendezvous. In my most rancid moments, I wondered what was the sexual or marital equivalent of doing what we all did after crossing the border into our native region: lapsing or rising into Swabian brogue. Away from home we continued to talk, whereas sexually most of us went dumb.

Once I became used to this severance from all I loved and revered, I banished sensuality and love together, like some sort of lighthouse keeper, thrusting images of both samite skin and slightly haughty good humor into the mind sludge of daily work, even reaching the point of giving up one Christmas leave so that a fellow officer could go home. The Stauffenberg of those days was an automaton of energy and good will who cheered himself up by saying, "The flow of personality cannot heed the snipers on the embankments; even an enforced virtue must have its due." What *she* made of *that* idea, need one even say, was crisp and right: "Phooey, Claus! Don't be so solemn. Life's more humdrum than you think it is. Life's always badly combed."

5

Occupations

◆

Asking my acute and studious brother Berthold in 1938 what sort of figure I really cut, I at once felt dispossessed; the image he sketched was of someone else, not the person I thought I was.

"What are you worrying about?" We were sauntering through woodland, he with his somewhat rolling gait, slim and preternaturally fresh. He looked too young, though older than I was, to be the skilled jurist, the man whom Dag Hammarskjöld's brother had offered a post with the International Court at The Hague in 1931.

"Your way of talking," he said with an almost prim laugh, "is soft and clipped. Yes, and you almost always contrive to smile when you speak. *Very* winning!"

Whatever smile was on my face waned there and then; was I *that* eager to be liked?

"And you walk with a slight stoop, as many horsemen do. I can always pick you out by your laugh, even through the thickness of a wall! I mean a wooden one, at least. Say the partition of a train compartment. Eyes: let's see, this isn't exactly the light to test them by." We paused while he peered gravely. "Metallic, dark blue. Face broad and neat without being round. Nose a touch aquiline. Your jaw's much less developed than my own." I let him run on, holding up to me a mirror that had nothing in common with the mirror I shaved at. "Jutting high cheekbones—no, too strong. I mean imposingly evident. Smallish forehead such as some professors or intellectuals have, and a bit of a cleft chin. Doesn't that mean double identity? And you have little bulges over your eyebrows, a sign of all kinds of things. Tenacity. Keenness of observation. Quick thought. Not to mention disgraceful will power! Quite a brother, in fact!"

On he went, now as if quoting a school report card. "His rather wavy dark hair shines and has been brushed down hard. He is capable, without warning, of long surging mental voluntaries which wash the listener off his feet and deprive him of all critical faculty. Retains a certain pallor from infancy, boyhood, during which years he was rather sickly. In many ways is coming to resemble, facially at least, his ancestor Neithardt von Gneisenau. Destined, as the poet Rilke wrote to the mother, for a spectacular career. The bristles in his clean-shaven upper lip grow in thick and heavy, while his nostrils reach back deeply into his face." He cracked out laughing, urging me to a similar chore with cries of "Now me, Claus! What am *I* like?" He sounded so young, so giddy, so eager.

It was hard to refuse him, but I said no: I wasn't in the mood and I might say the wrong thing. Mine, I later saw, really *was* the head that poor Frank Mehnert had used as a model for his statue of a young sapper briefly erected on a bridge over the Elbe at Magdeburg. Mehnert himself had helped them to put it up, but vandals had smashed it at the beginning of the war, at which point everyone had lost interest.

As we walked home, Berthold kept giving me sidelong glances full of amusement and concern, worried that I should *care* how I looked, no doubt, whereas I truly wanted to see myself through others' eyes. Not to chasten myself, or because I didn't even have a rough idea, but to remedy the feeling that I had no special face at all: only something out of an almanac, a snippet from a coat of arms. Sculptures were one thing, photographs another; I had seen several heads of me and countless snapshots, but I wanted something ordinary that said I was always there, at a basic human level not worth noticing by sculptor, photographer, or even a distinguished elder brother who was another brother's twin, an international jurist and (on the quiet) a new biographer of the Spartan kings Agis and Cleomenes. Perhaps, all along, I wanted someone to be *my* twin. Was that why I felt so opaque? Is that why I wanted my face to be the authentic bearer of my soul?

Would I know myself in the street? I would, but I mightn't want to get to know me. From the clues I kept assembling, I knew I had an effect on people while remaining, to them and myself as well, rather woolly.

"Nice chap," they'd say. "You'd like him."

Or, "*Very* dependable. You can count on Claus."

And worse: "Splendid type, a real live wire."

Was this the null rhetoric of those who didn't want to hurt a fathead's feelings? I was a *type*, it seemed, an empty heart raised to abstract maximum: the third brother, who tagged along behind the bigger twins.

I set the whole thing aside: if I had indeed come unstuck from one side of a medal, then I had, and I'd live on, with generalized immobile hair, an etched deadness in my gaze, no Adam's apple, and a date engraved beneath my shoes.

No wonder, then, after October 4, 1938, when my division moved into the Sudetenland (after grouping, ostensibly for "exercises," in the Greiz-Plauen-Chemnitz area), I felt at home in my *role*. This was not autumn maneuvers, it was occupation, undertaken during the apparent détente after the Munich conference, whose results became public on September 30. In the town of Mies, we were met with cordially bestowed bouquets; each vehicle had its own "shower of flowers," as the division's war diary expressed it. In Nurschan, however, next to Pilsen, the people were Czech and thus far from glad to see us; indeed, the British mediation team, with a Czech staff officer, showed up and insisted we evacuate the town, since it was not part of the area ceded to Germany by the Munich agreement. What ensued, or did not ensue, the war diary told with laconic impersonality: "The division replied that any area once occupied by German troops would not be relinquished." Presumably, then, if we were able to enter, say, Tibet, Antarctica, or Tasmania, the same would be true. If it was not a formula for peace, it was certainly one for roughshod extending of pastoral care according to S'gruber.

My own hands were full, however, with the mundanest jobs imaginable, yet so close to what I had learned while growing up in Lautlingen. It was a farming area, but no one was working the fields. Both horses and vehicles had been requisitioned. Since the Occupation, Czechoslovakia had cut off all supplies to the Sudetenland, and supplies from Germany proper were only trickling through. So there had to be yeast for the making of bread, and hands to dig up the potato harvest and store the wheat, and trucks to deliver beer. I assigned one supply company platoon to an estate manager to help him with the harvest. To prevent the spread of foot and mouth disease, I appointed a temporary veterinary officer to the Mies district. I arranged for brown coal to be shipped to the glass factory at Hermannshutte. The region needed all the gasoline it could get, as I reminded those who attended my special conference on October tenth. Butter and milk destined for Pilsen were going bad, so we opened up the new frontier, through which also passed hundreds of workpeople equipped with permits I myself had signed. My hand grew weary, but I rejoiced in the thought that the family name was cruising back and forth, several hundredfold, across the border. In a word, we were being useful, and I thought local mayors had never been so efficient as in those early days in the Sudetenland, and a peaceful takeover had never had so genial a face. It was almost as if we had decided to behave like boy scouts, prepared to win the sap from the land and ensure it did not go to waste. General Hoepner said as much in his order of the day praising the work of the rearward units I commanded. Then we were gone, moving back into Germany on October sixteenth after our pragmatic near-idyll.

The invasion of Poland was different, however, and Freiherr von Loper (who had replaced Hoepner at year's end) was always saying that the entire campaign had been ill-conceived, if planned at all. We were always on the point of running out of supplies, but we never quite did, even when we had excessive numbers of prisoners to feed and civilians as well. After the campaign was over, I sent out to everyone from the commanding general to the most junior private a questionnaire about important matters—weapons, supplies, vehicles, treatment of wounds—and then assembled the responses into a long report. I had become a weird combination of merchant, organizer, and go-between, almost as if war weren't war at all but some quarrel about groceries. The Polish campaign was a bloodbath, an orgy of impromptu atrocities that became more systematic the longer it lasted. I saw none of the horrors inflicted on civilians, but I was close to one which stood for hundreds more. Early in September 1939, in Wielun, a town southwest of Lodz, a sergeant major had arrested two women for signaling with flashlights from the ground floor of a house.

"Directing enemy artillery, obviously," he told his superior officer, an old friend of mine. "What shall I do with them?" The story came equipped with dialogue.

"Oh," the answer came, "get rid of them." That was all.

The sergeant major had the two women shot, little knowing they were well known locally as rather simple folk; all they had done was to hide from us, using the flashlights to see their way. They had not been signaling at all, as would have become clear if an inquiry had taken place. The ensuing court-martial reduced the officer's rank, but did nothing else. I saw how cheaply mistakes could be made, how on a mindless whim people could be swatted out like flies, and I heard how Polish Jews were being herded into ghettos in the larger towns. SS formations were committing unheard-of depravities behind the lines, and those army commanders who opposed them were being "dealt with," either by means of a bullet or demotion to dealing with rations and supplies, the role in which I myself began, and stayed.

In Wielun I began to form the habit of envisioning horrors I hadn't seen, making them even worse in order to punish myself for being so remote from where they were taking place. The two executed women haunted me, laughing simply at the machine pistol some oaf of a sergeant aimed their way. They wanted to frolic, to dance, to hide and go seek with this burly, hairy, gruff, beer-stained, bloodstained man, who blew their brains out even as they started toward him with slack-jawed crow cries and nervously talking hands.

"Take me there," I told my driver.

"It was yesterday, Captain. There is no hope."

When I insisted, he drove me in the little dun scout car about half a kilometer to a burned-out cowshed.

"Are they buried?" I asked a young lieutenant, who answered without removing his eyes from his binoculars. "We have other things to do. Our own dead are rotting in the sun. What d'you expect?"

There in the scorched deep grass they were, one of them dumpy and bran-faced, with much of her jaw shot away, and one hand frozen in a lunge at her groin, the other thinner and taller, but folded almost double, her long fair hair covering her bare feet. I smelled manure and sulfur. "*This*," I called to the intent lieutenant, "is *soldiering?*"

"No, Captain. It is war. Forgive me, I'm busy."

From torturing myself with what I imagined, now I did so with something even worse, and in the days that followed I imagined it in even extremer form, with smoke coming from the women's ears, blood clots falling from their eyes like raisins, and, behind the ruined face of each, weirdly showing through like a satanic watermark, S'gruber's own tight, meager, toothbrushed head. These women had died because of him; he enabled people to get careless with other people's lives.

Telling Nina how steeply the Polish autumn shaded into winter, I asked her to knit me some gloves and pick up a sleeping bag. Incessant rain kept me from sleep and I yearned for a small samovar in which to brew something hot. Longing for home, I faced that fact only when we seized an undamaged chateau crammed with exquisite Empire furniture and found beds to rest in. On the way to one, hidden from the main road by cliffs of trees through which a narrow coachway ran, we passed the remains of an entire column shot to bits, with at least a hundred dead horses along the roadside, and I thought what madness, what waste, what insensate ruin. How abominable to lay waste the blessings of the land, churning the soil merely to get those slaughtered out of hand out of the way. If this was the military vocation, it reeked, it smoked, it paddled in its own pus. In fact, I spent some of the poorest hours of my life during the Polish campaign, and, although I never told Nina and kept up a fresh and lively front ("Claus is always in the pink," my fellow officers said), I concluded that I was too softhearted for the mauling of Europe, befouling it from end to end in order to gratify the demented dream of a failed painter and wallpaper hanger.

But what else could I do? The things I loathed had to mask the things I craved, and I went through the motions, in France actually sipping coffee for three days with von Ribbentrop, (a man of anemic, arrogant finesse who doted on the *von* his adoptive aunt gave his name to suck on). I quaffed the best champagne and breakfasted on eggs we'd "commandeered"; I grieved at the first (or last) act of the British tragedy unfolding at Dunkirk.

"People expect me to come on strong, like a lion," quipped Ribbentrop, being one of the boys for a moment, and I pointed to a woodpecker we'd just disturbed, leaving us with a single tweeting *pip* sound. "Or one of those," I said heedlessly. "Pecking grubs from the cores of wooden crosses."

He stared his parched stare and swigged a mouthful of the

coffee the French made from dandelion roots. I had opened my mouth before, in sudden reckless bursts, as if something foul had welled up from within and had to be spat out, come what may; perhaps I wanted to be called into S'gruber's presence to explain myself, but I wasn't that important. Perhaps I wanted a bullet in the back of the neck, to efface an insoluble problem. All I got was a reputation for raffish, impetuous, and *entertaining* talk; and cryptic miserable asides to S'gruber's Foreign Minister got me into no trouble at all. What a rain-coated, withdrawn, aseptically powdery temperament Ribbentrop had! I never did find out what this former champagne salesman was doing so near the front lines.

Yet he was no odder than I, who, hearing on the grapevine I was going to be transferred back to Germany to a staff post, felt a pang that I'd be going back into the monster's mouth as an ordinary captain, no longer *Rittmeister*, Captain of Cavalry, a glamorous title from the Age of Gold! A touch of the courtly cowboy lingered in me still.

On the face of things, the mild military career begun as a Ib staff officer (Supply) with the First Light Division at Wuppertal had hummed with fire. I'd served in the Sudetenland, Poland, and then with (although always somewhat behind) von Manstein as he carved right through the Ardennes to reach the mouth of the Somme at Abbeville in May 1940. After three campaigns I'd developed a personal style, at least as a supply and planning officer: holding conferences at any time of day, letting the others wander in at their own speed, settle down with a drink, a pipe or a cigar, and listen casually as I held forth about the bakery and trucks, rations and fuel. There was usually a storm of talk until, at some indefinable point, they were ready to listen to formal proposals as I sauntered up and down, left hand in my trousers pocket and a glass in the other hand, punctuating my stroll with halts at this or that person.

"Well then, I think we'll do it this way" was my only formula as I went back to the map to check various positions. I never gave formal orders, but rather let them develop inevitably from the to and fro of talk; nor did I find it easy to get my thoughts together, preferring to hand out the necessary pieces and let the others combine them at will. It was a highly unmilitary way of doing anything. I was thirty-two, not exactly a beginner, and there I was, camped out in a bivouac near Saint-Omer, not far from Dunkirk, thinking I could sniff the sea, and trying to tell myself that, as long as I myself did nothing pernicious, it wasn't immoral to serve those who'd turned Europe into a slaughterhouse. If I could persuade myself of that, I'd be able to persuade myself of anything; but I couldn't, I knew something was racing through Europe like a virus, and every ten minutes I caught sight of it in the corner of my mind's eye, pulsing and swelling, venting slime and splitting down the middle.

Then what was I to do? My training hadn't prepared me for such an eventuality. There was no manual. There was no protocol for aversion, no map of the ways back. Next thing, the order transferring me home to the Organization Section of the Army General Staff, at just about the time the British were getting away from Dunkirk in May of 1940, sealed up my dilemma and, in removing me from the scene of immediate action, gave my lingering conformism a new lease on life. The textbook in my head actually led me to tell Nina, after the battle for Dunkirk, that S'gruber had thus far run his war pretty well; he was, after all, the supreme commander.

"That man's got a nose for military matters. Whereas the generals didn't know, he *did*—he knew the Maginot Line could be broken through. Admittedly, he bungled the enveloping movements at Dunkirk, but he won't do that again." In her unspeaking face I saw the woman fight the loyal wife to a draw. She heard the soldier speaking, not the humanist, and she knew that *I* knew S'gruber's early victories amounted to more than an act of upstart gymnastics. She looked away, heavy-faced.

My bookseller in Wuppertal, however, from whom I'd bought a load of books to take to war with me, was quite outspoken. When last I'd seen him I'd told him, "War is hell and horrors, I know, but it's a relief to be on the move at last. We're a soldiering family. There's no getting away from that."

Now, as if closing the cover of some book he'd found vulgar and sensationalist, he said, "You've changed in ways I can't understand. You're *for* him! I don't believe it. Don't you remember how he crushed the so-called Roehm revolt in 'thirty-four? Two hundred dead, murdered, including a lot of his friends? He's been chopping heads off ever since. It's nearly two years since they set fire to the synagogues and made the Jews wear yellow stars. Half of Europe is drenched with blood—and you stand there singing his praises! What's happened to you? You always used to curse about him and say you could never bring yourself to serve under a petit bourgeois like him."

Acid, he might have been saying, burns; don't bathe your eyes with it. What I said was "That man's father was no petit bourgeois. That man's father was *Mars*." The part of me that spoke was the part that never, never wanted to see Germany defeated; I was a professional soldier. The part of me that smarted when my friend answered was the part that doted on poetry.

"Then you've never read *Macbeth*," he snapped. "Let me sell you some books in exchange for your Leibnitzes, pray." I had never felt so secondhand in all my life.

In his face's ironic incredulity, I saw again the censorious smile of Stefan George, a smile made up of a dozen different elements that hardly seemed to belong together. In George's face, when the mouth smiled, the bottom lip implied something else, while each eye seemed to go to sleep, engrossed with a separate caustic thought.

I had already heard similar rebukes from Uncle Nux, my mother's brother, and Fritzi von der Schulenburg, since 1937

Deputy President of the Berlin Police. "*Urgent* business," said Fritzi, nicknamed "Sphinx Face," down his broken nose.

"Someone," Uncle Nux said, "has to try to put a stop to him. This country's one big concentration camp. Poland's a cemetery. And there's a damned sight worse to come. Things are bad, very bad, but it isn't too late yet. An opposition is forming, as I'm sure you must have heard. You should contrive to arrange a posting from which you might do something useful. To stop him dead." I demurred. Convinced as I might have been by their gravity, their facts, I was merely a paperwork officer.

"A paper*weight?*" Nux was pungent when he wanted to be, but Fritzi winked, as if to say *Your uncle meant to be more tactful*. Sphinx Face had cracked.

"*I* can set nothing in motion," I went on. "I am not God almighty. Nor is there the faintest likelihood of my being offered any such posting at a rank high enough to give me any freedom of action." All the same, even as they asked and I responded, I felt the remnants of *that thing*—military totemism, addiction to heroics, the itch to move across border after border—begin to blow away, or to erode, only to be replaced with an acute sense of helplessness. I groped for that old image of the cell malefically dividing, and reversed it: the multiplied separate parts of myself were coming together at long last, not neatly, not pleasurably, but with imperious gradualness. I was losing a cozy simplism without finding the means to a complex act. After a long abeyance, in a flurry of muddled metaphors that matched my selves, one of me was testing the weather like some animal whose hibernation was over, but couldn't fathom the blizzard that whirled where the sun had been.

So, after Nux and Fritzi had gone, I tried to catechize myself, saying again and again: "He is vicious. Schicklgruber is death. He is death for Germany, for Europe, for my wife and children, for all of us. He is the supreme commander who is the supreme fiend. I will *not* be his paperweight."

Then, more violently, I set him up to strike him down, marvelling that Nux's plea had begun to germinate so fast, only to realize he'd tapped black filth that I'd been pushing out of sight for years. I'd sooner have no career at all than help the paperhanger. *S'gruber,* I murmured, *is the foul brown pus of a cancer run riot.* Then, more rationally: *Undream him now. His is a death's head. Be a count and not a slave. You belong to Germany, not to him.* I knew then where I stood: I knew, I *knew.*

After that, it was easier to hate; much harder to find out what I could do from where I was.

Like a professor of futurity, I had a chair and I sat at a desk that was much less a chunk of wood than a receiving station for wounded ideas. At the time, the army was hurling itself about over the map of Europe, whereas my own concern had to be with regrouping what would be left after hostilities ended, which in its way was a visionary challenge. I missed firsthand contact with troops (there was nothing more disabusing), but I realized that someone had better peer through the long tunnel to the Germany of, say, 1950–1960, in charge of which S'gruber, I knew, I just *knew* it, would not be. It was one thing to be out there among troops who were giving their all, and quite another to be among flag pinners and map measurers.

That was the nightmare, just being part of the General Staff treadmill, where I was Stauffenberg the improviser, puffing away at a black cigar, my office wide open for all callers at all hours (until two A.M. anyway), or marching up and down the room while dictating to whoever was at the typewriter. It became a matter of pride to be able to resume dictating, exactly where I had left off, after answering the phone. The scene would have graced a fairground; everyone came for advice, an interview, a signature, and the more traffic that came through my office door the more complex the chess game became. I not only had to think several moves ahead, but also to take into account other games that were being played elsewhere, with

possibly unorthodox pieces making illicit moves. It was a job
that called for as much imagination as skill, as much the capacity for interlocked dreams as that for knowing what, down
to the last letter, was in each of a thousand different folders.

How stealthy it all was. I was being a small boy again,
curled like a worm on the rim of the gigantic fireplace in
Stauffenberg Castle in 1262, envisioning medieval tourneys in
the flames and distressed heroines in urgent need of rescue.
For the time being, logistics remained the bureaucratic form
of wood-smoke pipe dreams in which a sometimes ailing boy,
his mind like a green Alpine pasture in which Christmas trees
twinkled red and green until his retinas, overloaded from the
colored lights of previous years, could stand no more, went to
scythe imaginary winter hay on the slopes near the Felsentor.

Logistics was only the military version of what my mother
in particular had always done in and around the estate at
Lautlingen, visiting the old and the sick, ensuring that no one
went without, or felt cut off from the rural community. The
family mansion was bang in the center of the village and there
was no way of being aloof even if you wanted it. Peasants lived
on either side of us, and, when in 1933 the cult cry became
"popular togetherness," my mother observed that we had been
practicing that sort of thing in Lautlingen for centuries: "We
were never anything but one family."

I knew she included those dead and gone, both of our own
and of the peasantry, in what she said. No two ways about it: I
grew up with a responsibility to care for others, something between shepherd and welfare officer, and the role extended
even to the beech forests and the region's folk songs. Nor was it
onerous to be responsible for so much, or for so many. Lautlingen was full of young children named after Alexander, Berthold, and myself, which almost meant you were never quite
sure where the villagers left off and you began. Is that how
God feels, I wondered, about the universe? Arrogant as my
analogy might have been, it was meant humbly: anyone in-

deed is part of everything, I said, and everything of anyone, with the same atoms everywhere. There is nothing one can do that does not affect somebody somewhere. Logistics, so-called, was almost the most conjectural form of affection.

All I had in my room at the hut in Mauerwald headquarters was a bed, a table, a chest of drawers, a picture of Nina and the children, and a couple of books: a Leibnitz and a copy of Stefan George. One day, though, I added something. Tapping away with nail and boot, I hardly heard the door open and an old, loyal friend enter. A gasp of amazement preceded even his greeting.

"Claus, what on earth are you doing?" He blinked hard.

"I can see you're impressed, old friend!"

"But why? I thought you hated the man and the rabble round him." With one hand he flat-palmed S'gruber away.

"I *chose* this picture," I told him, puckering my face with loathing as I spoke, "and I've put it up so that whoever calls here will see the man's insane expression and the total lack of any kind of balance. I have the same picture in my study at home, for the same reasons." One last tap with my boot, and the vile ikon was firm.

"*This* is exorcism," he said, with sly smile but grave of voice. "Didn't know you went in for it."

"Not with pictures, I don't. Explosives, perhaps. To me the devil has weight, an alimentary canal, blood pressure—the lot."

Then he told me it was neat, that I could have done nothing more subtle—provided I meant what I said.

"Surely you don't think I've gone over? To *Him!*"

Laughing away the very concept, he spoke of horses, of *passage* and *levade*. "I still try to take my early morning ride," I told him, dimly aware that I was going to say something exaggerated. "At least once, in the old days, before soldiering became this serious, I rode in three days from the Swabian Alb to Bamberg, just to be at home. Right after maneuvers! In this place"—headquarters was forever on the move—"I need a three-day ride before breakfast each day, just to keep sane."

That tickled him, but it piqued me; I wanted to have said something more accurate about the constant muddle, the red tape, the incessant subdividing of subdivisions.

"Your trouble, Claus," I heard, "is incurable." He gestured at the insane face on the wall: a face as mediocre as vain, as foolish as demonic. "The difference between you and me, old friend, is that you have no confidence and mine is ill-founded." We opened a bottle and, while I was reading to him from Stefan George, he fell asleep amid assorted chuckles and sighs.

Once again I was alone to fret about Nina and the children. Like some family in a nursery rhyme, we kept multiplying, with a new child every two years. What faith in the stability of the future that implied! Or was it, rather, an intimate means of humanizing time, regardless of the consequences? *Three blind mice*, I thought, as my three sons came to mind, the big one running like a splay-footed demon, the middle one bombarding with questions every adult he could find and sticking his nose into every cupboard he could open, and the youngest yelling to them to wait for him. I suddenly saw my children as my emissaries to a so-called normal life I was increasingly denied, which, when I re-entered it on a few days' leave, seemed charged with the supernatural. Even our untidy walks in search of mushrooms and bluebells, or their brisker winter equivalents (games of tag, and faked or genuine pratfalls into snowdrifts), had a legendary quality, whereas life "at the war" seemed humdrum. At home, something both majestic and horrible seemed to thrive behind the simplest appearances.

A thrown ball, thumping against a ground-floor window and bringing from the boys jubilant cries of relief, introduced me to the sounds heard during my absences: the same. My presence was unnecessary to those callow cries.

At times, Nina seemed to be assessing my reading of her reading of my mind. Not a word did we exchange; but we did

our worrying in parallel, each's notion of the humdrum contradicting the other's. War to her was exotic, not quite an affair of bugles and drums and flags, but not quite *not* that either, whereas war to me was work. Home, on the other hand,
was idyllized novelty to me, but for her the lovely physiogno-
my of her domestic timetable. When I stared at the blanched,
light-splattered undersides of the leaves, she respected the
near-ecstasy, but admitted she'd seen her share of trees and
wanted a bit more social life instead.

Flying out toward the front, I felt somehow that I was being
an escapist. Flying back to an office in the rear, I actually felt I
was doing something more dangerous, just because it didn't
quite fit the image of heroic war.

I could always envision her at her chores, but could she envision me at mine with anything like the same degree of detail?
I doubted it. A staff officer is a bit of a nanny, at the best of
times, and his image is hardly that of martial valor. Besides, I
kept the horrors from her, those I'd seen or heard about, from
shockingly wounded men to the mass graves behind the lines
in Poland and the women of Wielun.

One topic, however, came up again and again.

"As for the Führer, so-called," I told her, "I've a dreadful
sense of having been taken in. The man's insane and has been
all along. He has no horizons, and all this time we've been
dead wrong about him, Nina. He's a sadist, a butcher, a man in
love with death. I've learned to hate him, I've taught myself
how. If you *love life* you have to *loathe him.* He's—well—the
personification of our death, our degradation. In slime."

She grimaced. "It still isn't too late, if enough of you are of
the same mind . . ."

"On the same day, you mean," I said sarcastically.

"Are officers *that* fickle?" She clipped a rose.

"More so than chorus girls." I'd seen more officers than I'd
seen chorines, but I let the image stand and took the rose, flick-
ing off its velvet perimeter a tiny toiling spider.

"How many's a quorum, then?" I had no answer and inhaled the rose, once, twice, three times. "As many as possible."

Such exchanges as these hovered like St. Elmo's fire over the intensified relish of our intimate life, always under pressure, always for the next-to-last or the last time, supercharged with the sense that we had become fractional strangers. Infrequency had conferred on us something almost illicit. Or it felt that way, even more so because we each anticipated seeming strange to the other. As a result, we often detonated our uneasiness in laughter, especially when it became plain that, in some elaborate rigmarole of cannily uttered prudences, one was trying to cater to a reserve the other didn't even feel.

"Stop thinking my thoughts for me!" she'd say, having just thought mine for me.

"I didn't, I was only—"

"Never mind." She smiled like a rampant child. "You're fighting Hitler's war. *Germany's*, anyway."

"No, it's his alone," I told her. "He's settling old scores on the global scale." We shut him out and murmured ourselves to sleep.

6

Tables

◆

All the time, I had too much to do, emplaning and deplaning, trying to sleep on slower-than-slow trains that creaked across Germany, talking supply and reinforcement until talk seemed a new form of foot-in-mouth disease. Otherwise I answered the telephone nonstop behind mounds of paper, pencil in hand, laughing or cursing, dictating to my clerk during the lulls. My working day was often sixteen hours long and I drove my staff relentlessly until the rings under their eyes became the only message the loyal wretches had left to give me.

I became well known. Someone who is everywhere is someone nowhere, but in my own case the adage failed. Everyone had my ear. Even generals came to sound me out. "What's going on behind the scenes, Stauffenberg? Is headquarters rank with defeatism?" If I was late for lunch, it became traditional to say, "Oh, he's got some general crying on his shoulder again." I took an interest even in things which were not my proper concern, little heeding "Basic Order Number One," which, displayed in all wartime offices, reminded us that no one, however senior in rank, was to know the slightest bit more than he needed for the execution of his duty. I became, as they say, well informed; I had all the names, numbers, rumors, the trouble brewing and the spilled milk.

After a while, I discovered what image of me fellow officers had: I was candid; I always stated my own view, but without gush or malice; I listened to everyone who came to my door; I never told tales; I laughed mightily at matters most serious; I took trivialities to heart on behalf of those who dumped them on my desk; I was the only officer with whom Colonel General Halder would do business directly—no doubt because we were at one on the question of S'gruber, who had actually attacked him with clenched fists and foaming at the mouth. Thinking of this, I looked at Halder's schoolmaster's pince-nez and sleek brush-cut hair, half giggling. Halder had style, but his style quivered, his mind was wax.

"You see, Claus," he said in his odd, pent-up voice that made even a bleat sound militant, "the man's just a vulgarian. I think at one time, in my salad days, I actually looked for signs of *genius* in him! I did my best to be impartial and honest with him, and never to be blinded by my sheer *de-tes-ta-tion*. Well, I never found that genius; I never found talent, or ability, just something diabolical and infernal. You can't deal with that on a military level. You can only go home and pray, and sink your teeth into some soft white bread, and hope to get away with all the ghastly mistakes you've made because you wanted to believe in a certain leader—because you had high hopes for a new Germany, fresh out of the Ark." Indeed, I had several times found him in tears, moaning "That *Emil*, that *damned* Emil," using a nickname-codename to keep his Führer remote, much as I myself did, on the quiet, pondering alone like a night-wolf, in a fit of hungry nerves. "We can't expect him," Halder said, "to be everybody else when he's so good at being himself." Did that apply to me too?

When I sat down to write my regular letter to Nina, I had the shocking idea that I'd become someone who made no sense, at home at least, save as a correspondent. You told the news. You explained your work. You reported you had no leisure and therefore nothing to say about your off-duty hours. And off went the envelope, by motorcycle and aircraft, full of trivia, while the real man slipped through a crack in the flap and stayed behind. Letters didn't work, but neither did anything else. I knew that some great and lasting relationships sustained themselves on paper, were even better thus; indeed, some correspondents never met. For some reason, though, my letters were stiffer than I ever was in person; they sagged with heavy and righteous philosophizing, addressed to a woman who, deep down, was quietly trying to adjust herself before the event to how familiar things at home would look after I had been killed in battle or some silly car smash.

Look: the picnic table adjoining the splashy yellow patch of *gentian lutea* needed a fresh coat of weatherproof stain. *Today he is alive,* she'd think, *wherever he is. Tomorrow, he might be killed, and I wouldn't know for days, and the picnic table would look exactly the same, and the birds would go on cruising through the centuries-old trees and the boys would need to be fed. Carp, small sausages, and potatoes mashed with cream.*

She'd finger the crumbling wood of the table's corner, but it knew nothing of her or me and existed only to have emotions successively fixed upon it: just a table, inert and nerveless. Yet our tables survived us all.

I could hardly write such things to her; I couldn't bear to formulate them to myself. I worried about the bombs that fell near home, but that wasn't the stuff of letters, so I ended up, as on June 21, 1940, writing *epistles* according to several prudent formulae, on that occasion droning away about the Treaty of Versailles when my heart was intent on the picnic table and on how tables didn't care.

"We must teach our children," I self-consciously wrote, "that salvation from collapse and decay lies only in permanent struggle and a permanent quest for renewal." Such verbal wool! Two *permanents* in one sentence! To be sure, I was no Rilke at letter writing; I had neither his finesse, his tact, nor his ceremonious purr.

Then, as if paper had undergone alchemy, I saw within the page, marooned in shallow letters on a marble block the size of a pocket hymnal, my sons' names and dates of birth.

> Berthold, 3 July 1934
> Heimeran, 9 July 1936
> Franz Ludwig, 4 May 1938

A few months more and the number would be four. Was that why I so ponderously theorized, in a letter that Nina copied out for her mother and my in-laws to conjecture over? I let out an all-encompassing dismissory sigh befitting someone advanced in years, and my heart thumped away. I kept saying, in scores of letters, nothing that mattered: neither the love nor the fear, nor even (for good reasons) what I felt about the abominable paperhanger himself. I should have written boldly, from the marrow, mincing not a word.

Dearest Nina,

Although the rest of the world might think we have been bewitched, and irrevocably so, by this demonic upstart, we have *not*. There is no question of loyalty; all that remains is to get *rid* of him, cost what it may.

It wouldn't have been news to her anyway. She *knew*, but what she didn't know was the day-to-day progress of the aversion, of the resolve to do away with him.

Dearest Nina,

For years, some of our most senior officers have been intent on removing this cancerous hooligan, in whom, as you know, even *I* (shame, shame!) had hopes. I am the *latest* of their converts.

Ah, the letters unsent! Unsent because unwritten, but hot inside me all the time, throbbing year-long in the aorta.

Dearest Nina,

Ever since he came to power, there have been schemes and plots to depose him; but the sheer *variety* of his evil ways has hindered his coming into proper focus—it's like trying to look at a pack of yelping dogs all at the same time. I sometimes think he's brought the idea of the devil-incarnate up to date. *Seven* attempts on him before 1940, I think, and in 1939 even the British Military Attaché offered to shoot him from a well-placed window. Bombs. Knives. Explosive clothing. Revolvers. Poison. Nothing works. Georg Elser, a cabinetmaker, came closest, with a bomb fitted into a cement pillar, but it went off fifteen minutes too late. S'gruber had gone. Good God, back in 1926 there was a journal called *Resistance*. Blow up his private train: that was Halder. Seize the Reich Chancellery and shoot him out of hand: General von Witzleben. But nothing works. Not much actually happens. He seems invulnerable. A wraith. A myth. And just hating him isn't lethal.

Yes, I thought, such a letter in the wrong hands could get us all beheaded. I kept my dark thoughts darker still.

On November 15, 1940, Valerie, my first daughter, was born. Added to my three sons, she entitled Nina, a *Countess von Stauffenberg*, to the piece of trash called the "German Mother's Cross in Bronze" for bearing four to five children. It was a pretty enough bauble, heaven knew, of white-trimmed blue, with a narrow white ribbon that had one broad and two narrow blue stripes. So blue was the color of fertility! Indeed, to become thus eligible was in itself a penalty, an insult; we had been making children for reasons of our own, having nothing to do with S'gruber, and we would go on doing so, never mind how many Mother's Crosses we had to refuse.

"Such," I told Berthold, to whom I became closer and closer, perhaps because his quiet and retiring ways exemplified what I myself really wanted to be like, "is the cross a mother bears! In all ways." He grinned gently, putting all my meanings together and storing them against some rainy day when we might need a witticism to get us through. Having named my first son after him, I had two of him to rejoice over, and back in Lautlingen there were Bertholds by the dozen, just as there were Clauses and Alexanders. Our own people commemorated us, indeed multiplied us, almost as if we were loaves and fishes.

After the first, successful winter (1941–42) of the Russian campaign, I still thought that the only way to rid Germany of S'gruber was, first, to create a backdrop of military advantage against which to stage a coup. Then we would be able to negotiate from a position of some strength and self-respect. After a while, however, given the increasingly incompetent leadership in the General Staff itself (which I was able to observe at close quarters), I saw that the war could no longer be won. I gradually relinquished the pipe dream of a military settlement first and purge of the brownshirts second. Yet, whatever I thought privately, I always insisted in conversation on the chance of a military—rather than a gangsterish—way through. I knew about the horrendous edict from S'gruber concerning summary execution of Russian women and children, and I had learned a new word: *pogrom*, a label for a new act. My own childhood had been nothing like this. My adolescence, all classics and poetry, had been safe from the midnight knock and a visit from two robots in outdated raingear. I had been allowed to grow pink and chubby, then lean and pale and tall, and then broadly muscled, and it was comparatively late in life that I recovered a specter which my family's religion had always offered me among its props: the vision of evil, new-minted, with selected guinea pigs made to lie in snow or ice water; or to tear themselves to pieces in vacuum chambers ostensibly to help the useless Luftwaffe to learn about high altitude; or to receive poison- or mustard-gas bullets. My head filled with innocent people, with whom until now I had nothing in common, forced to become the subjects in gas-gangrene tests or made to live in saltwater. I saw excavations full of crisscross corpses and I knew that, slow as I might have been on the uptake, I was now once more in charge of my brain.

One group of Russian peasants, saved from the SS by army officers, expressed their gratitude by catching crayfish for us for a whole night, and this incongruous, histrionic act stole my heart. Against any such decency there stood the oddly named "Night and Fog Decree," ordering that all persons endangering German security, except those to be executed forthwith, should vanish without a trace. It was tantamount to saying that a suspect had two fates open to him: death and death. This was no writing on the wall; it was a series of ghoulish headlines giving the outright lie to all those antique rigmaroles of officers mounted on horseback for mainly social reasons. In the long run, we were supposed to ride over the bodies of others to a questionably glorious death.

Fritzi von der Schulenburg, forever showing up with Nux on this or that pretext, had shed any Nazi sympathies long before I met him. What an amazing man he was, whom Nux had taken such a shine to. In spite of being nearsighted and night blind, Fritzi had once led a patrol through a forest crawling with hostile troops. "Tell me what you can see!" he'd kept on telling the soldier beside him. In the very midst of war, he'd learned the second part of Goethe's *Faust* by heart, this unkempt, insolent, ponderously spoken Junker with the big delicate ears and a nose flattened years ago by a mishap on the sports field. Up went his clenched fist when he spoke, and people heard him out, I among them. After a farewell party in Berlin, he'd ended up, God knows how, across the lines of the electric railway in a suburb he otherwise had never been near, with his monocle still in place. A train was almost upon him when railroad workers pulled him clear. That was Fritzi, who stuck through thick and thin to the same grocer and newspaper seller, but gave up S'gruber like someone ascending from the kingdom of the dead. So too did my staunch old friend Ali Mertz von Quirnheim, in his brisk and affably matter-of-fact way; once Ali knew, he knew forever, and he jogged my elbow unceasingly, squinting through his glasses (and even seeming to squint with his wide thin mouth) into my less than nimble brain.

"Think, Claus." He spoke it as a professor of classics would address someone who had misconstrued an easy passage in Caesar. *Pensat*—

"I *am* thinking."

"Harder, then." Glasses off for a hard polish.

Was it then? Was there a click? I awoke with nerves and gullet recoiling, head laden with a truly historical hangover, and in front of me a fuzzy objective that got clearer day by day, like a mirage in black and white becoming a didactic woodcut. I never slept soundly again, but only moved from nightmare to nightmare, with a chauvinist's last gasp.

I forgot the names of the flowers on the family estate. A somnambulist me died as I recalled, with stark pathos, a teenagers' game in which a youth kissed a girl's nose while she kissed his chin, and then vice versa, like pieces of a jigsaw failing to mate. Now I knew the truth, any other thought was preferable: any image, any shout, any motion.

For some reason I could not visualize S'gruber; I could hear him only, in maniacal crescendo, hectoring the rabble. He sounded like acid in motion, hate's ejaculate.

"Burnable refuse," Fritzi was saying, dumping the syllables down like clay. "Any farmer would see to it."

Once again I needed my photograph of Corporal S'gruber; I had got the point but mislaid the example.

Then Ali said, "The truculent offendedness in his eyes—" and I saw S'gruber again, a worthy opponent for the likes of us. A chain linked itself up. A message came from my cousin Hans Christoph to Berthold. I answered guardedly, but my mind shone like fresh-cut sodium.

Thanks to me, the responsibility for Soviet prisoners enlisted to fight against the Russians now lay with army headquarters, and not with the SS. The army had already become a rabble, with military formations composed of Armenians, Turks, Georgians, Azerbaijanis, North Caucasians, Turkestanis, Volga Tartars, and Cossacks. It was more of an opera troupe than it was an army, but we needed every anti-Bolshevik we could lay our hands on, and even S'gruber had to keep quiet about the eventual political effects. Were there, he wondered, Germans in our own ranks just as eager to fight against *him?* Into the bargain I was arguing that the volunteer formations should have their own uniform and their own officer corps. When he forbade any further recruitment, on February 10, 1942, I watered the order down to exclude only Balts and Ukrainians; and, a few months later, at a conference held in Quartermaster General Wagner's Zossen office, I managed to prevent the subject from being bandied about at a higher level.

"Gentlemen," I said, after extemporizing a few provisos concerning equality of treatment for volunteers, "if you have misgivings, please express them here and now; and, if you have none, please endorse my proposals forthwith. Otherwise, the tampering will begin, and in no time at all we'll have a hundred experts converting a simple instruction into a Joseph's coat." And that was that, even down to specific instructions having to do with badges of rank, family allowances, canteen goods, pay and working conditions and dress. S'gruber, true to form, had actually proposed that each prisoner of war should be tattooed on the right buttock, which meant of course (as I facetiously told a solemn friend) that if we met anyone postwar in Unter den Linden we should have to ask him to drop his pants to prove he wasn't a Russian POW. I even arranged for volunteers to be eligible for the Iron Cross and, on another occasion, was able to prevent Turkish battalions from being sent to the front without adequate winter dress.

I was doing my old thing in good company; I was *looking after people,* the role to which I'd always presumed I was born, whether the people were at home in Lautlingen or here in Russia. I argued that the Eastern peoples were certainly not, as National Socialism claimed, creatures of a lower order, and at the Vinnitsa conference in October 1942 blew my cork during a half-hour off-the-cuff speech against German policy in the East. There must have been forty officers present to hear me lament that Germany was sowing the seeds of Eastern hatred. "Our children will reap the reward of this, one day soon," I said. "It seems to me a scandal that, at a time when millions of German soldiers are risking their lives daily, no one can be found among the senior commanders with the courage to put on his steel helmet and go and tell *the Führer* to his face about these things, even at the risk of losing his life."

I could hardly sit still. In January 1943, I visited Field Marshal von Manstein in Taganrog to inform him that a coup d'état was overdue, only to be fobbed off with the old tale that the army would mutiny once the Eastern front collapsed. "*Mutiny,*" he intoned, with slack neck skin ajiggle, as if addressing someone who was a soldier only and not a soldier-conspirator. "If, after the war, a coup seems either possible or imperative, then I will undertake it myself." His downturned mouth sagged even further, his slit eyes tautened.

What a fraud the man was. "Major," he went on, "I sympathize. It is a sensible plan. But I can't act against the man without orders from above. I too am a soldier. I could only make an attempt on him with orders *from him!* Don't you realize that there are five men above me: the Commander in Chief of the Army, the Commander in Chief of the Armed Forces, the War Minister, the Chancellor, and the President? And *he* is *all five*." It was like listening to a professional sophist or a drawing-room comedian. No doubt he was being ironic, but certainly he was trying to duck the whole thing.

I had one last go at him, almost shouting: "If we don't do *this*, it's no use doing *anything*. We won't be an army, we'll be a bunch of stooges and bootlickers babbling to our nurses about love, food, and lessons, in that order. The Führer has to *go*, and he won't go willingly." For once Manstein's wattles were still.

"Then . . . you want to *kill* him?" He shook his head.

"We do, *Herr Feldmarschall*, like a mad dog!"

"Then that is your affair, not mine. Good day, Major."

In a blistering ill-humor I flew back to Army High Command, frustrated and more than a bit disgusted, but also tentatively entertaining the notion that, if somehow someone could get an order into Manstein's skull (which he recognized as something he must obey), he'd comply like a wound-up musical top. Such an idyll had no starting point, however, and it never would have. I looked through the frost of my exhaled breath at the smeary sunset, thinking: The sunset belongs to nobody at all. It was a suitable image for the unattainable. We were flying at about thirteen thousand meters, and the sun was where it was, handy but taboo.

In the end, I got into the habit of telling any new recruit to our plot, "Is the door shut tight? Good. Now, let's get down to brass tacks, my friend. I'm doing my damnedest to commit treason. Undermining from within and collaborating with the

enemy. *Both* kinds of treason, see. Now, how about you? Let's
see what we can get you involved in to stop your life from being so dull."

Things I'd heard repeatedly had made me bold and rash.
For instance, I could never forget something I had been told
but had never seen with my own eyes. Stacked up on the
thickly sawdusted floor of the carpenter's shop in Plötzensee
prison, there were two kinds of rough-cut coffins, those in the
one stack about twenty centimeters longer than those in the
other. The longer ones were for those of the condemned who
were hanged, the shorter ones for those beheaded. Each coffin
of either kind, my informant said, held two bodies always.
There was no wasted space. What a cruel perversion of the
Ark, yet perhaps not as awful as what invaded my mind's eye:
all that sawdust from the woodwork being brushed up, then
shoveled into boxes, and moved to the death shed itself, where
they spread it over the floor, so thick that if you tiptoed across
it your toes would be hidden. I knew what the sawdust was for,
at the guillotine or beneath the hooks, and I knew about the
washbasin, the glasses, and the bottle of brandy for the witnesses, the wide heavy black curtain.

I knew, and yet I did not know: at any time when my duties
brought me back to Berlin, a brisk stroll or a short drive
through the Tiergarten and up Strom Strasse into Moabit could
have opened my eyes for ever and ever. I stayed away, though,
in almost superstitious obliviousness, at the same time wondering with the innermost part of me why any political system
under the sun should create so many corpses in one of its suburbs. There was never that much crime in any city, any nation;
there were never that many eyes to take an eye for, never that
many teeth. The only wholesale criminals were those sponsor-
ing the Plötzensee bloodbath on the gently sloping floor, and
they seemed invulnerable to any legal process. We shied from
the truth as if it were a sewer, taking light lunches at semi-
suave restaurants with officers from the Reserve Army HQ in

Bendlerstrasse. We kept our imaginations sweet, hoping rather wanly that the courage of our friends, the dead, would give us strength, whereas the zeal of the butchers should have seared our hearts. *(Dying away)*

7

Nux & Co.

◆

Still reliving my past in anesthetized delirium, and aware in the present only of split crescendos of pain, I almost died right there in Carthage. The only hope was to send me home to Germany, although the trip itself might finish me. On April 21, 1943, shortly before my division surrendered, I arrived via hospital ship and train in Munich, where Dr. Ferdinand Sauerbruch completed the multiple operation my wounds required. My high temperature lasted for weeks. Time and again I almost slipped away into death, and every stage of recovery brought new complications. Pigheaded as ever, I refused painkillers and sleeping pills, which meant I hardly slept at all, less even than I had in Poland and France.

General Zeitzler, Chief of the Army General Staff, came to my bedside to present me with the Golden Badge for War Wounded and a box of cigars, which was like a love apple from a toppling god; Zeitzler (who'd succeeded Halder in September, '42) was already out of favor with S'gruber as a socalled defeatist and backslider. Other senior officers paraded past my bed, eager to enlist me for their staff; but I told them all the same tale while they gaped at my brown-flecked bandages. "Thank you for your concern, gentlemen," I stiffly said. "But it's for my superiors to worry themselves about my future duties. I . . ." The unspoken words left the question open, and my face alive with surplus pain must have daunted them; they never asked again, and I was left in peace to wonder why a scarecrow should be so much in demand.

In June I was able to attempt my first three-fingered letter, which naturally enough went to my wounded predecessor in the desert, Wilhelm Bürklin, now well on the way to recovery. "My dear Bürklin," I wrote, gasping with strain, and feeling grotesquely off balance even while sitting up in bed, "I am now to be operated on for an infection of the middle ear. I have only recently been treated for my knee injuries."

Then my brain seemed to ooze away; I wished I'd dictated the letter to Nina instead, as I'd managed to do in May. A sudden bout of fever stayed my hand for a while, after which I resumed, gasping away as if trying to lift my own body's weight, telling Bürklin, quite needlessly, "In my state, one always has to bargain for complications and setbacks." He, of all men, didn't need such verbal suet; but it was all I had to give. I thought in circles, formulas, and quips.

When, later on, he asked me why I wouldn't spare the time to have an artificial hand fitted, and an eye, I told him, not without some trumped-up comradely levity, which he enjoyed more than my straight-from-the-shoulder maunderings, that I was fine as I was.

"Really," I chaffed, "I can hardly think what I needed as many as ten fingers for in the first place!"

Two hospital visits from Uncle Nux straightened me out no end, though. "You *remember*, Claus?" I remembered, in perfect detail, how I'd schooled myself to hate S'gruber and to justify on moral grounds any action taken against him. "In my book, my boy, you're still the finger on the trigger. You still rate tops with me. We'll get you well, and then . . ."

Did he see that tear of joy? "Uncle," I told him, sore-throated, "there's only one difference. Now I'm three fingers on the trigger. Just you wait. I'll be your man yet. I'm going to be better than ever." I felt I was growing up at last.

After three months in hospital I went home to Lautlingen to be nursed by my mother, who decided to heal me by quoting long chunks of *her* favorite poems, and washed and dressed by

Uncle Nux's lined, dry hands. On I plugged, gradually learning to feed myself (almost everything save the cutting of meat,
of which we never got much anyway), to wash with a special
sponge, and even, after a while, how to knot a bow tie simply
to prove I could. Perhaps I was a born ascetic after all. Even
the gifts from admirers upset me; I didn't want things given *to*
me because I'd lost a hand and an eye; I wanted to *give myself*
to whatever duty I could manage. Yet for hours on end I felt
like a swab of cotton waste, within but not of that beloved fa-
milial world swarming with relatives and helping hands. My
head throbbed non-stop. I boiled with tears. In one half-lucid
interval I again wrote to Zeitzler, recklessly asking to be posted
back to the front, a request I regretted during an interval in
which I almost thought clearly. Was I shirking what I'd promised Nux? Or what? Zeitzler replied, saying, "The right assignment for you is already arranged, with General Olbricht . . ."

Then the throbbing faded and, on most days, especially
after a nap, I was good for hours of exacting talk. In fact, by
then everyone seemed tenser than I was, Nux in particular, no
doubt because he spent hours making handwritten marginal
notes on military and political papers of mine in his safekeep-
ing. From time to time, in an amateurish way, I'd set down my
prescriptions for a better Germany, and Nux would add or de-
lete an ideal here, a name there. When he seemed especially
tense—with a crinkled hesitancy in his face as if a tic had frozen—I made my laugh boom, even if it reminded me how
poor my hearing had become. Then he stopped scribbling,
perked up, and launched into talk that was a series of emotional lunges, releasing him and making his cheeks flush.

On one occasion he said, without preamble, "I'm an old
man. My main job nowadays is looking after you. And that's
enough. Have you met General Beck?"

I had not, but I knew he was an intense, grave, decent man,
long out of favor with S'gruber and eager to see him go.

"Or Goerdeler, the former mayor of Leipzig?"

"Not yet, but I no doubt will. There are dozens of people to meet now I'm back."

"What I want you to do, my boy," he countered in a hoarse rumble that seemed to come from behind him rather than within, "is to focus on the madman. *Him.* Never forget why he has to be expunged. Butcher. Sadist. Devil. A bloody corporal! To hell with religious scruple. You were never much given to that anyway. Do you know, I sit by myself for whole hours and just *foam* with loathing, I pour with the sweat of hate. I wish that, many years ago, we'd managed to get our hands on his pregnant bitch of a mother and shoved a flamethrower up her drain."

At that point he stopped using recognizable words and lapsed into a growling croon, addressed not to me but the middle distance, and I realized that he was cursing, raving, getting it out of his system in a different way. When the men in our family made those strange noises, I at last recognized, they were lambasting the world with sulfuric oaths, in syllables so foul they had no place in ordinary invective, but had to be pitched out into the air like dollops of filth, never offensive because always mumbo-jumbo to everyone else.

I must have drifted off even as he vented his hatred in that peculiar way; his uncouth ragings had become my lullaby, and that they remained for several months as I went from strength to strength, schooling myself all over again from suspicion to certainty, from there to condemnation and loathing, and from that to an imperative criminal act to be done by one of us on behalf of all, making us all both guilty and innocent in one stroke. But Nux was ahead of me in one respect: he saw me as his private candidate for national glory, the *key man*, whereas I thought of myself as only one of several recruits to a gathering conspiracy, a planner at best, at worst a human relic who might get in everyone's way during the crunch.

Alone in my bedroom, lounging in a light silk robe, I could not read with my remaining, bloodshot eye, not for more than a few moments. It teared non-stop, but I could focus on my dress uniform where it hung, out of the sunlight, in an alcove of my dressing room. There on the rough cloth that officers and men both wore (gray-green jacket above slate-gray trousers) was the chromatic embryo of a military career. Someone had brought the ribbons up to date; the medals were tucked away somewhere in a drawer. A hardly visible white trim ran down both sides of the black Sudetenland medal, which had a central red stripe. Oddly enough, this bauble, known officially as the "Medal in Remembrance of 1 October 1938," was the same as the medal that commemorated the Anschluss on Austria in March of the same year. Depicted on both were a large Germany figure, with a furled banner, and a small Austrian or Czech figure trying to ascend a tower. The large figure was of course assisting the other, and both were allegorically moving to the left. How typical, I thought, of S'gruber and his regime to come up with a category medal for benevolent invasion! In *his* mind, Austrians were indistinguishable from Czechs, March's territorial incursion from October's.

To the left of this ribbon was the so-called Service Medal, given in 1936 for stock reasons and never much esteemed; the ribbon was cornflower blue, this being the favorite flower of William the First and therefore a Prussian fetish; the medal itself, since I had put in twelve years, *just*, was bronze. To this one's right was the Eastern Medal we irreverently called the "Order of Chilled Beef," or "Frosty," for the Russian campaign of 1941 and 1942; I was entitled to wear that crimson ribbon with its central black stripe trimmed with white. But nobody at all was entitled to wear the next one along, and the last, which happened to be the German-Italian North African medal prematurely struck for the Axis entry into Cairo. Its five equal stripes of black, white, red, white again, and green on a cheap-looking ribbon stood like a denatured rainbow above the medal's highly stylized entrance to a tomb or pyramid, with fasces on one side, the swastika on the other.

"That," I told Nux when he looked in, "has to come off. Not only have we been routed in Africa; not only did we not take Cairo; the ribbon looks much too much like the Italian flag. I wouldn't wear that rag on my chest in any case!" My good eye squirmed, watered.

Mouthing with deliberate uncouthness, he explained something about "these patriotic wartime maids, with no experience. She saw the ribbon-stick and pinned it on. These blasted maids. *Urgh!*" Grunt, rumble, he was off again, frowning vocally like my father and his kin, but whatever he meant eluded me. Had he had a stroke? Or merely cursed the maid?

"Translation, please," I quipped, making my whole body sting as I began the first tremors of a chuckle.

He made the noises again, evidently unimpressed by my contempt for the Cairo medal. Humph-haug-haumph, he went, as if masticating a golf ball. "Save your strength, my boy. Germany needs it." He was mumbling from embarrassment.

I nodded, wondering if he knew that I had written in vain, in a daze, begging Zeitzler for a fresh posting to the front; I hadn't then realized that my next tour of duty, already fixed, was to place me at the center of conspiratorial events. I thought back over Zeitzler's picturesque arrival at my bedside in Munich, bearing the golden Wound Badge that now gleamed dully just past the doorway of the other room. For one or two wounds you got a black badge; for three or four, silver; and for five or more you got gold. My eye, hand, fingers, my ear, and my knee (twice) added up to six, and hey presto there it was, delivered by a highly strung general. You wore it ribbonless on the breast like the star of an order. Its oval showed a war helmet in front of crossed swords, and the whole was surrounded by a wreath of laurel. Thank God, I thought: my tunic won't look so bare. The ribbons are drab, especially without the hoax derived from Mussolini's flag, but the Wound Badge is for something *real*.

It dawned on me that my bits of colored ribbon honored me for two things only: for being somewhere, as a tourist is here or there, and for having been a passive recipient of aircraft fire. The record contained nothing about initiative; I was a competent manager, that was all. I had *led* no troops into action, although no doubt I had drafted orders which had got men killed. It was as if I lacked a dimension, and, as a paragon of mere geography and blatant wounds, I would have to assert myself even more. Otherwise the face of my career would have no nose.

According to some of my fellow officers, I resembled the so-called Bamberger Reiter—the Horseman of Bamberg—which had stood since the thirteenth century in the cathedral of my native city, but I could never spot the resemblance: those matted, coiled pageboy locks weren't mine, and the Horseman's features were much more deeply chiseled than my own. Not only that: the statue's face lacked sensitivity and had a lumpish jut to it that would never be mine. I might have been keen, lugubrious, and suave, and dark and intense, but never like that rustic Hun, chubby under his studded crown of flaking stone. Could it have been Uncle Nux who held me high, at arm's length, for my pudgy infant hands to feel the statue's shaven face? Had I ever been that high? Was I that high even then? Did I stand atop a column of rising air instead of on Uncle Nux's shoulders? I chuckled at a big nose so knobbly, at eyeballs that did not even flinch as I scraped them with my tiny nails, and then I screamed as I almost fell, or felt I was about to fall, deep into the naked shoulder.

"There, Claus! Down, down *down!*" His face gave way as I clawed at it, and, puny as I was, I knew he was frailer than the riding man of stone. The foggy mumble of his voice was full of love: love blazing and devout, the beacon of the family's core.

Pain-hindered as I was, I felt my loathing for S'gruber even more strongly; indeed, the pain fed the other, and thoughts of him made the pain worse. Yet I wasn't Fritzi, running the Berlin police, with armed men at my disposal and an entrée into the anterooms of power. I needed a gang of my own.

When Nux went out to look for a handkerchief, already making the motions of using it and breathing with fierce brevity, Nina walked into the room with an even, gradual stride that seemed the culmination of a long walk, whereas she had been in the house all the time. In those knowing, evaluative eyes, something like radiant metallurgy teemed.

"Can I still work?" I asked in a tone that said *"Do* things?"

"You will," she answered, converting advice into prophecy without a hint of condescension. She knew me like a text. In Rome she'd read my mind with ease.

"Will we reap the whirlwind?"

Her lip flared a little at the callow metaphor, but the expression in her eyes said, Reap it if you must, and of course you must, you aren't debating choices any more. I take that for granted, whatever else I say.

The decision was made, but I kept repeating the preludes to it like an infant mismanaging his first solid food.

"Of course you can still work, my dearest man," she told me next, "but this I'll do myself." She clipped, filed, and buffed my fingernails, then with the scissors' points trimmed each cuticle in turn, snipping away, where I could no longer see anything at all, at the frayed stub to get it level with the skin.

"We can't have you going out like that! What people are going to focus on has to be presentable." She spoke, *she loved*, as if I had shed not a hand and an eye but thirty years, and, even more amazing, as if my physical image had enlarged and needed only a bit of extra polish to be the Bamberg Horseman all over again.

She was gone by the time Nux came back, his eyes teared and his cheeks purple from heavy blowing. "Well," I told him, with exhausted finality, "the generals have done nothing so far, so I guess the colonels *are* going to have to do it themselves."

"You *are*," he said with a brimming, august smile that seemed to occupy his entire face. His head was big, his eyes were always aimed at some point above the horizon, and his features were small and neat. He always reduced amiable categories to downright, painful particulars, saying "you" and "he," or citing the exact time, temperature, or someone's name in full (as if they might be hiding behind a nickname or a title). "Your new chief, Friedrich Olbricht, head of the Army General Office, is one of the main conspirators. I think you deserve to know that. He mourns his soldier son in a Saxon drawl."

He might have been telling me the time of the next train. What a relief to know about Olbricht. Hundreds of thousands had been getting themselves shot to bits on duty while a few Neros whistled their way toward the middle of the century. When a man attained a certain military rank, I'd decided, the rank and the man fused, and then he must have no second thoughts about expressing, and enacting, the mature consensus.

What we had was a retinue of butchers, bakers, and candlestick makers dressed up as generals, who drew their pay, did their sycophantic duty, and held their breath until their next leave or until the next time they could divert a Heinkel 111 from an official mission in order to make a one-night stopover at home and conjugally resume while others went without. Military high priests, fat on venison, cranberries, and red cabbage, they got homesick on a weekly basis.

What a way to run a country.

Manstein wasn't the only rubber lion in the camp. There were scores like him, hedging, yes-but-ing, and prating about "a breath of fresh air" at the front as if death were calisthenics and mutilation a new way of standing erect. I had finally come to my senses, and *come to* them as if from a long way off, Angola or somewhere equally remote, enveloped in a wave of friendship and love, whose cruder embodiment was all those gifts pouring in from France, Italy, Greece, even the Ukraine, from men with deadly business on their hands, but whose subtler one was the new way in which people looked at me, a living relic from the fiery furnace. Had I become a better man? I dared to hope so, basing the hope on some belief that the inessential me had been burned away.

8

No More Romps

◆

What a convenient thought. I had been honed like a razor, but perhaps now, in her heart, Nina found me repulsive. My eye socket leaked fluid and I had to dab it with a wad of cotton. I wore the patch, but it chafed, so I wore cotton inside the patch, and that chafed too. I acquired a glass eye, which fitted quite well, until I lost it somewhere and had to get another, which didn't feel right. Dab, dab. Rub, rub. How could she look at me without wincing? As it was, she never gave a sign that I had changed, but matter-of-factly and with a face of calm concern provided pads of cotton when I needed them. The worst part was that the hand which reached up to mop the eye was a scarecrow remnant, evoking its missing partner, so that almost everything I did reminded my family of what else was wrong with me. At first gravely impressed, rather than horrified, the boys and little Valerie began to regard me as some special phantom, almost a big toy to be appreciated since there were so many ways in which they could help me, guide me, see me through. Other fathers were much less interesting to look at, they felt, and I suddenly realized that, in some bizarre way, I appealed to the side of them that responded to little steam engines, model planes, the erector set which made bridges and tractors bloom in strips of perforated metal.

"They don't seem to care," I told Nina. "I mean *worry*."

"Children have open minds," she whispered. "At least until a certain age."

"And you?" My question was too blunt, too much the product of sleepless nights thick with black misgivings. "I seem to have gone through a metamorphosis. How can you stand it?" I was the man in the velvet mask, a mere echo of myself.

She inhaled deep and long, then expressed herself with definitive, warm concision. "I could be accused, I suppose, of consciously never mentioning what's happened to you. I've adjusted my eyes, though. Let's say you've been lifted above the common level of men. You bear marks of *distinction*. A woman can accustom herself to anything in time. If you'd been injured by a car in a Berlin street, which caused you the same or similar injuries, it might have been harder to accept. As things are, however, my *idea* of you—of all you are and have been and will be—is far stronger than incidental changes in your appearance. One's parents get older. They change. One's children grow up, and quite unpredictably. Life *is* change, anyway, and only a very narrow mind balks at that. After all, Claus, change is a challenge, isn't it? If things, if people, didn't change, I wouldn't think I was altogether alive."

And she dabbed away my tears with a mellow caress, using an exquisitely embroidered handkerchief. "You're alive," she said, "I'm grateful for that. Your eye is *your* eye, your hand's *your* hand."

Not quite believing her, I nodded, and like a child laid my head against her arm to be soothed, as usual keeping that one hand away from her, she as usual tugging it toward her and stroking it until, especially in the dark, it almost felt whole again, and knew no diffidence at all.

Sometimes, however, I added up the losses.

No more romps on the lawn, in the playroom.

"Wind it, Daddy!" little Franz Ludwig pleaded, with his

model Tiger tank in hand, but I couldn't, nor even lift him skyward.

Nor catch a ball. Nor cup a breast, a cheek, an elbow.

Humming a military march, I tried to fold a paper airplane, but botched the first diagonal fold of the wing, unable to hold the paper firm while smoothing the crease. As best I could, I screwed it into a ball and pitched it behind me, managing next with combined teeth and fingers to make a boat that looked more like a paper hat. The children giggled. I put it on, heaving with sweat.

But I could still tickle, though a bit painfully at first. And stroke hair. And pat on the back. And put my hand in my pocket to bring out a surprise: a coin, a piece of candy, a glass eye.

The world fell into place again, and Uncle Nux made me aware of it, driving me to an even more murderous stand, indeed coming after me now with a diligent emphasis he wouldn't have brought to bear on a man intact. I wore my eyepatch rather high, covering more than a centimeter above the eyebrow line, almost as if to suggest that the eye wasn't quite so bad after all. I had a look of raffish availability; and, lolling back against a garden chair, with an armful and a lapful of children with thick bangs down to *their* browlines, noticing how the boys' belts were too long, and so had tongues that dangled, and how at times Valerie's neat round face developed a slightly puffy abstractedness full of obscure pain awful in one so small, I knew I had to work for them as well as play. And work meant kill. How quaintly they tugged at the empty sleeve as it flapped in the country breeze; it was another prop to toy with, like my suspenders (which they twanged against my chest) and the eyeflap, which they patted straight with tender awe, making me feel like a doll whose cap had slipped. After such tolerance, I had to make a gesture back.

"You're perking up," Nina told me without lowering her shrewd gaze. "You have become a count again."

"I am," I said. "From now on, I'm not going to get much reading done. Or convalescing, even." She looked away.

On August ninth, I returned to Munich for yet another operation, the one preparatory to the fitting of my artificial hand; but Italy had fallen on the eighth, so, blaming a bone splinter, I canceled the surgery, and my carefully rehearsed accommodation to the role of Frankenstein monster—the first synthetic colonel—had to wait its turn.

Then I went to Berlin, hampered and spectacular as I was, summoned by Olbricht. In the sleeping car, a fellow officer sympathetically offered to help me undress, but I gave him my best cynical chuckle, told him to see how it was done, and in a trice undressed myself with three fingers and my teeth! Never had I been so agile, or so deft. "Time me," I said. "I break my record every day!"

I pledged myself to Olbricht, who had the face of an introverted, somewhat shifty cleric, given to fits of righteous intensity. Then Sauerbruch looked me over again, humming out of tune. I told him I had urgent work of much importance ahead of me. The operations would have to wait. Sauerbruch was aghast. "You're not fit to engage in any such thing." He knew exactly what I had in mind. "And—you might very well crack up at the wrong time. You need to convalesce for a year at least."

"No," I said. "We're going to amputate from the trunk of Germany the arm that gestures *heil*. We're going to blind the eye beneath the brushed-down forelock. We're going to give *Germany* the chance to convalesce. You'll see."

For two short spells in August, I was able to be a husband again, visiting Nina in Bamberg, and during a second stay in Lautlingen I had some searching talks with brother Berthold. Everyone treated me with lovely, casual naturalness, referring only tacitly to my condition and dealing with me throughout as with a man intact. Against all the odds, I had been saved, quite possibly to no purpose. If that amounted to self-importance, I pleaded guilty, as I told Berthold and Nina.

Sauerbruch's own son, himself a colonel, understood precisely what I meant when, in one of those oral plunges that compensated in part for the second-to-second control I had to exert over my shoulders, my leg, my cheek and eye muscles, I told him, "Peter, I could never look the wives and children of the war dead in the face if I didn't do my bit to stop what's going on. I *couldn't*." I used not to sound so earnest.

To acquaintances and strangers, I must have seemed over-animated, possessed of some seething ambition or some demonic hunger for power. Men intent, or hell-bent, on building cathedrals, painting murals, composing symphonies, exploring the Amazon, flying all the way to the sun, must have impressed their fellow men in a similar fashion. The same was true of demagogues and mountebanks, but I was neither of those. A new Germany was my not-so-distant goal, but I knew also that, come what may, I would never believe all men were equal; I put my trust instead in the ranks passed out by nature itself. My dream was a Germany whose people accepted their rootedness in the soil, something as sacred in our hands and under our plows as our very presence on the crust of this planet. I wanted a Germany led by men from all classes of society, men committed to selfless high-mindedness. The nobility's role was to serve, to give a lead, and even to provide examples for emulation. No snob, I was no pawnbroker of my own class either, but I did believe in the upward social motion of those who combined natural vitality, keen mind, public spirit, and a capacity for civilized ease.

In this sense I was acutely old-fashioned, as were my methods, but I had seen what the euphoria stemming from rootless acquisitiveness could do, and I wanted no more of that. No rabble of workers, no new trumped-up elite of opportunistic psychopaths, but a federation of states in which each state had considerable autonomy, so that local dealings remained local, had a flavor, and grew out of communal contact with the region's soil. It sounded slyly righteous.

All of this, in some shape or other, I explained to both Olbricht and Henning von Tresckow, finding the latter especially
receptive. I'd seen photographs of him in this or that illustrat-
ed magazine, especially one in which he had tucked his thumb
inside his tunic, his other hand in his trousers pocket, while he
gazed out slightly to one side, his small mouth tautened, his
prematurely bald head giving his expression of bashful indeci-
siveness a weird look of slack seniority. So I was astonished to
find the man, when I first met him, back in 1941, piercingly
severe (until I got to know him), and not at all diffident, slack,
or boyish. War had honed him and responsibility had sapped
the facial pudginess. In a word, Tresckow was stern civility
with a mellow hand. It was in profile that his face impressed
me most: there seemed an enormous distance from ear to
cheek, as if his face had begun to flow forward led by his
slightly convex nose, while the streamlined bulb of his forehead held the motion intact and firm. His wife, Erika, had sad
eyes in a jovial face, or was it just their heavy lids that made
me think so? A good sport, as the saying went, she smiled most
when he frowned, the point being that his frown had a genial
recoil. His frown was when his mind paused between reflex
good will and a thoroughgoing intellectual salute. I felt truly at
home with him; he was a firm and unfanciful enthusiast with
pensive, kindly eyes.

Now, because he said he was going to be in or near Berlin
for fully ten weeks before assuming command of his regiment
(he had already been promoted colonel), I canceled the hand
operation altogether. As discreetly as we could, we worked together on such things as occupation plans, mobilization timeta-
bles, and secret operational orders, he living meanwhile with
his sister in Neubabelsberg, a suburb of Potsdam, while I grew
strong in the garden suburb of Wannsee.

"So much to tell you," he began at our first meeting. "A lot
happened, or almost happened, while you were in Africa.
Kluge, the new C.-in-C. of Army Group Center in Russia,
came over to us, at least insofar as Kluge comes over to any-

thing. Clever Hans, we call him. Last October he accepted a gift of 250,000 marks from his grateful Führer, and I told him 'History will never forgive you unless you took it to defray the expenses of our coup d'état!' Anyway, our beloved Führer was due to visit us in Smolensk on March thirteenth, this year, and we knew he wears an armored cap and a bulletproof vest. 'Right,' I said, 'let's shoot him in the mess while he's troughing.' 'No,' said Clever Hans, 'it isn't seemly to shoot a man at lunch. Besides, think of the risk to many senior officers present.' Some men are like antique furniture. In the end, von Schlabrendorff and I rigged up a double bomb disguised as two bottles of Cointreau and asked Heinz Brandt—a colonel in the divine entourage—if he'd take it to Colonel Helmuth Stieff out in Mauerwald. He agreed. Why not?"

"Fabian von Schlabrendorff," I said. "The very name seems like slate: a promise of success!" The man's image came before me: big jug ears and rippled septum, poring over a detonator through round glasses, like a saint in an updated stained-glass window. He'd popped his head in and said hello, then gone his way, on the track of more explosives.

" . . . Jodl, Zeitzler, SS bodyguards, doctors, photographers, Party hacks, his personal cook, and Kempka, his personal driver, all in three Condors, with a fighter escort." Tresckow had hardly paused when I spoke, and now his burly yet sensitive face under the jutting bald frontal lobe gleamed wet with indignation. "Brandt of course got into Pollux's plane," he went on, using one of the several code names for S'gruber. "Half an hour later the bomb was supposed to go off, but it didn't, and I suppose Brandt was lucky."

"What happened?" This was the closest I'd been to an actual *attempt*, and my pulse was moving fast.

"We eventually heard that Pollux had landed safely at his Rastenburg headquarters. So now Stieff, who at that time wasn't involved in the conspiracy, was due to receive a dangerous present. I called Brandt and told him to keep the package.

'There's been a mix-up, old man, and we've sent you the wrong stuff.' Fortunately Brandt hadn't made the delivery. Next day, Schlabrendorff took the routine courier plane to East Prussia, looked up Brandt, who actually juggled the damned time bomb in front of him, joking, even as he accepted the package of real Cointreau."

"And?" I was there with Schlabrendorff, doing it, retrieving the dud.

"Off he went to the night train for Berlin and locked the door behind him. There in the Korschen siding he opened up the package with a razor blade. The little capsule of acid had been broken all right; he'd used a key before handing the bomb over to Brandt. The liquid had eroded the wire. The pin had sprung forward. The detonator cap was burnt and the detonator black on the outside, but the charge hadn't gone off. The cause must have been the severe cold in the Condor's cabin. Maybe the heating failed. As we found—Schlabrendorff and I, that is—after our tests in the Russian forests, time bombs take longer in cold weather. That's all. We'll never know for sure. After a quiet night riding in the Berlin train alongside the unused explosive, Schlabrendorff took it to a meeting of the senior conspirators and showed them why what might have come to be known as 'Cointreau Day' never happened."

"Brandt," I murmured, "still doesn't know?"

"No. But Stieff does. You'll meet him any day now."

"Damned bad luck. A mere matter of temperature."

"I'll tell you," Tresckow said in a curious tone, like that of placid fury, "the only way we'll ever get him is to have the assassin invited to one of Pollux's nightly gatherings of cronies. Or ordered to attend one of the military conferences at Wolf's Lair. Schlabrendorff's gone over his daily schedule with a fine-tooth comb, and there's no other way. Take it from me, Fabian's accustomed to looking for loopholes; he may be a bit of a crusader, but he's a lawyer after all. He's right."

It sounded like the end of everything. "Isn't there anyone

with access?" I asked him. "Can't *anyone* get in there and deliver?"

"Only Meichssner, who's with Operations Staff, you know," he said with a wry grin. "And *he's* a bundle of nerves, as near an alcoholic as a man can be. Will *you*," he continued, changing tone from exasperation to jocund teasing, "have a go at him? Will you talk him round for us?"

"Lead him in," I answered, much too fast. "I'll do my level best. If I can't sober him up, I'll drown him in it. We've been really close to each other in our time. Surely he'll do a favor for his old pal Claus. I'll swing him round all right. You'll see. I've done it before, and now I look so *different* no one seems able to refuse me a thing. I know Joachim through and through. His father's a fanatical pastor of the Confessional Church, forever getting onto him, prodding him to do this and that. I think our man's *used* to being prodded. Tell you what: I'll use the bony end of my short arm!" Tresckow gave me his *grand seigneur* look, as if to calm me down, but all I did was to grin gauchely at him; I finally had something *to do*.

Without Tresckow, backing us at a distance with messages and reminders from the Russian front, like some intuitive force of nature in which an iceberg, an unrelenting tundra wind, and a tiger's muscles combined, we might have come apart at the seams. Tresckow, the former stockbroker, was decent, brilliant, and hard-working, a casually noble man who had uncanny power to get the best out of everyone merely by implying how unworthy the alternative would be. He steered us into useful ingenuity we never knew we had. The steady boyish rigor of his gaze was the only truly military thing about him. Too civilized to be the major general he became, he loathed uniforms, formulas, and regimentation of all sorts. Wholly without ruthlessness, he was a past master of coaxing, which was why his assignment was to win over to our side as many of the military high-ups as possible.

His erudite, cordial glow had bowled Cointreau Stieff over

at once; in fact, Tresckow was preaching to the converted, and Stieff had already made up his own mind about the SS atrocities in Poland. "I am ashamed," he said. Tresckow would have won him over anyway, just as he did Generals Fellgiebel, Wagner, and Lindemann (though not Guderian). It was unthinkable to give Tresckow a nickname (he was too diagrammatic, too much the embodiment of his correct name minus its military rank prefix, for that), whereas Himmler and others called Stieff "Poison Dwarf," which quite wrongly suggested he was deformed or had a vicious tongue. Far from it, he just happened to be short with a slight hump, yet trim, and his habitual demeanor was casual and spry. His big eyes bulged a little, giving his tiny neat face an innocent look, and his thin black plastered-down hair seemed brushed severely back as if to clear his view as much as possible. Even his voice was dapper. He might have been a jockey or a stunt man. Amused, although just the slightest degree appalled as well, to have been the pretext for Schlabrendorff's bomb, he'd murmur, "Cointreau, gentlemen?" and spread his mouth into a keen, ironic grin, wondering perhaps what might have happened if the "wrong" package had actually reached him via Colonel Brandt, who knew no more than he about the real contents. When we reassured him, he smiled even more jauntily, reasoning no doubt that, bomb or no bomb, dud or no dud, he'd been preserved for better things, which included of course the two genuine bottles that Schlabrendorff had taken to headquarters on the regular courier plane.

"We are purifying ourselves," Stieff liked to say. I knew what he meant, though the term sounded racist as well.

When Tresckow eventually passed to me a package of captured British explosive (hexogen) in Berlin, I took it out to Stieff in Mauerwald camp at Wolf's Lair. He then kept some of it by him in his quarters and some in the headquarters building, after which he transferred both the explosives and the fuses to Major Kuhn, who, with the assistance of Lieutenant von Hagen, concealed them near one of Mauerwald's wooden watchtowers.

Formerly, if passers-by had looked hard at me, it had been because I was a passable-looking young officer who did the usual things, such as bearing himself well, although not too well groomed, but now I was a garish exhibit, a tribute to cannon fire and Browning machine guns. The eyepatch made me twist and wrinkle my cheek. My knee made me limp. And my three-fingered hand, rather than the one completely gone, seemed to hypnotize those who caught sight of it and sent them into trances of muddled aversion.

I had work to do, however, and constant journeys to make; I noticed the stares less and less as the summer wore on. In Lautlingen I talked repeatedly with Berthold, concentrating on the actual coup itself. At Sauerbruch's home, I got Olbricht and General Ludwig Beck together, I who had never met Beck, our head of state designate (though I knew him well as the man who, at the War Academy in 1935, had spoken out strongly against creating a vast mechanized army for which there was *too little oil*, least of all an army intended for attack rather than defense).

"We need officers," Beck had said on that occasion, "with strong enough character and nerves to act according to the dictates of reason." Men like himself: that's what he meant.

He knew all about monsters.

Between 1934 and 1938 he was granted an audience with S'gruber only once. This "Cunctator" or "Slowpoke," as he was known, was a worthy silhouette of a man, at least, like an entry or an emblem from a book of models for personal behavior. I could see him doing things he had not done and saying what he had not said. I transposed him, transplanted him, and made his image work on my behalf until it groaned.

9

The Go-Between

◆

With my three remaining fingers, I practiced non-stop. My
pen began to speed. "I will be back for active duty," I wrote to
Olbricht in September, "in three weeks' time." And I was: I
had something to do, and it almost seemed as if I'd had to lose
manual dexterity in order to lend a helping hand, smothered
as it was, early on, in bandages. Such grisly turns of thought I
kept from Nina altogether, though; she had enough to bear as
it was; instead, my talk with her was uplift, almost debonair.

"Nina," I said to her, not without a certain sense of heady
grandiosity, one day as she sat by my side in Bamberg with the
French windows wide on an afternoon of unusual heat, "it's all
fixed. It's *on!*" Sometimes very much a countess, she gave me
the mother-of-pearl look that was her visual nod. "So, Claus,
the world is round. Good."

"We'll use a bomb."

She knew and went straight on. "You and—"

"Yes. The old team. The Bamberg Horseman. Stefan George.
Tresckow. Fritzi. Beck. Schlabrendorff. Olbricht. Ali. And others. *You* know." Surely there were others?

"A team that grand," she quipped, but with fidgeting eyes,
"has no need of you. I'm glad." My joke had palled.

"I'm the go-between," I said wanly. "I'll be that."

"No, Claus, you're the sacrificial animal, you're the only one
of them who's really in this world. *Don't.*" The word dangled
in mid-air, like a tassel, until "I have to" flicked it away.

She shook her head with regal hesitance. "Just look at you

now," she whispered, "a tower of strength if I ever saw one. Do they *all* need *you now?*"

So I blathered what, in my mind's ear, had become the standard speech. "It's up to us General Staff people now. Nobody else. We'll have to take the blame, one way or another, so it's better to have been not exactly passive. For the record, I mean. And, who knows, we might even pull it off." Would it have sounded better in a theater?

"Why you?" She forced her lips together slantwise.

I shrugged one shoulder, but she either didn't notice or refused to construe the movement.

"You've done enough already." Her hands unfurled.

"I haven't done anything that matters."

"An eye—" Pointing at her own.

"A *country*. Ours. Yours. Mine. *His!*" It was as simple and unavoidable as that; I had begun, even then, succumbing to an honorable fatalism I didn't want to talk about. One can go on, however, only until stopped, as along certain mountain roads that worsen as they wind even higher until they end in a gnarled white stone which, telling you how far you have come, orders you back with its cold face of a *thing*. On, Stauffenberg, I told myself. You have nothing to lose. It was an obscene lie, but the truth made me tell it.

On October first, I took up my duties as Chief of Staff to Friedrich Olbricht. The Zeitzler plan was working out. I had spent a busy, improvisatory summer, in part trying to correlate an essay I had written on home defense against enemy parachute troops with our plans for insurrection. If you knew how to repel the enemy, you could also discover how to let him in. In this instance, he would be coming from within, but the same principles held, and I began to take a mild pride in the finesse with which an operation designed to protect could be adapted into a secret weapon. By now, good old Tresckow had left Berlin to take over his regiment, and I was virtually on my own with all the proposals for the military coup. We were so far ahead in our planning, in fact, that I at first thought we could go ahead in early November. It was mere self-delusion to try and win the war beforehand; no longer was it a matter of putting first things first. There was only the first thing—the eradication of S'gruber once and for all—followed by the second thing, which was the seizure and retention of power. My ears tingled as I realized the utter lack of alternative. Things had reached this point and there was no going back, just as there was only one way forward. It was no use soliloquizing, or debating the ethics of murder; we had a common purpose and, from this point on, we seemed to begin speaking the same language.

Once I was breakfasting on my Wannsee balcony with Ali Mertz von Quirnheim. It was a bright, spacious-feeling day with a unseasonably warm sun, but wasps came after the honey, and I giddily fled indoors, calling through the French doors, "One of the big advantages in being wounded is that you can confess your phobias openly. No one blames a disabled veteran for ducking a wasp!"

"What, then, about the converse?" called the pensive Ali. "If you get badly stung by wasps, are you exempted from being blown to bits? I mean, is it then all right to admit your terror of high explosive if you've faced wasps with courage?"

I had no answer, even when I resumed my breakfast. We talked then about my brother Alexander's poems, which a friend had brought to Berthold and me, and I sat wondering over what was left of the honey (Why had the wasps left?) if symbolism can be propagandistic; if what is moderate can actually sway readers; and if all poetry should not be punctuated in a private fashion like that of Stefan George.

On that same balcony, during a starlit night after a fearsome air raid which had left one third of the landscape in flames, I looked out over Wannsee toward the city—northeast—and quietly spoke some lines to myself. Then I noticed Berthold's wife, Maria, watching and listening, her face all wry indulgence.

"Practicing?" She whispered more quietly than I had been talking to myself.

"Not really," I told her. "Soothing myself is more like it. Look at the fires. Berlin is burning. Again."

"Stefan George," she was saying. "You quote him to win men over to the cause. Does it work?"

"If it doesn't, the headlines will. No nation doing as well as Goebbels claims can have so many fires nightly."

She knew, anyway, as well as the fact that copies of the poem "Antichrist" went from hand to hand as a means of conspirators' identifying one another. It was an innocent enough thing to have in your pocket: what harm could a poem do? To whom?

One night, on my way to visit Beck, right in the middle of an air raid, we heard that his house had been demolished.

"We can't get through to the Goethestrasse," Schweizer, my driver, said in the lovable broad phonetics of the Swabian Alb. "Several streets are impassable with debris and craters. What shall we do? I've already entered the address in the logbook."

"Do, man? We shall hurry," I told him. "There's always a way through or round. Let's see what we can do. There's all the more reason to get there fast."

Off he went as if hedgehopping a small fighter plane, until he turned round aghast and cried, "Look!" The drawn-back convertible roof of the car had caught fire and was blazing away merrily behind us: a veritable box kite of flame.

"A bomb!" he yelled.

"The Royal Air Force can hardly see *us*," I bellowed forward. "Drive even faster to keep the flames behind the car." He did and we survived uncharred and Beck was all right although his house was much the worse for wear.

"Nothing is ever fast enough for you, Colonel." Poor

Schweizer, had he only known how time dragged between one July and the next; I felt distended with impatience, itching to go and do, but overcome daily by the same awful sense of viscous slow motion, as if our limbs were crammed with tar and the future were banned. In such a mood I had conned the amiable medical officer at the Bendlerstrasse into passing me fit for active service.

I wished that wishing might make it so, unable to master twinges of inexpressible grief that flashed through my core, as never through the core of a "fit" man. A few lines of an old Brazilian song, "Tarde Azul" or "Blue Dusk," unmanned me as I paused at a café door, and quite beyond the power of the words themselves: a dream taking place in the azure light of dusk, in which the lover-dreamer cried out:

> So far from you,
> wanting your warmth,
> that whole sweet hour,
> I yearn to find you . . .

In some small, damp cavity in my chest, the song was singing itself, inaccurately but with unendurable pathos, as if the whole of life had gone to waste, and I was on this earth only to be brave, lonely, helpless, done for, and forgotten. Give me, I prayed mutely, only a matchbox to move about in; only give me some scope. Otherwise treat me as a plant, and plantlike I will hold my peace until I blanch.

Only three weeks ago, in twenty-four groups, the Plötzensee hangman had finished off 186 prisoners, between seven-thirty in the evening and eight-thirty the next morning. I felt a caustic nausea. An American colleague at staff college had told me about the stockyards at Chicago; but this was unspeakable. The prison pastor had heard about the mass execution only just before it began. The convict-librarians made their lists complete, typing the surnames with double spaces between the letters, the first names with only single spaces; then they pasted the typed slips into the prison deathbook next to lists of names hand-scrawled. As each group met its doom, a line went through the name or a tick affixed itself: job done. Only the women had no numbers, having been brought there from a different jail. Some prisoners were hanged by mistake, but it mattered little: Röttger, the hangman, perched on his footstool, had worked up a rhythm, laughing and slapping his three-quarter-length leather jerkin. Four minutes was all he took with each.

The bodies lay in the open air, inside the walls of a demolished storehouse: a big one, since the body count was now 300. Destined for the Institute of Anatomy, they had to be transported, but there were constant air raids. The weather was warm and wet. Finally the bodies disappeared, ending up in a mass grave somewhere near Berlin. The work of removal had been so unpleasant that those doing it had received a special bonus. The Minister of Justice had granted the extra money just a week ago.

Sickened beyond shock, yet also vindicated, I tried to keep some sort of equilibrium. The work to be done was not to feel nauseated, but to reach S'gruber just once. For this, we would have to keep our heads, in more ways than one. Anger would blur our judgment, so I believed what I heard, but went on treating it as a rumor. So as to be crisp, practical, swift, when the call to action came.

The recent dead had joined S'gruber's other dead, and we the plotters were not quite as alone as it sometimes seemed after too much coffee, too little sleep, no good news, and the unending nervous strain that made you feel as if someone had slapped nettles across your eyes and the tops of your cheeks.

Preposterous as it seemed, between 1936 and 1938 I was right there, in the same suburb as Plötzensee Prison itself, at the Staff College. The guillotine and I were neighbors, both then and again when I came back to Berlin to work with Olbricht in the Reserve Army HQ in Bendlerstrasse. I never heard its dry clack. I never saw them sweep the slop along the sloping floor into the manhole which an iron lid concealed. Nor did I see them snag the clothes of the condemned on crude little peg hooks let into the walls. The only two windows in the shed looked out onto the garden, but I had no idea if the victims faced that way or inward, where the heavy black curtain hung, with the remaining condemned in a line behind it, awaiting their turn. I did not even see the guillotine after it had been wrecked by Allied bombs, which was when the hangman really came into his own again. Was the hangman the headsman also: the *guillotineur?*

"Come on! Come on! Come on!" he'd bellow as he went past the opened cell doors, leering and joking, with here a slinky motion and there a hopping jump. For each victim he received eighty marks, while, for bundling a victim into the execution chamber, each of the two warders appointed got eight cigarettes. Ridiculous to say, when I first heard about these devilish premiums, I wondered if someone paid him eighty-*one* marks, or the warders *nine* cigarettes, they would take the prisoner back to the cell, to remain there until the next bargaining began. But of course no one came back from the trellis that graced the entrance to the death house, with its twining creepers arranged along the wooden uprights that stood before the seven-barred windows, the half-open portal, the ugly brickwork of the walls. The feet that walked along the path from the cells, in wooden clogs, did not come out again, at least not vertical.

I shuddered. The "Gate to Eternity" they called that thing behind the iron bars. It might have been an ante-chapel, an ill-designed and wretchedly built shrine attached to some not very well-to-do monastery. If so, this order had thousands of brothers and sisters, fathers and mothers, impeccably austere anchorites of the fetter, and steeled visionaries of the erect head during the last walk.

10

Conspirators

♦

In early October 1943, Nux and I sat out one day in the rose garden in Wannsee, a small samovar of hot coffee between us. At some distance my mother was trimming bushes, almost, it seemed, a leaf at a time, her mouth in constant movement as she talked to herself or recited, from time to time tossing us a fragile vertical wave of the hand. Tilting it against the faint breeze, which made it buck and flutter, Nux held a desk blotter with a large sheet of paper neatly fitted into its four corners.

"My design for the perfect Germany," he chortled. "Young Schulenburg and I cooked up some of this five years ago. Now: who says Germany has no prophets? Don't you remember when we came to see you, when you were a cavalry captain in a garrison on the Rhine?" I did: it was the winter of 1938–39, a lifetime ago. Oddly enough, Nux's paper was covered in unrecognizable faces drawn in spidery cursive lines; I couldn't decipher his writing either.

"How's it going, Claus? You come and go like a salesman. Schulenburg's got a list of a thousand names."

"Plans, Uncle," I told him. "It's all plans and winning people over." In fact it was just the type of work the army had trained me for, I mused, but Nux was already reading aloud from his blotter.

"Head of State: *Beck*. Of course." Beck, sometimes as aloof as a dying star, sometimes just an amateur gardener. "Chancellor? It says Goerdeler here. I've ticked Beck. Do I tick Goerdeler too?"

"Over my dead body. The man's a bureaucratic prude. A

swiveler. He'll back down from the bloodletting. No, *my* man's Leber. Met him through Fritzi. Leber said he'd make a pact with the devil himself to rid us of—Pollux."

Nux grinned impishly. "Pollux, ah yes. *Him.*" He put a line through a name and deftly erased a face with a rubber finger-stall worn just for that purpose. "You know the code name for you? One of the names, anyway. No, you wouldn't. *Zollern-dorff.* Now, what shall we put *him* down for?"

"Contact man," I said wearily. "No. Put Leber in for Goer-deler." Leber's dark granitic, slablike presence had haunted me since our first meeting. Usually we met at his place, but when the air raid alert went I got out fast, lest a bomb hit the house and reveal who'd been there. "His head burns coal," I said, "he has such energy."

Nux had already moved on, muttering, "Foreign Minister? No, sorry, Minister of *Interior!* Does it really take all these bloody people to run a country of the mind?" He barked a few short, nasty syllables even as my mother floated toward us with a yellow rose, which she tucked into the top of Nux's blotter.

"Interior?" I said. "Fritzi, of course. Our wild man of the woods. Our Red Count." Fritzi already had the new German constitution in his head, and no doubt Nux had written it down in his own wayward fashion. My mother backed off, caution-ing us to face the sun as it moved.

"He's down for Food as well." Nux popped an index finger between his teeth. "*Food.*"

"Good God! *Very* Interior, I'd say."

"Politics," Nux groaned. "I say, Claus. Let's kill off the Nazi bastards and *then* make plans." But what would he do with his blotter in the meantime? "Ass-wipe it," he answered. "Old men have to find something to do. I'd be as well off with toy soldiers and a fort. I'm a retired colonel, damn it."

"You'll be liaison officer for Bohemia and Moravia, Uncle. Just wait awhile, and you'll be busier than me."

More grunts, then: "Let's make a list of whom to kill. I can draw them and then erase them as they go."

"The list," I told him gently, "is too short to make. Only one name on it. Well, maybe three: Himmler, Göring, too."

"Then who," he almost snarled, "is going to do it? Are you going to phone Pollux for an appointment? You didn't shoot him over his soup, and you didn't blow up his plane. Perhaps you could talk him into growing his hair long, and then stuff it down his throat until he stopped breathing."

"Uncle," I nearly exploded, "it's no good going off half cocked. There are proclamations to be typed. The secretaries in the Bendlerstrasse type them in gloves. Tresckow will soon be off to the front. Hardly anybody has access to the target. Only Stieff. And Meichssner, whom I'm supposed to win over. I can't do everything. I can't be everywhere. The imponderables are sickening."

"Then cut through them," he said as he got up to go, "and live dangerously. You can quote me to anyone."

For hours I dictated the plans for Operation Valkyrie while three brave women—Ehrengard, Countess von der Schulenberg; Margarete von Oven; and Tresckow's wife, Erika—took them down. Once S'gruber was dead, the code word "Valkyrie" would go out from the commander of the Home Army to the district commanders. Or it would *appear* to do so; emanating from General Fromm, Commander of the Reserve Army, only a few doors away, it would come from myself. Fromm wasn't one of us, and was unlikely to be, but we had to use his name to preclude suspicion among the troops. The orders said the SS had mounted a putsch, which had been suppressed. Reserve Army units were then supposed to disarm the SS. A second order would come from Field Marshal Erwin von Witzleben, who was to be Commander in Chief of the armed forces. He had in fact signed it a year ago, without a moment's pause. It proclaimed a state of emergency, and it banned arbitrary acts of revenge.

Witzleben was just what we needed. Not a complicated

man, a reader, or one given to tortuous political finesse, he was happiest when hunting, and he genuinely had no non-military ambitions. His word was his bond, as everybody kept piously saying, and he enjoyed reading adventure tales. When he lost his temper, the crow's-feet under his eyes stood out like twigs and his wide forbearing mouth became almost lipless while his deep-set eyes felt into you.

We slaved away, drafting and checking, ferreting out an ambiguity here, something long-winded there, until the text was as good as we could make it. In that Indian summer the faces of the women gleamed as if polished, and the paper they wrote on formed moist dimples under their wrists. I did all my composing on my feet, almost as if orating, but able to speak only in a percussive whisper while staring at the gloves Fräulein von Oven wore, so as to leave no fingerprints, and the typewriter that was locked away as soon as finished with. No wonder she looked harassed, though her demeanor was flawless. One day, after meeting both myself and Tresckow (whom I now referred to as "my instructor") in the Grunewald, during one of his quick trips to Berlin, she was walking down the Trabener Strasse with us, and under her arm drafts of various orders for the coup. A car full of SS drew up beside us, and they all jumped out, taking no notice of the three of us, and entered a house nearby. When we heard the brakes grate, we thought the conspiracy was over and that all three of us would be arrested. We were both, she told us later, as white as sheets, war-hardened as we were.

"No, all three of us," she disarmingly added, knowing she'd been saved for months more of work under impossible conditions, with both the mails and the telephone out of the question for arranging meetings, and all forms of public transportation disrupted by air raids. I had the sudden dreadful thought that we should have destroyed all the typewriter ribbons as well, and the platen too.

Better to be Beck, in dark glasses, sitting in his garden under the watchful eye of his widowed daughter, inhaling the scent of blossoms and listening to the blackbirds, mallards, and doves. Beck's art was never to be wholly of this world. In the old days, strolling away from an autumn commemoration ceremony at Berlin University, he asked someone on Unter den Linden, "Did you know the last piece of music they played?"

"The chorale from Bach's 'The Art of Fugue.' "

Beck sighed in delight. "That was the most otherworldly thing I have ever heard. Very remarkable." A hundred meters farther on, he spoke again to his companion: "One should take note of that—for *all* eventualities, don't you think?" Trying to entrap him would have been like selling rosaries to the Angel of Death; he knew the technical terms of all the philosophical systems, the esoteric lore of rose-growing, and how to talk to himself while giving the illusion of talking to others.

Trying to accomplish so many things all at the same time, in the same hurry, in the early autumn of 1943, we ended up with a harvest of ideas but not enough accomplished. And one example rebuked us, as it should have done. Late in October, Nina herself took with her to Bamberg, to burn, a rucksack full of incriminating papers. All the way from Berlin to home, she had these early versions of orders and proclamations with her, each one a potential death warrant. Our only alternative was to burn the drafts sheet by sheet in a lavatory basin, flush the ashes away and wipe away the black rim on the porcelain. Since the offices we worked in were centrally heated, we were always accumulating large quantities of typewritten paper, and it was as if, burning it on the premises or removing it to Bamberg, we were incendiaries to our own recent past. Only the most recent draft mattered, only the current plot.

Was it during these awful, frustrating October weeks that I first developed the notion that this was all my life was going to be? These would be the friends I made, these would be the only enterprises. It felt reassuring to have things so fixed, but demoralizing to know that all those possible other lives one dallies with, and saves up for next year or the year after that, were never going to be. The so-called joys of anticipation became crystal ciphers, more relevant to someone as yet unborn than to myself, and with that began my extraordinary sense of having been dispossessed by my future. Not quite an automaton, I nonetheless felt more abstract than any person should. And in the long run I knew only that the name Stauffenberg stood for a certain line of force, a pressure exerted, a will gone rigid as wood. Again and again I wanted to do something irrelevant, something that had nothing to do with S'gruber. What a good time, I thought, to begin a stamp collection, or to become an authority on index fingers; but such folderol was out of the question. We were in an unspeakable, fatal mess: the very thing we pledged our lives to, the assassination, seemed impossible, and until we had accomplished it we could do nothing else. I became more irritable and volatile than ever. Something akin to the fetishist's precision, such as attaches itself to the cult of dueling scars on or near the cheekbones, kept getting in our way. What we desired, deep down, was almost heraldic: an ikon as tiny and complete as a boutonniere.

Preposterous? Of course. No one impartial would have thought us wise or even competent. Religious scruples got in the way as well. My own adjutant, Werner von Haeften, who arrived in November, was eager to volunteer. He had been severely wounded himself, was no longer eligible for service at the front, and he knew—as it were—the currency of weaponry. But his brother, Hans Bernd, a man of sensitive and acute intellect who had studied law at Cambridge and other places, confronted him with telling objections, asking in particular if he, Werner, could be certain that this was a demand made of *him* by God. "We should not use gangster methods against gangsters," Hans Bernd told him, and this holy imperative converted into an objection on the grounds of logic appeared

time and again in Werner's insistence that even a distant accomplice cannot go untainted. "If we kill him off," Werner
said with the pensive but far from solemn crispness that was
peculiarly his, "then we're murderers, and we can't deny the
fact and we can't refuse to bear the guilt—and all its consequences."

Had he not, last February, at the house of Pastor Zimmer-
man, talked with Dietrich Bonhoeffer only two months before
the Gestapo arrested Bonhoeffer? "I shall be with Hitler tomorrow," Haeften told him. "Shall I shoot him?" The answer
he got was prudently worldly.

"It's not simply a matter of killing him," said the author of
the uncompleted book called *Ethics*, "but of keeping in mind
what will happen *politically* if you do. There must be a proper
government ready to take over. Otherwise the results will be
catastrophic. No one has the right to tell you to shoot him or
not to shoot him; in the end, this is a moral choice up to the individual concerned. Situation ethics, I call it. Above all, you
must be deeply and personally convinced that so dreadful an
act is morally inevitable and therefore right."

That was earlier in 1943, and the conversation no doubt af-
fected Haeften deeply. My own view, arrived at after agonizing sessions alone, and also with Berthold, was that Christ's
commandment to love referred to the millions of Germans and
others whom S'gruber's regime had degraded and slaughtered;
to love *them* was to hate *him*, and to kill him was to manifest
commanded love at large. There were circumstances in which
a deed of blood was allowed, and several of my fellow plotters—men just as devout as myself, though I knew my defi-
ciencies—felt much the same. "We *must*," I said, "read 'love'
hugely."

With some success I tried to cultivate the art of sleeping
right through an air raid. When my telephone gave its quiet
click, advance warning before the sirens began, I roused everyone else, then went back to sleep until the alarm sounded, at

which point the others woke me and down I went, my boots squeezed under my arm, to the shelter. If I were blown up, it would be as S'gruber's assassin, not as an air raid victim. Of that I was convinced, hence my cavalier attitude to vertical bombs. One of Berthold's friends, Alfred Kranzfelder, who acted as liaison officer between the Foreign Office and the Naval High Command, once regaled us during a raid of ferocious intensity with his experiences, only a few days earlier in Paris, at a Bach and Mozart organ concert: a cool customer, humming and whistling snatches of melody while the bowels of the earth heaved, but also the man with whom I and one other walked in the forest of Eberswalde in bitter November.

"Claus," he said several times, "someone's behind us. I keep hearing steps." All I could hear was aircraft high up.

"Walk faster, then wait."

When no one came, we started off again.

"I can still hear footsteps," Kranzfelder whispered. "They're closer now." Then I too heard, but the "footsteps" were the flapping sounds made by his own leather coat as he walked. He buttoned it up with an abashed chuckle.

It was already winter. My wounds ached as if newly angered. The rest of my body filled with odd, dragging neuralgias, perhaps because of the strains created by amputation. Air raids came nightly and it was hard to sleep, even out in Wannsee, a fairly peaceful place, deep in my little haven at 8 Tristanstrasse. On the morning of my birthday, November fifteenth, I looked out at the thin snowscape as the wind flung a parabola of snow past a tree, and for a moment it was as if a human silhouette had lunged at speed across that space, hardly blocking the light but leaving a distinct yet utterly blank retina image that haunted me for hours. I'd just seen my thirty-fifth year vanish; and, look again as I did, several times while shaving, I never saw the wind repeat the original configuration. The few snowflakes that made it up had long ago dispersed, never to recombine.

How petty the time scale we lived by: month to month, birthday to birthday; and yet how grandiose our presumptions about Naziism itself. We were like astronomers, we plotters, waiting for a star to cool and die within a few months, whereas it was working on a time scale of a billion years and would not be rushed.

11

Dead Ends

◆

The next phase was one of good ideas miscarried. In November, Stieff told me, "I've tried, but I simply can't get near the conference room. It's hopeless. I'm not sure there's any point in my holding on to 'the stuff.'" So we found a volunteer who, involved in a demonstration of warm tunics for the Russian front, would wear a bomb in his uniform and clasp S'gruber in a fierce embrace, thereby setting off the fuse. An air raid destroyed the demonstration tunics, however, and our suicidal volunteer had to return to combat.

Next I talked to Major Freiherr von Leonrod, in mid-November.

"Will you help us with a coup d'état already in the works?" My lines came pat to tongue, treasonous and crisp.

"I'll help you with the raising of Atlantis, if you need!" He was given to devout hyperboles, but he never fussed or prevaricated.

"Later," I laughed. "We may need you for something smaller by Christmas, O.K.?" We did, but he was off on other duties when S'gruber summoned Olbricht to Wolf's Lair at Rastenburg for a conference on manpower reserves. Olbricht begged off sick, and so I had myself deputized, complete with bomb in my expanding yellow briefcase, but when, early in the morning of December 26, 1943, I arrived in that dank, lugubrious redoubt hidden in the depths of a pine forest like the witch's home in *Hansel and Gretel*, I found S'gruber had canceled the whole thing and gone off to spend *his* Christmas on the Obersalzberg. What a fool I felt, taking my bomb home, like some spurned Santa Claus; I winced at the coincidence of the names. I hadn't even been able to look around, though I'd found out that the different parts of the encampment were connected by tunnels with ventilating machinery. Could we use those in some way? Maybe *gas* everybody?

A row with Goerdeler followed, who still wanted us all to march in to S'gruber and state our grievances; then S'gruber, as a rational man, would get the point.

"You did nothing," he brayed. "Nothing." Hysteria *ponderoso*.

"There was nothing to do. He'd gone." Goerdeler was the man who thought silver cigarette cases a corrupt luxury and didn't allow into his home any woman who'd broken her engagement. . . . Why was I dealing with such dodos?

"I briefed all the political people. Dangerous information for them to have. I do think we need another way," he whined. "I do not like your bombs." Dear sir, he'd tell God, you're lewd.

"No, we'll kill him, even if I have to do the thing myself." But what I had in mind was getting a message to Winston Churchill (who might understand), without mentioning it to Goerdeler, who was becoming a chronic civilian pacifist pain.

For a while we marked time, managing only to cheat S'gruber's order that Allied airmen should be shot; I obtained from POW camps the names of airmen who had died, and then used these "dead souls" on the lists of those reported shot. Early in February S'gruber was due to inspect the Russian tunics again. We got ready, with yet another volunteer, but the demonstration never took place. A young captain, ADC to a field marshal, got his revolver as far as the anteroom to S'gruber's map room, only to be turned away by the SS officer on duty: "Sorry, no ADC's to attend the meetings today. *Restricted.*"

It was just as well, perhaps; the officer class was never especially good at pumping bullets into maniacs at close range. By this time, the Gestapo had arrested some of our civilian fellow conspirators, and, worse, Himmler had ousted our old friend, and his rival, Admiral Canaris, from the Wehrmacht Intelligence Office. Canaris flashed before me: groomed, delphic, pliably clever, a man of incessant mystery who doted on dogs. Never would he feed us information again or bamboozle his Führer. Now Beck became gravely ill and had to be operated upon. Goerdeler went on complaining that nothing had happened and that no one told him anything any more; I sent him my word of honor that something would come "of all this," and at last went after Meichssner, on the train to Berchtesgaden, plying him with two bottles of burgundy in the presence of another officer. As he was leaving my compartment, I said, "See you soon, Meichssner? *Y'know.*"

"One *never* knows," he said, slurring it. "Thank you for the wine." His slightly bulging eyes rolled, trying to hide.

"You see," I told the other officer, "it's crystal clear. He doesn't want to play our game any more. His liver's cold. No one wants the dirty work, as they call it. They all want to keep their uniforms clean for the victory parade. They don't seem to believe Himmler told his masseur that after the war he'll stage a mass execution of the aristocracy in the Lustgarten. 'The lords are no better than the Jews,' he said."

"*Who*, then?" he asked with a look of sardonic bewilderment. I thought of names, old friends, new ones, but getting them into S'gruber's vicinity was next to impossible. Twice Tresckow had tried to arrange himself a posting to S'gruber's staff, but all he'd achieved was a promotion to major general.

In April I visited the estates of various friends in and around
Berlin, glad to get away from the constant brick dust in the air
after RAF raids, and anxious to thrash things out with Count
Hardenberg at Küstrin and Fritzi at his brother-in-law's place,
Trebbow, where instead of taking things easy we stayed up all
night trying to come up with a name.

"Adam Trott's going to Sweden in June," I said. "He'll find
out the Allied attitude and pass my message to Churchill. I
can't think the British, anyway, would insist on an unconditional surrender if a successful coup takes place. Even though
the British think we Germans are a warmongering lot." Trott,
whom I'd met through Haeften's brother, was our Oxford man
and knew exactly how to phrase things to the island people
he'd come to love so well. Bald and saturnine, he'd get things
right; he had presence and brains, brains, brains.

"God love us, Claus, you're a trusting bugger," Fritzi answered. "They'll rub our noses in it and, mark my words, insist
we surrender to *all* the Allies, the Russians included."

"Oh, the British *act* tough," I said, "but they won't let Europe turn into Russian real estate. I'm convinced they'll make
a deal with us. An honorable peace, so they can play us off
against Russia." When Trott returned, however, he brought
bad news. No deal. No, the Allies would not refrain from
bombing Berlin. No, they'd rather see Germany surrender in
toto than negotiate with the German resistance. Shocked, I
nonetheless told Trott, "Wait and see. Churchill will change
his tune once the war is won. Now let's try Eisenhower or Be-
dell Smith and get the fighting in the West stopped right
away." I drew up an eleven-point plan both fatuous and blasé,
requiring "1. Immediate cessation of air warfare. 2. Cancella-
tion of Allied plans for the invasion of France. 3. Avoidance of
further bloodshed. . . . 5. No occupation of Germany." Number 8 was the kicker, though, and it made Adam hoot and
Fritzi snarl, asking that Austria and the Sudetenland remain an
integral part of the German Reich!

"Claus, you want to keep the loot and make them choke on it! That's not how the world runs." Adam was aghast.

"The bastards will bomb us twice as hard for even asking. *Incredible!*" Fritzi roared. "Does the rapist, after being pardoned, get to keep his victim as a souvenir?"

And Leber chimed in, "You'll never be able to use Germany as a wedge to split the Allies. It just isn't on. Whatever we do, we're going to have to do it alone. First, find an entrée to the swine, kill him, then take our chances. *You can't negotiate the risk out of it. You can't.*" These were three wise men and I was a proven idealist, a naif, through and through: a planner, yes, but a diplomat never.

Then three more events: Stieff gave me back the bombs, which I then gave to Olbricht's adjutant, Colonel Fritz von der Lancken, to keep at his home in Potsdam; behind the scenes, S'gruber's chief adjutant, General Schmundt, recommended that I be transferred from Olbricht to energize the becalmed Fromm (from a friend to an enigmatic boor); and (perhaps this third caused the second) a weird exchange took place between Himmler and General Guderian.

"Who's to succeed Heusinger as head of Army Operations?" asked Himmler.

"Why, Stauffenberg," said Guderian. "He's the best horse in the General Staff stable."

Himmler smiled that wintry smirk of his, like a wound reopening. "Agreed. I've been hearing quite a lot about him. All of it good. He's impressive. One of the *useful* lords, whom we can use now and deal with later. Yes. Let's put our money on Stauffenberg. And get it back later."

Was I *that* good? Quickly, basking in hearsay that filtered down from high places, I assessed my own mental and emotional advance, from being utterly taken in by S'gruber back in my Staff College days, to being of two minds about him during the Polish and French campaigns, to finally seeing the truth dawn and beginning to loathe him more and more, to the complex long act of learning to hate him through and through, in a crescendo, and then learning not to keep the hatred in a vacuum, but to air it, mobilize it, use it, after which there was the whole business of an ethics that transcended ethics, culminating in a deed of homicidal saintliness, not an end in itself, but the prelude to a just polity, a decent policy, a new Germany. I'd come a long way, round many corners, just to be one of the killers in order to stay sane.

Feeling obliged to make contact with the formal structure of my ostensible religion, I went somewhat shamefacedly to talk with Conrad Preysing, the Bishop of Berlin, at Hermsdorf Hospital. It was a tense encounter, mainly because I had come to discuss the effect on me of a cause I couldn't reveal, so that we conversed in mental gestures, I in biased hypotheses, he in the minutiae of principle.

I began uneasily. "Might not a man undertake something evil for a virtuous purpose? Bad means, good end? A change of regime, say."

"Many do. Some even do a good thing toward a bad end. But you're forgetting something, aren't you?" The massive black mantelpiece behind his chair shone like a mesa of coal, reflecting the dense greenery of an apple tree in the tiny oblong garden outside the window. "Colonel, you are asking if someone might do such a thing without losing his immortal soul. The man might be considered separate from his act, which would be an exception, *within* his spiritual system, but not *of* it, like a bit of . . . like a foreign body lodged in the stomach, round which nature forms a clot of slime." He half-smiled an apology.

I leapt at the offer. "And which, like a tiny bit of shrapnel, say, eventually works its way right out?"

He knew better. "Not necessarily. It may remain within forever. One may bless the, ah, host *qua* man without sanctioning the act. I bless you, as a priest; the Church does not." It was enough. I went away into the world's new warmth with a lilt in my gait.

So much for what was serious. Other things, almost farcical

in nature, were going on; for eight months I'd enjoyed my post with Olbricht, who in his ironic way was content to take a lead from such a junior as myself. Now his boss, Fritz Fromm— 2.04 meters tall, vain, addicted to hunting, and a gourmand with enormous square white teeth, about which he sometimes boasted—insisted on having "the toy" for himself. I was my *children's* toy, on account of my lopsidedness and bizarre patch, not to mention the thrusting gyrations with which I overcame my disabilities while walking about, and no one else's. Fritz Fromm, already in Keitel's bad books, would have done better to mend fences than to requisition for his fun a disabled man. Then I saw the silly side of it, which was just as well, because Fromm eventually got his way. What he never knew was that Olbricht and I had begun to get on famously, even to the extent of his mimicking me and asking for orders, all in a deft imitation of my habitual short-phrased patter. Or so I was told by officers who witnessed these bits of byplay, one of whose functions I believe was to show me that Olbricht didn't in the least mind playing second fiddle to me, at least as far as conspiracy went. Tall robot that Fromm thought me, I was winding myself up to an intensity that would make me human twice over.

On June sixth the Allies launched their Normandy invasion; I hadn't thought it would come so soon or go so well. The situation was miserable. What was the point of a coup now? Why risk civil war during defeat? "There's no way out," I told my cousin Peter Yorck, who answered, "We can still do something symbolic, can't we?" Then I sent a message to Tresckow, who wrote back in terms so pungent and final I never asked him anything again. He wrote from the midst of a massive Russian attack.

> The assassination must take place *coûte que coûte*. Even if it doesn't succeed, the Berlin action must go forward. The point now is not whether the coup has any practical purpose, but to prove to the world and before history that German resistance is

ready to stake its all. Compared to this, everything else is a side issue.

That does it, I said mentally. We are not baboons. Nor are we prisoners of war—yet.

On the next day, quite without warning, while I was mulling over Tresckow's message, Fromm whisked me off to S'gruber's Alpine HQ in Berchtesgaden, where I actually conferred about a memorandum I'd written. The whole thing was like a nightclub tableau, with Göring in lipstick, Himmler antiseptically sighing and nodding oily nods, while S'gruber bullied everyone into agreement. Only Heinz Brandt and I stood up to him. The air was stale, especially near S'gruber. At one point, while everyone was poring over the maps on the situation table, S'gruber seemed to blanch, then raised a trembling right hand and looked down the table right at me, as if I posed a threat. The blue and brown splotches that usually discolored his face had gone.

"*Stauffenberg*," he barked dryly. "There you are."

I had not moved since I came in. "*Jawohl, mein Führer*. Is there some question?"

"You can see from there?" His right hand seemed to shudder as he pointed to the map.

I reassured him with a few taut syllables, after which he grunted, "I *do* have your attention, then. It is hard to tell, Colonel, if you are looking one in the eye or not."

Bolder than ever, with Heinz Brandt glaring a plea for caution, I told him, "The one eye does the work of two; sometimes it overdoes it, out of eagerness. May I perhaps come a little closer to the Führer? On such a privileged occasion, I don't want to go and miss something. Another meter or two would do it."

The unsteady hand beckoned me, and toward him I marched, crisp and quick and ultramilitary. Strange to say, with me closer to him, he seemed less anxious; I presented no danger at all; in fact, I found I could move about easily, without requests or commands, in his immediate vicinity. But he'd smelled some threat, all right: from that day on, he and he alone decided on transfers of personnel within the headquarters and gave express instructions about the scrutiny of briefcases.

Then, chill of chills, Himmler helped me into my coat and lifted my briefcase for me, only to set it down quite roughly. The bomb was there, all right, but I had it with me only to test my nerves, which Himmler did to the full. How courteous we were, tilting our heads and saying our thank yous, each pausing for the other to precede, as in a music-hall farce, and paying empty tributes to the mountain air.

On my way out, at the bottom of the ornate, echoing outside staircase, I paused for a moment with Speer, Minister for Armaments and War Production, whom we actually had in mind for a slot in the conspiracy's cabinet. His name was on Nux's list, and Fritzi's too. I'd sat right by him at the big round table in the Berghof salon, my briefcase by his foot. "Hitler himself," he was saying, "urged me to consult with you confidentially as often as I want. You're well in, my friend. I may even wear out your telephone!"

"I don't mind talking to you," I whispered. "I'm glad to, Herr Minister, any time. But the rest in there, they're a bunch of idiots. Criminals and psychopaths. How can you go on dealing with them? They're fawning yes-men, the whole crew."

"*La sagesse,*" he murmured, being fancy, "*se fout.* Wisdom screws itself. I mean it has to look after itself when it's surrounded by nodding donkeys." Had that eerie mountain air gone to his head?

"Thanks for the translation," I told him. "Be seeing you again soon, no doubt." I hoped so; Speer was the architect I'd once wanted to become.

"Inevitably." He looked so dapper, so buttoned-up, that one almost looked for the key that wound him, the table on which he'd dance. "Even if not at this bloody weekend bungalow!"

"The Führer will remember you," Fromm scoffed after our plane had taken off from Freilassing airfield. "You impressed him. Heil Hitler!"

"With my memorandum on parachutists?"

"With your velvet eye! I think he'd like one too. He lives in a dream world, and when things go wrong he looks around for scapegoats. But first he scares 'em to death, and looking like you, with *his face* to begin with, would help! Instead of the forelock that dangles over *his* left eye, a black patch! Yes."

Fromm roared with ghoulish mirth, glad he was back in favor after two years in the cold. Being needed made him salivate. A weather vane, an opportunist, all the way.

After that I managed a quick visit to Bamberg to see Nina and the children. When a quick shivering fit, no doubt the result of fatigue, came over me, she held me tight for a full five minutes, her knitting perched high from one hand like a bedraggled flag. Was it reaction from my first close-up of the devil himself? If spying out the land made me quake, what would I do once the coup had begun? Go catatonic for months on end? I'd been with him only an hour.

"Now, Claus," she was asking, "tell me all about it. What was he like? Were the eyes impressive?"

"No, not in the least. Nothing at all, there was nothing in them or behind them. His eyes were kind of veiled. They expressed nothing at all. Gray, dull, deadened. The whole atmosphere seemed degenerate and rotten with lipstick and perfume and nail polish. They're all psychotics except Speer, who seemed ordinary enough and almost sane. And Brandt, the one who carried Schlabrendorff's Cointreau bomb. Imagine, all the filth and mess, all the depravity in Europe, comes out of the conversations held with him in that room or one like it elsewhere. It's a kitchen of horrors."

Nina seemed oddly relieved. "I think it did you good to go there and actually see him. You've broken a spell. What a pity all of your friends can't go there too and see the root of all this misery." With her free hand she scooped the invisible root out of the ground and held it up for view, then resumed her knitting; ever since I'd had cold hands in Poland, she'd knitted gloves for me all year round. "I feel closer to you, doing it," she'd said. And now, although her work was halved, and more special, she kept at it, tenderly practical as ever.

On June fifteenth, promoted to full colonel, I took up my new post as chief of staff to Fromm. "Good organizer," he said to me as if commenting on someone else. "Just the man I need." Now the Reserve Army, which Fromm commanded, was really within our grasp; *he* was the man *I* needed, and I tried to win him over at once.

"The war is lost. The fault is one man's alone."

"My own appraisal," he said in a gulp, "is not so radically different." I told him I was planning a coup. "Thank you for your candor. Just go ahead as you think fit, and get on with your normal work as well. And for God's sake, if you go through with your ridiculous coup, don't forget my good friend Wilhelm Keitel. Don't forget *him*, please!" He sounded almost plaintive; but his fat poignancy disappeared into the mound of work he then assigned to me (Fromm delegated nearly everything to his staff while he read hunting and shooting magazines).

Within hours, however, I forgot Fromm in the wave of pain I felt when news came that two of our civilian co-conspirators had been condemned to death by the so-called People's Court, notorious for its phony trials and automatic sentences of death. It was all very well, after Tresckow's resonant call to arms, to think in terms of proving, even if only to history, that some of us dared to seize whatever initiative remained to us; but I wondered how much longer the rest of us would last.

I remembered that the tall, blond, young-faced, and blue-eyed Nikolaus Halem had called S'gruber "the mailman of chaos" and, in fierce arguments with several of us, had argued the futility of looking for a military assassin. In 1938 a close

friend of his had been found floating in the Danube, murdered, and another had been sent to both Dachau and Buchenwald. Halem went his own way, on one occasion helping a Jew
to escape to Czechoslovakia who lost his nerve at the wheel,
streaked through the German frontier barrier and rammed
into the Czech one. Arrested, Halem talked his way out of
trouble, as he so often did; but, unable to talk *us* into finding
his kind of assassin—a thug, an inveterate criminal—he found
his own in the person of Beppo Römer, whom the police soon
picked up, and then Halem himself (in February of 1942), together with some hundred other plotters, including Halem's
friend Mumm, the diplomat. The death sentence was handed
down, abusively, on June sixteenth. They had both been tortured for months on end, but implicated nobody; their friends
Fritzi and Schlabrendorff and my cousin Yorck went free.

"You military types will never kill him," he'd told Fritzi.
"He's got you mesmerized. You ought to pay some bum, some
lout, to do the dirty work for you; and, if you don't, I will."
Nothing that we did, no crime that we committed, would be
worse than doing nothing at all.

Then Tresckow sent another message, asking me to go to
Paris and visit General Speidel, Rommel's chief of staff, sug-
gesting he open a gap in the western front for the Allies to
march through; otherwise the Russians would sweep right
through Germany and seal it off. How much I wished my "instructor," as I called Tresckow, were there in Berlin and not
occupied with the futile battle against the Russians in the East.

On June 23 I was talking to my old chum Colonel Eberhard
Finckh in his office on the Rue de Surène in S'gruber's Paris,
where "Ebo" was supposed to foul things up while going
through the motions of being Quartermaster West. Much to
Rommel's annoyance, and some clinical amusement on the
part of Speidel (who knew about our conspiracy), Ebo had
managed to "misplace" the bargeloads of ammunition and
fuel which Rommel had rushed to Normandy along the

French inland waterways. Well briefed before he left Berlin, Ebo was doing his job well; if we wanted the Allies to break through, it was no use letting our own troops have supplies.

"It's a bit calmer here, Claus," he said with his old jolly bluster, "than in the old Stalingrad days! Warmer. The feedbag comes round more often." White-haired, whiter for being next to his youthful rosy complexion in which a blush hovered, Ebo was family, producing a bottle of perfume for Nina. "Xaris." He chuckled. "I know the brand." Astounded, I sat down, pushing my brow sweat upward into my hair.

"No," he cautioned me, "let's get out of here. Find a place we can talk in." He stared at me with eyes that said, I can finally acept the way you look, whereas back in Berlin, only a few weeks ago, his eyes had fumbled, his hands had dithered, when he first saw me. "Oh, Claus, I'm sorry," he'd said. "It's *wrong*. It shouldn't have happened to *you*. It shouldn't have happened at all. You're too . . . . An eye's awful, but . . . . I'm *so upset*."

"Not here?" I motioned at his big mahogany desk, the rugs and bamboo screens, the purring coffeepot, in his barn of an office, flashy with new cut lilies and Nazi flag.

"I'm in enough trouble with Rommel as it is. He wants to fire me, and if I go what use will I be then? Besides, this place isn't as private as it looks. Walls, as the British say, have ears." He winked at the big lilies.

His driver took us to the Jeu de Paume, a pavilion cut off from the Louvre by the Tuileries Garden, and full of Cézanne, Degas, Gauguin, Manet, Monet, Renoir, Rousseau, Toulouse-Lautrec, and van Gogh. Strolling at connoisseur's pace through the arcades of ravishing color, and sighing a bit in that clammy indoor summer air, we got to our main topic.

"You know, Ebo, we haven't any real field marshals left. Whatever their wallpaper hanger wants, they all shit their pants and do it. Nobody has the guts to stand up to him. We have some two thousand generals and field marshals. Imagine that. *Two thousand*. My God. Silence is golden, I've heard.

Well, in this case it's rancid, putrid. Their guts are in their drawers."

Ebo shushed me, then motioned with his eyes at a tall fair-haired man in a dove-gray suit, standing in front of van Gogh's self-portrait of 1889, better known as "Vincent in the Flames." At a discreet distance a uniformed chauffeur hovered. We'd come here to be *private!*

"SS," Ebo whispered. "Visiting SS. It's General Stundt. Just *look* at him." What was astonishing was not the presence of an SS general in mufti in front of van Gogh's mastered churning misery, but what the general was doing, literally trying with finger and thumb to halt a galvanic tic that dragged his face awry in electric convulsions which sucked flesh and skin from bone. The whole face broke up into uncoordinated fits while Stundt tugged at his chin, his mouth, his eye, as if manipulating rubber. To no avail. The chauffeur leapt forward to help, only to be shoved back with appalling force. The general then dry-washed his entire face with both hands, letting out a series of quite different sighs and, finally, addressed van Gogh direct at eye-level, obliviously mouthing words that fell from his face like slabs.

"*Ja.* The Titan. The Grail Knight. *Panzerfaust.* Wolf!"

Passwords? Slogans? Curses of enigmatic force? "Wolf" was one of S'gruber's nicknames, but surely Stundt had someone else in mind, or something. The only other "Wolf" I knew was Helldorf, head of the Berlin police. I felt uncannily upset. Ebo was still gaping as we moved on past the general, who still hadn't stirred, or said any more.

"Rommel's different," Ebo whispered, reverting to my own outburst about generals. "He's against assassination, Speidel says, but he'll join in a coup all right. He's a bit prim. . . ."

When I got back to Berlin, I realized that the assassin I'd been searching for was myself; I'd never thought of it before because I had to run the coup. At the end of an agonizing process in which those with access to S'gruber found excuses and those without it were full of suicidal zeal, I found myself, in more senses than one. There was no more time to comb the lists of personnel. If we didn't act at once, we wouldn't even achieve something symbolic, which meant that if *I* didn't act *I* wouldn't achieve, in this mess, even the faint impact of a punctuation mark at the end of a sentence. All of me began to flow to a point as I told Berthold, Yorck, and the two Haeftens.

"You'll have to be in two places at once, so to speak, anyway," Berthold said coolly. "Is that wise?"

"No, but that's how it's going to be. I'm sick of mucking around. The war's almost over. I have access to him. I can arrange more access than I need. I have the bomb, or rather von der Lancken has it in Potsdam. I'll take the first chance, and then rush back to Berlin. My God, I'm not that indispensable, am I?"

Face crumpled with bleak insight, Berthold just went on murmuring, "I think you are, I think you are, I *know* you are, you are, can't you see it, I know you are, don't you realize what it means to be indispensable in *two* places? *Claus?*"

I was miles and years away, a small boy emerging from an attic in a corner turret, where I had a desk and a stool and a camp bed together with a broken cello, to sneak into my mother's weekly salon, where loud field marshals and well-razored diplomats were holding forth over white wine and cream cake. Lined up by the wall, in white gloves, the servants stood like heraldic waxworks, even as I padded behind them, my breath held, and one-handedly snipped off the tails of their coats with an outsize scissors, after which I fled to an old nut tree and raked the distance with my battered telescope: cows, a ruined tower, picnicking lovers, a glacier, my mood one of sweet indignation: not having been caught, I'd won no praise or blame.

"Claus, come back!" I lay down supine on the little rug of our Wannsee apartment, slid off my eyepatch, wiped away the mucus from the lower lid, and sank into sleep through a puddle of unfallen tears.

12

Berlin

◆

The weird backdrop of everything we said and thought was droves of bombers which flew right across Germany to hit Berlin. We hardly even looked up. A year ago we always had. Nowadays no fighters droned up toward them, and the antiaircraft guns were almost ineffectual. We didn't care. What we called a "mild" attack was one that hit somewhere else in the city. Raging fires and streets jammed with rubble had become so commonplace, like the jumble of toys in some untidy nursery, that we hardly looked at them twice, and the only time the chronic destruction obtruded was when it prevented you from driving along a certain street or destroyed a file of essential documents. *Narcosis* was the word that came to mind: Greek for "making numb," and numbed we were, yet hectically alert at the same time, on behalf of the majority who were too numbed to care.

We became blasé even about the devastation of our homeland, our capital city. The Jeremiahs among us used to prophesy that the bombs would rain down on us for another year, day and night, after which there would be month after month of street fighting, which would precede a return to normal. Millions of us would slither back into view from under the rubble and, although in a sketchy fashion, go about our business as usual. Londoners had been doing just that for years already, and surely not only the British could be phoenixlike. Perhaps those I called Jeremiahs were prophets of a new golden age instead.

The staggering thing, in the immediate present, was what

happened after the "all clear" sounded. Squads of laborers shifted the rubble. Stretcher bearers wove their crazy patterns through the crowd. Next thing, the trains were running again and mail deliveries had resumed. The bombing fused the people together into a self-righteous acquiescence that needed only a public appearance from Goebbels to refuel it. He personified maniacal will and handed out bits of his unholy grail in the shape of handshakes and autographs, telling everyone there was plenty of food and medicine. It took no great intelligence to discern that any revolt would have to come from above. Tired, disaffected, and sickened as the populace might be, it would initiate no revolt of its own. What people needed more than a new regime was a good week's sleep.

Then there was the weather, sultry and unvaried. People slouched from place to place, looking mostly down, occasionally standing still to wipe a forearm across the brow or to pinch the bridge of the nose as if to bring their eyes back into focus. Where tar remained on the roads, faint mirages danced and hovered above it while it melted. And it was heat with dust, adding new threads of pink to eyes bloodshot already. In another moment of history, such weather might have been sublime, an urban reminder of all the richness the harvest contained, of warm water to swim in, of evenings just a few degrees cooler than the day had been, and sleep under one thin sheet. Instead, it was a drab inferno, blurring the minds of those who needed to think most clearly and twisting the overwrought nerves of furtive conspirators to murderous new tensions. The hot, muggy air seemed an additional presence sent by the Gestapo to overhear us and, instead of functioning as an element breathed in common, drove us apart in search of a cubic foot that was cool and free of another's body heat. Tiffs occurred that would have been impossible had the weather been ten degrees cooler, or the humidity lower. All we could do was to tell our brains that we could transcend anything: the muttering thunder between our ears had nothing to do with what went on in the clouds through which the bombs and the lightning fell.

There was one innocent episode during the same month, however, that strengthened me no end. I had of course given up riding altogether after being wounded, and Jagd and I lived in separate dimensions. A maimed man has no light touch left to him, but I did hear of a fellow officer who, in spite of having *two* artificial arms, had managed to ride again, at least without intolerable difficulty. "I'll never manage anything like that," I told Nina. "I'm not *that* resourceful." That was my attitude when I visited the cavalry school at Krampnitz, commanded by my old friend Colonel Harold Momm.

"Try again," he urged me, "just for the record."

"No," I told him. "It would be humiliating."

He nonetheless had a horse led out in front of the officers' mess. Somehow I mounted it and, glory be, got it to do a piaffer, like a blind man doing acrobatics, a deaf man singing perfect pitch. It was as if my hand were not my own but, guided by some reins I could not see, did things perfectly in the fashion of a marionette. I had never felt so stranded, so frail, so feathery, and there I was making the horse tromp the sonnet of dressage, high-stepping in place with a dozen young officers looking on. It was a levitation. A miracle. A lift. And, even as the horse executed its maneuver, I felt strange in the extreme. My second attempt went less well, however, as if the first one had been an unmitigated fluke. All of a sudden I was butterfingered, unable to drape the reins through my hand. I wobbled, I almost fell off, I was completely off balance. I was like someone trying to knit one-handed. My unattuned mind sent a message to my other hand to help the one that fumbled with the reins, but no hand answered. So, as increasingly often, I used my teeth, grimacing at the taste of soiled leather and at first losing the reins altogether. The horse just grazed. Then I overused my knees, I leaned forward when I shouldn't have, and he took off in a spry canter while I flailed about trying to get a proper hold of the reins again.

Then I realized I had learned a new and just as intricate discipline. I had acquired the finesse of living lopsided, and the little shuffles I made, and the awkward compensatory strides, amounted to a new kind of dressage, practiced on myself this time. There was an art to merely getting about, and on a horse there was a newer art of adapting *that* new skill to the old discipline. I no longer excelled. If I did well, it was by accident, when the horse actually misread my moves and executed what turned out to be the best maneuver. I tried again and again to do things with average competence, grateful for the quiet bravos of Momm and his staff. I was in the saddle again, and it was bliss.

On my mount I smelled ammonia and saddle leather, bran and hay, but from all of Germany quaking and undulating around me I sensed a viscous bubble of panic ready to burst. At this very moment of precarious, almost tightrope-walking ecstasy, some rough-handed lout was hosing down the guillotine in this or that crowded jail, and several of our number were being dragged in spiked handcuffs from their cells to the interrogation rooms where loud military marches were already playing (or, perversion of perversion, recordings of children's laughter played full blast). There was always a smell of burning on the wind, mingled with cordite or sulfur. The distance boomed. The sky droned.

I dismounted, assisted just a little. Of course I was overjoyed, but I had no time to go home to Bamberg to ride Jagd. The balance regained, or the sense of mental equilibrium that came with the physical one, would enable me to do something more daring than a piaffer. In this new mode of cavalry attack, a man was his own horse and could not afford to be seen getting used to his mount in public.

My Nina was pregnant with our fifth child, who was due

sometime in January 1945, emerging into a better world. Or so I hoped, miserably beset by the notion that, like some gruesome equestrian assassin, I was mounted on my children—ages ten, eight, six, three, with one unborn—and no longer allowed to gallop back.

"There's something I want you to see," Berthold said on the phone to me one evening. "Something you *have* to see. It's dangerous, but I've managed to arrange it." His voice sounded clogged and drab. I agreed, and Haeften drove us from the Bendlerstrasse through dwindling light to an ugly rococo building with a shrapnel-pitted façade, at the most fifteen minutes from my desk. My stomach gurgled away, empty and tight.

"Have *you* seen it?" I asked in a tone of ill-disguised querulous mystification. "Why all the cloak-and-dagger? Why don't you tell me now?" Frowning, as if from some mellow but undeniable pain, he merely said, "Have I *seen* it? I've seen *enough*. According to some it's a national treasure. Here, let me give you a hand." Up the broken steps we went, onto a stone landing that felt oddly hollow under its coating of rubble, and through a door that opened even as Berthold reached for it. All I could see in the gloomy hallway was a male figure in a smock receding from us with a nimble lurch. No words, no introductions. The building seemed empty and smelled of metal polish with, mixed in, another, sweeter aroma like that of freshly opened canned ham like that we'd plundered in Poland. After two more doors, each with frosted glass sheathed in wire grids, Berthold ushered me into a big-feeling chamber that had an echo and the sound of dripping taps. Apart from one small lamp at head level just inside the doorway, there was no light, but I could see what looked like a gigantic crate or a medium-sized van in the center of the room. The smell was vile: not acrid or sweet, but rather like chlorine.

"Over here," Berthold whispered, tracing out the route with a flashlight masked in red. "On the wall." I could just make

out some sort of display case and was half expecting to see revolvers, rifles, gas guns, when the rosy beam began to outline
the skeleton of a human hand, then an elbow, several feet, and
a perfectly cleaned pair of femurs mounted toe to thigh. I
could hold my breath no longer. "Where are we?"

He made no audible response. That grisly mural would have
been enough for me (though I had one fleeting, ridiculous
thought about knowing where to come for my replacement
hand), but Berthold was motioning me to the crate-shaped
thing, a head taller than I was, and, swaying a little, up a small
stepladder I went, suddenly realizing the wall was metal, the
smell that of rust and moss. The flashlight found my hand and
I stroked it downward, then held it still, aghast to see three
partly dismembered bodies, all female, floating in what must
have been alcohol. Voluptuously built, these women had a
flawless poise, and one, with her head far back, in frozen motion seemed to cup her stomach with one hand. I looked on,
awed. Then I saw that the woman on my left had no head at
all and that, afloat between the legs of the one in the middle
was a torso with breasts but no legs, no arms, no head. The skin
had a zinc-white cast that seemed to flush as I moved the beam
of light to and fro, like a schoolboy at some penny peepshow.

"Jews," Berthold whispered as if shivering, though the
dreadful room was warm. "They measure them, then gas
them. But some from Plötzensee come here too, especially the
beheaded. I thought you needed a postcard like this, right behind your eye. It won't ever go away, Claus." He prodded my
hip.

"Don't say my name in here," I snapped. My head felt
numb, my knees felt superlubricated.

"Another tank is full of imbeciles' heads, all in alcohol. Mon-
gols, macrocephalics, half of them children—*everything*."
Helpless, I retched dryly over the tank, almost toppled off the
stepladder, and without thinking spat several times into the
tank. Then I realized what I had just done.

"Now they'll *know.*" I would have scooped it back, but when your only hand holds the flashlight . . . Next the red light came from my mouth as I leaned over hunting for the scab of vomit, bile, or whatever it was; and I could see nothing but big white thighs and pubic hair in a dead float like some sea fern delicately grafted. I thought I heard a gurgle: my stomach?

With my eye closed, I trod back down, the flashlight still in my mouth, even as Berthold raved on in an uncontrollable whisper. "They throw some into freight cars spread with quicklime, and it takes them days to die. In the camps, tiny flakes of scorched skin come floating in through the bars of the cells. And when they slaughter them in hundreds in pits, the condemned have to stand on the dead and dying, and they caress them while waiting to be shot. It goes on all the time. *Anatomy!* Why, this is nothing. The whole of Europe's thick with blood."

I wiped the flashlight on my sleeve and gave it back.

All I could think just then was *It's no use being alive.* Maybe a hundred years hence, mankind will have improved, will be—humane. Yet I doubted it; the monster which had slithered out of the abyss would not go back, any more than my lost eye would grow in again like a crab apple in late May.

"Let's get going," Berthold said quite loudly.

"How did you arrange it?" I had no voice, no tones, at all, and I had to ask him again. My heart was under water.

"Influence," he said glibly, almost serenely.

"I thought *I* had all the influence."

"I know some people you don't." Said like an elder brother.

"That mess in the tank," I fussed. "Won't they see it?"

"To hell with it." He made it sound reverent, biteless.

"All right, but I still feel guilty, as if I've defiled something." I had heaved upon the dead in their mutilation.

Berthold lit the way to the outside door. "No, you cared enough to throw up. Handkerchief?" The door closed behind us as if by remote control. I wanted to scream or yell, somehow to discharge the nauseated tension of the last quarter-hour. One definitive vignette of the Third Reich had unmanned me quite, and here I was envisioning an act of murder, my mind obsessively hunting a tangent that returned me to Sauerbruch's office, in a closet of which there sat a cardboard box full of plaster heads replicating those of burn victims, which he had tinted himself in ghoulish watercolors. Noseless, lipless, eyeless, chinless, mouthless, these makeshift gargoyles were his "teaching aids," but he loved to show them off to guests as well, and no doubt patients seeing them felt less sorry for themselves. Yet Sauerbruch's box was a heavenly pasture compared to the vat in the anatomy institute.

All the way home to Wannsee, I kept wondering why the concept of beauty is so arbitrary, why exposed intestines are called ugly but the amputated Venus de Milo its opposite, and on and on, and so forth, all of it maudlin, trite brooding out of trauma by disgust. The floating women had come home to roost all right, and, I harangued myself as the warm air laved my face, they even had an unearthly beauty which reminded me that life is not essential to the body's beauty—oh no, nor human to land- or seascape, nor God's blessing to a planet empty of humankind. I wanted, right there, the end of humanity, by whatever means: incineration by the local star, or mass suicide. Then, soothed by extreme fantasy, I came to life.

"I hope you've not overwound the Toy," I told Berthold, who didn't answer or even turn to look at me.

"Things are so bad now," quipped Haeften by the car, feeling out of things, "the generals stab one another in the front."

"Clever," I sighed. "Very clever. I am thinking about Macbeth's hand. No, *Lady* Macbeth's hands." But I could fix my mind on nothing that dispelled the floating Jews adrift in a private fluid dimension in which they had a dignity denied them in their lives, and us in ours.

13

"Stauff"

◆

Late in the afternoon of July fifth I strolled through the unbombed gardens of Wannsee with my longtime counselor and friend, Professor Rudolf Fahrner, who had arrived from Athens at the end of June, and since then had been sharing the flat at 8 Tristanstrasse with Berthold and me, working on various proclamations.

"Nothing much has happened up to now," I told him as a clutch of little girls in frilly dresses hurtled past us giggling. A couple of them turned round and pointed at my eye until their teacher shooed them onward. "But the waiting's over. Just one thing. I've decided to do the damned thing myself. D'you approve?"

"The war is almost over. Didn't you tell me we've lost over a dozen divisions in the latest Russian offensive?"

"If we act now," I told him, reciting something I'd told myself over and over, "we'll save a lot of lives. The point is, though, we'll have to do it out of self-respect anyway. I'm supposed to run the coup here in Berlin, so how the hell can I be in two places at almost the same time? Should I go and do it? We *should* have done it in *1938*."

The whole of his special subject, German language and literature, seemed to pass in review before his eyes before he answered with gruff reluctance, "Yes." That was all. The rest of the day was given over to telephone calls—some of which I made while lying flat on a table—wine, and poetry. Fahrner was witty, Berthold in the grip of some exaltation other than wine, and I, I was full of talk, my head felt aflame.

All my previous worries seemed like squashed wasps, and I even launched forth about my ancestor, Gneisenau, a biography of whom Fahrner had published in 1942. "After all," I told them, "Mother's one of his great-granddaughters. His name was always coming up at home. Maybe, unconsciously, I keep trying to be like him, at least in some ways. If I remember rightly, Rudolf, I even tried to talk you into changing your version of him and soft-pedaling his revolutionary, populist, side. Sorry! None of my business, I suppose, but he was family, so I had a right to be a bit possessive, and if not that, well—finicky. Revolt from within is the business of responsible people in high places, not of the people at large. Agreed?"

Giving me a bemused, indulgent look, while his hand made some motion in between a wave and a slap, Fahrner saw Berthold glance away, and brought his hand abruptly down. Clearly, on that unbuttoned night of nights, I was not to be chided for going off at the mouth. Not only had I interfered with his book while he was writing it, intruding my own night-thoughts into literary history; I now saw his book as the prospectus of my future, six or seven years hence, twisting what had begun as hero-worship into prophetic self-importance. And when, at last, in mellow exasperation, Fahrner fetched the book from his suitcase and read a certain passage aloud, to ease the tension, I felt it was me he singled out, like a boar against snow.

" 'His was not a spirit,' " he read with a rather nasal resonance, " 'which was prepared to bow to what to others might seem the inevitable; his mind was busy thinking how, by his own exertions, a man might liberate Prussia.' " He paused and looked right at me. "Well, Claus? For *Prussia* read *Germany?*" I needed no second bidding, and it was dawn before we turned in, talked-out.

Next day came the news that Julius Leber had been seized by the Gestapo, Leber who had once beaten his way through a mob of brownshirts with a chair leg in each hand. I couldn't believe he was in prison again, he who'd spent so much of his life already on a bare floor without coat, blanket, or even straw at a temperature below freezing, in Sachsenhausen camp, and had come out after four years, saying, "No fate is quite point-less." Now they had him again, the German Lenin with the broad shoulders and the Gibraltar build.

"I'll fetch him out," I babbled, "I'll get him out, I won't leave him there," but I had little idea of exactly how to man-age it. Who had betrayed him? How safe were the rest of us for how long? I felt as if a Stauffenberg carousel had been set to run inside my brain, confusedly chanting, "I'll kill S'gruber, I'll *kill* him all right. The only decent thing now's to commit as much high treason as we can. If you're going to be a traitor, be one all the way. And we'll *get* Leber out. They won't touch a hair of his head."

On July sixth I flew with Fromm to S'gruber's HQ at Berchtesgaden, complete with my bomb. "I've got the whole bag of tricks here," I told Stieff. "Interested?" He seemed to waver, then shook his head vigorously like a wet dog and made some joking excuse. Himmler, Speer, Buhle, and Fromm held two hour-long conferences, one running from five to six in the evening, the other from midnight on. I had no chance to do anything; I thought Stieff would do it, but he didn't, nor did he make the attempt on the following day when S'gruber in-spected uniforms at Klessheim Castle nearby. I smarted with disappointment and rage, then flew back to Berlin in a loud, drafty Heinkel. It was impossible talk over the engines, and Fromm merely *saw* the wheezing laugh, so close to tears, that I resorted to.

Going to the mirror in my bedroom, I took off my eyepatch and looked at the gristly little clump of what remained. There should have been some brown and white, but everything was red and suet-colored. Such an act corresponded, I supposed, to gaping at your own genitalia; but I just wanted to see if all the

seepage came from a stopped-up tear duct. It didn't. Some of
the liquid was lymph, and there was even a trace of blood; if
the eye had been intact, it would have been bloodshot, like the
eyes of the people in the Berlin streets, like the eyes of my fellow conspirators. As it was, I had outlets rather than a self-con-
tained tracery of tiny capillaries, and constantly having to dab
away at what they released did not improve my temper. Indeed, an itch had developed, as if a dozen needles kept making
fleeting contact with the nerves, and then it became a feathery
sensation, after which I seemed to have an eye socket full of
dust. This itch woke me from what little sleep I got and, in the
long run, set the whole cheek twitching in a muscle spasm of
its own. No doubt observers interpreted the phenomenon as
they chose. It certainly fitted in with the general report of a
Stauffenberg more and more nervous each day.

My minor behavior had become somewhat erratic. A faint
strut had invaded my natural gait. I gesticulated more. I
looked, smirking or smiling, down at rugs, floorboards, or the
smashed concrete of the sidewalk. When speaking, I had no
stammer, but my brain itself seemed to have one, which, by
sheer effort of larynx and tongue, I prevented from reaching
the outside world. My voice was even hoarser, as if colossal
nervous strain had sapped it of resonance, but all I had was a
severe case of relaxed throat, easily remedied by gargling with
port wine, of which we had none, just as we had no ointment
to still the itching in my eye.

We were making do. We were making history. It was no use
fretting about incidentals unless, of course, they prevented you
from laying your life on the line with maximum competence.
Just dying in any old fashion was merely histrionic.

About this time I became more patch-conscious than usual,
taking elaborate care to ensure an air space between the rim of
the velvet and the left-hand side of my nose's bridge. Otherwise the salt of perspiration made the other seepage worse. It
was a soft, soothing patch, ridged with swirling corrugations

across which a fingernail could run with a faint *zip* noise. I had often wished for a patch I could wear as a monocle, but there was no such thing in the National Socialist heaven on earth, so I wore a strip of black elastic across my right temple and above my left ear. Fingering it abstractedly, I sometimes drew the patch upward and back over my head as if masking a succession of sockets that climbed up my brow into my hair. Then, abruptly, I slid the loop down again, having in the process given my eye socket a thorough airing. It was also, I found, a useful way of emphasizing a point, and I had even seen people agree with me because, in a fit of ostensibly preoccupied pique, I began to slide patch away from eye, threatening them with vacancy, and God alone knew what besides. Conjunctivitis only.

Of course, the other eye at once became mesmerically terrifying, just because it was there, and I learned the difference between a patch that is no eye at all and an eye remnant. With one eye open and the other clad, I was normal; with one eye open and the other naked, I was an off-center Cyclops, yet with no more fearsome attribute, thanks to modern explosives, than a hypersensitive little pucker in the cavity. I could not even blink to soothe it.

Of course, my depth perception was uncertain, and sometimes the good eye gave out under the strain, and I conducted my business in a steamed-up blur, balancing a mirage with a blank, and thankful I was not a Luftwaffe pilot, although it wouldn't have mattered much one way or the other: there was no fuel, except for communications planes, and what was left of Göring's vaunted air armada sat creaking and clicking in the July sun.

On July eleventh, with Captain Friedrich Karl Klausing instead of Werner von Haeften, I once more flew to S'gruber's headquarters in Berchtesgaden.

"Damn, *damn*," I whispered to Stieff before the conference began at a few minutes past one P.M. "*No Himmler.* Good

God, shouldn't I go ahead and do it anyway?" I had been certain Himmler would be there. When *I* was there, so should *he* be; we were supposed to work things out together. Otherwise why have a conference at all? I telephoned Olbricht, who said "No, you mustn't," and at once set about canceling various preliminary measures he'd set in motion. What a fiasco.

Late that evening I was back in Berlin reporting to Beck and Olbricht, who both agreed with me that we would never again hold up the assassination because Himmler wasn't present.

Beck was in a strange, divided mood. Right on top of insisting we must act forthwith and (he quoted Clever Hans Kluge's newest opinion) send "outstanding negotiators" to London and Moscow, he swung to abstracted pensiveness.

"Tomorrow," he said gently, "the Wednesday Society meets. The speaker is the eminent physicist Werner von Heisenberg, and he will address us on the physical structure of stars, the nature of the atom, and the use of atomic energy and cosmic rays. I'm doing a little bookwork beforehand! Imagine: the Society goes back to 1863, long before *all this!*"

"Good God, sir," I exclaimed, as if echoing my outburst to Stieff earlier in the day, "I think history's more present for you than the present itself—what's going on, or not going on, this very second! I don't mean it as a criticism, I'm just a bit envious of your capacity for moving outside time, for always managing to see the here and now as just a little fidget—a hiccup, a cough, a bad local smell—in terms of something vast that's available to you alone. Yes, I'm really envious."

Beck's ditherer's eyes opened and closed, then opened again full of new-lit zeal, but his mind was cruising high above Greenland, and mechanized warfare was the merest of modern vulgarities. Whatever was he going to come up with now? A man with more time than I would have begun to write at least some of Beck's Beckisms down.

"God." He sighed. "I think you said *good* God? I suppose it's possible to think of God as a *thing—ein Etwas—*but not as some gigantic gaslike formation that acts on us somewhere in the hidden depths. Oh no. It's only useful to think of God as a thing when you mean God is *not nothing*. We cannot *experience* God in the same way as a piece of chalk. We do not *experience* God, the assembler or convener of the universe; we make our peace, or not, only with our own notion of that being who is not nothing. People have to realize this. Do you think Olbricht's grasped it? Does he care? Do *you?*" He grew suddenly mischievous. "Claus, every bellyache has a silver lining—I've had enough stomach trouble to know! Now, Godspeed. I must rest."

As I left, one of the coarsest Beckisms came back to me, but I realized it was just as abstruse as crude. "Claus," he'd said, several weeks ago, "the whole world's got the jitters. We're so jumpy we even rush through defecation, and cannot savor—I suppose I mean *ontologically prize*—the minutes during which what's used and dead slips away from us, who are still to be used and go on living. When that dead stuff falls away, the part of me that's half-dead pays homage to the half of me that's still alive. There! Am I an overgrown schoolboy with a penchant for filth? Or am I becoming the latest philosopher of body chemistry? Who am I to quibble when, I gather, somebody high up's been conning Himmler about how to exploit the stars for the war effort? The SS will soon be purging the Milky Way, at this rate, of dwarf stars and deviant binaries and God knows what else!" I left his dark walnut of a soul to creak and tighten; Beck fingered the texture of being as if it were God's eyelid, and no one could prove him wrong.

"Are you all right, sir?" Schweizer asked as I slumped into the car. "Was it a bad interview? You seem unsettled."

"I'm fine," I called forward to him. "I've just been made aware that the way we live our lives, most of us, is a waste of life itself. You know what life *is*, Schweizer? It's a damned good thing, and the universe has no time for Oliver Twist. Now, please don't kill us by driving too slow."

Then we flew over craters round which we couldn't drive.

The day before my next attempt, S'gruber moved his HQ back to Rastenburg in East Prussia, heedless of the oncoming Russians from the East. This time, Saturday July fifteenth, I again went with Klausing, since Haeften still wasn't fit. I was beginning to feel repetitious, trapped in a fathead's pattern; I'd already been to Berchtesgaden three times, and once before to Rastenburg. I'd become so accustomed to carrying a bomb around in a plump, yellow briefcase that I felt ungainly without it. Could a tilted walk, even by a disabled soldier, give him away to the Gestapo? *That man is accustomed to carrying a bomb*, they'd say. *Follow him until he collects it again. Then pounce.*

We landed at Rastenburg soon after nine-thirty A.M. and were met by Lieutenant Geisberg, who drove us bumpily to breakfast in the Kurhaus mess in Area 2 of Wolf's Lair. An aroma of genuine coffee hung on the sultry air like a reprieve, and I thought, the "Cure House" is well named. It's a spa, with caffeine, whereas "Wolf's Lair" is crass and that "Eagle's Nest" thing at Berchtesgaden's inane.

Then, it was the coffee's fault, I was longing for home, and local carp cooked according to arcane Bamberger recipes, and small Frankish sausages, and a special smoky beer, all of them as far away as Shangri-la.

At eleven, however, Geisberg drove us off to meet Keitel, Fromm's "good friend," who found no order too vile to pass on, no bond too precious to break in the interests of self-advancement, medals, and money. He knew nothing about strategy and had no effect on the course of the war, but he was just what S'gruber wanted: a pork butcher in uniform, well deserving the dainty pun that discerned the lackey—*Lakai*—in his very name. Fortunately, before becoming entangled with this rancid figurehead, I'd been able to put through a call to Stieff in Mauerwald camp, not far away.

At 1300 Fromm, Keitel, and I went to the so-called morning

briefing, held in a hut near the visitors' bunker in which S'gruber slept. There I stood, gazing upward at the wires and cables, the camouflage nets and ropes, which festooned the trees. The grass was neatly trimmed, the gravel of the paths was quite unworn, and not far away the bunker entrance gaped like the entrance to some pyramid or (the image crept back into my mind's eye) to the ziggurat on the bogus Cairo medal. Keitel and I were making diligently trivial conversation with Luftwaffe General Bodenschatz in front of the entrance when S'gruber came out, accompanied by Admiral von Putt-kamer, one bodyguard, and his chief photographer.

". . . my own suggestion that you be ordered to Wolf's Lair to advise us," Keitel was saying. He'd just described Eva Braun as "a very, very nice person, dark blond, reticent, retiring sort, with quite nice legs, oh yes." Bodenschatz came to attention as S'gruber approached, and Keitel stiffened, then began to gush. "*Mein Führer!* How wonderful of you to come outside! General Bodenschatz, Count von Stauffenberg, and I are sampling the summer air. Good German air!" The photographer took aim. The click caught Bodenschatz bowing slightly as he shook hands.

Then, while his Führer stared at him with glacial patience, Keitel rambled on about his last birthday, his face haggard but his eyes all joy. "An utterly German occasion," he was saying, "in the Tavellenbrück game area at Ibenhorst. I was with Scherping, Master of the Hunt, looking for elk. Nothing but pastureland, dense alders, giant hydroceles, for two whole hours. But I potted one in the end, felled it with my second shot, a huge beast taller than I. After that I just had time to get back and change for dinner with the Führer himself! Ah, what a day that was, *mein Führer!* Stauffenberg here doesn't hunt, but he still rides, I think. . . ." And there he left his gaffe, sud-denly recalling that S'gruber loathed horses; Keitel, the farmer and landowner, was the fidgeting toady once again, proud of his elk only because S'gruber had helped him celebrate the kill. The photographer snapped us again. We kept on making chit-chat so as to seem alive in the pictures, but S'gruber, having shaken hands with Bodenschatz at length in order to defer his second contact with me, no longer had Keitel's dithering nostalgia to lean upon. The hand that might just have been lifted out of brine or isinglass jerked, then strayed toward me even as its owner stared past my neck at the ghost of Keitel's giant elk, killed for the Field-Marshal's sixty-first year on earth.

All I could think of, in the anticlimax of it all, was how poorly a one-eyed man judges distances. When S'gruber once again shook *my* hand—barely suppressing his wince of revulsion as my three fingers grazed his knuckles—I shoved out my hand too far, and not merely because it felt so light. A man whose mission is to arm the fuse of a bomb should have better depth perception than that, I told myself, even as S'gruber snapped his hand back and twisted away, his eyes the color of rained-on lead. And he kept looking back as if I were stalking him, or some invisible bird hovered above his ear huffing at him and tumbling the hot air about his cheeks. Then I thought forlornly of the copper wire umbilical that linked me to Berlin, where some of the older conspirators in our group were dusting off their stamp collections, or practicing holding themselves erect on well-groomed green lawns, or coining epic little speeches.

Next, we all went inside and "briefed" S'gruber for about half an hour. A special conference, on stragglers and reinforcements, began, followed by yet another, in which Fromm was the centerpiece.

I felt wretched: I'd had no opportunity to arm the bomb by nipping the neck of the fuse with pliers; none beforehand and none now, even as the final briefing began to wind up around two-thirty. Only a fool would have stood in front of the briefing hut with the fuse already going, just in the hope that S'gruber would show up on time. Equally, however, we had long ago decided against the instant fuse that enabled one to take advantage of sudden opportunity. I, the bomber, had to survive to run the coup. It was like being the prisoner of specialized time: you could not prepare to act any more than you could act without preparation. A second briefcase was with Klausing, parked in the same place as before, so he could be of no help, and I certainly couldn't carry both briefcases—someone would be bound to offer to help, even to open it up for me, when the bomb wrapped in the shirt would be impossible to overlook. No, we had saddled ourselves with the wrong method, unless we could find some way to get the fuse going in private: some pretext, some excuse. Besides, Fromm was on top of us, and he couldn't be trusted to keep quiet, still less to shield my action as I wielded the pliers with three fingers.

As it was, back in Berlin, Olbricht had alerted the Guard Battalion and the army schools for eleven A.M., a superbly reckless thing to do if the entire operation depended on Himmler's being present. It was worth doing this only if I were to make the attack on S'gruber regardless of any other factors; but one of the senior plotters, Quartermaster General Wagner (who last year had visited me in hospital), had sent a colonel with us to remind Stieff and myself in particular that there must be no assassination without Himmler. Hearing this, Beck and Olbricht backed down when I made a telephone call to report the fact (as well as to say that S'gruber had called on me to make a presentation).

"Ali," I said to Mertz von Quirnheim, who held the phone at the other end, in the Bendlerstrasse, "you know that in the last resort it's only a matter between *you* and *me*. What do *you* say?"

There was no delay, no wavering. *"Do* it," he said, but when I got back to the scene the second conference was over and I had to prepare for the third one, with Fromm watching my every move. Why had I called the Bendlerstrasse? In the first place, I was being obedient to the wishes of Wagner, Beck, and Olbricht, hoping against hope they'd forget about Himmler.

My main motive, though, was to report that there seemed no way of attempting the assassination that day: I was too hemmed in, too much in demand, and in any case saddled with the wrong bomb. To Ali's "do it" I would have responded heart and soul when I got back to the conference hut, but there was no opportunity, and indeed no chance of getting away before the bomb went off: I would never have been allowed to excuse myself while occupying S'gruber's undivided attention. The conference hut smelled of petals and chalk mingled with some sort of disinfectant, and it was that smell which I took home in my nostrils, thinking assassination might be something you learned as you went along, but not something you discussed long-distance while actually engaged in the attempt.

That same day, Saturday the fifteenth, Ali telephoned his wife in Harnack-Hause to tell her the attempt was off. She at once wrote down in her diary the gist of the fiasco, bit by bit, evil turn by evil turn, quietly dominating what had dominated us. Her prose nested us as we fell. "Stauff," she truncatedly wrote, "had called him after the start of the conference with the Führer to say that Himmler once again was not there." *Had* I? "A. reported this," she went on, "to Olbricht, Beck, and other gentlemen who were waiting there together. There had ensued a rather long and, as A. thought, deliberately prolonged exchange of opinions and additional telephone calls, all of which gave A. the depressing feeling of finding himself alone when the courage and determination to take the plunge were required."

So, I was not alone: I was not alone in feeling alone.

Frau Mertz continued writing with the same stately pungency; it was the way she talked, and here she was setting it on paper in the quiet suburb of Harnack-Hause while the birds of summer tootled and the undemolished chestnut trees creaked as the afternoon heat began to relent. "So he was forced to tell Stauff after a valuable half an hour had elapsed that the generals were opposed to carrying out the attack if Himmler was not there. But Stauff had replied," as I well knew, " 'Ali, you know that in the last resort . . .' "

That brief, vivid, yet ultimately pointless exchange of words coursed through my mind again. *Do it*, Ali had said. And do it I had meant to. Now Hilda Mertz von Quirnheim conducted me out to the end of my penultimate endeavor, in words that proved all over again that neither Ali nor I was alone; there, on wartime paper bound in heirloom leather, with her broad but secretive nib dipped in diluted ink, she had seen me through, saying, "From that moment on he had waited, with Siebeck" (Ali with a friend, that is) "in maddening suspense, until finally the news came from St that the conference had just ended as he had returned to it. This was the third time since I had been in Berlin that Stauffenberg had gone down this horrible road in vain." How true: she had only been in the city since early July, when Ali had moved out from living with Berthold and myself. I liked being "Stauff" in her mind's ear, but her one use of "St" reminded me of how I would inscribe "Gf St" on my war diary, with unenigmatic allusiveness; "Stauff," though, perhaps because it evoked *Staub*, the word for dust, gave me the right post-mortem feeling of elusiveness: dust in S'gruber's eye, ground out by the mills of God.

First thing on July sixteenth, as on every Sunday, I put through a call to Nina, wanting to say everything, not in detail, but compressed into a phrase: *I am on the very edge*. Instead, I became prosaic.

"I wish you wouldn't go through with the trip to Lautlingen. Stay in Bamberg with your mother." How tell her the rest? "There are good reasons," I lamely added.

"But I already have the tickets and passes. We'll have to go on the eighteenth, as planned. Does it really matter that much?" When she became concerned, her voice developed a grave lilt, and I knew she would consider seriously any *serious* reservations I had.

"Yes, it really matters." I was hoarse again.

"Then what? Oh, I think I know."

Risk it and tell her now, I thought. No: *don't.* My mother wants to see the children.

"It's blistering hot here and muggy," she said while she waited.

"Here too." I was insulting her good judgment, on a seeming whim asking for a serious change in plans. When a woman traveled by train in wartime, with four children, it was almost like moving an army. "Well, in that case"—I wrenched the words out—"you'd better go ahead as planned." I wished I could, for once, explain to her in full, pouring out heart and mind in a wash of fervor, relief, and love; but to do so might empty me of momentum. I'd kill him in my mind and then not do it on the day. I'd never felt so fraudulent, so secretive, so little her lover, her man, her rock. Here I was, giving myself quite inadequate reasons for not telling her, whereas, in my deepest self, I'd become voluptuously secretive about the whole thing, as if S'gruber were mine, *mine already,* to be shared with no one, not even the woman in whose arms I'd dreamed the evil dreams of convalescence, from strangling him one-handed to shooting him through the eye. Life had become a ferocious lull in which, against my nature and my will, I thought most clearly about murdering him when I was being hugged tight, and so, in my mind's eye—that lewd little cockpit where a maimed midget swung an epic broadsword—I felt most loving, most grateful, most tenderly reciprocal, only in the act of dreaming his death. I could be human again only in and after the few seconds of that murderous feat. Unhugged, I couldn't get his death into focus; but, with his death in focus while Nina held me tight, I was gentle as a baby. Had I been in her arms instead of on the telephone, I'd have told her, for sure; our intimacy made me feel safe enough to be fierce, in all ways. As it was, the wire made me dumb, and deceitful too. Surely the Gestapo heard everything we said?

"Claus, is there something you're not saying?"

"Just one of those hunches I get. I'm just fidgety, darling. It's the damned weather. Who can even *think?*"

She waited for me to say more, sensing I still might come through with it; but I said nothing, and just sighed into the Bakelite hole of the receiver, which mouthed a rigid, unending "Oh" of rebuke at me.

"I'm lying in your arms, again," I burst out, "and I'm dreaming deadly dreams, awful dreams that won't go away. It's like right after being wounded, all over again. In a weird way, I seem to be done for. *Kaputt.* A ruined, insane baby."

"What, Claus? What's that about a baby? The line's bad."

"Things are all mixed up. I used to have a clear head, and now I can't even fathom a routine journey. I want to make so many changes, being so changed myself, that nothing seems fixed. I've only you to hold on to."

"And you will again. Big silly. It won't be long."

"Of course not," I said, and I knew then that I'd never tell her. At once I felt glad I hadn't infected her mind with the moral slime I paddled in. Was a liar ever so smug?

"Claus, be good. Don't rub your eye so much."

"I'll be the best. Only, sometimes, my head is like a war. My head needs an armistice fast."

"Don't do anything rash. Be a good colonel now."

"No, only what's utterly considered, and maybe not even that. I'll just sit tight, until the next kiss."

"A warm, soft, long, open Roman one."

I made a kiss-cluck down the wire, where it mixed with all the noises-off and got lost. "God bless," I blurted.

"Yes," she called. "And Claus will explain everything to his Nina very soon. *Au revoir,* dearest. Be good."

Instead, I did my full explaining to Ludwig Beck.

There the target had been, grimacing, raving, squinting, twitching: only a matter of meters away, but the act remained undone, as Beck reiterated throughout the evening. For a man who understood so well the role of patience in human affairs (he wasn't called Slowpoke for nothing), he waited with re- markable discomfort. "While I was telephoning," I told him, "Stieff took the briefcase out of the conference room, maybe to take care of it. Who the hell knows? Who can read Stieff any more?"

"Yes," said Beck, "Olbricht admits that there were some mishaps." Then, in a tone more like his usual even, measured drone, he went on, well rehearsed. "You realize that various parties have once again suggested that we abandon the bomb strategy and arrange instead for our western armies to—well, surrender. Your stock as a planter of bombs has been going down steadily, and I have been under considerable pressure to have you bypassed. Colonel Hansen of Intelligence has already offered to put his plane at our disposal with a view to persuad- ing Kluge once and for all. Not only that: we could foment a civil war at once, and that too would put paid to your bomb. I must in all conscience tell you that unless you explode your bomb, as distinct from merely traveling around with it, in the next few days you will probably no longer have my support— although my admiration and esteem will continue. We already owe you much, but you are not the only means at our disposal. Not quite, anyway." If he had not looked so weary, he would have looked the personification of quiet, festering anger. How pale he was, how drawn.

While Beck droned on, I looked down at my big suntanned hand, what was left of it. Those three fingers had to do three times more work than usual. Indeed, more than three. I won- dered if anyone had ever speculated how Stauffenberg shaved (in a posture of seemingly languorous delicacy I did) or adjust- ed his dress (contorted like a marionette I did) or cut his meat at table (when there *was* any, I did, pressing the knife down on the meat to hold it while I sawed away, thus preposterously trying to combine steadiness with motion). The bombers had arrived early that morning, twice in fact, and the sirens sound- ed so often that I actually heard them, inured to them as I was.

There was much to be done, and yet nothing truly new. The robot would go through his paces once again, after which they would put him away in a museum for curiosities, among the toy trains, the multiple gyroscopes, and the tops that played tunes from Mozart. Yet it was without either relief or anticlimax that I envisioned my final attempt. The most interesting thought I had, confronted with the assassin's schedule and tableau that had become peculiarly mine, was that the French, in just such weather as this, had stormed the Bastille. The heat then, in that July, had been oppressive, and look how well the French had done. Surely we, just as zealously, could bring about a military coup, and then all those big, salmony-apricot sunsets, which seemed like God leaking into view, would be ours, at least to love if not to keep.

That evening, Berthold, Fritzi, Adam von Trott, and my cousin Caesar von Hofacker (a Luftwaffe lieutenant colonel on Stülpnagel's staff in Paris) came to my rooms in Wannsee to thrash things out. Ardent and persuasive as ever, Caesar had ideas galore, first of all pouting his almost rosebud mouth and then letting rip. "Oh yes, Claus, we'll have to divide Germany into north and south zones. I was talking to Ebo the other day, and he agreed. I think Stülpnagel and Speidel will go along."

Adam glared, but that meant he was thinking hard about something else, and Caesar bridled, flushing throughout his rather chubby face even as his wide-open, tired eyes seemed to mist over; he seemed hurt.

"Sorry," Adam said, "believe it or not, I was just thinking one should carry with one everywhere a case of mounted butterflies to remind one of life's fragility!"

"Very poetic," Caesar said. "Here I am, I keep coming and going. I bring you word that *Kluge* will cooperate once Hitler's dead. You send me away to ask *Rommel* to send Hitler an ultimatum saying the war is lost. And *you fellows* sit around polishing maxims. All I care about is that bomb and the moment Ebo Finckh phones me to say, *Exercise all ready?*"

As best I could I soothed him. "I'll phone you myself, Caesar, on the day. You first." His blush wanned, his eyes seemed to focus better, and he became less overwrought. We talked until midnight, converting hope into the politics of exaltation, with our miracle just round the corner, needing only a push.

14
Weep Work

◆

Tuesday, July eighteenth, was torrid, and rather peculiar too. Everyone seemed on edge and talked too loud. According to one of our confederates, Fritzi's boss, the debauched Count Helldorf, who had been Police President of Berlin since 1934, "we must on no account trust Major Remer," who commanded the Berlin Guard Battalion. An ex-Hitler Youth leader who had won the Knight's Cross, Remer had only just arrived after being wounded at the front while performing somber, concentrated feats of courage; he was still regaining his strength, but he was every bit a soldier, a Nazi zealot, and a conscienceless automaton.

This latest complainant was a spectacular man, but hardly the one to appraise Knight's Cross majors. Ferried back and forth on dark expeditions by a chauffeur with the exquisite name of Kelch (Chalice), Wolf Helldorf held orgies at his Wannsee villa in the course of which, I'd heard, pretty actresses under hypnosis emitted for the company the sounds of physical love. The hypnotist, a fake Danish aristocrat with hair dyed blond, was "Erik Jan Hanussen," formerly a muckraking Viennese journalist called Herschel Steinschneider who had been in the business of debunking spiritualists and fortune-tellers. Even S'gruber had resorted to him. The unwise "Hanussen" had been in the habit of lending Helldorf money in exchange for IOU's, which he then kept in his wallet; his bullet-riddled corpse was discovered in the woods, but his IOU's were nowhere to be found. Helldorf conducted his Venusbergs unfazed, although with fewer hypnotic trances; the sounds heard were merely genuine, one gathered.

Looking out at the festive chestnut trees along the Landwehr Canal, I smiled to think that, not far away from the rooms Berthold and I occupied in Wannsee, Helldorf's servants were deftly wiping away the smears from the night's abuses while he himself was busily denigrating a brave young officer. No, that was too naive a view of the matter: Helldorf was a debauchee and Remer was a dutiful clown, that was all; it was silly to assume an exaggerated moral stance, as if trying to arbitrate between a man whose favorite word was "shit," whose deputy as commander of the storm troopers or brownshirts had been the bellhop-bouncer Karl Ernst, and a man like Remer who had been wounded eight times and had received his Knights Cross with Oak Leaves from the hand of S'gruber himself. Helldorf liked flesh and Remer liked blood. *That* was it, and we needed them both for the time being, although Helldorf surely realized that, after so long a career in the SA, his post-coup future would be limited. He was too compromised, and Tresckow would succeed him, whereas Remer would either join us or be shot out of hand. Yet Helldorf was vivid, you had to grant him that. A live ant roamed, trapped, in the hollow of his navel, kept in with a disk of adhesive dressing, presumably to create some mildly intolerable itch that was also grossly stimulating to his eroded palate. Some SS had actually seen, or even provided, the ant.

"Gentlemen," Helldorf went on, in that oddly bragging tone of his, "there is no need to use a bomb after all. Hear me out." I marveled at his gleaming image: shaven, talced, perfumed, laundered, coiffed. His leathers and his buckle shone. His white shirt had a luxurious softness which regular military issue did not. I could see the ceiling of my office in his high-buffed patent leather toecaps. "I have it on the best authority, from a recent houseguest who knows the Führer well, that his only form of sexual gratification is to have Fräulein Braun relieve herself into his mouth. I shock you? Wait. So as to have something on him, in case he ever tired of her, she had one of these love encounters secretly filmed through a hole in a wall. My suggestion is that we get hold of this film and show it in every theater in the Fatherland. I very much doubt if he'd survive. Sometimes she faces him, more often not, and mostly clad except for her underclothing. He pleads and whines for it, and she pretends disgust, but he never allows her to void until he's achieved a sufficient degree of excitation. Afterwards, they wash each other and cuddle. I wouldn't, myself, have credited our Führer with such highly evolved sexual tastes, and I wonder what bearing this bit of news could have on the famous dictum of Clever Hans Kluge that one shouldn't shoot a man while he's having lunch. Well, my hearties?"

Blushing, the curly-haired Haeften looked beseechingly at me, his face asking *How do we get rid of this man?*

Trimly, as if unsickened, I said "Otto Strasser peddled that story for years. Myself, I prefer the bomb." Then, sarcastically, with a quick glance at Haeften, "You never know. Maybe the public would cheer his moral courage in revealing his perversion. Far from foolproof. My God, a new cult might start, and *he*'d take the credit for it." Having complained about Major Remer and dropped his pellet of obscenity, our Black Prince from Sodom took his leave with a bow, a spring-loaded heel-click, and a lazy *Heil!*

About six in the evening, I went to see General Wagner, now Deputy Chief of the General Staff, at Zossen. How calm we both were, taking coffee in the anteroom with his aide, von Kanitz, then, after Kanitz suggested it, like professional beaters driving rabbits out of the bushes behind the bunkerlike huts.

Kanitz did the shooting with the general's shotgun while the two of us, flailing away and laughing at the incongruity of the whole antic, chatted casually about the job to come. We worked up quite a sweat in that muggy evening of high summer. Turning away from Wagner, I grinned at the unruffled Kanitz. "How relaxed and genial he seems," I said in an undertone. "Nothing on his mind at all."

"Always the same before he makes an important decision," Kanitz told me cheerfully. "But he never quite achieves your own look of . . . well . . . radiant enthusiasm, especially when the tension is high." I felt embarrassed and was glad to scare out a few more rabbits, as if translating the mental build-up into prosaic action. I left Zossen just before eight.

Finally I called Bamberg; having heard nothing from Nina, I spoke with her mother, who confirmed that Nina and the children had set off for Lautlingen in good time. Bombs had fallen, however, in Ebingen, and the civilian telephone circuits were out. There was no talking to Lautlingen, from anywhere, and the only way Nina had of reporting her safe arrival was to send a letter. In fact the circuits stayed out, or restricted to military traffic, not only from the eighteenth to the nineteenth, but into Thursday the twentieth, and beyond. Instead of the conversation we should have had, I mentally rehearsed just about every word we'd ever exchanged, worrying myself into a fit of nervous stomach, and exhorting myself non-stop to hold on: If you get distracted now, by anything, you'll fail. If you don't keep your mind on the job, you'll bungle it, and then Nina and the children will *really* be at risk.

I thus performed my duties with my mind and heart invested in another planet, from which no news came, six hundred kilometers from Berlin. Envisioning a fast plane that went from Berlin to Leipzig, thence to Bamberg and directly home, I almost lost my sense of mission, and when I regained it I felt as if I had killed them off: wife, children, the whole family. It was not a night to be alone.

Next day, Wednesday the nineteenth of July, we took care of all the last-minute arrangements, grateful that the end of the long haul was in sight. I ate sandwiches for lunch and dinner, devouring both meals with a telephone in hand, and got away from the Bendlerstrasse only at nine in the evening. I asked Schweizer to stop in Dahlem at Adam Trott's apartment, where Adam, in high mental gear, showed me the bucket and the box of matches he kept by him to burn papers in if an emergency arose. There was smoke in the air. Had he been practicing?

"One more time, Claus, eh?" he said with palpable sadness, then seemed full of new exhilaration.

"I'm obsessed," I told him. "I'm a ritual killer. Will I ever be normal again? After something so awful?"

"*You* will always be *you*," he said, "to those of us who know you. What the rest will think won't matter."

He could always, through his job at the Foreign Office, have left us for a neutral country such as Sweden, but he never had. "A sower is reluctant to leave germinating seed for others to tend," he'd said on more than one occasion. "Between sowing and harvest, there are storms galore." It did me good to look at his glowering aquiline face, the capacious bald dome beneath which his eyebrows nearly met. Easily the most brilliant mind among us, he'd appealed to Roosevelt at the beginning of the year, asking him in vain if he'd support a clean new regime in Germany; Roosevelt, like Churchill, tarred us all alike.

Quietly we rehearsed what would happen tomorrow, and then went through the bad news. An Allied plane had strafed Rommel's car, and now he had a triple fracture of the skull. Had he been part of it, our conspiracy would have been like a child bereaved. Goerdeler, after a night in the cellar of some friends, was now marooned in hiding some two hundred kilometers southwest of Berlin, in Westphalia. And General Falkenhausen, who would have given us support in Belgium and northern France, had been abruptly dismissed. Always I had too many people to keep in mind, too many names to juggle, too many crises to fit into the general puzzle.

"I presume your 'report' is ready!" Adam joked, but there was no hint of humor in his dark, somberly analytical face.

"Never readier." I winced. "God, this bloody waiting makes me sick. Never again, I don't care what happens tomorrow. Never."

"Leber's right," he said, pursuing thoughts of his own in a murmur of intense forlornness. "After you get *him*, there will be a power vacuum. It'll have to be filled at once or we won't have gained a thing, and the Russkies will move in. I *studied* political theory, but Leber's got it in his bones. He knows without having to find out."

"*After* the bomb," I said. "I just can't see beyond it right now." I felt peculiarly desolated, a feeling that not even the best company, which Adam was, could shift.

We embraced without a word further, and Schweizer drove me to Pastor Niemöller's church in St. Anne's: a gesture, inasmuch as Niemöller had been in one concentration camp or another since before the war began. A small service was under way, a tidy fluctuating hum, and I knelt at the back for ten or fifteen minutes, telling my maker that I'd never kill again, I'd never even hate, but on this occasion I would. I wanted holy auspices for an unholy act. Then Schweizer drove me home to Wannsee, he who'd chauffeured me back and forth at all hours, to villas and country houses and woods and airfields, waiting around in all weathers while mysterious people came and went. If he wondered why my duties required such a round-the-clock onslaught, he never said, but just logged everything in his grubby, much-thumbed duty-book to keep things straight, at least from his chauffeur point of view. If he was ever baffled, he wrapped that feeling up in a big broad Swabian smile and a cordial grunt, then put his foot down to get me somewhere even earlier than planned.

Later on, Berthold arrived and stayed the night, remaining

with me in fact until my aircraft took off the next morning. I had not seen Nina and the children since early June, and yet instead of remembering our most recent exchange—"I wish you wouldn't go through with the trip to Lautlingen. Stay in Bamberg with your mother." "Does it really matter that much?"—I recalled a much earlier one, from the palmier days before 1944, and the best words we spoke together limped around inside my head: words which, ages ago, in other circumstances, we chose—arranged, modulated, left ambiguously hovering, *whatever* the process was—to be suitable for "last words" or merely words until the next time. What we said had a both provisional and terminal quality. The condemned man had clearer auspices under which to compose his final say, whereas the man who had a chance, the wife who might not be widowed after all, had to walk on the water of futurity.

Did all couples always say goodbye well in advance?

"It may be a very long time. Longer than either of us thinks." I was going to North Africa. My leave was over.

"Yes." Her image of North Africa was already clear.

"I . . . all . . . everything . . . with all my heart and with a full spirit I thank you, my dearest, for everything." No line was private, but all they could have made out was that Stauffenberg, the notorious dashing extrovert, was cringing just a little. "For everything."

"Claus, Claus, we have said it a thousand times."

My head was full of caustic *buts*, about which even in February 1943 she no doubt already knew, except for the finer details; I saw flame racing across a void blue sky, those nearest and dearest to me transformed into agitated marionettes tugged by rough string, and S'gruber raising his sooty head from my very own pillow. Now my good eye did the weep work of two. My hand and my wrist shook to different rhythms. I almost dropped the phone. The line went dead, but in my mind's eye she reigned absolute, someone in stained glass who, for never fussing, had the stable gravity of an alp.

Needless to say, I also treasured and pondered our last exchange, perfunctory as it was, a mere scurf of itself. Some farewells were unsayable, after all, which is why I kept trying to say *that* one, without ever hitting on the right words, the right stance; and I concluded that such farewells came about by the couple's passionately dwelling on each other in the worst moments, almost going in a trance until each, for opaque reasons, knew the other's overwrought image of him or her had functioned, all of a sudden, as a shred of utterly coherent light. The one image saw the other in pinpoint valedictory and, indeed, if both were lucky, each image stayed on the retinas of the other image like those images recoverable from the retinas of the dead.

What, if the lost eye could not weep, was it doing? And what did it usually do? The socket filled with salt while the brown glove, fitted where the hand had been, absorbed a tiny leakage of blood. A woman loved this eye, this hand, and went on loving their possessor almost as if he had been somehow *improved*. I had not. I was worse than useless. I belonged to one of two human groups: those not very good at murder, and those very good at it indeed, who thrived on death. The whole way, I'd had to *force* myself. I wasn't a *soldier* at all.

Staring at my hand in front of me in the dark, I willed myself to lose consciousness, and with the third or fourth attempt, after fixing hard on Jagd, the Felsentor, Stefan George's face, then Nina blushing to the sun of Rome in September, I drifted off, vaguely aware that we needed the familiar sounds of Allied bombers in order to sleep. The only bomb in our vicinity that night was on the other side of my bedroom wall, ready but inert.

For once it wasn't one of those nights when I woke with a fast-banging heart. On those nights, I knew it would stop, and then oblivion: no place, no one, no be. Perhaps I slept well because, on the one hand, I'd become sheathed in a bizarre identity, and, on the other, because I might not have to sustain it long. Slumber came from the brevity of the assassin's role. After the next day, I'd be a new man or none at all. I had no dream for in between.

15

Wolf's Lair

♦

I rose early, well before six, in much the frame of mind of someone who, knowing the day will soon be torrid, wants to get his work done in the few cool hours. It seemed to me that today would be my fifth, or fiftieth, venture into S'gruber's headquarters, almost as if for years I had been seeking an audience of a special kind. I smiled at the fanciful bombast of the phrase "Wolf's Lair": the man was less a wolf than a spider, into whose web—all those cables and wires, ropes and cords, among the camouflage nets—I was willingly setting foot, thus far to no purpose whatever. In my mind's eye I saw once again the beech trees, the birches, and the darkness-loaded pines of the East Prussian encampment, wishing I had other duties to perform, indeed a destiny less repetitious. No use: this roundabout was mine, just as dismal and yet as promising as when I first became briefcase bearer to the future Germany.

I tugged my shirt on with the delicate teeth hold I'd developed in only a few months, and tapped on Berthold's door; but he'd been awake for some time, he said when I entered, reading the *Odyssey* in preparation for a new bout of translating.

"Any appropriate quotations," I asked him, "for the day's doings?" His brisk, somehow denuded grin said no, but one never knew what Homer might say next. This was amusing; he knew at least the *Odyssey* by heart.

"Then," I said over my shoulder, "we must invent our own motto. How about *Semper fidelis? Forever faithful?*"

"*To . . . ?*" was all I heard as he scrambled about getting ready. A cup of sawdusty acorn coffee awaited him. Somewhere in Berlin, somewhere in Germany, in Bamberg or Lautlingen, I hoped, someone that instant was drinking genuine coffee.

"Berthold," I told him, my voice gravelly with sleep, "we're finally going to do this thing . . . In God's sight . . . And according to conscience . . . Blow the swine sky-high . . . I can't reach Nina. The lines are down or something."

The laywer groomed at four universities nodded his brimming assent.

Even at dawn the heat was unbearable, and the weary, haggard Berliners trudging among the ruins and the dust had a phantom poise. Well, today we might just do something for them as well as for ourselves. Berthold came with me, and I was glad of his steady face.

At Rangsdorf airfield, after a drive of about three-quarters of an hour, with Schweizer displaying exceptional finesse at the wheel, I stared at the waiting Heinkel 111, General Wagner's private aircraft. The nose was almost entirely of glass. Its feline contours included some wedge-shaped gaps under the fin and at the rear of the wing root. The camouflage evoked an underwater world with its pale green lozenge shapes, and the entire airplane seemed to be rippling gently in the heat. There was a strange hole at the very rear where the fuselage tapered to a sharp point, and I thought of a tortoise tail even as I realized that, now the first flurry of energy wore off, I was half asleep. I had little sense of what the outcome would be, whether something fiendish, out of bad luck by protocol at its most inane, or something glorious, worthy of Homer, out of good luck by initiative at its most sublime. I smiled at myself for coming up before breakfast with so many horse-breeding images, and Haeften returned the smile.

"Ready for anything now," he said. Compared with his brother, who had come with him in the little Mercedes, Werner had a faint suntan, and I wondered where he'd been.

Off gallivanting, no doubt, with Frau Bredow's daughters, Kranzfelder, and the garrulous Hungarian count, von Welsburg. Life went on, including an occasional picnic too. I felt a bond with him, not least because he too had been disabled in action; a shattered pelvis held him back from many things, he who was not even a professional officer but a businessman. It was eerie how putting the world to rights had become the special charge of certain *mutilés de guerre*. No doubt the existentialists in the circles that Beck moved in would commend our greed for action, for—What was their phrase?—redefining ourselves instead of settling for a second-best life as a paper shuffler, a Tarzan of the telephone.

Haeften bade his brother Hans Bernd a swift goodbye, extrovert to introvert, both with slightly receding dark hair, the one thirty-five, the other thirty-nine. The Brothers B, I thought, in each case the intellectuals of the family, the less bumptious, the less headstrong, the less airy. How lucky both Werner and I were to have brothers of such restraining sagacity, who went along with us nonetheless, but without ever losing their analytical command or their gift of almost holy joy.

"Tell Corporal Schweizer," I instructed Haeften as my reverie snapped, "what to do in the meantime."

At once he did, concluding, much to Schweizer's amazement, "Then go to the clothing store in Spandau and get yourself a new uniform."

"Yes, sir, but why?" Poor Schweizer took a pride in his appearance.

"Never you mind," Haeften told him. "You'll be getting much more than that in the long run. You'll see." We got into the Heinkel after our last handclasps with our brothers, and Schweizer, still bemused, handed me the briefcase containing the bombs, and I handed it over to Haeften and took his.

The car, however, waited until we had taken off, and in fact there was a delay, during which Stieff showed up with a Major Rall and climbed aboard. Supposed to leave at seven A.M., we didn't get off the ground until eight. Then Berthold and Hans Bernd went off about their own business, Berthold to the naval headquarters in Coral Camp and Hans Bernd to the Foreign Office. Fortunately the Heinkel was much faster than the lumbering Junkers 52 courier aircraft we might otherwise have taken, had not Wagner been helpful, and would speed us over the 600 kilometers from Rangsdorf to Rastenburg in just over two hours.

Everyone had waved goodbye, but with restricted, subdued gestures. A family outing was over. Another was about to start. By now I was a familiar figure at the airfield, briefcase in hand, and perhaps those on duty assumed I was directing a large part of the war.

Next thing, I was looking down at the gutted façades of a bombed-out city as the Heinkel banked, its twin engines quarreling for the upper hand, and then leveled out over the River Spree, heading northeast to cross the Oder and the Vistula, with our nose aimed at Lithuania. My *machine infernale* was beside me, or rather both *m.i.*'s were, the one with a half-hour fuse (the backup bomb, to be used in conjunction with, or instead of, the other, whose fuse was fifteen minutes). If Haeften and I succeeded today, there might just be no more bombs dropped on the pumice-stone wasteland unrolling beneath us. I already felt like a phoenix and was aghast that anything so sturdy and intact as the Heinkel and its passengers, its crew, should have soared up from the rubble called Berlin. I should have recognized this landscape after other take-offs, but today felt like a special day, and I had a specially sensitive eye and ear. How astonishing to find that the Prussian plain, beneath and before us, looked less dreary than the city behind us. All of a sudden, the barrens were hospitable, the metropolis repelled, and not for the old pastoral reasons.

We touched down at Rastenburg about ten-fifteen after a bumpy flight during which I saw before me, more vividly than during any other absence, Berthold's face, unshaven and puffy, as if he had been in a fight soon after dawn.

"From twelve onward," Haeften told the pilot, "you must be ready for immediate take-off." No delay this time.

In a car provided by Captain Pieper, we lurched along the awful road as far as Queden Farm and then turned northward into Area 2. We conversed in snatches only, still not quite awake, and mesmerized by the swollen dark green of the foliage, the rich overlapping sounds of birds and invisible animals. It was a July idyll fit for the lid of a chocolate box, but it was also a landscape which never quite rid itself of the lugubrious, tainted air it had in winter, when the snow didn't so much blanch it as wrap it like disused furniture in dust sheets. That is more or less how it felt, like the Ardennes in summer, and nothing like southern Germany at all. After all, this was Prussia, and Prussian I was not.

What a long drive. We had to pass through the same checkpoints as on the fifteenth: first of all at the main perimeter gate, where pillboxes and minefields reminded you that this was the Outer Wire, a mere beginning. This time through, I noticed an entire system of concentric fortifications. I smelled sulfur, from what source I had no idea. Then we came to the Inner Wire, likewise mined, but also fortified with an electrified barbed-wire fence. Before a car could set off for Checkpoint (or Sperrkreis) 2, Checkpoint 1 phoned the dramatis personae forward. Some 1400 meters beyond this lay the so-called Officers' Guard, where the car park was and the camp proper began, its actual nerve center being some 300 meters farther in. Ringed with a tough wire-mesh fence two and a half meters high, patrolled non-stop by SS guards and secret service agents, this was the compound known as Sperrkreis 1, containing only three buildings: the Führerbunker 1, S'gruber's living quarters, heavily reinforced; the briefing hut, otherwise known as the map room or the situation hut; and, from the sublime to the tender, the big wooden kennel for Blondi, the Alsatian bitch given him by Bormann to lift his spirits after Stalingrad. No one had a pass into this holy of holies: you either got a temporary permit or that cowboy *manqué*, SS Oberführer Ratten-

huber checked you in personally, but only after you were
frisked for weapons. Never before, in one half-hour drive, had
I seen so many slit trenches, machine-gun towers, and fire positions; on July fifteenth my mind had been on other things,
but today I was keenly aware that this was going to be the escape route.

"How odd," I whispered to Stieff before Haeften saw him
off to Mauerwald, "to be enclosed in radio terminology!
Sperrkreis means 'rejector circuit,' doesn't it?" At this, his
jaunty expression intensified, but Haeften (who'd heard me)
had no expression at all.

I went on to the Kurhaus in Area 2 and took an overdue
breakfast at a table fastidiously laid under an oak tree. What a
hubbub! Captain Pieper was present, as were Dr. Erich Walker, the senior medical officer; Dr. Wagner, head of the dental
clinic; Captain von Möllendorff, the personnel officer; and
Lieutenant General von Thadden with a staff officer. Some of
these dunderheads had been there breakfasting since nine
A.M., the scheduled time of my arrival; but, I joked to Pieper
and Möllendorff, perhaps the whole thing was an experiment
for the benefit of Walker and Wagner, a medical-dental test
case.

The coffee here was real, as well as a couple of hours strong,
and I began to wake up, to feel a slightly manic glow. In good
spirits I telephoned Keitel's adjutant, Major Ernst John von
Freyend, to rearrange my meetings for the day; and then,
about eleven A.M., feeling quite refueled, I stood up to go and
even let the duty officer, Lieutenant Jansen, carry my briefcase, something I'd always been loath to do, whether it held
bombs or not. We had a short walk of some hundred meters
before us.

"How heavy it is." Jansen smiled, fully aware that I rarely
accepted physical help from anyone.

"It contains specimens from the Armaments Office," I told
him, with an equal smile, wondering what he would have

thought had he lifted Haeften's briefcase, which at this point held both bombs. Indeed, my remark applied to *that* case and not my own, heavy as it seemed. Thinking of so many things, and recharged by caffeine, I was splicing thoughts together, only to unpick them at speed.

"There is a lot to talk about today," I added as I shook hands with the insipid but good-natured General Buhle, half wondering if the Buhles of the world weren't the life and soul of any dictatorship. Then Haeften arrived from a washroom somewhere, and, with Buhle, von Thadden, and Colonels Lechler and Kandt, I went into the sweltering Army High Command hut marked OPERATIONS STAFF. For half an hour we discussed the creation of two new East Prussian divisions from Home Guard reservists, and I became testily bored.

"Something has to stop the Russians from marching right into the Führer's enclosure," I said, willing to say anything on this day of days. "Germany mustn't scrape the barrel, though, merely to provide cannon fodder." The bullet-headed Buhle gaped, von Thadden mumbled, and Haeften disappeared into an ocular glaze at which he was becoming most deft. Half an hour of all that prattle was enough, for me at any rate. Then we all adjourned to meet with Keitel in the building opposite Jodl's, quite a walk away.

Keitel smelled of warm, wet wool, which of course was the effect of the heat; his face was scarlet, his eyes were veined, his nose seemed blocked. He'd hardly begun to bore us when S'gruber's valet, Linge, called up to remind him that Mussolini was visiting Wolf's Lair later that day. From then on, Keitel behaved like a cat on hot bricks, adding peremptoriness to his usual sycophancy. Soon after midday, the railroad shuttle between Wolf's Lair and Mauerwald brought Lieutenant General Adolf Heusinger for the briefing conference, and I braced myself for two ordeals: the first the usual one of hearing experts brief "Wolf" in his "Lair," until he ignored them by yelling orders of utterly capricious fatuity; the second, the last act of our slow-grown, almost dithering melodrama.

"Almost time," Keitel told the group in his office. "General Heusinger is already here. The Duce soon will be."

Everyone looked flustered, but nobody moved; then we all seemed to budge at once, almost colliding in our anxiety not to vex Keitel further. Yet no one left.

Haeften had been obliged to cool his heels in the waiting room in the same building, or to wander up and down the halls in a tense patrol. Why, I suddenly wondered, did they never inspect our briefcases here, as at the Berghof? It was incongruous to check your clothes for arms without inspecting what you carried.

Now Haeften, the bombs, and I were reunited. The whole enterprise was becoming something apart from us, like a mathematical equation obligingly working itself out. Not only that: we had that good non-hissing British fuse, and there was hope in the very fact. Yet hope was not enough, nor had it been enough throughout the series of heroic but bungled attempts. This, it was clear, was an opportunity to do not just anything but something perfect, taut as a sonnet, neat as a rapier flick.

Fondling my eyepatch, I fixed my mind, as if in broken promise to myself, on some irrelevant but sustaining images of wolfhounds; then of oath-taking recruits laying their left hands woodenly on the regimental colors in 1938; then of a cherished heirloom, a silver breakfast tray smeared here and there with strawberry preserves and butter; and most of all a line about a burning corral from one of Stefan George's poems. This being my fifth recent attempt (June 7, July 6, 11, 15, and now 20) I should have seen a pentagram in the palm of my hand, but the hand held the briefcase, and its partner, God help it, was somewhere in North Africa. When a fighter strafes your car, you cannot expect to get away with too much. A husk of a man had come to blow a windbag to bits. A remnant had come to liquidate. It might not have been poetic justice, but it was rough enough justice for S'gruber and his ilk.

Did I look as hot and flushed as I felt? My underwear was already stuck to my groin. Perhaps, because I was tall as well as hefty, I seemed only more ethereal, bathed not in perspiration but in noble dew. But that was too fancy a thought for such an occasion as today, and I put it aside for the time when the archconspirator, already a legend, settled back, smiling broadly at his accomplices, his mind a jumble of prayers, bangs, cheers, and toasts. *Heil, Stauffenberg!* No, it would *never* come to that.

Never mind: all my men were primed. That precisian of the written or transmitted message, General Fellgiebel, our wry grammarian of the airwaves, stood ready to flash the news to Berlin that the bomb had gone off, then obstruct all further communication as much as he could: a sketchy thing to count upon, but we had nothing else.

I actually felt as if I were not going to do what I knew I would. Chatting, leaning, murmuring, almost like a male model showing off fashions for the maimed, I worked my way through the half-hour to twelve-thirty second by second, heart at a giddy race. For a brief moment I had visions of removing two dictators with one bomb, but I realized that S'gruber's conference would be over before the Italian loudmouth showed up. Indeed, it was going to begin half an hour earlier than planned. Keitel said so.

"Present your report concisely, Colonel," he said with his usual acrid snap. Sometimes a colonel had to know his place, and keep it. Very well. My place today was alongside S'gruber, but only briefly, or it would be my last. Very well. Mussolini's feet smelled like roaring panthers, anyway. I would be healthier at a distance. I was the military midwife, hands ready to be daubed with blood. I was glad I'd prayed the night before; it was the only kind of talking I hadn't tried over the past year.

16

1242 Hours

◆

Keitel couldn't take his eyes off the clock, being nothing but a factory worker at heart. Then he told us it was time to go. At last!

"The meeting, gentlemen, will once again be in the briefing hut, one of those reinforced by Herr Speer."

I suddenly remembered that Speer was due to address practically the whole of political Berlin, some two hundred, on the subject of armaments, in the hall of Goebbels's Propaganda Ministry. At eleven. That's why he hadn't been able to accept our invitation to lunch at the Bendlerstrasse. He had no doubt already finished his chore, whereas I— Something tiny snapped inside me. I had been in the Speer-style briefing hut only last week, and I knew what it was made of: plasterboard walls reinforced with fiberglass, then a layer of wooden planking, the whole sheathed in bulletproof material the name of which I did not know. It was a flimsy place; a concrete bunker would have suited our purposes much better, confining the blast and making it lethal, but I had vowed to set off the bomb regardless of circumstances, and it was no use quibbling now, even with myself. There would be no telephone calls this time; there would be none of the umbilical dubiety that had tied us all in knots. Thus nourished by the clichés of the chronic conspirator, or of the repeated incompetent, I moved into the hallway with my briefcase of documents.

There I asked John von Freyend where I might refresh my appearance, and he directed me to a small lavatory. When I emerged, Haeften was there in the passageway with the other briefcase. I then asked John von Freyend where I could change my shirt, (meaning where I could arm a bomb), at the same time wondering if they ever tried to imagine how a maimed man does something that mundane. John von Freyend showed us to the waiting room, a bare roomette requiring only the presence of an enclosing train to justify it and, I thought in a giddy second, Fabian von Schlabrendorff to open up a bomb package with a razor blade! But this time it was I doing it, with special pliers whose jaws Berthold had encased in rubber to give a better grip and whose shape resembled that of a distorted spur meant to fit over the apex of a wedge-shaped heel. A man with only three fingers needs unusual tools. I crushed the glass capsule that released acid onto the wisp of wire which released the detonator. In fifteen minutes (or less: the day was hot, at least twenty degrees Celsius, and probably twenty-five, and fuses ran faster when warm), the acid would eat it through. If not— Someone rapped on the door just as Haeften and I were restowing the shirts that both hid and cushioned the bombs. I saw one of John von Freyend's senior NCO's.

"Sergeant Major Vogel," the man said out of his imposing thick neck. "General Fellgiebel has telephoned for you and asks that you please return his call at Colonel Sander's extension." Fellgiebel had been camping out, unwelcome, in Sander's office since eight in the morning.

"In addition, Herr Oberst, General Keitel's adjutant asks if you will please hurry. You will be late for the briefing with the Führer." I had seen this fellow lurking in the hallway and eyeing both Haeften and me with uncommon interest verging on suspicion. Now he stood peering into the waiting room through the half-open doorway.

Just like any other harassed colonel, I bit his head off. "I am coming at once!" He made no move to depart, though, and he would actually have been in my way had I left the room forthwith. Haeften's suntan had vanished, but his hands were steady. There was no time to arm the second bomb, not with the first one already live and Vogel hovering in the doorway. We closed our briefcases at speed and moved to the door. The instant I stepped into the corridor, I saw John von Freyend, hot and agitated at the entrance.

"*Stauffenberg*," he called, almost pleadingly, "come along, *please!* It's past 1230 hours. The meeting's already begun!"

I hurried after the blunt, coarse figure of Keitel, with John von Freyend at my side. Haeften went his own way, with the second briefcase, to see about the car for our return journey.

For some reason I found myself able to converse animatedly with Buhle, which was like befriending a waxwork. Then Lechler offered to carry my briefcase, as did Freyend, but I refused, weirdly haunted by the expression on the sergeant major's face: not suspicious, but one of exultant esteem, part obsequious, part stern. I had been looked at in many ways; but only on trains, undressing myself with hand and teeth, had I seen just that same look. Perhaps, even now, having realized what I was doing, and in spite of himself and his admiration for the hare-brained pluck of such a deed, he was phoning his superiors with the news. Whatever he did, the bomb now had a mind of its own.

The next person we encountered was an aide who told us that S'gruber was already in the briefing hut. The target was within reach at last. Warm in my uniform, as well as from the heat and the excitement, I felt inside as cold as a stoat: blasé in my inevitable murderousness. Then John von Freyend asked me once again if he might carry my briefcase, and this time I accepted.

"Could you please put me," I asked him, "as near as possible to the Führer so that I catch everything I need for my briefing afterward?" My hearing, of course, was none too good, although it used to be crystal-sharp; so that was a genuine excuse, as was my need to know what the madman said. The principal reason, however, was to get as close to him as soon as possible.

We were almost sprinting. S'gruber awaited us; and while you might keep the millennium, the decline and fall of the West, or the solar system dancing attendance on you, you did not dawdle when dealing with *him*. The merest unwise move might lead to the guillotine, or to the end of your career. Not that it mattered in this instance, but it was best to keep up appearances all the way to the wire.

We advanced down the same broad hallway as on July fifteenth, and entered the conference room through swinging doors. All the windows were open, which was no help to my bomb, and unavailing against the intolerable fug of July. The meeting was indeed under way, with various officers either at the big oaken map table or standing around the room. Under the table there must have been a dozen stools. S'gruber himself sat at the table, facing north, with spectacles and magnifying glass at the ready. No Himmler, no Göring. We must have been four or five minutes late, interrupting Heusinger, who had the floor, while S'gruber turned and hesitantly shook hands when Keitel made a superfluous introduction.

Time halted as I touched that hand again and saw him tense it, as if schooling himself not to recoil, but not to prolong the contact either. A dry hand, a small hand, a pale hand with the blood of millions on it. He spoke the minimum of words in greeting. "You will have to wait, Stauffenberg." It was logical enough, but his words came from another world. "I want Heusinger to finish first." Then he turned back to the map, dabbing his hand at some already nonexistent division.

Heusinger was explaining, from S'gruber's immediate right, the calamity on the eastern front. Outside, in the entrance hall, the sergeant major in charge of the switchboard knew that I was expecting an urgent call from Berlin containing information I needed to bring my report right up to date. My line of retreat awaited me, although it must have seemed odd to Keitel, the "telltale toady" as most commanders called him, that a mere colonel should contemplate leaving the conference room before being dismissed. But special facts, such as I was supposed to present, required special procedures; Keitel remained unsuspicious. The two premature Valkyrie drills had puzzled him, but it was Fromm rather than he who had become watchful, and Fromm as ever was waiting to see which way the wind would blow, so his suspicions would remain with him until it was to his advantage to express them to the Gestapo.

All this time the bomb was ripening inaudibly. There were only six minutes to go, and the back of my neck felt as if someone were scoring it up and down with a fork. On Heusinger's right was the amiable Heinz Brandt, who gave me one of his measured smiles, not so much a smile as a rictus of sly exactitude. I responded with what I hoped was an affable nod; the air in that room was awful, and trying to breathe it was like inhaling through a rolled-up decaying sweater. The bright-check drapes hung dead.

Now the obsequious Keitel, after a few mild excuses, took his post on S'gruber's immediate left, next to Jodl. There was still no Himmler, no Göring, and I presumed they were holding themselves in readiness for Mussolini; but there must have been a dozen and a half other officers grouped about the room. Only S'gruber and two stenographers, Berger and Buchholz, were sitting down.

Once more John von Freyend enacted the role of chivalrous gentleman, asking Rear Admiral Voss, the Naval Commander in Chief's headquarters man, if he would vacate his place for me.

"The colonel," John von Freyend said, "is not quite as agile as he used to be ... among company!"

At once Voss went round to the opposite side of the table, murmuring with a smile, "Quite right, quite right." What wasn't so right was where I had to stand, between Heusinger and Brandt, who were on S'gruber's immediate right: both my blind eye and my deaf ear were toward my target, presenting him with a null silhouette. It would have mattered in quite another way if I had intended to brief him and Heusinger; but, while Heusinger's voice came and went as if blown on a non-existent summer breeze, I had to move the briefcase from where John von Freyend had set it down, pretty much where Voss had stood. Now I had someone unknown, with mint-fresh breath, right behind me. I felt dizzily hot, almost at the start of a reeling motion; and, looking downward, I could see nothing of S'gruber at all. Elbowing my way forward a little, so as to come flush with the table and thus shield my movements, I pretended to push the briefcase out of everyone's way, toeing it this way and that. There was no hope of undetectably easing it leftward, either behind Heusinger or in front of him, until it sat right at S'gruber's feet. Nor could I judge distances much, least of all those to my left. In the end, I left the thing barely under the table, to the right of the fat oaken support known as a socle. Only six people could stand at the table's long sides, and there I was, opposite the socle, with only Brandt farther away from S'gruber than I. Time was short. Yet my mind lingered, wishing that the conference had been held underground: not because I wanted to compress the bomb blast, but because it would have been cooler. I felt drenched, and there was still a long way to go.

Clearly, S'gruber, a man given to constant paranoid changes of plan and location, had weighed the chances of there being an air raid against those of feeling bottled up underground, and had plumped for a summer's day. According to our sources, this was not unusual anyway: he held most of his conferences in the briefing hut, and the fact that his underground bunker was being repaired had nothing to do with his being on the surface today. He sweltered not because he chose to but because he was following his usual scheme of evading predictable patterns. Some of our informants had been wrong and should have told us that, to guarantee his presence in the bunker, we should have staged an air raid, which would have grounded him fast, underground repairs or no, where clearly a desire for comfort could not drive him.

My mind filled with speculations it was already too late to

consider, but that was perhaps to lull myself, to persuade myself that I was still in charge of events. I was not. I couldn't stop the bomb now even if I were manacled to it. And that truant mind of mine could only think, Yes, if S'gruber hadn't made the Luftwaffe convert those superb new jet fighters, the Messerschmitt 262s, into fighter-bombers, Germany would by now have had complete control of the skies. In which case the air raid we had failed to arrange could not have happened in any case. . . .

The map engrossed them all, as it should have, being an elegy in two dimensions. The Russians had broken through and were not going to waste the breach. It was all over, bar the next few thousand explosions.

Signaling to John von Freyehd, who so readily assumed others' troubles, I made an almost Masonic sign. While he made his way round the table to my side, I turned to Heinz Brandt and whispered, "I must go and telephone. Keep an eye on my briefcase, will you? It has secret papers in it." Why should he not, he who had agreed to ferry fatal Cointreau aboard S'gruber's plane? Once again, poor Brandt was unwitting neighbor to a bomb. I was looking at a dead man. He would be dead at twelve-forty-two. I could even smell the leather aroma of my hands. For once I had no qualms; I was immune.

Then I made a quiet, perfunctory excuse to Keitel. "Field Marshal, I am going to make a quick call and come straight back." I *told* him, I didn't *ask*. I was going to call no one, nor was I going to come back. John von Freyend and I then walked out together into the passageway, where I told him that I wanted to return Fellgiebel's call, the call which Haeften and I had learned about from Sergeant Major Vogel while arming the first bomb. At once he asked the telephone operator, Sergeant Major Adam, to put me through. When I picked up the receiver, John von Freyend went back into the briefing, and then I put the receiver down again. The sergeant major frowned, confronted as he was by a man who, having come

out unbidden to take a call that he in fact made and then ignored, moved hatless and beltless at a good clip down the passageway to the outside world. On I strode, quivering with fatigue and elation while Sergeant Major Adam called out to me
from behind.

At that moment, the war and the lives of a good five thousand fellow conspirators and their relatives trembled in the
balance. Yet the day was far from over; this was merely Scene
1 of the first act. I tried to think of no one at all, out there in
the suffocating heat, so bemused that I began to wonder if I
were dreaming it that Fellgiebel had left a message with Sergeant Major Adam, asking me to go to Colonel Sander, the
Wehrmacht signals officer, as soon as the conference ended.
Or was I reading all of that into Adam's mutinously baffled
face? No, he had said it, and I had registered it subliminally
while thinking about something else.

I increased my stride, beltless, hatless, and briefcaseless as I
was. No one else called after me, but outside the entrance I
met Lieutenant Colonel Borgmann on his way in, en route perhaps to a nasty death; but by now I was case-hardened, or I
hoped I was. Even with my aching knee, I could be with Fellgiebel in a couple of minutes after a short climactic walk.

The car was already lined up, the driver waiting. After all, a
man as disabled as I was entitled not to have to walk, even
after planting a bomb.

When I arrived at Sander's office, he was busy telephoning
for a car. But I already had one, and a driver as well; Second
Lieutenant Kretz had waited for us since our arrival. Fellgiebel and I went outside and stood in the sun on the turf in front
of Bunker 8/13, where I lit a long-craved cigarette. The per-
sonable Haeften looked frozen.

"Only seconds to go," I told him, with heart hammering.

I had never seen Fellgiebel look so self-possessed in that
coarse-skinned way of his. "Sander," he grumbled, "he's been
fidgeting about all morning. He has made it very clear, colo-

nel-to-general style of course, that I'm merely a guest and a
visitor at Wolf's Lair. I've interrupted his work, cramped his
style, made him uneasy. He feels *monitored!* Perhaps that's
how all permanent residents of Area One become after a
while. Paranoid. Stauffenberg, I have never seen you gulp
smoke so!" Deep into my throat I drew the smoke, wondering
why time, so famous for doing all kinds of things, did not
elapse. Back in the briefing hut, Heusinger said something im-
precise, and someone suggested asking me.

"Stauffenberg will know. It's his sort of thing."

Then they looked for me. Buhle went outside the room several times and finally asked Sergeant Major Adam where I
was. "He has left the building" was all he could find out while
Keitel fumed: not only had I been late; now I was missing, and
his well-planned morning was a shambles.

Out came Sander now from his office, rigorously polite.
"Colonel, I have arranged it. Your car—"

"Is already here," I said as silkily as I could, resolved to
match him in finesse; Stauffenberg retained his manners for as
long as possible. Sander must have believed in his own magic,
assimilating the ostensible fact at speed and rereminding me
next that the camp commandant, Streve, expected me for
lunch. "He asks you not to forget. He would be chagrined if
you missed it. Or if you had to walk." Eyes on the briefing hut,
I mumbled something agreeable.

So far, no explosion, but Heinz Brandt had already tried to
get a better look at the map while Heusinger, to whom he was
adjutant, went from point to point explaining how things in
Russia had come unstuck. Then Brandt, who found my briefcase in his way, finally shoved it forward with his foot, not far
at all, in fact a negligible distance—he who had juggled with
the Cointreau dud in front of Schlabrendorff! A twice-doomed
man, he gained essentially nothing, at his very last immobile
with his arms full of maps and charts for Heusinger's use.

Admiral von Puttkamer, the lissom and fair-haired arriviste

who had talked S'gruber out of invading England, was ensconced on a windowsill, wondering if he should make a Stauffenberg exit too, but merely in order to go change his pants for Mussolini's visit. S'gruber himself, chin in hand and leaning on an elbow, was craning over the map as if it held answers and he could brush back into his lap, from its pin-pitted surface, the divisions he had doomed in Russia. Heusinger still had not finished his pessimistic briefing, but he was winding down. Buhle was strutting about, as if to discharge through movement the pique he felt at no longer being able to produce Stauffenberg. Once again he went out and asked Sergeant Major Adam if I had returned; once again he went back in, shook his head at the enraged Keitel, and took up his position near the windows, where there was room to stride about under Puttkamer's amiable gaze.

Poor Heusinger: we were supposed to warn him before we made an attempt (he was rather more for us than he wasn't), but his contact, Tresckow, was again away at the front, and in any event Heusinger had let him down by failing to arrange for him to be anywhere else, such as Wolf's Lair, or Berlin. Now Heusinger, somewhat hoarse, was saying, "The Russian is driving with strong forces west of the Duna toward the north. His spearheads are already southwest of Dunaburg. If our army group around Lake Peipus is not at long last withdrawn, a catast—" Only a few syllables after he thus prophetically said the diseaselike name of the lake that lies southwest of Leningrad, our bomb went off among the twenty-four men present.

I trembled with self-loathing and delight; I had just converted human beings into flame and charcoal. Faces had turned into a flash of light traveling much faster than their minds had. The texture of the explosion was that of a shredded rainbow pouring upward as a reverse waterfall. I thought I felt the heat. I knew I smelled the reek of burned hair, and my first thought, pardonable in an assassin, was *That is S'gruber burn-*

ing; his ideas are shriveling on the pyre of himself, his mus-
tache has gone, his eyes are like those of a dead lake trout,
matt and grayish green. I could taste his death on the still
summer air. His sundered heart was lodged up in the treetops
with the aghast birds. Ants already floundered in his half-con-
gealing blood. The trademark forelock had gone off with a
foaming crack, like guncotton, and the outside snakebite of his
nostrils no longer channeled air. Others lived, but clearly he
was dead, destined to befoul us no further, with his mouth, or
his mind, or his hands, or his traumatized eyes.

Out came the longest sigh of my life, as if I'd been holding
my breath since the first of July, and the full volume of it hovered in front of my face, a cloud of virtue amid the railroad
smoke of the bang itself. He'd *gone.* We were going to have
our lives again, in peace. Now for the living, the living, the living; the life to come in a dignified world. We'd all be able to
open our mouths again. No more of us would die.

At the bang, Fellgiebel almost lost his composure altogether,
and I myself jumped violently, but Sander just puckered his
mouth and said, "Animals in the minefields. You get used to it.
This place is full of alarms of one kind or another. Perhaps
someone fired a gun."

I looked at Fellgiebel, to whom in Sander's office only minutes before I had said, "Just reporting for our talk, sir." Then
we had gone outside to watch.

Now I said to him, "I think it is time to go to my lunch with
Lieutenant Colonel Streve. I won't be able to return to the
briefing session, I'm afraid." Haeften had tightened his jaw
enough to alter the sit of his mouth, which looked almost withered. He got into the rear of the waiting eight-cylinder Horch,
briefcase in hand, and I climbed in beside Kretz, the driver,
who at once said, "Sir, you have forgotten your cap and belt."

"Drive," I told him. "That is what you are for. Just see that
you make a good job of *that.*" How rude. The man had waited
for me all morning, and here I was ill-mouthing him for his

considerateness; people are always looking out for the interests of a man with one hand, one eye, and a missing briefcase, cap, and belt. My head felt like a gymnasium full of dead birds.

I marveled at the human body, the room it occupies in space, collapsed on a sofa or overflying you at several thousand feet with its fundament pointed downward through the metal seat of a Heinkel; always displacing air or water and, in its bulbous, muscular, soft-cored way, so emphatic, and so perishable; so inflammable, so magically gross.

It had names, which fit it well or ill, and it did or did not pass through barriers; when they wouldn't let you past Checkpoint 2, say, as with myself at Wolf's Lair on that awful day, they were saying no to your veins and arteries, your intestines and your teeth. A sergeant major, having heard an explosion, was not about to let anyone through without considerable military fuss. (Heart of oak it may have been, this rank had all the grandiosity of archdukes without their chic.) Once again on the telephone—although on this occasion not to the Bendlerstrasse, where they were all hovering in an agony of anticipation—I did my uppish best.

"Colonel Count von Stauffenberg, speaking from the outer checkpoint, Captain. You will recall that we took breakfast together this morning. A pleasure, indeed. Because of the explosion, the guard refuses to let me through. I am in a hurry. Colonel General Fromm," I lied, "is awaiting me at the airfield." Then I hung up, told the sergeant major that everything was in order; but the officious oaf went and telephoned for confirmation, which the camp commander's aide, with whom I had indeed breakfasted, readily supplied. He must have been bored with the whole business, but I had in fact hung up before he gave me the go-ahead. We were on our way. Shortly before one o'clock, Haeften and I drove up to the waiting Heinkel 111, after another rough ride, and climbed aboard.

Unfortunately, one of S'gruber's adjutants, only minutes after the bomb went off, cut all communications between

Wolf's Lair and the outside. Fine: we had planned to do so ourselves! Then he told Fellgiebel what he had done. All Fellgiebel could do was to phone Olbricht at the Bendlerstrasse and then black out communications entirely. He was in no position to blow up the entire Rastenburg message center, housed as it was in several underground bunkers, heavily guarded by the SS, and he did as well as he could. One of his slips, however, enabled Fromm to talk with Keitel even as our plane headed west over the dried-up dismal flatlands of East Prussia. By then, Keitel knew that I was not, as first assumed, among the severely injured who had been rushed to the hospital. The telephone sergeant had told how the "one-eyed colonel" hurried away, heedless of his expected phone call. Already the bits of the second bomb, which Haeften had dismantled as we sped toward the airfield and had thrown to the side of the road, had been found and identified.

How strange: Wolf's Lair was a scene of hectic recovery and speedy analysis, whereas at the Bendlerstrasse nothing was happening at all. The main switch centers went off and on, like some form of marine life, pulsing and flashing even as our Heinkel churned through the up- and downdrafts. Luckily the first order for my arrest never reached Berlin, thanks to Fellgiebel; but neither Beck nor Witzleben, who should have been issuing orders and proclamations like the titular heads they were, had even shown up. Operation Valkyrie did not begin. Olbricht knew only that something had happened at Rastenburg, but not exactly what. He couldn't, for a third time, act on a presumption, never mind how much he itched to get things under way.

As for me, with the heroic or manic side of my mind, I told myself that everything had gone as planned; I had no need to see the corpse. S'gruber was *dead*. Back in Carthage I had prayed to live, and now I prayed again: this time for speed through the air, speed at the Bendlerstrasse too, and, after a decent interval, a hero's welcome home in Bamberg and Lautlingen. Maimed for nothing in a desert war already lost, I wanted to come unscathed through the biggest thing I'd known or done; Claus the ogre would be the young prince once again, admired and loved.

17

Boomerang

♦

Would I care to sit up front, in the cabin, asked the co-pilot. No, I told him. I couldn't bear to see where we were going. Nor did I wish to sit where I already was either; I didn't want to be anywhere, in fact. I wanted to be consumed, transubstantiated, made into a knightly flame of hymnlike dignity, with no airspeed, no ground speed, no future. I was twitching like mad.

Next thing, I'd changed my mind and was groping forward inside the Heinkel, half afraid I'd stick a finger through the stressed-skin fabric of the fuselage. I wanted to be going *somewhere* at my own speed and steered by myself, not by a Luftwaffe jockey. I ended up in the wholly glazed-in nose, staring forward at the pale green of the plain, with the sun on my left. It was like being inside a conical porthole, with a tremendous wind blast hitting the glass non-stop and the metal parts oddly cold to the touch.

I sighted along the offset machine gun, arranging my eye behind the spike that hovered uncertainly against the silhouette of the ring at the barrel's end. Why, even the gun moved unstably in its ball-and-socket mounting. Who would want to be a gunner here, or a bomb aimer, in this lethal greenhouse? I knew that casualties were high; there was no protection whatever. This flight, though, was over theoretically friendly terrain, so for a while I enjoyed the sensation of being prone in the bullet's nub, teeth into the splintery slam of summer air.

In the haze over on the right, to the north, was Danzig, and beneath us Schwetz or Graudenz, and that inert-looking coil was the Vistula. Halfway home, I thought: it's been quite a day so far. Something *happened*. All of a sudden I felt utterly removed from the roar of aero engines. I sometimes called it my Bruckner mood: lumbering, rhapsodic, voluminously grave, and to hell with S'gruber's addiction to the same composer. My mood told me that I didn't wish to become a politician at all, but a military poet, neither count nor colonel. I yearned for ovations of the soul. I groped my way back. Haeften had ruddy cheeks again.

When you are quaking from head to foot, drenched in perspiration, can hear your stomach churning and boiling, and your head has a piston-throb ache, then you solace yourself with minor matters, even if only to prevent your spirit from shaking itself out of the body's armature.

Were all those minor matters that I'd been brooding about? In the context of one thing they were, and that was my new status of successful assassin. I had just *killed*. I could never go back on that; my life had changed irreversibly. Where, then, was the exultation? We'd been waiting for years to wipe him out and I had been the instrument. Not only did I not feel glad enough, I wasn't even aware of the deed as a fact. It was too soon, my body was a web of pain, I had other things to do. Yet it was vital that I recognize at once I was no longer like other men, men who hadn't killed. Something should be flowing through me: some juice, some electric elation. Perhaps I'd burned out my nerves on the bomb itself and had nothing left to relish it with. Or perhaps I had only to relax and begin to tutor myself: *You did it, you didn't buckle, you didn't shirk it, you got away from the bomb with a full minute to spare. You wiped him off the face of the earth, and others with him, no doubt; but never mind, think positively.* He would never be photographed again. He would never make another orgasmic speech. He would never sign another order, or lose another army, or call another conference. Something foul and rank had gone, a fungus kicked off a tree trunk. He was gone and I was new. My mind warmed up, and that entire sense of having done things by remote control faded away. I was Claus. What a bomb had blown apart didn't come together again. Very well, then: I was ripe; I was top dog; I was the only one in the whole world who had ever killed him, shredded him, peeled him, splashed the bright-check curtains with his blood. It was time to take pride in what I'd done; but what grew first, and fast once it had started, was relief that I'd never have to do it again. Many killings would have to follow, but that would be others' work, not mine. The murder of Wolf in his Lair with his whelps was mine alone: more than enough to haunt me, never mind how many confessors I had.

As the Heinkel plowed on toward Berlin, Haeften looked both glum and cocky. I tried to take a nap, but there was too much noise and motion, and I had so much adrenaline flowing through me that I couldn't sit still, but tapped my foot, flexed my knee (which had never been right since first being wounded), and tried to bite the little strips of skin trailing from my cuticles; they tore and bled and I licked them raw.

Next thing, I was on the ground, but where was Schweizer? Our first idea had been to have an armored car waiting at another airfield: Tempelhof; but we scrapped the whole plan once it became clear that Fromm would not be going with me to Wolf's Lair. Instead, Schweizer was supposed to be available from about one in the afternoon. After all, I had had no way of knowing whether or not S'gruber would call a conference or a briefing earlier than scheduled. He was forever doing just that. Where, then, was Schweizer? Had he misunderstood? He had never proved unreliable before; and it was no use wondering if he had gone to one of the other airfields discussed as a means of shaking off pursuit: Staaken, Adlershof, Gatow, or even Tempelhof; he had not been privy to our talks.

Our Heinkel had landed at Rangsdorf shortly before four in the afternoon. A trip that should have taken two hours at most had taken almost three, and I could only conclude that, with the air so turbulent on such a hot day, we spent much of our time moving upward as well as forward, and then dropping suddenly. Whatever the cause, that vertical zigzag had much to answer for. Other things, at least, would have happened on time. Wagner would have phoned Ebo Finckh in Paris with the key word, "exercise," meaning the bomb would explode today, and then again, with the same word, meaning get the plans for the French takeover out of your filing cabinet, and put the French part of our plan into action. Get Kluge moving. Hitler is dead.

"Phone the Bendlerstrasse," I told Haeften breathlessly. "*Tell* them he's dead. Now, where the hell is Schweizer? *We have no car!*" Haeften spoke to Olbricht, who went in to Fromm and asked him to set things in motion; but Fromm had just spoken with Keitel, who said S'gruber was alive and then asked about my own whereabouts—and not in any spirit of affable concern. Fromm refused to budge.

"Fromm won't sign," Olbricht told Hoepner glumly; but Klausing, only minutes later, strode into the signals center at the Bendlerstrasse and handed the vital message to the signals traffic officer: "The Führer Adolf Hitler is dead." Operation Valkyrie, codename for the emergency mobilization of Fromm's "Reserve" or "Replacement" Army, could now begin, on paper at least. It was a signal that explained Klausing's wrought-up face, the edginess of his hands, his omission of a security grading, for which the signals man ran after him.

"Yes, yes, put it in yourself," said Klausing gruffly. Had the signal been less secret than what the signals officer scrawled on it—"Most Immediate/Top Secret"—it would have gone out faster, via the so-called round-robin circuit. In fact it took Ol-

bricht's two secretaries, Delia Ziegler and Anni Lerche, over
three hours to get all the teleprints out, which is to say until
nineteen-fifteen or thereabouts.

With minimum fuss I obtained a Luftwaffe car and left
with Haeften at once, my last sight of the airfield being someone agitatedly waving at us from behind a hedge that flanked
the road. Ten minutes later I identified the face as that of an
old friend, Dr. Franz Bäke, no doubt eager to offer us a ride
into Berlin. Too late. I wondered if he knew why I appeared to
snub or ignore him, even presuming I had recognized him at
once.

The usual rough ride ensued. Again I bit my abraded
tongue. Haeften looked exhausted yet oddly blithe. Neither of
us knew for sure that S'gruber was dead and done for, but
pragmatic hope filled out the facts. Streaming with perspiration, we wound down the windows and tried to bask in the
draft as it veered and slackened, then picked up again when
the car went straight. Despite craters and potholes, we were at
the Bendlerstrasse by four-thirty and my great moment awaited me.

Without so much as a hello, I strode into my own office,
where Berthold, Fritzi, and some others had gathered, and
with outrageous assurance told them, "He is dead. I saw how
he was carried out." A guess, but was it better to walk in and
start quibbling? "I saw the whole thing," I went on as they
gaped almost serenely. "I was standing outside the hut with
General Fellgiebel. There was an explosion inside and then I
saw lots of medical personnel come running up and cars. The
explosion was just as if the hut had taken a direct hit from a
fifteen-millimeter shell. I'm sure no one survived it. They're
all quite dead." Dead, *dead*, quite dead. I used the word to an-
nul the part of my mind that worried, but there they stood—
Berthold working his jaw this way and that as if to free it of a
cobweb, Fritzi inhaling hard to catch a crystal of truth free-

floating in the air beneath his septum—unable to credit the most beautiful piece of news since the Resurrection. Well, if not *quite* that, it was manna: otherworldly, indigestible, and sleek. I had just delivered a Platonic form to men expecting a mere semblance of it, and their stunned eyes impressed me no end. When I phoned Hofacker in Paris and said, "Conquistador! A big fat flame. The way to action's open," he cried, "Wonderful, wonderful! We're really in business now."

But not for long. In came Klausing with another paper, which I signed, although ostensibly it emanated from Fromm, a man without whom we might have done very well indeed. Already, Olbricht told me, Fromm was on the go; he had even decided to arrest the unswerving Ali for authorizing the Valkyrie alarm without permission. So in we went to the tub of lard himself.

"Stauffenberg here," Olbricht began, "confirms the Führer's death." His oversensitized face quivered in its sheen of wet.

Booming nasally, Fromm addressed the wall: "That is *impossible*. Field Marshal Keitel has just assured me of the contrary."

Then it was my own turn to play, and what seemed a trump. "Field Marshal Keitel is lying, as usual. I myself saw Hitler being carried out dead." I almost added, *his body mangled into forty or fifty pieces the size of small hens*, for effect, but held it back just in time. I brimmed with invention. Bits of scenario kept entering my mind's eye. After all, *I* had stage-managed this event, and in a keenly intimate way it was *mine*.

"Under these circumstances," Olbricht began to say, "we have given the order for a State of Emergency."

Fromm saw it differently, however. "I am in charge here," he said, hardly breathing. "*I* give the orders. My subordinates do not. Yet"—and here he began to bellow and to pound the flat of his rosy hand on the table—"here you are, simply doing whatever you want—WHENEVER YOU WANT TO DO IT!

Not only is it insubordination, it is treason and revolt. The penalty is death. Now: who gave this Valkyrie order anyway?" His jowls heaved and rippled.

A touch sheepish, Olbricht said, "Mertz, my chief of staff," but somehow divining he should have been able to say, I myself did it, and undo it I will not.

"Then go and get him at once!" roared Fromm, flushing with vocal percussion. In came Ali, stern-faced but calm. "Very well," Fromm declared, adding decibels with each syllable, "you are all three under arrest. You will soon see what happens next." What a dolt, what an officious ox.

Now it was my turn. "On the contrary, General, it is *you* that is arrested. I myself set off the bomb, and I know for certain that Hitler is dead." Fromm gasped and, with a porcine snuffle, hunched his shoulders, hoisting muscle, fat, and epaulettes. "You might as well face the fact, beginning now." From being a tiger of wrath I had turned into a horse of instruction. "He was blown to bits," I added hotly.

"Count Stauffenberg," he blustered, "the assassination has failed. You will have to shoot yourself at once." Poor Fromm, eager to wipe out all who might blab about him and his fellow-traveling ambivalence: one damned among the doomed.

"No, sir," I told him with clinical hauteur, as if refusing to go to bed early on one of those magnificent bird-murmuring, squirrel-busy summer evenings in Swabia, "that I will not do. I am a Stauffenberg of the Gneisenau line."

Dumbfounded and then puce with rage, Fromm blundered to his feet and came at me, fists flailing, mouth slack and foul. Haeften and young Kleist drew their pistols and tugged him back, at which point Kleist rammed his pistol muzzle into Fromm's stomach. Had Fromm also reached for his pistol at the beginning of that sudden liquid movement, and then reached Stauffenberg too soon? Shoved back into his chair, and disarmed, he became almost catatonic.

"Colonel General," I told him, "you have five minutes in

which to think things over." He would join us or not. A bunch
of crueler plotters would have shot him out of hand, there and
then, one bullet into the stewed slush of his belly, then one to
cleanse the filth of his head.

When Olbricht asked him his decision, Fromm spoke with
almost courtly finesse, choosing a term from billiards. "Under
the circumstances I regard myself as in balk."

Olbricht asked Beck to try to persuade him, but Beck refused: "I don't want to seem to be forcing the fellow's hand; it
would not *do*." I sighed, but with all the ungainliness of one
unaccustomed to doing so. All we did was to bundle Fromm
and Bartram, his peg-legged aide, into Bartram's office, which
adjoined the butler's pantry and the anteroom registry. We
disconnected the phone and stationed guards at both exits. It
was about five o'clock, and soon Witzleben would perform his
first act as commander of the Wehrmacht by appointing
Hoepner temporary commander of the Reserve Army.
Hoepner, being Hoepner, insisted on having his appointment
confirmed in writing; it was Hoepner who had suggested delaying the Valkyrie order until I actually put in an appearance,
but Olbricht (and he no ball of fire!) disregarded him; and it
was Hoepner whom, during the next few hours, we would
come to know better than almost everyone else. He really
wanted to survive. Witzleben was overdue.

Now began a farce with uniforms. Beck had put on a brown
lounge suit so as not to provoke comment when he climbed out
of Schwerin von Schwanenfeld's car. Told to put a uniform tunic on Beck, a captain lifted one out of a locker and put it on
Hoepner instead, who didn't seem to mind. The man didn't
know Beck, anyway, and might have thought he was some distinguished but anguished-faced sanitary engineer making a social call on the new regime. He soon realized, however, that
this was the man who would replace S'gruber as head of the
Reich, and thereafter could not remove his awed gaze from
him. Hoepner, that quite different kettle of fish, had also come

dressed as a civilian, and so clad had taken a jubilant lunch with Olbricht; but now he went into the lavatory to change into the dress uniform he had brought with him in a suitcase, unworn since S'gruber cashiered him. So now we were all, as it were, dressed up, even brother Berthold in his naval blue, even Peter Yorck and Hans Bernd von Haeften looking like chocolate soldiers. What we lacked was a tune to dance to, over which to trip.

Now Hoepner, during the lull as we awaited the arrival of troops in Berlin, went in to Fromm and apologized: "I'm sorry about the way things have turned out."

Unmoved, Fromm explained the idiocy of the day to him. "Well, Hoepner, I too am sorry, but I have no choice. In my opinion, the Führer is not dead, not dead at all. Keitel told me so. Marshal Graziani was with him at the time, while the Duce was with the Führer. You're in the wrong."

Then I called General Wagner in Zossen camp and told him S'gruber was a goner, but Wagner sounded oddly reluctant as I handed the receiver to Beck, who said something about the assumption of plenary power. "Witzleben will be there shortly," Beck said with a minatory cough. Sadly, Stieff, fast going bad, had called Wagner, branding the whole coup "total madness."

Wagner's response had been simple. "Tell Keitel at once," he told Stieff. "And tell him that all kinds of peculiar calls keep reaching me from the Bendlerstrasse." What could we expect, after all, from a man with a name like that? He was Hitlerian before he began. He had something against rabbits.

"For me, this man is dead," Beck insisted, telling Helldorf in particular, but as it were guaranteeing us all. "Whatever you hear to the contrary you must ignore. If we believe in ourselves for the next few hours, we shall prevail."

What had already been, by almost any standard, a Promethean day was beginning to develop a shape, a spearpoint. Out of a thousand things' combining, the coup began to begin. Helldorf nodded at Beck, promising, "I will telephone the

Bendlerstrasse every twenty minutes," and went off to alert the Security Police. I heard how Klausing had summoned the younger officers from their place of waiting in the Esplanade Hotel; how Beck and Schwerin had driven by them on the Bendlerstrasse, Schwerin motioning to them to hurry; how it had finally been decided not to bring Goerdeler in too soon (no one could find him anyway). Now Otto John of Lufthansa telephoned, heard Haeften tell him, "We have executive authority; come straight over," and rushed in from his office at Tempelhof only to run into an odd tableau on the second floor.

What he saw was an SS officer (Oberführer Dr. Humbert Achamer-Pifrader), sent to arrest me, but instead deprived of pistol, cap, and belt by one of our own officers, who put him forthwith in the keeping of two steel-helmeted sentries with fixed bayonets. Only those bearing an orange identity card signed by myself got through the main door, and one of these the unutterable Pifrader lacked.

Smiling at being so taken aback, Otto asked how things were going. "Hitler is no more," said the loyal Haeften, with whom, it seemed years ago, I had planted the bomb. "Keitel insists he's not dead, but only slightly wounded. It's not true." Then Schwerin briefed him more fully, explaining, "Beck's determined to press things through to the end. Is there any news from Lisbon?" There was, and it had to do with an Allied demand for unconditional surrender, bad news that Otto would have to give Beck in private.

Even now, Eugen Gerstenmaier, our martial theologian, was coming to the Bendlerstrasse by streetcar, as if it were the most natural thing in the world to go commuterlike to the hot fulcrum of a revolution which, on your arrival, appointed you military plenipotentiary for cultural and church affairs.

Non-stop I used the telephone, urging, pleading, bolstering, methods far from those envisioned by Gerstenmaier, who had both a pistol and a Bible on him. "There's got to be some shooting," he told me during a lull. "Wonderful to talk, but essential to liquidate. If we don't . . . " I heard him out, agreed, but had no one shot, not even General Kortzfleisch, who had come to see Fromm and started to shout, "The Führer's not dead; the Führer is not dead!" Pretending to stay, he suddenly burst from the room next to Olbricht's and raced down the hallway.

"The general's gone!" yelled von der Lancken, our keeper of bombs. Young Hammerstein called, "Look out at the exit!" They did, and Kleist with an NCO held up the general at gunpoint, eventually returning him to the care of Hammerstein, who had to listen to his ravings all evening. "My oath as an officer!" yelled Kortzfleisch. "A coup's not for the likes of me. I'd rather go home and weed my garden. Now, if you *insist* on keeping me here, then look after me properly, as my rank requires."

Why had we not put Fromm, Pifrader, and Kortzfleisch in the cells attached to the guardroom, along with those known to be diehards? Why did we allow Hoepner to play the role of courtly captor, bestowing wine and sandwiches in a belated effort to be worldly? Hot lead, said Gerstenmaier, is what they deserved: an apocalyptic, final bellyful.

Major Oertzen handed me a list of all the donkeywork to be done: agencies, offices, centers, posts, ministeries, institutes, and depots to be occupied, even the "Research Office" devoted to telephone tapping. It was like trying to improvise a complex parlor game from scratch, with the grand prize the arrest of Goebbels, and no autographs allowed. Streets had to be cordoned off and barriers set up on the Berlin circular autobahn. I signed passes in a blaze of penmanship, phoned up leaders and intermediaries and flunkies, felt the third total drench of the day stiffen into the first and second in my evil-smelling tunic, and prayed for temporary luck. But already things were going askew; commanders could not fathom orders received from

Witzleben, then Fromm, then Hoepner, on top of which orders began coming through from Keitel which said S'gruber was alive.

"We no longer have the vital fifty-one per cent chance of success," fussed Hoepner.

"Could we even now, still, call the whole thing off?" (Olbricht)

Only Beck held firm, saying, "Let us be strong for Germany, let us be firm, *whatever* happens."

And I fervently backed him, sprinting from room to room with a ha-ha here, a bravo there, here a poo-hoo and there a long, intense, yearning, empathetic, wet-eyed nod.

"*Murder*, Gerstenmaier! We don't murder. We try before a court." Goodness, how many I had killed that very day, blowing them to shreds and smeared collops.

"Yes," to all and sundry on the phone, "all orders from the C-in-C Reserve Army are to be obeyed. . . . Seize all wireless stations and information centers. All SS opposition must be polished off." I had said it all a million times, like some fathead draping a giant spider's web over his face against the midday sun. Of all men, I was the most naked, in the open: the killer pre-eminent, but also the rhetorician of the coup, its referee, its plumber, its confessor, its alchemist. I had nowhere else to go, no one else to be, no other chance to set off a bomb. In other words, the premise was fixed, and the outcome was beginning to shrivel into permanent identity.

Then another blow, below the belt. Beck spoke to Kluge at La Roche-Guyon, pleading with him to get the revolt in France under way, only to have Kluge shift from evasive to querulous.

"Is he really dead? How can I be sure." One could always count on Kluge to twitter: he, who wouldn't shoot S'gruber at lunch.

Beck was having none of it. "Are you prepared to place

yourself under my orders or not?" He pouted gravely into the phone.

After a pause, Kluge promised to call back in half an hour, no doubt intending to go out and buy some crafty punctuation; the call never came, and Beck's face began to sag like crepe.

"*Kluge*," he sighed. "His yes is no, his no is yes. He's afraid to live, to die. Afraid to be afraid. A touch of cancer might perk him up, at least to existential opportunism. His son-in-law, who runs a military hospital in Paris, has provided him with seven ampules of waterless acid cyanide. *Seven!* No, he didn't tell me just now. Bits of information come my way now and then. Kluge belongs in Byzantium. *Yes, I mean more or less*, he blathers. *For God's sake, let me think a moment. Let me be judicious, let me be military! The world is bigger than our cause.* He's turned honor into theological stylistics. Kluge—Kluge is a swan. And I, my dear Stauffenberg, what am *I*? I am the crown prince of Denmark. The cannons roar. I am in constant pain. I have none of Halder's sarcasm to spike my speeches with. I'm an old, black, slimy sea lion who's overstayed his welcome in this zoo. Didn't you just fly over the Masurian Lakes on your way back? Down at the bottom of one of *those*, I might feel whole again, and good—anywhere where's there's no Kluge. What a dithering trimmer, forever yes-butting. There you have him. Clever Hans. He's shy of life, that's all."

"Sir," I tried to say crisply, but I only mumbled it, "you know we love you as sons would. *We* are yours."

"You, my sons," he said with a slanted grin in which pain and fatalistic poise mixed drably, "will kill me in the end. No, Claus. I'd rather you fellows than anybody. Beck's proud, even with his Maker, who's just a mediocre yellow sun."

18

The Violet Hour

◆

The violet hour was just beginning to lose its pink, but the gorgeous swollen summer made night hug the ground, shredded and wafting about. That sapped violet was one of the scenic marvels of July; it was also the picture postcard of our greatest day, and suddenly I went out of myself—away from the mess of aches, nerves, pangs, jerks, gasps, I'd been—and beyond all such stances as the daring man vindicated, the officer proved, the family man on fire. I turned into a contraption that spewed out what I wanted done.

"Stauffenberg speaking. *Jawohl. Ja.* All orders . . . All radio and news-reporting agencies to be occupied. . . . Of course! All resistance to be broken. You'll probably get counterorders from the Führer headquarters, but they're not, do you understand me, *not* valid. Ignore them. The army has taken over. No one's authorized to give orders except us. As always in emergencies, soldiers have to do the dirty work. Yes, that's correct: Witzleben has been appointed Supreme Commander. No, I don't give a damn what your opinion is—it's a purely formal appointment, see. Now get on with it and occupy those radio relay stations. You understand? *Heil.*"

While talking to one man, I still heard what I'd said to the man before; I'd become something briefly inhuman, a cone-shaped grid with radio waves blaring zigzag from my head, still warning fellow conspirators and urging, urging, urging, in an eternal present tense. Bleats in vacuo.

The dreadful messages came through still, dreadful although compressed or oblique. Appeals without a home.

"Sorry ... Claus ... call ... back ... later. ... *I'll* phone."
This was a former colleague pretending he had a bad connection.

"Mertz has railroaded me." Olbricht thinking aloud.

"A disgraceful attempt on our Führer's life has failed, thank
God. The plotters are *here in the Bendlerblock itself.* Our job
now is to sever their lines of communications. From now on,
everything signed Witzleben, Olbricht, Stauffenberg, goes into
the enciphering trays for a day or two in quarantine. *Everything.* We'll choke these swine at source." That was General
Fritz Thiele, chief of signals, to his staff. A curly worm of human slime.

"They're crazy," Stieff told Wagner a bit later.

"For me this man is dead." Beck, ever and ever.

Then one of the silliest exchanges of all, between Hoepner
and Panzer General Veiel:

"Veiel here. Who's that?"

"Hoepner here, Veiel. What's up?"

"It's all right."

"What do you mean—'It's all right'?"

Veiel: "Well, it's all right." Both afraid to speak.

Then Hase, the City Commandant, referred to "a fatal accident," in order to avoid implicating anyone.

"Stieff too is now a defector." Stauffenberg during the early
evening.

"All this is no good any more," said Fellgiebel to Olbricht,
meaning *Stop talking; do something.* And Olbricht put down
the receiver, said like an oaf, "There's the first one to defect."
No, *Stieff;* Fellgiebel never.

Hans Bernd Gisevius, a lanky delphic accomplice from Admiral Canaris's Intelligence network, was staring at me with
wry impatience. "Don't you see what kind of duds you've got
around here? They haven't the faintest idea what to do. What

we need is some corpses: *now.*" Those bloodthirsty civilians made me sick, but I wondered if Gisevius was right. An ex-Gestapo lawyer surely knew.

Later in the evening, Otto John decided to leave the Bendlerstrasse, since we had nothing for him to do. "If you call early tomorrow," Schwerin von Schwanenfeld joked, "we'll know what's up." In the hallway John met Werner von Haeften and told him, "I'll phone at eight tomorrow morning."

Haeften, with a stern chuckle: "Perhaps we'll have been strung up by then. *Auf Wiedersehen.*"

About 7:55 P.M. Beck spoke to Army Group North, which was almost surrounded by the Russians. "Withdraw immediately." He then ordered that, "for the sake of future historians," his instruction be recorded. "No one can tell what might happen in the next few hours." Old Beck, ogling the scholars of posterity!

Nine-thirty P.M. "Everything was in total confusion and disorder. The City Commandant's headquarters is a complete muddle." Young Kleist after coming back from a mission of Olbricht's.

Not much later. "Come here." An order from Hase, still City Commandant, to Remer, who was now with Goebbels.

"*You* come *here*, to Dr. Goebbels's home." Remer to Hase: a proposal only, of course, with two sergeants for escort.

"Please remain." Goebbels to Hase. "I'm running things now."

"May I have dinner, then?" Hase to Goebbels.

"Hock or moselle?" Hase dined at a table overlooked from the door by SS guards while Goebbels rattled off countermeasures into his phones.

Arriving at the Bendlerstrasse gate, Witzleben and his host, Count von Lynar, ran into the bespectacled, ascetic-looking Captain Cords, who refused to let them pass. "Everyone entering must have an orange identity card signed by—" and then he said my name in full, stating both my rank and title to give the occasion its due.

Witzleben let out a bellow. He had come in medals and full uniform straight from Wagner's office, where he'd heard how the assassination had failed, and he was shivering with several different sorts of rage. Now the knife was twisting in the wound. "I," he told Cords in a bullying hoot, "am Field Marshal von Witzleben."

"Of *course*," von Lynar huffed. His monocle flashed.

"How do I know that? *Sir*." Cords had given Helldorf the same kind of trouble earlier on; people either had the heavy orange linen paper pass or they did not.

When he phoned, I told him, "Yes, yes, the field marshal is expected. He is a famous man accustomed to being recognized. Let him through at once." An impostor? Surely not.

In he stormed, cap in hand, his face purple or beet, and his baton swinging cursively with unspent spleen. Heels clicked and everyone stood. I approached him and saluted.

"A fine mess, this," he growled. Gisevius shook his hand, the only one of us to do so. Then Witzleben saw Beck, his superior at least as far as the rebel hierarchy of the coup went, and addressed him in a tone of pungent surliness: "Reporting for duty, sir." The two of them went into Fromm's room, where a grand old row developed, into the midst of which Schwerin von Schwanenfeld and I were summoned.

"Fine way to lead an insurrection!" Witzleben banged his fist on the table. "How *dare* you involve us in something so dubious? Is he dead or not? Are we dealing with facts or with boyhood suppositions? Is it too much to ask, or do you know what the truth is? Are there *any* facts at all? Our necks are in the balance!" Bang went the fist again and his eyes, always half closed, clamped tight as if to hold in steam and shut out the sight of the failed assassin, whose chest all day had been going in and out like a bellows. God, I felt tired.

"As for you, sir"—he glowered at Beck—"why in the name of all that's military haven't you—"

"I," said the shadow regent of Germany, "have no troops at my disposal. *I* am a *civilian*." His cheeks grew even whiter and the muscles round his mouth tugged this way and that in little aborted tics.

In the brief silence that followed we could hear Olbricht and Hoepner having their own row next door.

"There's a risk in every coup d'état." Olbricht, fierce.

"Yes, but one must have a ninety per cent probability that the putsch will work." Hoepner sounded oddly choked.

"Nonsense, you'll never have such odds. Fifty-one per cent is quite enough."

"Nowhere near enough. Say eighty."

"How do you expect to get eighty?" Olbricht seemed almost to be trifling with him, but Hoepner was incensed in his morose way.

"There you are! Not even eighty. Then you *can't* go ahead. . . ." Only hours ago they had lunched amiably at the Casino Club.

"Bickering as usual," snarled Witzleben. "Too much talk, too few facts, and too many damned sandwiches and bottles of wine from the officers' canteen!" Even then, as we jawed on, Fromm was having a frugal dinner while under arrest. As if taking impetus from the two next door, Witzleben started all over again.

"One of Keitel's lies," I told him.

"Guesses, guesses," he raved. "How do you *know*?"

"The evidence of his senses," Beck murmured, trying to intervene. Then he said it again loudly.

"Evidence of things *not seen*," sneered Witzleben with uncommon allusiveness; he hardly ever quoted, but what was he quoting from? Not his favorite schoolboy stories, for sure.

Five minutes later Witzleben calmed down enough to say, "I wash my hands of the whole affair. You *gentlemen* are not

fit to run a sideshow full of monkeys." Schwerin and I stood
there like marble columns. Beck sighed with a calm face. All
along, we had believed in the assassination, but had we ever
believed we could pull off the coup?

"Idea men," shouted Witzleben, still hauling us over the
coals. "*Planners!* When you say you have killed, then YOU
SHOULD HAVE TAKEN SOMEBODY'S LIFE. There should
be a corpse. Someone should be dead beyond resurrection. Is
that too much to ask? *General? Colonel?* Am I dealing with
real soldiers? Or chocolate ones on a very hot day? Answer,
gentlemen: I am damned if I deal with you at all, any further,
in this. And damned if I don't. Damn the lot of you. You have
strung us up. Bombs! Poetry! Colonels! *Counts!* I would have
done better to train a squad of thoroughbred dogs. Goodbye.
I'll see you when the hangman entertains."

He didn't just storm out of the room; he erupted past us all,
raving acidly, his eyelids working as if on strings. He had aged
ten years in the past hour without changing hue.

Now he and von Lynar drove off in their Mercedes to tell
Wagner what was up. Yes, I thought as he left, if he'd given us
more of his time, he wouldn't have had to use his mouth so
much in the last half-hour. There would soon be more shit-
heads than you could count on two hands.

On I went, bedraggled in my white summer tunic and my
red-striped breeches, using two telephones, one on my own
desk, one on Fromm's, trying to be—in one breath—humane,
masterful, brisk, persuasive, and always expeditious. The
whole day's doings amounted to a bedlam hurry.

"Keitel is lying, of course. Hitler is dead. I can count on you,
can't I? Make sure your chief stands firm.

"I'm counting on you. Stieff has let us down. Please, Hayessen, don't you do the same. We must hold out, we *must*."

Then, to several others: "Stauffenberg here. Please hold
firm."

And, to everyone: "If you give up now, we're sunk. For God's sake, if you've any respect for me at all, *trust* me. I'll see it through, just give me today."

White-coated orderlies came in at Olbricht's request and set the table. Everyone sat down to eat except Olbricht and me, but the only one who showed much appetite was Fritzi Schulenburg, savagely caricaturing the meal: "We must empty the cup. We must sacrifice ourselves. Posterity will understand. . . ." The smile vanished faster than usual from his heavy, rugged, sword-slashed face; he no longer walked up and down with rapid small steps. Only days before, he had thrust a twenty-mark bill into someone's hand, saying, "Buy some roses for Frau Leber," who was lying in a hospital bed under supervision, well aware that the Gestapo were on the track of her arrested husband's friends. There he was, not only fishing crumpled money out of his perpetually unbuttoned tunic, but also on July eighteenth walking from Schwerin to Trebbow to celebrate his wife's birthday one day in advance. She got the children out of bed and he stayed the night, after which he drove away from them waving his cap madly at the laughing, gesticulating children. He bowed low from the driver's seat and was gone, only to be told on his arrival back in Berlin that his brother had been killed in Normandy. That was only yesterday he had such news, and here he was dining with enormous grave relish. How close we were, yet how distant from each other he and I had become, as if already encased in our futures. A mute black suction. Each felt the shadow move upon him and cool him, tempting him into thoughts more inward and self-involved than were seemly; but what else? It was a funeral meal, cut across by rotten conversations.

Klausing, the cleft in his chin deeper and his mouth somehow shriveled, offered an answer.

"Everything going all right?" someone asked.

"Hard to tell. It's always the same. In combat too. You fire and you never know whether you've hit anything. You hear about it afterwards. You're always in the dark until you get the complete picture." That night there were many such hollowed conversations, but what was audible was more like individual voluntaries addressed to no one, not even as lively as Hans Fritzsche's half-hourly check on the sentries guarding our prisoners: Fromm, Kortzfleisch, still rumbling, "Don't you dare touch me!" and Pifrader, who, I could not forget, had successfully exhumed and destroyed the corpses of some quarter of a million Jews killed off in the Baltic zone.

"What are your orders?" Fritzsche yelled.

"Our orders, sir," the sentries responded as one, "are to see that these men don't escape and to *shoot* them if they try." A fine sentiment, less decisive than what Gisevius said about the flashing black apparition of the butcher, or grave tumbler, Pifrader, whose buffed heels clicked together like a pistol shot and whose growl, even here in the plotters' den, took his eminence for granted.

"Stauffenberg," Gisevius asked, "why didn't you shoot him straight off?" I groaned at him; killing was no reflex of mine.

"His turn will come." I had better things to do, and I had faith in lock and key, in sentries, and in the legal way of doing things.

He persisted even as I turned away. "What if he makes a break for it? He'll have seen everything." The pudgy rosebud of his mouth flinched as if someone had tweaked the flab along his jaw.

"No." But we had also seized Pifrader's aide, his two toughs.

"Then if you won't shoot him, let's form an officers' troop and go shoot holes in Goebbels. Now." Yes, I thought, *Nux* would.

"I'll ask Colonel Jaeger about it," I said. "Jaeger's just the daredevil type we need for that." The voice I heard within my mouth sounded tired and sapped; I should have taken a sandwich with coffee, but there was no time. Not far away, northeast across Berlin, in police headquarters on the Alexander

Platz, the evil twins Helldorf and "Kripo" Nebe—Berlin Police President and head of the Criminal Police (a neatly ambiguous phrase to begin with)—were sorting out lines of their own, to be tried on Gisevius when he arrived.

"It's failed," Nebe snarled. "All very well for them to claim that Himmler would say Hitler was alive even if he were dead. That's logical. But I don't want logic, I want facts. And the facts are—Himmler's on his way to Berlin to crush the coup. Shall we intercept him and kill him?"

"No," snapped Helldorf, a man every bit as antiseptically trim and smart as Pifrader. "To hell with Beck and his friends. For years these generals have been shitting on us. They promised us everything. And what's happened today? Shit. Shit. Shit. *You* vanish. *I'll* bluff it out. I've always gambled. Why should I lose now?" Never had he been so satanically jaunty. "Impudence." He laughed. "We'll deny everything. Pretend that nothing happened!"

Yet these two, the flagrant count and the zealous ex-leader of one of the Jewish Extermination Commandos in Russia, were too close to such bloodsuckers as Kaltenbrunner and Group Leader (or "Gestapo") Müller to be wholly safe. One slip in so highly charged a context and they were done for; their very umbrella made their lives more dangerous. Yet Helldorf could not bear to wait. Earlier he had asked Gisevius to phone Nebe to ask what was going on, and Nebe had merely said, "Something strange has happened in East Prussia," then agreed to meet Gisevius at a rendezvous Gisevius so obliquely described that Nebe went to the wrong place, the Hotel Excelsior, while Gisevius cooled his heels in a restaurant frequented by Helldorf. . . .

I stared at the number on my secret telephone: 1293, slowly adding its digits up to 15 and then to a final 6. What did 6 mean, numerologically? Did everyone who needed this number know it? Or did they mistrust it as I imagined they did all the letters I "signed" with my special rubber facsimile stamp?

The orderlies came in again and cleared away the mostly untouched food, leaving an aroma of coffee, cheese, and sausage salad. Almost all the troops told to protect the Bendlerstrasse had been withdrawn on Goebbels's and Remer's orders, but the phone kept on buzzing even as we died on the vine. The radio station, which we should have seized but had not—the major assigned to it had inactivated a switch room and studios no longer in use, whereas the real thing went radiating into the night from a nearby bunker he'd missed—said that S'gruber would soon make a broadcast; Himmler was now appointed Commander in Chief of the Reserve Army; and General Reinecke, we gathered from incoming calls, had been ordered to storm the building, so clearly the handful of troops still at the main gate would now become the spearhead of the attack. Something leaden in my heart turned into an image from the first day of the month: Helldorf fulsomely congratulating me on my new appointment as chief of staff, to which I answered only, with amicable jollity, "Too kind, Herr Präsident, too kind!" Then I got rid of him on some pretext; but now his iterative, vulgar "shit, shit, shit" included me as well. Dismissed by the master of a thousand alibis, degraded by the servant of who knew how many deviant lusts, I felt oddly denatured, as far from my original or initial self as Berlin from Brazil.

19

Osmosis

◆

In the meantime, Fromm's aid, Bartram, his wooden leg notwithstanding, had managed to find a way out of the room in which we held them prisoner. Dagger in hand, Bartram pushed into a dark passage that led to an old stairway. Up he went and found Major General Kennes.

"There's a putsch going on! General Fromm says you must tell the infantry school to send troops at once."

Kennes laughed. "You're rambling, old man. Why not get a bit of shuteye? You'll be all right then."

"General Fromm *is being held a prisoner under double armed guard on the floor below.*" Bartram tried not to shout.

It was no use: Kennes didn't care, at least not until he came downstairs to attend a briefing which Hoepner and I gave for heads of groups. Now he realized that Bartram wasn't crazy after all, and, reluctant to use the phone, he tried to leave the building, first alone, then with other officers, none of whom got out, because they had no passes. Then they sent an officer to Olbricht to get some and, astonishingly, succeeded. The Bendlerstrasse was honeycombed with both structural and official exits. Next they all left at about the time Witzleben arrived, even calling on Fromm's wife at Lake Leber to say that he wouldn't be home that night. With so impeccable a domestic spirit among us, it was a wonder that Germany ever took the wrong path.

Bartram, however, had stayed behind, ferreting about, popping his head into this and that doorway with his horrific news, then returning to inform Fromm.

"Don't you think, Bartram," Fromm asked with blockish diffidence, "I should try to escape through the same place? You seem to have no trouble going to and fro."

"You are known," Bartram told him. "You are tall, and a colonel general in full uniform would hardly go unnoticed, whereas nobody knows who I am. I'm just a captain after all. Better to wait for darkness and leave through the truck entrance. Someone on Kennes's staff can alert your driver to wait on Tiergartenstrasse. I'll arrange it myself." Off he went through the hole, dragging his leg behind him with slightly dramatic gasps.

When he came back, Fromm ordered him to go to Hoepner. "Ask him if I might use my private apartment—on condition that I do nothing and certainly make no attempt to telephone. You *understand*." Again chivalry prevailed. Hoepner said yes; Fromm moved in, and an armed guard stood at his door. Now Fromm and Bartram discussed the situation all over again, Fromm speculating how they might evade the guards, Bartram with almost condescending tact pointing out that Fromm had just thrown away the perfect escape. "You—we—no longer have the use of the unguarded exit." Fromm pondered that for a while, his hand on a telephone he dared not use. Then he sent Bartram to fetch the radio from their first place of imprisonment and so thrust him into the main current of the developing counteraction.

S'gruber was not dead, *all* the radios said; and Himmler was now in charge of the Reserve Army. Puzzled, some of Olbricht's staff—Colonels Herber, von der Heyde, and Pridun, together with Major Harnack—went to Olbricht to demand an explanation, which he declined to give, instead instructing them how to safeguard the building. "Every officer must play his part," he told them. "The Guard Battalion sentries are no longer there. Normal duty is suspended herewith." He coughed, not so much nervously as to renew their attention. "I want six officers to take it upon themselves to keep intruders out. Colonels, majors, captains, lieutenants, any rank will do. Work out a duty roster, please."

Off went a couple of junior officers to Cords at the main gate, who had already had an interesting day, caught in some military osmosis that kept changing its direction of flow. Olbricht's words kept going through my mind; I had never quite realized what a genius he had for obfuscation, for transforming into august allegory facts he refused to state.

"But why?" someone asked, some lieutenant colonel. "Why guard the building anyway?"

"To avert a possible catastrophe. There has been a certain amount of indecipherable confusion, gentlemen."

"Who is involved? Is there a putsch?"

"The exact word," magnificent Olbricht pronounced, "will offer itself at the right time. Until then, let us be wary. Forces from out of the night are making themselves felt. Trust *us*—Hoepner, Stauffenberg, myself—to sort it all out. By telephone or otherwise. In a maze of orders and counterorders, rumors and counterrumors, some of them put out by people whose well-being does not necessarily imply our own, we have to be supremely careful. Before we put our fort in order, let us defend it like men. In an officerly spirit."

I almost cheered. Stauffenbergese was one thing—a brand of crisp but velvety persuasion (or so I hoped)—but Olbrichtese was codified mist, a sentimentality of the tight-wrung nerve.

"Responsible officers have seized the initiative," he said in conclusion. "Reassure yourselves about that. The matter is far from out of hand, and it will not reach that point." But his finesse could not stop them from grumbling. They felt they'd been had, and they were right. He terminated the proceedings with a salute, raising his arm. Only a handful returned the salute in the same way, most of them, Heyde included, reciprocating with a short bow.

Ah, they're with us, I thought. The end had begun, and once more we were working in the human domain; an idyll had begun to bloom. But whose? I no longer felt able to read the signs aright. Merely being busy made me feel better than I should have. After all, high spirits could have their fling on the next several thousand days of our lives, whereas today—today was blurred, untidy, and opaque.

On flowed the Nazi radio into the steamy night, serenading the coup before it began. The martial music was incessant.

Next thing, Herber, the former policeman, and some others confronted Olbricht again, Herber with earnest insolence asking, "What's the real game? Against *whom* are we to guard the building? Why? My understanding was that we were here to supply reinforcements or replacements to the armies at the front. In any case, what's all this stuff about a conspiracy?'"

Like a music box flicked on, Olbricht delivered more or less his previous speech, with only the merest flush in his cheeks betraying his annoyance. "Gentlemen, for a long time we have been observing the developing situation with great anxiety; it was undoubtedly headed for catastrophe. Measures had to be taken to . . . anticipate this, and those measures—those measures precisely—are now being carried out. I ask for your support. That is all." They knew, even those not in our confidence, that the leader of a conspiracy was right there among them in the Bendlerstrasse. So far there had been no overt arguments, although a certain amount of mumbling and fidgeting.

"A putsch is going on," Herber said in his gruff lilt. "That much is plain."

"And just as plain," said Heyde, half whispering, "that without being in the know or involved in any way, we are being railroaded into it. We are the subordinates of men who are implicating us, without taking us into their confidence, at just the time when the conspiracy or whatever it is seems to be failing. We should look out for ourselves. It wasn't our affair in the first place."

"We never opposed it," said Harnack, "in fact we never took sides." Actually, Harnack had sent out the signals for Valkyrie Stage 2.

Now the colorless Heyde, with whom I had been at the military academy, started up again, a talker but not much of a doer, on the day in question carrying a dagger instead of a sidearm, no doubt for decoration. "If we continue to sit on the fence, though, the SS will have our necks. Now is the time to take a stand."

Herber looked shiftier than ever, every inch a wheedler with close-set dark eyes, plastered-down black hair, and a bodily posture that seemed to say his hands were ready to receive whatever the world put into them: a prehensile cringe. "The *oath*," he said, as if vomiting the Holy Ghost, and they all adjourned into a nearby office, Heyde's or Pridun's.

"We cannot forswear our oath," said von der Heyde, who (true to form) had spent much of the afternoon tearfully grinding his teeth at the news of S'gruber's death. Although he refused to cooperate, no one arrested him, no doubt another gentlemanly oversight, and in the end he'd told Delia Ziegler and Anni Lerche that, having nothing particular to do, he'd go and have a meal somewhere. At this point I gave the guards at the gate firm orders to let no one out without a valid pass, which Heyde lacked. At least, unlike some others who, on hearing S'gruber was dead, had ripped the Nazi insignia from their tunics, saying they were with us all the way, he stayed constant to his misguided beliefs. True robots couldn't change their tune.

Of the six officers Olbricht detailed to guard the exits, four were Heyde, Herber, Harnack, and Pridun; with such to protect us it was little wonder that a truckload of arms got through and was promptly carted up to the second floor: submachine guns, hand grenades, and pistols. The *works*.

How did I feel? Worse even than I looked, as if a stomach pump had been at work on my innards, on the marrow of my bones. My knees were weak, my eye teared, the socket of the other itched unbearably, and, worst, the amputated part of my right arm seemed to be there again, its atoms clustering around a three-dimensional pattern, almost as if, for what remained of the surreptitious in our plot, I were to have an invisible hand, signing right-handed signatures that couldn't be held against me because they couldn't be seen, and shaking other hands without compromise because mine was the hand which, feeling, couldn't be felt. A terrible, giddy, sour pun came to me: I was the Phantom not of the *Oper* (opera) but of the *Opfer* (victim). And what followed this bit of levity was an acute sense that I was already less in this world than others thought me; I felt wanly subtracted from, full of shivers, no longer an entity but a mere quotation from myself, less *myself* than the eye that had gone shredded God knew where across Tunisia. I felt *dilute*.

It was now about 2245 hours, but the heat clung on. Cords at the main gate found a new crisis on his hands. A new platoon had arrived, but he persuaded them to take his orders.

"Now we have our own troops," he told Klausing with wry relief, only to discover, after he put the phone down, that a strong detachment from Goebbels and Remer had just marched up. The two groups confronted each other, some with arms at the ready, but it was no use staging a little war out there, so he had the gate closed and all other entrances guarded as closely as possible. Only the small pedestrians' entrance remained open; a large force could hardly use that.

Not many were in Olbricht's anteroom when Herber, pistol in hand and a hand grenade bulging in his trousers pocket, roared in with his associates past Delia Ziegler and Anni Lerche and confronted Olbricht all over again while Heyde aimed his machine gun at the others: Yorck, Berthold, and Gerstenmaier.

"This is against the Führer!" Herber blurted, incongruous indoors in his cap; his eyeglass was a porthole into the smallest mind in the world. "Something against the Führer's going on. My comrades and I remain loyal to our oath. We insist on seeing General Fromm at once."

Only faintly surprised, Olbricht answered, actually taking a step toward them, guns or not. "There has been a report of the Führer's death," he said stiffly. "There has also been news to the contrary. The situation is complex in the extreme." Olbricht's son-in-law, Georgi, nodded redundantly.

"Not good enough, Herr General. We must speak with General Fromm." Delia Ziegler rushed out to give the alarm.

"You," Olbricht told Herber, meaning them all, "are armed.

I am not. But first of all I ask you to come along with me and talk to General Hoepner." Now Delia Ziegler came at speed, almost skidding, into the hallway en route to Fromm's office, where Beck and Hoepner were. Instead she ran into Haeften and myself, who had heard the commotion of heavy boots pell-mell and Herber's pompous bray.

"Trouble!" she gasped. "Guns on Olbricht!"

Haeften's easy grin fell away like a veil.

Instead of pausing to analyze things, we ran toward the open door.

"—is cleared up, you will not be allowed to leave the room," Herber was saying. "If you try to leave, we shall shoot."

I looked in, saw what was afoot, and ducked out again as fast as I could. Then some idiot tried to grasp me by an arm I did not possess; I got back into the anteroom, and skipped through Ali's office into the corridor, gasping, "Quick!" to Haeften, who seemed more animated than he'd been in days. We ran, but there was a noise of shooting behind us and I suddenly jerked forward, backward, upright, wincing as something that felt ridiculously small bit through my left arm even as I yelled, "What's up? Who's doing all that shooting?" As many as ten rounds. Dozens of officers were milling about in the corridor. My blood was already pooling on the floor. A shot went through the ceiling, weirdly anonymous and invisible, aimed at nothing. Out came Herber, ducking low and twisting right as someone shot at him from within the anteroom (Klausing, I gathered), only to be knocked off his feet in the confusion as I, in squeezable pain, clamped my service pistol against my side with my stump and cocked it with the three fingers of my left hand, all of them thick with blood. Then I fired at Pridun, wondering had I been hit in the shoulder blade or the arm proper? The pain moved about as if looking for home.

"Under the table!" someone shouted to the secretaries, who were in the line of fire. Then a fusillade came from the vicinity of Olbricht's office. Out whizzed Georgi with a briefcase

stuffed with papers, then Gerstenmaier the theologian, gun in
hand, which he fired vaguely in the other direction. Georgi
vanished, Gerstenmaier went back in, no doubt in search of a
stationary target, I thought, but out he came again and hared
off after Georgi even as someone bawled, "For or against the
Führer?" from the other end of the hall. "You *swine!*"

Rotten shooting all of it. I alone had been hit, presumably by
Herber, whom Klausing had missed, as I had missed Pridun, as
Gerstenmaier had missed whomever he was firing at. Heyde so
far had not lunged with or thrown his stately dagger. Somehow, though, Klausing got out of the building, but they turned
back Gerstenmaier. The main thing was to get through to Paris, and, right there in the midst of that bloodthirsty commotion, Frau Alix Winterfeldt, Fromm's secretary, placed the
call. That much of the universe had still not fallen apart.

What was it that Olbricht had exclaimed as the first shots
sounded? "Now the damned fools have gone and shot old
Claus, who's had enough today!" How did he know? As fast as
I could, I told Colonel von Linstow in Paris, "It's all over, I
think. There's shooting in the Bendlerstrasse; I myself have
taken a bullet in the arm." Poor Linstow, already plagued with
heart trouble, could hardly breathe or speak as he reeled into
Stülpnagel's room on the fourth floor of the Hotel Raphael in
Paris.

"It's all over in Berlin," he wheezed as they helped him to a
chair. "Stauffenberg's just been on the phone. He told me the
terrible news. The opposition were shooting in the hallways
and hammering on his door." They gave him water and he finally went back across the road to the Majestic Hotel to get
more information.

I wanted to know nothing, not even the trivial things, such
as the secretaries huddling beneath the tables while the shooting went on, the gruesome, apelike bawling of slogans in the
corridors, the pool of blood over which Gerstenmaier had to
step, the rounding-up of almost everyone in the building,

Berthold included. Soon my arm would go numb, but it still stung and trembled, and I began to feel faint. Out of fatigue and disappointment, as well as (I realized) to indicate surrender, I slipped off my eyepatch—a painful maneuver that really set my arm and shoulder aflame—and aired the socket in sulfur, smoke, and the windless fug of a summer's day, still faintly charged with the scent of magnolia from the trees along the Landwehr Canal. No one even noticed. They were too busy accepting their lot.

Olbricht and Herber (a busy man that evening) had actually reached Hoepner in Fromm's office, where Beck, Haeften, and I had already taken up our station like figures in some medieval morality play. Now Ali, sweat pouring off his face, arrived just as Herber began to accuse Hoepner.

Hoepner shrugged. "I have no information. I am awaiting orders from Field Marshal Witzleben. Talk to Fromm by all means. He's on the floor below in his private apartment." Already Haeften had lit a small fire on the floor and was burning papers, index cards, and maps.

"They've all left me in the lurch," I told Alix Winterfeldt even as she stared unbelieving at the raw cavity where my eye had been. An unworthy utterance; some of them had never broken faith. Why, even the secretaries had shown more initiative than certain officers upon whom I'd thought we could count until the crack of doom.

Fromm meanwhile listened to the radio, guarded by Freiherr von Leonrod, at least until Herber, now carrying a submachine gun, rang the bell and was admitted by the one-legged Bartram, who then, as if exhausted, leaned against the wall. Leonrod moved off at once and Fromm came out, his giant's gait infected now with a bumptious strut. Once again power had fallen back into his hands, a situation for which—within the narrow confines of his weasel mind—he was well equipped.

When he entered, I glowered at him, I like to think, with

both eyes: the live and the dead one despising him in parallel. Brandishing a revolver, he inhaled deeply as if to prepare us for a long speech, and Haeften made as if to shoot him then and there, but I waved him off, sighing, "No use."

In the office next to Olbricht's, one of our prisoners, General Kortzfleisch, threw a typewriter through the window into the courtyard, then a telephone, thereby alerting the guard. "Come up!" he cried. "A general is under arrest in here. Come and free him."

Now the loathsome Pifrader got to work, phoning his chief, "Gestapo" Müller at about eleven P.M., reporting that shooting had broken out, and there was likely to be more.

"Damned idiots," Müller screamed. "I want *everybody* for interrogation." Always, before death, the Gestapo wanted the dance of death, the gibber, the shriek, the drooling blab.

Olbricht's last sight of his son-in-law, Georgi, had been when Georgi loaded his revolver for him at Olbricht's request: *Olbricht's* revolver. "I haven't used a weapon in many years," the father-in-law said. "I'm rather glad." 2315 hours.

There seemed less smoke in the room itself than in my nostrils: not just acrid, but with a fruity putridity like railroad locomotive smoke and tickling a memory that wouldn't come at first. When it did, I was once again within touching distance of S'gruber, whose meteorism (how could anyone forget?) made rank the air for several meters around him with his unique blend of stale milk and hen manure, a devilish aroma I chose not to mention when I reported to Nina, after my first meeting with him, the insane look in his eyes. It felt like centuries ago.

"I won't need that fast plane of yours to get me to East Prussia," Witzleben told General Wagner on arrival.

"We're going on home," Wagner said. "There's nothing else for it."

"Bloody stupid mess," Witzleben raged, little realizing that it might have been otherwise if, instead of snuggling with the dogs at von Lynar's estate, he had come in hours earlier to back up Beck. On his way in and on his way out, he had spent precious time with Wagner, impressing Kanitz, his aide, as old and broken and no longer spry, yet still patrician.

Fifty miles south of Berlin, where Witzleben was staying, von Lynar's wife looked aghast at the guest book she so punctiliously kept (our revolution was nothing if not bookish, or bookkeeperish), and decided it had to go.

"The hangman will be here tomorrow morning," Witzleben announced miserably, then settled down to wait. All I could remember of his visitation at the Bendlerstrasse was the click of false teeth as he opened his mouth wide to shout, and the weird black lines under his eyes, like those under the cheetah's, which absorb light. Orders had gone out above his name, but he hadn't signed, so perhaps that fanned his anger. Even so, something aloof and lackadaisical had kept him away from the Bendlerstrasse when we most needed him, and Beck was too diffident to call him in. Ulcers or hemorrhoids had depleted Witzleben long ago: he would have been better off out there, among murmuring birds, with his daughter and her three small children, *all day*, than embroiled in a fading conspiracy.

As it was, he had to tell Frau Reimer, his daughter, "Everything's gone wrong," like an eagle that had flown over an earthquake.

20

0021 Hours
(Quintet)

◆

"Put down your weapons!" Fromm bawled, perspiring and blinking. "Those in this room are under arrest. Now, gentlemen, I am going to do to you what you did to me this afternoon. How silly the likes of you must feel, knowing that such as I, given half a chance, will always do to you what you're too lily-livered to do to me." He offered no wine and sandwiches, though, to fuel our dismay; he never had much poetry in him, or much of the milk of human kindness. What had Speer ever seen in him?

Then he resumed, puffing his malevolence. "You have been caught red-handed in the act of treason and you will be tried at once by court-martial, which I now convene." A bandwagon jumper to the end, Fromm had finally found a speech that fitted his attitude to life; no more of that sardonic, lethal ambivalence ("If you go through with your ridiculous coup, don't forget my good friend Wilhelm Keitel!"), no more of the tacit agreement that fell short of active help.

Even with Beck he was unthinkably brutal, Beck who for so long had been the personification of German resistance to S'gruber, ever since 1938. Why, the man was a tradition in his own right; an introvert precisian of the old school, he had every right to linger on this moment, in cogitative, uncomprehending dismay. What had he said, a few weeks before, using an image that Fritzi had echoed or parodied during our hurried supper only hours ago? "It's no use," Beck had said.

"There is no deliverance. We must drain little by little the bitter cup down to the bitterest dreg. *That* is our destiny."

Now Fromm, the hulking opportunist, had *Beck* to toy with.

"Lay down your weapons." Fromm heaved. "For the second time. You too"—motioning at Beck, who at once laboriously cleared his throat and answered back, his clenched hands trembling. God is not, he'd told me, a gigantic gaslike formation somewhere in the depths; according to Beck, God was—but Beck was answering.

"Surely you wouldn't demand that of me, your former commanding officer. I will draw the consequences from this unhappy situation myself." Beck reached slowly for the shiny brown Parabellum pistol perched on the suitcase behind him (or was it on the office safe? I really began to quail at this point, weak and nauseated from that bullet in the back).

"I want this for private purposes," Beck told him. "You wouldn't deprive an old comrade of his ancient privilege."

All Fromm did was warn him. "Keep it pointed at yourself."

Beck sighed. "At a time like this, it's the old days I remember, when—"

Fromm cut the nostalgic preliminary short. "We don't want to hear about that now. I ask you to stop talking and *do* something." Fromm was in a hurry and Beck, with an ashen expression of the weirdest melancholic relish, like a clock finally being permitted to strike or an instrument being allowed to come in after a symphony had been going for a full half-hour, looked in mute farewell at each of us, with wavering hand aimed the muzzle at his temple and pulled the trigger. The bullet grazed his scalp and drew blood.

"Did it fire properly?" he asked, sagging sideways.

"Help the old fellow," said Fromm. Haeften and I moved. "Take away his gun."

"No, no," Beck muttered. "I want to keep it."

I saw again the Beck of old and the frosty demeanor within

which his honor stayed intact even when it split, as when he smiled shamefacedly for having made so many notes for every meeting. "A dangerous habit," I told him, but he was a paper shuffler by profession, he said. His was just about the only house on the Goethestrasse not bombed to bits, and he once spent the night helping his only other neighbor put out a fire, after which the neighbor took a glass of brandy with him and explained that the Gestapo had requisitioned the corner room in order to keep a watch on Beck and his visitors. It was Beck who thought Hoepner an egregious opportunist (Hoepner had been slated to replace Fromm). It was Beck who thought Goerdeler talked too much. It was Beck who would have become head of state in the new Germany. And it was Beck who defended me when they all turned on me for doing nothing, for making too many phone calls, for being rude and cryptic and overbearing. His small mouth tilting as if a current were going through it in a laboratory, he would grip my arm and whisper, "We men of action *know*." When, as now in his blood, he looked downward, he seemed hurt and unable to get over it (though he always did); but when he looked into the middle distance, his face tautened, the downcurve of his mouth rectified itself, and his eyes appeared to soak up power, or fuel, from some very distant source, which then fed into the rest of his face. A tense, refined man, he should perhaps never have been a general, but in being one he transcended the role entirely and brought to it a deep sense of historical aplomb.

"Take the gun away from him, he hasn't the strength." Fromm was doing all the talking now. Acutely faint myself, I tried to help Beck into a comfortable position in his chair, my blood mingling with his in some last complicity.

Beck held on hard to the gun, and I had the terrible thought: *as if clinging to his life itself.* The reek in Fromm's office was so pungent that several of us began coughing. Almost reeling, I gave Beck a final salute he saw.

"Very well," said Fromm with magistral coldness. He

looked up at the bullet hole in the ceiling. "Use it." With that he addressed Olbricht, Ali, Haeften, and myself: "And you, gentlemen, if there is anything you want to put in writing, you still have a few moments." Why didn't Beck shoot Fromm? *Now?*

"Yes," Olbricht said, "I should like to write."

"Then"—Fromm leered—"come over to the round table here, where you always sat opposite me, in the *old days*." Beck seemed to heed the phrase, culled from his own utterances, but fell back again, mumbling to himself. Then Hoepner too asked to write something down. Again Beck fired his pistol, I supporting him, and Fromm left the room with a grunt, and not so much as a glance at the old general in the act of suicide. Sickened by the mortal effrontery that gave one human power of death over another—S'gruber over millions, I over him, Fromm over Beck and Ali and Olbricht and Haeften—I tried not to be in the present, but only in times cold and dead, sucked away from us merely by the sun's rise and fall.

Beck was the man whom Franz Halder, my former idol, had replaced as Chief of the General Staff. Beck was the man who, marrying Amalie Pagenstecher in 1916, was a widower eighteen months later, with an infant daughter to rear. This doom-soaked man lived a quiet life, growing his own vegetables and writing military history. He suffered almost constantly from incurable toothache even while composing his essay "The Doctrine of Total War" and planning some great treatise on Robert E. Lee. When he went out to meet other conspirators, he wore dark glasses and baggy pants with blatant mysteriousness. I knew that, during the two weeks his regular housekeeper had been away, Frau Kuster, her stand-in, had noticed Beck's bedsheets were wringing wet each morning, as if he'd been tossing and turning all night in the unbearable humidity of his room. Or had he been drinking heavily? Had he cried out for Amalie?

Once again, even as Beck seemed to revive there in his

chair, I was sidling ghostlike through the ruins of Lichterfelde until I reached the piously named Goethestrasse. The doorbell of number 9 again failed to work. I pounded until the housekeeper came. Flawlessly on cue, she said Beck was not at home as I followed her in, a non-person to see a person not at home. And there he was, at his desk, looking furtive and sage and fatherly. A nonpareil with carcinoma. Aristocrat I may have been, but I was a hero worshiper at heart, not of the slavish kind, but rather a connoisseur of great men over whose potential, whose exploits, I pored as over a volume in some illustrious library, making notes with a shaky hand. I said goodbye to Beck by staring at his blanched, smeared face.

When Fromm came back he had with him officers from the assault party Schlee had led and the ex-commander of the Guard Battalion, Lieutenant Colonel Gehrke. Hoepner put on the table the page he had been writing, face-up; Olbricht asked for an envelope and sealed his letter in it. My own goodbyes had been said so long ago, so many times, in a babble of incomplete phrases, that the whole grisly business felt posthumous already. The Nazi hives were being purged, not for the first time, of solid men and patriots.

Only half conscious now, but still alive, having again not quite managed to finish himself off, Beck sprawled in the chair, his face thick with blood. Though I would dearly have liked to be at attention, I myself lay in another chair, supported by Ali and Haeften, an outsize piece of human wreckage with which, however, Fromm hadn't yet finished. The writing had occupied a good half-hour, and the "court-martial" ended first. *Who* had our judges been?

"In the name of the Führer," Fromm declared with a blast of fresh energy, "a summary court-martial called by myself has reached the following verdict: Colonel of the General Staff Mertz von Quirnheim, General Olbricht, the Colonel—I cannot bring myself to name him—and Lieutenant von Haeften are condemned to death." How portentous he looked. Ali shrugged and looked at the ceiling. Olbricht stood at stiff attention as if no longer in this world anyway. Haeften looked aggressively round him for some way out. I thought of Lautlingen, my home; Bamberg, Nina's; then of Nina homeless, my orphaned children, my mother, my dead father; a castle in ruins, an Alpine peak beheaded raw. My head exploded. The vision came to me of all of us, multiplied in our vulnerability through oh so many children, like a rich orchard awaiting the flamethrower; and, in no matter which direction the blazing gel squirted, it found some of us, male or female, big or small. We were too spread out. We had increased when we should have girded our loins. The fruit of our love had undone us all; but, then, we had never expected Naziism. No, that wasn't a good enough excuse, we'd gone on breeding to the last moment, perhaps deluded into thinking there was safety in numbers, whereas, when the numbers were mostly children, you had cut your family's throat.

We were a crop that lacked manure. Is that what the scratching pen of Olbricht was confiding to posterity? Was that the message in Hoepner's quivering, blurting face? No, no "von" embarrassed them on their identity cards making their names too long. *Count Claus Schenk von Stauffenberg,* I mouthed. *Adam von Trott zu Solz. Count Friederich Dietlof von der Schulenburg.* What the hell were the likes of us doing in the twentieth century, thinking we were flowers trimmed with steel? "If I get out of this lot alive," Fritzi had only just said, "I'll get rid of my title. I'll renounce it." It was far too late for anything so operatic. Our family links roamed abroad into England and America. We were just not organized, and, perhaps, in the old days, as no doubt always, we expected our *servants* to do our killing for us, which they'd have done only by running amuck, which German servants didn't do. They took orders, and we gave too few.

"There are things," Hoepner was telling Fromm, "I can say in my defense. I would like to have a chance to say them." He sat down and made as if to write again.

Then I somehow got to my feet, staggering a bit until Haeften caught hold of my right arm. "I assume the blame for the entire thing. These others have acted as soldiers and subordinates. They merely carried out their orders. They are in no way to blame." Fromm stared as if he hadn't heard, blocking the doorway as if he expected a last-minute charge followed by an exodus. *Were Nina and the children safe?*

"Are you finished, gentlemen?" Fromm crooned. "I must ask you to hurry, so as not to make it too difficult for the others." But again Hoepner was writing home. He blotted his letter with a flourish, as if his own name had been one of the four. If Nina and the children were safe, where *were* they?

"I had nothing to do with it," Hoepner said, "nothing to do with the whole affair. I would like to present my own defense." Were Nina and the children still *alive*, even?

Ignoring him, Fromm trumpeted the facts all over again, pointing out the four he wanted shot. "This gentleman here, the colonel; this general with the Knight's Cross; this colonel in the General Staff, and this lieutenant. The sentence of the court is to be carried out by rifle fire in the courtyard at once." He turned to Lieutenant Schlee.

"Yes," Schlee answered. "Captain Bartram said one officer and ten NCO's. I have detailed Second Lieutenant Werner Schady to carry out the order. He is ready in the courtyard below." Good God, I thought, people are always willing to kill.

"Schweizer is waiting," Haeften whispered against my shoulder. "We'll work something out." I said nothing, too weak even to walk. They led us downstairs, I leaning on Haeften for support.

"Give him the coup de grâce," Fromm said with a careless motion at Beck, as good as dead in his chair, but the officer addressed passed the order to a sergeant, who dragged Beck out and shot him in the back of the neck in the little map room. "And escort this officer to the military prison in Lehrter Strasse."

"No," said Hoepner. "I am not a swine. I am *not*."

"Take him away now," Fromm said. "I shall not be back to-night." Meaningfully he stepped out of the doorway.

Two faceless men helped me down the stairs, having shoved Haeften off, which perhaps gave him the impetus he needed to make a halfhearted lunge ahead, away from the escort; but they quickly subdued him and, in any case, he could only have reached the site of his execution sooner. There was nowhere else to go. Now I knew that, unlike certain prisoners of war who over the years compose chamber music in their heads which they agree to play together once released, we would have no such chance: no Stauffenberg on cello as we played our "July Bomb Quintet." Indeed, could the others even play? It had never occurred to me to ask. Let the secret die with us, I thought. Like so many. What use would a three-fingered cellist have been anyway? Let Berthold and Alexander play in my stead.

With my heart bouncing about in a weightless flutter, I longed for seven-hilled Bamberg on the River Regnitz, its moated castles, and its "Little Venice" where laundry hung out over the foreshortened, upside-down reflections of the fishermen's old houses, ocher and saffron colored with white window boxes of geraniums high above the water. In winter the chunk ice sailed under the bridge and through the town like a regatta of fallen ceilings, and I would see none of it again, not even in a dream, in a fit of desert melancholy, or even, airsick and worldsick and brainsick and cliquesick and bombsick, waiting out another three-hour flight to the scene of the next disaster. Never would I, like an Indian named Sequoia, invent anything so wonderful as the eighty-six letters of the Cherokee alphabet, or, like a Russian scholar, without ever leaving my study overlooking the icebound River Neva, manage to decipher the hieroglyphs of the ancient Mayans, after a quarter of a century's work.

Preposterous ricochets from a mind almost dead, these bitter yearnings came and went, while back home our geraniums were bulging scarlet against the big southern-facing windows and knew nothing of bloodshed. I saw Nina, Nina, Nina, detaching from an ebony picture frame a tiny wedge of plaster flake, like a dead moth, a miniature of me: I the face in the frame, I the moth-flake flicked aside, having learned how death cures all men of being metaphorical. *This* was how death was going to be, and no other way: the last of the deaths a so-called hero dies.

There was my own car with my own driver, Schweizer, and I had the pointless thought: Was he finally in his new uniform for this appalling event? Had he tried it on in front of some washroom mirror? Most ordinary corporals, I thought, don't have *this* kind of thing to do. My car's lights blazed amid those of trucks and other cars, all without their blackout visors, to illumine the mound of sandy earth in the courtyard; we were to be shot in front of a sandpile from some excavation or other. Looking up, I saw a flash of white face behind at least two of the blackout curtains on the second floor. *Witnesses!* There were always witnesses. This would be the fourth time metal would invade my battered body, the second time today; it was almost a relief to know that there would not be a fifth. The headlights were no more than ten or twelve meters away, and I tried to pick out Schweizer's face, but the light was too intense; indeed, as we arrived on the uneven ground, littered with broken bricks and jagged hunks of slate, various searchlights came on, quite blinding me and the other three. It was almost midnight: astonishingly, of the same day on which it had all begun.

In much the same way, we had been led out into the courtyard of 11-13 Bendlerstrasse by the same door we used to enter for the day's work. Behind the lights the big iron gate twinkled like something out at sea.

"Hurry up," someone called. "An air raid warning has come through." There were some disorganized shouts and I saw a face at an upper window. How chunky, how carved, the building looked. The firing squad lined up, jostling for position: a motley posse of orderlies and general duties NCO's, who swabbed floors and carried files by day and—blissful privilege—bumped off the General Staff by night. I almost vomited. Then I remembered Beck with the top shell of his head split open above his powdery-looking eyes. He was sixty-four, our leader-to-be crudely self-lobotomized. It wasn't a world worth lingering in.

They stood us to one side, men of contrasting heights, until everything was ready. I thought of putting my eyepatch on again as a last vicious piece of decorum, but my left sleeve was stiff with blood, and I couldn't be bothered. It was more important to stand erect between Haeften and Ali, the one with his face wrinkling and unwrinkling like a child's, the other impassive.

Take an eye gulp, I told myself, never mind of what. I forced my eye wide open in spite of the lights. The trees seemed to be crowded with gray birds, motionless and still, as if they knew that after the shooting there would never again be anything. The world would end. I saw Schweizer's face only twenty meters away, his head canted toward me. Two NCO's conducted Olbricht to the sandbags. A loud ornate sour voice that set my teeth on edge boomed an order, then another, and Olbricht jackknifed backward.

Now the two NCO's came for me and led me forward without touching me; Olbricht looked like a broken giant wren. Again that discordant voice. I would be dead before the bullets hurt. A shadow lunged in front of me, abruptly felled by shots. It was Haeften, who had somehow broken free. I stood my ground, shrugged at Ali as the firing squad again took aim, and with all my strength shouted, "Long live holy Germany!" I sounded as faint as Beck had. I stiffened my lips for the salvo and held them tight, at the very last, even after the crack of untidy rifle fire, kissing Nina's face at last. There was only a sense of being suffocated by fine-quality silk stuffed into my throat and down, into my throat and down farther, until there was no room for more. 0021 hours.

Ali was fourth.

Four crisp coups de grâce ensured that we would not rise up. Fromm stood on a truck and harangued the soldiers briefly, then drew from them three thundering *Sieg Heils* to his Führer. He gave a grotesque wave on stepping down, and some soldiers dragged our bodies aside.

Outside, in the Tiergartenstrasse round the corner, Kaltenbrunner, chief of the Gestapo, had parked quietly and was chatting with his subordinates in the gloom under the trees. From where they stood, the Bendlerstrasse building itself, lit by searchlights in the center of a blacked-out city, looked like something from an old movie set: a fort or a medieval castle, air raid warning or not. Next to arrive, Otto Skorzeny, the Viennese terrorist and supercommando who had rescued Mussolini, joined the Gestapo in their conversation. No one headed for the Bendlerstrasse, not even when Albert Speer arrived with Remer in a natty little white sports car, ambiguously saying, "I've come to stop Fromm's court-martial. We've just been with Dr. Goebbels."

"We don't want to get involved," they told him. "It's an army matter. We aren't going to interfere—yet. In any case, it's probably all over."

It was. A gigantic shadow poured and flapped across the ground toward them, at its advancing source a tall silhouette at the slow strut. Unescorted and in full dress uniform, Fromm was looking for his car, with an occasional half-stumble; his eyes hadn't adjusted from the glare of light he'd only just left.

Speer left the others and greeted his old friend, who answered, "The putsch is over and done with." He seemed to be suppressing a sob, or he couldn't quite get his breath. "I have just issued the necessary commands to all corps area headquarters. For a time, I was actually prevented from exercising my command of the Home Army. They even locked me up in a room—my own chief of staff, my own aides!"

"Well!" said Speer, impatient for details. "So?"

"As their appointing authority, it was my duty to hold a summary court-martial at once, of all involved in the uprising." Then he broke into an aggrieved slow murmur: "General Olbricht and my chief of staff, Colonel Stauffenberg, are no longer alive." In fact, S'gruber had dismissed Fromm by 1800 hours, since when he'd had no authority at all, least of all to have us shot.

"God, I wish you hadn't," Speer whispered. "Your own position will look most suspicious. Come on over to my ministry now. We'll work something out." Speer was loyal to *everybody*.

"No, I must call the Führer," Fromm said, even as he pumped the hand of Kaltenbrunner, who had walked over. "And see Dr. Goebbels. Then I'm going home. It's been a long day."

Kaltenbrunner freed his hand and nodded Fromm and Speer away while Skorzeny hovered, waiting for a change of plan.

For me, it was still 0021 hours. The sightseers could come and go in that dazzling slum of spent bodies and bloodied brick dust. I stiffened my lips all over again, long after there was need; but everything had been said, everything done. How vile to be dead so young, and so easily put down, like a hog.

VI

21

Casualties

♦

One travesty was over, but another still went on, whose origins went back to 1242 hours on July twentieth, when what happened at Wolf's Lair wasn't exactly worthy of our deaths.

First there came a pale yellow, bluish flash. A surging pressure wave rolled past. Men's hair lifted up and, in some cases, caught fire: SS Gruppenführer Fegelein's hair was a cap of flames. Many had blood pouring from their ears. There were wood splinters enough for a sawmill. Those not in jackboots had their pants in tatters. Those near the windows found their pockets full of glass splinters. Sonnleithner, the Foreign Minister's permanent representative to S'gruber, woke up knee deep in fiberglass. Nearly everyone was hurled to the ground by the force of an explosion which, in fact, cut a hole where my briefcase had been, flowed under the floorboards along the clinker foundation, and erupted into the offices at the end of the hut, where the lack of windows and the firmer walls had enabled the blast to do more damage than in the briefing room itself.

S'gruber's big map table was just about ripped in half. The window frames were twisted all ways. Out through the windows went those who could. Others remained, including John von Freyend, ever solicitous about my briefcase, who removed the severely injured Brandt and then cut Schmundt out of his boots: Cointreau Brandt, who'd befriended me and always been so affable, Schmundt who'd had me switched from Olbricht's staff to Fromm's, thus enabling me to take my bomb to Wolf's Lair in the first place.

A line of blackened men came stumbling out of the smashed shell of the hut.

"WHERE," Keitel was shouting, "is the Führer?" Almost at once he found him, embraced him hard, and yelled, "My Führer! My Führer! You're alive!" Keitel was a sycophant through and through. He would have fawned on the corpse to just the same extent, he who was sixty-two years old at the time, who lied and bowed and swindled, who smelled of wet wool and whom S'gruber spat at for having the brains of an usher, putting his arms around S'gruber right there amid the smoke and debris and, with incredibly improvised calm worthy of a mother with an hysterical child, leading him into the open by one hand while making faint guttural, prolonged coaxing noises that went on even after S'gruber recognized he was in the open air again in the thick of birds and trees.

All I had accomplished was the deaths of four insignificant Nazis: Dr. Berger, the shorthand writer (one of two), who had faced the bomb, had lost both legs; he died that afternoon. Heinz Brandt had lost a leg and he died two days later, as did General Korten, a big spike of wood in his abdomen. Wounded in the thigh, Schmundt would die in October. As for the rest, concussion, burst eardrums (except for Keitel), and painful injuries far from slight. A socle had saved Heusinger to bore people on another day. Two of the six men in the bomb's immediate vicinity had survived, as had eighteen others. It had been not so much a bomb as a warning, which we would have done much better to deliver by having a Fieseler Stork write it in smoke at a thousand meters above Wolf's Lair.

Fellgiebel had seen smoke soaring above the briefing hut, and then wood and paper fluttering through the motionless air as if something Japanese had come apart. Most of the room's contents went through the space left in the roof, while S'gruber himself sustained no more than a few bruises and burns, although later on his injuries became worse. Too late.

True, his hair stood on end like the bristles of a chimney brush; his pants hung in shreds and ribbons; his right elbow was bleeding; both his eardrums had been ruptured, which meant that he'd never again be able to hear such higher harmonics as occur in the prelude to *Lohengrin;* and the explosion had driven wood splinters into his legs. But, and this was the fatuous part, the trembling in his left leg had gone, weirdly transferred to the map lamp extender lattice that hung drunkenly from one wall.

In truth I had cured him instead of killing him. The table had saved him. He lifted up his torn pants and then displayed the square hole in the back; I had made a new martyr out of soot, plaster, glass, and timber, and who could count the cost?

Puttkamer thought the window heater had exploded. Someone yelled, "Fire!" How normal. Puttkamer leaped over the down-blasted door. Some eyebrows had burned off. Only Charlie Chaplin was missing. Otherwise the farce would have been complete. Damn S'gruber and his strychnine anti-gas pills. Damn his hypersensitivity to light. Damn his cracked lips and his defective sense of balance. Had he been less defective to begin with, I'd have turned him into pulp. Only two days later he was prating away like a connoisseur, telling someone, "I saw that infernally brilliant flash very clearly, oh yes, and I at once thought that the explosive must be British, since German explosives don't give off so harsh and intensely yellow a flame." He was right.

Had I had any sense of how things would go at the last moment, I would certainly not have stood there smoking outside Bunker 88 waiting for the bomb to go off, and, when it finally did, hearing that officious idiot Sander hold forth on forest noises, animals, mines, and trigger-happy highly strung green soldiers firing rounds at random. No, I would have walked, *marched,* back inside to hold the briefcase close to my own chest, still minus my cap and belt. Instead of finagling my way through the guard post at the outer wire, I would have gone back and armed the second bomb. History, however, does not allow for revisions; it accepts what happens, and there you are—if you're remembered at all—forever: like a wave coming in, uniquely formed, but once broken, never to be formed thus again. Forgive my drab egocentricity and the useless motion of my spray.

When I'd left him, right after the bomb's bang, Fellgiebel had begun to patrol the walk between Bunker 88 and S'gruber's private enclosure, wondering what on earth he'd see next. What he saw was S'gruber, whom he'd supposed dead, strutting about in the open, inhaling fresh air; but Sander, who remembered strict orders not to let the "defeatist" Fellgiebel, whom S'gruber loathed, come near S'gruber at any time (he was fractionally more useful than loathsome), urged him in the other direction, back toward Bunker 88. Blackout or no blackout, Fellgiebel then instructed Sander to call Lieutenant General Thiele, the senior signals officer in the Bendlerstrasse.

"There's a blackout in effect." Sander went by the book.

"So there is," barked Fellgiebel. "And it doesn't apply to senior officers. Now, will you phone General Thiele?" Fellgiebel had written the book which Sander went by. "And when you've done that, I'm going to start a blackout of my own."

"He isn't there," Sander said with touchy crispness. "His secretary is on the line."

"They usually are," sighed Fellgiebel. "Nobody's ever *in* who matters. Tell her there's been an assassination attempt, but that the Führer is alive." No sooner had Sander done so than Fellgiebel grasped the phone and told her, "This is vitally important news and it is imperative that you pass it on to General Thiele at once."

As soon as Sander left the building, Fellgiebel again phoned Thiele, found him in, and told him the worst, concluding, "It's too late to revise the manual now. The final chapter must stand as it is." It was a suitable enough code, although not up to Fellgiebel's usual standards of cryptic wit. He then phoned Colonel Kurt Hahn in Mauerwald, not far away, and said quite openly, "Something fearful has happened—the Führer is alive."

"What shall we do?" said Hahn in shock.

"Block everything," Fellgiebel told him, determined to hang for sheep rather than lamb. Hahn then phoned Thiele to confirm the bad news, and Fellgiebel left Area 1 just as Himmler arrived. He had already seen more than enough, but he had done his part, and his long day of frantic attempts to disconnect repeater stations, of persistent phone calls to this or that officer (who promptly whizzed off by motorcycle to plug up some leak), had only just begun. The initiative, such as remained, was now with Berlin and myself.

Indeed I was wanted now in two places. Toward two P.M., Sander went back to the briefing hut to check on the damage and there found Sergeant Major Adam, still somewhat dazed.

"This is not a rest camp," Sander told him brusquely, smarting from his prickly day with Fellgiebel. "Nor a wax museum. I presume you are waiting for the broken cables to heal?"

Straight-faced, Adam announced, "I have something to report, sir. I am in a position to see many things; I even sometimes make notes. Colonel von Stauffenberg left the building without his briefcase, his cap, or his belt. Surely it must have been he who planted the bomb. He rushed out as if there were only seconds to spare. I have already informed Major Wolf of this, but all he said was to report what I wanted to."

Now Sander let rip at him, converting the trials of his day into abuse, but also genuine in his indignation. "How dare you," he bellowed, "entertain such suspicions of so distinguished an officer?" After all, he had gone to considerable trouble to get me a car, even though I had one already. "I refuse to listen to such swill. Bomb or no bomb. If you must tell someone, tell the Security Police." He stormed away and, when questioned later, reported that as far as he was concerned I had taken lunch with the camp commandant, as arranged. In fact, Adam went with his tale to Martin Bormann, who took him straight to S'gruber. As a result, my doings of the day brought Adam a reward variously described as 20,000 marks and a house in Berlin, 30,000 marks and a house and promotion, and just 15,000 marks. Our plot's failure at least made one oaf comfortable for a month or two.

Next thing they decided to find and arrest me, which must have been between two and three o'clock, while I was flying over the slight variegations of the Polish plain, drab as spilled bran. But they were too bewildered to try hard, and the order to shoot down my plane lay unread on the desk of Major Georgi of the air staff, Olbricht's son-in-law. By then, not only Thiele (who had been absent from his office trying to walk off a fit of unbearable nerves) but also Olbricht knew that my bomb had exploded. Or did they? What Fellgiebel said to Kurt Hahn—"Something fearful has happened—the Führer is alive," spoken so as to suggest no period, colon, semicolon, or comma between the two parts of the statement—could have meant many things, including that I had been caught, that I had killed myself, or that the bomb simply had failed and everything was normal.

Was it a portent that egregious Percy Schramm, the war diary officer of Operations Staff, with whom I had chatted on my previous visit to Wolf's Lair, concluded his report on the search for Stauffenberg with a note on the Heinkel's take-off time from the Wilhelmsdorf airfield, which served Rastenburg, as being 1313 hours? Misspelling names right and left, as usual, he no doubt found it easier to tell the time than to recognize names. Did this mean that, as well as mutilating our names, just as the clerks in the execution prisons did those of the condemned, he saw our faces wrongly too, missing out here a nose, and there a cheek? He was only one among the many scribes of fate who, neither literate nor precise nor indeed much interested, managed to set down and irretrievably garble the events of that crammed and suffocating day on which, like a "drenched poodle" (as some wit recalled), I tried to roll a dead weight almost vertically uphill.

Fellgiebel had done his best, for which they made him pay. During the afternoon of the twentieth, the deputy head of the Security Service, suspicious of Fellgiebel's having been in Wolf's Lair for no good reason, "invited" him to come back there from Mauerwald, to which he'd returned after doing all he could. That's where he belonged; Wolf's Lair was Sander's job.

"Why were you here all day?" they asked him.

"Just looking in on Colonel Sander," he said, flexing his laughter lines, his worry lines, the eyes behind his plain-rimmed glasses full of combative civility.

"We will ask him. You signals officers are very social men."

"May I now go back to Mauerwald? I have duties—"

"Hold yourself in readiness, General."

In the late evening Keitel had him summoned once again to Wolf's Lair. "What's up, my friend?" Fellgiebel asked when Major Wolf relayed the message received by Sander.

"Orders from Field Marshal Keitel. You are to come back here, sir." Sander had covered well, but Fellgiebel had been with *me*.

"I'll be there in three-quarters of an hour."

"Have you a pistol?" asked Arntz, his aide. "I have a pretty good idea what you're in for. Those gangsters don't go by any military code. No Marquis of Queensberry rules to box by."

"Oh really, Arntz, one doesn't do *that*. One just doesn't *do away* with oneself. It's such a *solecism*. I'll tell the court-martial the truth. Then I'll get the firing squad no doubt. The main thing's not to let these vermin think we're scared of them! I've other things to think about now." He gave a terse smile. "Do you think there's such a thing as an afterlife? It's all rather convenient. If there is, you find out there is. If there isn't, there's no possible way of knowing it. It's worth thinking about, my friend. *If* I believed in another world, I'd say *auf Wiedersehen*. I don't. There's no hereafter in my book. So: we shall not meet again."

Off he went to Wolf's Lair, where he was arrested; his driver came back alone, in tears, to tell Arntz how it ended. For three weeks Fellgiebel held out under fearful tortures while Thiele, who replaced him at Mauerwald, reviled his name: "A blot on the German Army and the entire Signal Corps," he fumed before they arrested *him* as well.

Himself, Fellgiebel was amazed, not so much that he lived through so much torture without revealing any names, as that he'd survived since 1938 when the Gestapo began to tap his phone. A lover of horses, he'd laughed when S'gruber forbade his entourage to have anything to do with them.

"Emblems of the decadent landed upper class!" raved S'gruber. "I want no horses."

Fellgiebel merely listed his favorite hunter as a cart horse, musing, "He could have inspected it himself without knowing the difference. He wouldn't know one end of a horse from the other, whereas most psychopathic peasants might."

He had a leathery face, the jaw of a winner, the verbal habits—even during his violent outbursts—of the classical scholar, the man intact in his own mind, whereas Stieff, arrested in Mauerwald late that same evening, used a lifetime's build-up merely to say *miaou*. Stieff, who'd called S'gruber "the bloody dilettante" and "the proletarian megalomaniac," like Tresckow became a general only in late January of '44, which was perhaps why he played it safe. He cared, he backed off. He caved in with the frail, slack tap of an empty toothpaste tube hitting the bathroom floor.

22

The Small Hours

◆

Our bodies ended up on a truck driven by a sergeant to the Matthäikirche cemetery in Schöneberg, at whose fortresslike tower I'd often stared from my window in the Bendlerstrasse. The other buildings had been blasted away. Then they lugged Beck in his bloodstained brown suit and threw him on top of us. The sergeant found the cemetery gate locked, went to the sexton's house, and woke him up.

"Five bodies," he growled. "I have been *officially* ordered to bury them here. There will be no names mentioned and no one is to know where the grave is." The sexton opened up the gate. While the sergeant and another soldier were digging the grave, two police sergeants appeared, summoned to the scene by the verger, but their questions went unanswered. Our bodies merely accepted the beams of their flashlights, especially their interest in the scarlet stripes that three of us wore on our breeches as they stroked the lines of light up and down, making the red go pale. Next came the area superintendent, whom the sergeant swiftly persuaded to lend a hand. Soon all five of them were digging.

"Thirty more bodies are to follow. The grave will need to be really big." But the next bodies never arrived, even after the digging crew kept a death watch lasting several hours until our bodies stopped bleeding. When they slung Beck on top of me, deep in the trench, our faces brushed in a wormwood kiss. The closing of the grave, when it came, was hasty and careless, done with exasperated oaths.

"Go home now," the Bendlerstrasse sergeant told the three

local policemen. "Not a word." He made a costive frown.

"Nct a word, my eye!" said the superintendent. "In the morning I must write a complete report." A local doge.

"That's your lookout, then," the sergeant said with rough good humor. "My job's done." His frown flowed away.

Off they went, the three, stumbling over their own feet from fatigue as the truck roared back to the center of the city.

Was there ever a final resting place, though? Only two hours later the sexton had to clamber out of bed again. This time it was the SS, demanding their bodies back. By the straggly light of dawn, they took flashlight photographs of each of us for, it was claimed, identification, and then sped us off to the crematorium. What could they do with dust? Scatter it in the open fields, as Himmler insisted. Yet something survived. Our blood-streaked uniforms—how red the blood on the white tunic I wore that day!—went to Dr. Peter Boysen, the Bendlerstrasse group chief in charge of army clothing.

"These," SS General Rolf Stundt told him in a series of oral jerks, "you—will put—on permanent *display*—in—the basement here. Look." Stundt's aide handed him a big pair of wooden laundry tongs and lifted the cardboard box on to Boysen's desk. "*Stauffenberg's*," Stundt said, lifting my white tunic with the tongs. "That's blood. Traitor's blood. You also have Beck, Olbricht, and the other two in here. Officers will be instructed merely by seeing these things. See to it." Such was my last undertaker, but his orders misfired. Boysen left our uniforms in a wooden box in a corner until they began to smell and eventually went out in the garbage several months later.

Already Herber and his Bendlerstrasse vigilantes had worked up a vile momentum, inspired by having brought about five deaths. To and fro they roamed, brandishing their weapons and bellowing patriotic threats. Each one, in his own way, was hoping for an Iron Cross, of whatever class, whereas promotion they could now be sure of, and accelerated promotion at that.

With Yorck and Schwerin, Gerstenmaier burned as many incriminating papers as he could find, mostly in the ashtrays in my office. The smell of burned paper was like that of indoor fireworks, with something childish and nostalgic about it. Gerstenmaier stepped through the door, walked along the corridor, only to bump into Fliessbach, the procurer of arms, who at once put him in an NCO's office under guard. It was from here that he heard the blast of rifle fire and my own final cry, although he wasn't certain who was involved. He heard a shout and formed his own conclusions about how certain persons were being dealt with. From what he overheard—Herber and Fliessbach talking together—he realized that he would be in the next line in front of the firing squad; but, before anyone could conduct him downstairs, the Gestapo and the SS halted all further executions and confined him, again in my office, along with Berthold, looking more obstinate than ever with his jaw thrust upward and out, Fritzi (whose sardonic serenity had not wavered), von der Lancken (whom Remer himself had arrested), and poor Bernardis, whom they had found writhing in pain somewhere with one of the heart attacks he'd endured since 1942.

"Gentlemen," announced the cautious-faced, puffy-eyed infantry general Reinecke, "you are under arrest." What an anticlimax on top of the violent salvos from the courtyard below; but only Gerstenmaier had an inkling of what all the gunfire was for, while the others assumed that the same struggle as before was going on elsewhere, and this heartened them somewhat. "You will hear your sentences," Reinecke went on, less loud, "from the Führer himself." Bernardis looked at death's door already and Peter Yorck, who had been to a wedding with his wife and Gerstenmaier (taking the train back to Berlin at two A.M. on the twentieth), was worn out from lack of sleep, whereas Gerstenmaier—the impetuous and sometimes drastic

Swabian nurtured on Kant and Hegel—from time to time whistle-seethed his breath through the spaces in his wide-set teeth; it was the only comment the situation deserved.

Toward one A.M. the famous Skorzeny broke into the building with a strong force of SS, who occupied every office and stood guard on every exit. They soon had the big iron box that Olbricht had kept in his room. There was no more covert or open burning of documents. The paper chase could begin and the kite of reprisal would fly.

Herber and Heyde briefed Skorzeny and Kaltenbrunner, the so-called soft Austrian, on what had been happening. "You can't go around shooting people just because," said Skorzeny with heavy emphasis, "you want to seem loyal. Things have to be *proved*." Now he began to move through the building on a painstaking tour of inspection. Eventually he reached the room in which Kleist was being held prisoner.

Ruffian that he was, yet ever correct, Skorzeny gave a slight bow to the officer he saw sitting there: "Skorzeny," he said gently, introducing himself.

Kleist got up and, with a duplicate bow, said his name too. "Kleist!"

Then Skorzeny saw the handcuffs and, murmuring, "Oh," turned his back and got on with the impossible job of getting the Bendlerstrasse back on an even operational keel, impossible because various departments no longer had effective heads. So next he personally searched the suspects for weapons, ripping off their orders and decorations with his bare hands and tossing them into an upturned steel helmet behind him. Then he made them listen to S'gruber's triumphant early-morning speech of vengeance, turning the radio up full blast.

"My comrades, men and women of the German people ... By now I do not know how many times an assassination has been planned and attempted against me. If I speak to you today it is first of all in order that you should hear my voice and know that I am unhurt and well, and secondly that you should know of a crime unparalleled in German history."

It might have been a robot addressing them, the tone harsh and bald with just a touch of whine like a malfunction. On he went while Fritzi stared his open-eyed myopic stoicism at Berthold, who had kept asking about his brother's fate without receiving an answer. "The bomb planted by Colonel Count von Stauffenberg exploded two meters to my right. It very seriously wounded a number of faithful members of my staff. One of them has died. I myself am absolutely unhurt, except for a few minor scratches, bruises, and burns. I regard this as a confirmation of the decree of Providence."

Twice he had told them he was all right, but with an increasing list of the damage to him; presumably, if he went on long enough, the list would become so long that he would succumb, after all, merely from reciting it. *Two meters* was all I'd missed by. Convinced that the bomb was the work of the British secret service, he ordered a maximum V1 attack on London that very night. "I want continuous fire at maximum tempo with unrestricted expenditure of ammunition. I'll teach John Bull about bombs." (Some four hundred V1s in two nights showed Londoners how he felt until the canny Kluge had the bombardment stopped, hoping to win favor with Eisenhower, who'd noticed *my* bomb only to the extent of exclaiming, "Holy smoke, there seems to be a revolt going on among the Krauts!" and Churchill, who, during a sing-song aboard the cruiser *Enterprise*, had scoffed, "Well, they missed the old bugger again," and then recited a stanza from "Rule Britannia.")

One military march later, Göring spoke his unctuous blather, all the way from "saved by a miracle" to "exterminate these traitors with utter ruthlessness." Doenitz was even worse, invoking "holy wrath and immeasurable rage" as well as "characterless, craven, and perverse cleverness," although it seemed to smack more of original phrasing than anything either S'gruber or Göring had said.

Goerderler was now in hiding at Baron Palombrini's estate at Rahnesdorf, while the Gestapo did its best to run him down.

Our colleagues in Paris stood beside their undrunk champagne in the dining room of the Raphael. Away at the Russian front, Tresckow had gone to bed, worn out with waiting for news, at least until Schlabrendorff heard the broadcast, or about it, and told him the worst. Rommel, head full of shrapnel, lay in the Luftwaffe hospital at Bernay, as good as dead. And all over Germany, the SS preened itself, dusted off its contraptions, and prepared for a big catch of not very contrite fish; but Pifrader hung his head, savagely rebuked by Group Leader Müller for not having forestalled the executions in the Bendlerstrasse courtyard.

"You," his chief hammered away, "deserve the brass nozzle of a fire hose up your rear end, full force. How the hell do you expect us to interrogate the dead? With toothpicks and holy water? Have you no use for the living at all? Know what you are, Pifrader? You're a corpse man. Your personal file proves it."

S'gruber was howling again. "The circle of the conspirators is a very small one. It has nothing in common with"—a burst of blessed atmospherics blotted him out—"gang of criminal elements who will now be ruthlessly exterminated." More, more about Providence, the Creator, Germany, Conscience, followed by an avalanche of Wagnerian music, buttressed the image of Keitel as handmaiden nursing S'gruber's fist on a slow walk out of hell into the glory of the summer day, like shy lovers from some mediocre opera. What a panicky speech it was, but enough to alarm the men standing in the Bendlerstrasse, now handcuffed together, awaiting a bullet, torture, mere questioning, they knew not what.

"In the end," Schwerin said to Gerstenmaier, "one can do no more than die for the cause. Give me your hand."

"You already have it, we're handcuffed together, my friend!"

"I forgot," said Schwerin. "*Now.* What does that prove?"

At Goebbels's official residence in the Hermann Göring

Strasse the phones rang until dawn while Goebbels and Himmler pursued their interrogations. Hase they already had, quaffing *Sekt* with his frugal dinner. Helldorf arrived unsummoned.

"I came to offer my services," he told Himmler. "What the hell is going on?"

"*Your* services were used up long ago," Himmler murmured; then to the guards, "Confine this officer in the music room."

Steaming with heat and exertion, Fromm in horn-rimmed glasses bellowed, "*Heil!*" phoned his wife, and accepted a bottle of wine.

"You were in a tremendous hurry to bury living witnesses," Goebbels trilled at him. "I smell cowardice and panic." Fromm sulked. "It is not right for you to address me so, *not right*."

"What bothers me now," Goebbels told Himmler privately in his usual rasping lilt, "is that there may be a *second* attack on the Führer, by whom I've no idea." His fist roved about.

"Better worry about the generals on the eastern and western fronts. Look at that shit Fromm: he behaved like an extra in some lousy film." Himmler had lost a piece from his mental jigsaw puzzle and kept groping for it in mid-air with floating gestures right in front of Goebbels's face.

"Oh well," Goebbels blinked, cheering up. "We haven't done too badly. It was a revolution of the telephone, stopped with a couple of shots. Yes"—as if he'd only just heard what Himmler said about Fromm—"and that other fathead, Hoepner. How could they possibly win with such goons in charge? But with a bit more ingenuity they might have pulled it off."

Toward four in the morning, Goebbels saw Himmler downstairs to a waiting car, shook hands, and walked back up, pausing at every third step to savor the night's doings. In front of the door to his private quarters, he jumped onto a small table, letting his feet dangle, and with a sly light laugh lectured his aides, who, having paused on the stairs with him, now tried to muster dignified stances in front of their squatting, toe-swinging chief.

"It's been like a summer storm," he said, leaning his arm on a bust of S'gruber. "It's cleared the air. When the dreadful news began coming in right after midday, who would have thought things would end so well, so fast?" He fished his two cyanide pills from his pocket, eyed them against the light with a creamy smirk, and put them back. "We did have a couple of bad moments between then and now, take it from me. This is the . . . sixth attempt on the Führer I've had to soldier through with him. Oh yes, I haven't ducked my duty, I can tell you. The other attempts weren't half as dangerous as this one, but it took us longer to finish them off. If they'd gotten away with it, we wouldn't be sitting here. You can imagine what would have happened to me, and you."

Having turned to stone to wait him out, the two aides now awoke. "Shot out of hand," gasped Naumann. "Hanged in Plötzensee," von Oven whispered in irate relief.

"Right," laughed Goebbels. "They wouldn't have tortured us except for fun! We know nothing we haven't told them already!" Then he stood. "What a bunch of incompetents. Except that Stauffenberg. What cold-bloodedness. What intelligence. What an iron will. It's almost too bad about him. It's quite incredible that a man of such caliber should have surrounded himself with so many idiots."

I had one admirer, at least.

23

Romans

♦

That night, both my old Bamberg friend General von Thüngen and Major von Oertzen, a longtime crony of Tresckow
sent to join us, came under suspicion, and von Thüngen was allowed to go, but not before (in the incestuous game of mirrors
that now began) he had interrogated Oertzen!

"I agree," Kortzfleisch said to Thüngen, ready with cap and
briefcase to get away. "In spite of all his inconsistent statements, he seems to have become involved in the putsch only
by accident. He'd no idea what was going on. All the same,
he'll be held in protective custody."

Off went the sharp-featured Thüngen, his sorrowful eyes
packed with foreboding. Although technically a conspirator,
he'd done nothing on the twentieth but dawdle around the
Bendlerstrasse.

"Under arrest," a colonel told Oertzen. "Give me your pistol." When Oertzen was at his toughest, his face seemed to
quail; the staid, expressionless dark eyes backed away into a
glazed modesty, and you noticed how trim his haircut was,
and how he had shifted the parting of his hair away from his
left temple so as to brush one piece of hair leftward to cover a
bare spot. You would have thought him doomed to a secretar-
ial post, shuffling manila files and escorting riffraff in and out.
In fact, he had been a horseman and a racing driver; he
thrived on excitement. After handing over his pistol, he
bunked down for the night as best he could, knowing he would
have to get busy on the next day, Friday.

Soon after he woke, Oertzen went to the toilet to burn and

flush away various incriminating papers the previous day's search had missed. Even more enterprising, at least from his desperate point of view, he got his hands on two rifle grenades, which he concealed in sand buckets in the corridor with an oddly boylike motion: playing games.

About ten A.M., he asked his escort, Hentze, "Do you mind if I visit the toilet again? A bit of trouble. Breath of fresh air'll do me good. How stuffy it is in here." Before anyone so much as noticed he was doing anything unusual, he had seized one of the grenades and set it off next to his head. Hentze was wounded and Oertzen collapsed, presumed dead, but able to crawl a little farther to the other sand bucket even while a doctor was on his way to the scene. Then Oertzen put the second grenade in his mouth, literally blowing off his head as the officers milling about him leapt for cover.

"Died like a man," said fire-and-brimstone Kortzfleisch when he arrived, looking right through the bran and maroon slush on the floor and the walls, popping an austere glance downward as if seeing the exact outline of the trunk, which orderlies had removed.

Hentze was to blame, of course, but no one could prove it. Oertzen knew names and their whereabouts, and now he had taken them with him past the barbed wire of infinity. No paladin had ridden or driven so well, slithering and grappling his way to a second chance, as if in posthumous rebuke to the thrice-shot ghost of Ludwig Beck. Oertzen was the classic liaison man who brought to his inconspicuous role a touch of Promethean mischief best recalled in his flourishing in front of one eager young officer a briefcase from which he tugged a small bomb, whose works he then explained, concluding: "Whoever has the bomb should conceal it under his tunic, activate it, then throw his arms round Hitler from behind, and hold him until—*boom!* Like this." Oertzen had left this world as if fulfilling one of his own instructions, after planting the seed of his undoing first in this sand bucket, then in that.

An hour's drive away, Witzleben knew none of this. At 1100 hours, General Linnertz, officious as a butler, came to arrest him, and the whole thing went off with gruesome decorum. The Gestapo arrived soon after, but by then Countess Lynar had destroyed the guest book. How typical of us all: we may have been incompetent, but we observed all the decencies, we conducted ourselves like knights, almost as if—preposterous thought—our whole enterprise had been esthetic or meant as an acme of social bravura. Click-click went the heels. Up went the arms in salute. Some even bowed or got themselves escorted to death by a hand gently cupping the elbow as if in an underwater dream.

"Field Marshal," said Linnertz, "I am under orders to ask you to escort me into the city."

Witzleben: "Just so."

"I regret the necessity."

"As I regret the cause. Duty is duty."

"Then . . ."

"Of course, I have been expecting you since ten o'clock last night. No, everything is ready."

"Your *baton*, Field Marshal." Such severe civility.

Throughout the evening of July twentieth, out at Group Headquarters on the Russian front, Tresckow and Schlabrendorff had waited for news. Eventually, exhausted with waiting, Tresckow went to lie on his bed. "Like the husband in the adultery farce," he joked wanly, "we're always the last to know."

When Schlabrendorff heard S'gruber's radio speech, he went and told Tresckow the miserable news. "It seems to have flopped altogether. Stauffenberg, Olbricht, Mertz, Beck, dead."

"Then I'll have to shoot myself," Tresckow said without moving. "They'll soon find out about me, and torture me for names. The only way to forestall that's to put myself out of harm's way. Oh yes."

On through the night they argued, Tresckow inert as something carved, at ease on his bed, Schlabrendorff mopping his brow and polishing the thick lenses of his glasses. It was stifling in Tresckow's tiny room.

"I must," Tresckow said in a monotone. "I've no choice."

"Not true," countered Schlabrendorff the attorney. "Please think again. It may not come to that at all." He plucked the skin along his jawline as if testing it for flaws.

"No, I can't risk everyone else on a remote chance of their not finding out about me. The chances are far greater that they will."

"It doesn't follow. The Gestapo is remarkably incompetent at times. And, as well, they sometimes look the other way, especially if someone's indispensable."

"Good try, my friend. Don't try to blind me with the science based on exceptions."

"Gestapo power isn't absolute," Schlabrendorff said pleadingly. "They do foul up."

"Too many lines of investigation lead to me," Tresckow told him. "I may have been on the perimeter of things all year, but I'm still a central figure. One of the main criminals."

"But please. Sleep on it, anyway." Schlabrendorff wiped a tear.

"Don't tell me my good old loyal Indian elephant guide is weakening," Tresckow said with affectionate weariness. "I want you to stay alive as long as possible. With me gone, you're safer. And you can incriminate me as much as you want. I'll be beyond reach."

"You always called me that—Indian elephant guide, your *Kornak!* Odd how soothing it's been to have a role with a *name.*"

"I'll sleep on it, but I won't change my mind. Nor will you. Not even Claus could. He called me his 'instructor.'"

"Wait and see. Tomorrow's always—"

"My last day. I promise. As I said, I want *you* to stay alive as long as you can"—as if addressing a superior form of life.

Early on the morning of the 21st, Tresckow reiterated his decision. "Now they'll fall on us like wolves and smear us all over the landscape. But I'm convinced we did the right thing—tried to do the right thing. *He* is the archenemy not only of Germany but of the entire civilized world. In a few hours' time I'll be facing my Maker, and I'll have to answer for what I did and didn't do. I think my conscience is going to be clear. God promised to spare Sodom for ten just men. Well, I hope He'll spare Germany on account of what we almost did. Nobody's any business complaining. Anybody who joined the resistance movement put the shirt of Nessus on. Damn it, it's no use having convictions if you aren't willing to put your life on the line to back them up. Erika knows already."

Schlabrendorff wept openly while shaking his head in little dissenting jerks. "Don't. *Wait.* Think it over."

"God bless you. I must be going." They embraced with mild, stunned reserve.

In front of the army barracks at Ostrov, Tresckow's big car flashed in the humid sunshine. The driver stood idling and breathing deep while a young officer theorized about the effect on morale of steamy weather.

Out strode Tresckow, his chin high, his eyes unusually intense, the rings under them dark mauve.

"Would you care to accompany me this morning?" Tresckow asked the officer. Flecks of tight-coiled cloud, high, high.

"I have just received orders to wait for the field marshal." That was Walther Model.

"I am truly sorry," Tresckow told him with light composure. "Come over here a moment." They stepped out of earshot and turned to face westward, roughly toward Stockholm. "This is going to be my last day on earth—forgive the stagey way of putting it—and I should have liked you to be the witness of my death." The rhythm of the words invited him to dinner.

The young officer gasped, went red, and shook his head stiffly. "What do you mean?" He tried again. "*You*, General?"

"I have no intention of letting *that* lot get their bloody hands on me, now or ever. I shall go to the Twenty-eighth Rifle Division and walk forward some distance with a rifle, some grenades and two pistols. They'll hear a lot of shooting and conclude I ran into Russian partisans. Quite simple, really, and just as plausible. I just *might*." He sighed wryly.

The young officer's lips quivered and sagged. "Out there? General, don't."

"*Au revoir*, then," Tresckow said, "in a better world."

At that point, Major Oertzen was still alive, but only by a few minutes.

Tresckow took Major Kuhn with him and drove to the forward area, where they left the driver behind and advanced to reconnoiter on foot. The birds were raucous.

"The map," Tresckow said, almost to himself, murmuring.

"The general's map!" Kuhn shouted, turning back toward the car, from which the driver emerged, map in hand. Tresckow was out of sight, in the nearby wood, from which there came the sounds of gunfire and explosions; using his two pistols skyward, he had simulated an exchange of shots with partisans, as promised, and had then set off a rifle grenade next to his head, which the explosion demolished.

Now Schlabrendorff, who only hours earlier had heard Tresckow's last words, wishing they were just so much rhetoric, was given the chore of taking Tresckow's body home to the family grave in Brandenburg for honorable burial. Something obscene in the entire episode dried up his throat and made his eyes twitch. Tresckow was safe from dangers that might never have come his way, but how prove that?

The morning of July 21st found General Karl Heinrich von

Stülpnagel beginning to obey an order to report to Keitel after the miserable outcome of the day before. Of all our officers, he was the most efficient, having managed to arrest the leaders of the SS in Paris, only to be obliged by the dithering Kluge to release them. On the evening of the twentieth, he and Kluge had dined together in silence as if sitting in the house of the dead, after which Kluge accompanied him down the stone steps to his car in the castle courtyard, saying, "I think the only thing you can do now is to change into civilian clothes and go into hiding."

No handshake, just a curt exchange of bows, Stülpnagel as usual supporting his back with his left hand. Then, in the brief flash of headlights as the car realigned itself, he saluted and Kluge bowed once more. The car slid out of the black shadow cast by the gigantic chalk cliffs of La Roche-Guyon. Already Stülpnagel (always deft at gathering French hostages to shoot) had locked up some twelve hundred loyal Nazis, arranged for the drumhead court-martial of the worst among them and their execution against sandbagged stands on the courtyard of the École Militaire. His lunch, he said, he'd taken with an expert on "Goethe and the Generals." He'd even taken a stroll on the roof garden of the Hotel Raphael. His day had been full and already his career as military governor of Paris was over. Civilian clothes and a hiding place were not his style; a Prussian officer did not undertake such flummery even at the worst of times. "Regard yourself as suspended from duty," Kluge had said. All that was left was the letting go.

Shortly before retiring to bed at 0130 hours, Kluge put through a *Blitz* call to Rastenburg and told the agitated Jodl, "Stülpnagel, I'm afraid, charged ahead like a bull. '*The swine is dead*,' he said. Yes, arrested all SS and SD, even Ambassador Abetz. All that has been put right. I have suspended him from duty. We can't help him, of course not. I agree. I have sent a signal to the Führer himself, expressing my relief and gratitude. Some of us are loyal to the end. For us there will be no repetition of 1918. *Heil Hitler!*" As he slipped between the cool sheets, he heard gunfire slewed by distance and cupped both hands over his groin, where a tiny amaryllis threatened to bloom, so rousing his day as commander-in-chief had been.

Back at the Hotel Raphael in Paris, Stülpnagel told his waiting officers with a wave of the hand, *"No. Kluge refuses."* His eyes were dull and his cheeks had a raging flush, but he was as casually elegant as ever, and it was hard to believe he had brought the end of their new world. Military marches from the hotel's radios almost blotted out the clink of glasses, the expostulations of dismay. Then S'gruber spoke and Stülpnagel held himself erect at cold attention, his fists clenched. What had he told the writer Ernst Jünger not so long ago in the old abbey at Vaux-les-Cernay? "There are occasions when it becomes the duty of an honorable man to live no longer." He conferred in the foyer of the Raphael with newly released senior SS officers whose death warrants he had all but signed. Over champagne he formally shook hands with SS General Karl Oberg even as Caesar von Hofacker slipped away in disgust.

Next morning he informed Berlin that he would report in about nine A.M. on Saturday.

"Private plane? Official plane? No, neither. I'll come by road." He gave no reasons. Berlin wanted him to fly.

"I'm sorry," he told his secretary, Countess Podewils, "I won't be able to lunch with Captain Jünger. Give him my best and tell him . . . I'm off to Berlin. Fate has decided against us." She saw his meaning and winced openly.

Then he took a quick snack in the hotel bar, empty save for himself and one other. He filled a thermos with coffee while making scrappy conversation, and then walked out, down the short flight of stairs to the doorway. Countess Podewils came clattering down the stairs from above, three or four at a time, and caught him up on the outside, crying *"General!"* once as if to halt him in his tracks forever. They shook hands again. His hand felt hot. She turned away to hide her tears. The sentries

at the ornate gateway giving onto the Avenue Kleber presented arms. The car headed off in the direction of the Étoile and
disappeared.

Champs Élysées. Place de la Concorde, with the Ministry of
Marine on its north side, the German flag rattling in the rain-
strewn wind. Shops and ambling crowds as heedless of the rain
as the lines of German soldiers, camouflaged trucks and rumbling panzers. A French policeman saluted. After the northeas-
tern suburbs they increased speed toward Metz, but the engine
stalled at Meaux, and Stülpnagel slept on a mattress in a ga-
rage until another car arrived. At three they set off again, soon
dipping into the Argonne Forest, infested with French partisans. The drivers tested their weapons and Stülpnagel aimed
his revolver at a tree without leaving the car. Traces now of
the previous war: dugouts, collapsed trenches, ruined woods.
Sergeant Major Schauf, the driver, increased speed as the car
entered the overhanging shade of lush trees. Back in open
country, they soon saw Verdun, crossed the military bridge,
and entered the shell-hole terrain of World War One, now a
charcoal green.

With the Meuse crossed, Stülpnagel amazed them by ordering a detour to the region north of Verdun, where, as they realized, he had fought as a young captain. They saw the old
German front line, then some gray stone houses.

"Stop," said Stülpnagel, map on knee. "I need a little walk.
You go on to Champs, the next village, and wait for me there."
He was humming something they couldn't identify.

"The partisans—" the sergeant major began, but Stülpnagel
cut him off with a good-natured grin. Left hand to his back.

"To Champs!" Stülpnagel's thin, patient lips were working
tensely beneath his smudge of short-clipped mustache. Schauf
halted the car at the next bend in the road and got out with Fi-
scher, the general's orderly. Better to disobey.

Two shots. Or one? Snapping the silence of bees and birds.
Back they went, but Stülpnagel had gone. Over the ridge they

stormed, toward the towpath that flanked the canal and its se-
date green water. A field-gray uniform was floating past, its
red facings bright in the waning sun. Stülpnagel's hands were
at his throat, the water round him was crimson. Schauf waded
in, crying, "In God's name, General, *what* . . . ?"

The head was a mess. An eye had gone with a bullet that entered the right temple. Stülpnagel was choking on fluid, but
they bandaged him, looking over their shoulders for partisans;
but only spiraling harsh crows interrupted the evening hush.
They lifted him into the back seat, noting that his belt had
gone, as well as his Knight's Cross and cap. Off to Verdun they
raced, arriving at a hospital just before sunset. Back in Paris,
Linstow and others checked Stülpnagel's office for papers, but
there wasn't a single incriminating word, whereas the previous
night in the Raphael and the Majestic hotels half a dozen officers had spent hours tearing everything into tiny pieces and
flushing it away while, downstairs, the reprieved SS drank
themselves into sentimental joy.

Quietly the sandbagged execution stands came down.

Stülpnagel was blind, but made a statement to Oberg at
Verdun, and like everything else he said thereafter it was curt,
precise, and alert.

24

Two Wolves

◆

Now the bloodbath began to fill. Interrogation rooms reached
round-the-clock use. The third floor was one constant round of
screams audible in basement cells full of men and women tapping farewells or reassurances through the walls. Old hands,

dropping *j*, had divided the alphabet into five groups of five letters, so Gerstenmaier's name, for example, began "2:2, 1:5, 4:2"—two taps, then two; one tap, then five; four taps, then two. In fact, Gerstenmaier was not only tapping but also singing "A Mighty Fortress Is Our God," as if daring the hangmen to come and get him so that he could prove his point. For those next door to him, his voice was louder than the screams, but farther away the screams were always louder than the tapped-out messages. Number 8 Prinz Albrecht Strasse was an inferno of sound, but only a hint of things to come.

Meanwhile, at Wolf's Lair, two linked scenes began to enact themselves. Two human instruments had arrived, in order to be briefed. Ushered into the infernal presence first, befitting his rank, Freisler, President of the infamous People's Court, bellowed, "*Heil!*" with a ceremonious downcurl of his mouth, then bowed low, seeming to sweep an invisible judge's robe to the side in doing so. His face was not so much a face as it was a shell; he would have survived easily on the sea bottom, a hard-horned predator, vulnerable only to inbuilt gradations of decay. Or dynamite. Since 1934 he had been dealing out the death sentence, but his eyes showed nothing of that, only an implacable zeal which resembled hate, although he was rarely angry in any genuine sense; just one of the best-lubricated opportunists in S'gruber's chamber of horrors.

"Our Vishinsky!" S'gruber greeted him with a faint simper. "Versatile, devilish, and loud!"

Freisler bowed low. "The Führer is too kind." The hooded eyes almost shut in rapt smugness. A former communist and bolshevik commissar, Freisler knew how to frighten, how to reduce men to silence or stammering, how to bully, as well as how to wrap unspeakable travesties of law in erudite flapdoodle about justice.

"Freisler, I want the first trial to be a model. Intimidate them all you want—insult and interrupt, ridicule them and call them names—but make sure they are tried at lightning speed. No grand speeches, no slobbering self-justifications. As soon as they start any such thing, stop them at once, I don't care how. They are to be tried as civilians and condemned as scum, as a clique of sewer rats, as gobbets of slime from the festering bowels of the royalist aristocracy, as something foul which the German nation has coughed up like black jelly from its purely breathing lungs! They tried to *kill* me. To *kill* ME! And if they think I'll wait around until more of the same swinehound breed make a second attempt they're mistaken. I want them hanged without mercy, without the slightest mercy, within two hours of the verdict's being handed down. You understand? You have to deal once and for all with such off-scourings from a dead past. *You* do. Do not let me down in this, Herr Freisler; I want an exemplary process, after which they shall dangle and twist like fresh meat on hooks. I will hang *everybody* involved, I will *hang* as no one has ever hanged before, and I shall *see*, Freisler, I shall *see* it, every twitch and squirm, and when they try to run, and when they whine and howl and vomit and befoul themselves! Vengeance is mine, as their Bible says. All I ask of you is speed, force, and that enormous voice of yours. I want them strung up like butchered cows."

All this Freisler followed with cursory twists of his mouth and eyes, as the puny arms began to flail and a colorless foam gathered at the corners of the madman's mouth while his undernourished eyes plunged and roamed through a terra incognita of malevolent ingenuity. Now S'gruber's tinny, high-pitched, querulous *vox inhumana* hit a new register.

"Freisler, pronounce the word 'guilty' as you will, on all eight."

He did, slightly louder than conversational tone, having practiced it many times in court and in the mirror.

"*Louder!*" shrieked S'gruber, brandishing a white fist like the bulb at the end of a stinkhorn root. "Put some lung into it, man."

"Guilty, Guilty, *Guilty*, GUILTY, GUIL-TY!" Freisler, yelled in obedient, accelerating paroxysm, as if to parody that other cry, "Praise him, praise him!"

"Ah," wailed S'gruber in vitriolic contentment, his face bunched awry round a lethal smile. "That will make them think. That will be the *first* noose."

Unbidden, Freisler tried again, inhaling stagily and now flinging that invisible red robe forward in a wing wash of extermination; yet his ogreish leer had a touch of malice in it.

"Hanged!" he cried to the ceiling, nothing if not a ham.

"Strangled," S'gruber echoed, hoarse with pleasure. "And with no filth of priests attending them." He fingered grossly.

"No priests," Freisler chimed back. "No rosaries."

"And no letters. No wives. No journalists." Again Freisler played his part, repeating the cry word for word then adding his own forensic curlicues: ". . . and no hair-splitting overtures to martyrdom, *mein Führer*, but only the barest formula to take them off with." Gloating at the prospect, he failed to see the change in S'gruber's blood-choked face.

"Herr Freisler," the thin voice snapped in a tone utterly removed from the sadistic roguery of only a moment ago, "did you not, on June sixteenth, in sentencing Halem and Mumm to death, say to the accused, Halem, that pimp of assassins, 'See what you have done: you have sunk yourself'?" Freisler quivered just a little; a vein in his temple began to beat unduly, his enormous ears flushed red.

"Of course—" An oral thunderbolt cut him off.

"AND WHAT DID *HE* SAY TO *YOU?* What was the trash he said?"

"As I recall—"

"He told you straight out that 'A ship can sink, but it need not haul down its flag.' Herr Freisler, you are a good man in your profession, although there is communist slime and bile, grubs and beetles and lice, in your file; but do not ever again provide *zoo animals* with metaphors they can turn against you! You may use unanswerable metaphors, *unturnable* ones, but none other. I do not want the People's Court turned into a debating club, I will not have it made into a forum for treasonous hair splitters. As soon as they appear, indeed long before, these men are dead, and their minds must be schooled into being dead. I want the death of the mind evident to all present—the long harsh dying of the dull mind, with maggots in the air and worms in their mouths, their words decomposing before you and NOT, Herr Freisler, making a mockery of all we stand for. Let me make it clear: ships may sink, and ships will sink, but YOU will haul down their flags for them and stuff them into the mouths of these plutocratic psychopaths. Is that clear?"

With a contraction of his chest, Freisler said it was.

Dismissing him, S'gruber called out, "I will be watching. Do well. A maggot mourns no one, Herr Freisler, not even you, not even me. Save your energies. Avoid sexuality. Be pure in doom. Wear your best robe. Make them quake. I am your main audience, my dear fellow. Why are you dawdling about there? Away with you, eat some soil, inhale some fire. Judge them fairly and think of your Führer!"

The tired *jawohl* was cagey too; clearly, as Freisler saw it, he was fortunate to get away with as mild a going-over as this. But there was more to come.

"Herr Freisler," S'gruber called even as the two SS guards stood at the door to remove the ostensibly distinguished visitor, "remember a beautiful, poignant truth, which knocks the arrogance, the heroism, out of all men: All men have family *somewhere*, ready for the plucking, and not only the Stauffenbergs, the Hofackers, the Becks, the Stieffs, the Witzlebens. Both infants and the senile are relevant to our main purpose. *We*, like the Christians' God, demand the whole man, the entire family."

"But I—" Freisler began, then thought better of it. He finally escaped, determined to take out his humiliations on the accused brought before his unspeakable court.

The next visitor, Röttger the Plötzensee hangman, was cruder by far: a man accustomed to wearing a jerkin and encased for this event in a badly fitting brown suit and, almost as tight around him as the suit, an aroma of mothballs and celery. A leerer, he managed to cringe boldly while shifting all of a sudden from one foot to the other like a boxer feinting at shadows. S'gruber advanced and, without so much as a word, felt the man's arm muscle, hummed a maniacal word or two to himself, then transferred his grip to the throat, hoisting the jaw backward and upward in the gap between thumb and forefinger splayed wide. "Slow, slow," whispered the madman to the ghoul. "Above all, Witzleben, Hase, Hoepner ... Stretch them, my bully boy, make them feel their full length. I want them to linger. I want them all naked as well. After all, they will end their lives as film stars! *Hoepner* especially must feel the slowness of time."

The red-faced, sweating hangman could not speak, his eyes aimed upward as if some altogether milder being had been struck dumb by the Milky Way in summer, lustrous as an elongated wheatfield in the sky.

"*Mn Fhr-r,*" the wretch gasped.

"They are not to fall with sudden force."

The other nodded, dribbling on his Führer's hand.

"Ease out a footstool from beneath them. Ha!" At once he released the throat, slapped him on the back, cuffed his buttocks, jabbed him in the portly belly, and instructed him to procure cognac for the state witnesses, even as the hangman, in a fit of obsequious mimicry, tugged an invisible body tight between his hands, twisting and twirling and emitting, much to his Führer's pleasure, a throttled sigh as of someone whose voicebox had been surgically removed. For a full minute the two of them mimed at each other with unseen rope, unseen footstools, unseen victims, each countering the other's most sibilant wheeze with something fiercer yet even more debilitated, as if determined to turn asphyxiation into an abstract art of bisected whispers and demi-semi-quavers of impeded breath. Circling each other thus, they belonged in a madhouse, the superhuman devil just as much at ease with the plebeian of doom as the plebeian with his lord and master, except he mixed his gruesome foreplay with relief; even he knew how easy it was to slip off the greased plank of S'gruber's favor. It was almost as if, to keep well in, he should hang himself in a tour de force of diabolical black art.

"Hands," said S'gruber. "Let me see. Well?"

The hangman wiped both hands on a red and white handkerchief before presenting them, two massive engines of roughened flesh, black-nailed and warty, rank with stale carbolic soap, and as heavy in their hovering clutch as udders. S'gruber stroked them, first the left, cooing and chuckling, then abruptly let them fall and whisked his own hands through a drill of pointing, waving, clapping, fist-hammering in midair, and in the end a gesture so obscene that the hangman gurgled, although straight-faced.

"*Hands.* It's a crime to let them just hang there. Hanussen, the seer, taught me how to use *mine.* Hanussen, the fake Danish aristocrat, otherwise known as Herschel Steinschneider, a Viennese crypto-Jew, now dead. He had a place on the Lietzenburger Strasse. Did you— No, the likes of you would not. Yours are hands for delivering deformed foals from diseased mares belonging to aristocrats and then ripping the guts apart. You smile. You think it a compliment. It is *not.* If you were soap or dung, I would call you soap or dung." Then the gathering shriek as some tiny irritant exploded in his paranoid's brain and the crescendo of vituperation began with the hangman in retreat to the door, ducking his head and trying to hide his hands behind him. "Why do people never see that I do not *pay compliments,* I propound diagnostic truths! I shall be watching for you, *mein Herr,* on film, and may the devil himself help you if I catch you putting a hand wrong. Any of those swine

get off too easily—I mean with a sudden drop—and you yourself will eat the meal of your private parts fried in machine
oil!" At that point, the hangman vowed to be himself only
when not on camera; he didn't want the Führer to hear his
usual leering jokes, but one perverse part of him couldn't help
wondering what it might be like to undergo just what he'd
been told, provided he was conscious, of course, and knowing
he had nothing to lose. What was a *diag-nost-ic* truth?

I'd love to hang the Führer too, he told himself as the SS
marched him out; *in this world it's no good going halfway in
anything. I'd love to chop the Führer too, before frying his
bits up in the oil; which means I'd have to gentle him bit by
bit on the rope to keep his juices in and sweet. I'd do him like
a feather angel, that I would, and keep his big pebbly eyelids
fluttering for half an hour at least. Pride, that's what. Some
folks have none at all.*

Thinking his interview over, or that he was at least out of
earshot, Röttger convulsed when he heard the brassbound hysterical voice pour after him in a parting frenzy.

"That damned Stauffenberg, *mein Herr!* I wish you were
going to deal with *him* as well. He should at least have had the
guts *to stand next to me* with his briefcase. The bullet that
killed him was too good for him by far. Deal with them all, my
friend, as if you had Stauffenberg himself between your
hands! *Langsam,* my swine! *Lang-sam!*"

This time Röttger walked on unharassed, but confounded by
a weird sense of having heard S'gruber aim something at him
intended for someone else, not present.

Far away in Berlin, Gerstenmaier was still singing, as if to
abolish the horrific interval itself, about which he knew nothing, which meant he was singing in order to blot out a gruesome, symphonic guess in which all the inmates of the Gestapo
prison came together, voiceless or loud, half strangled, or
merely dry throated from intolerable fright.

25

Sippenhaft

◆

Quoting the Germanic sagas, Himmler invoked the doctrine of *Sippenhaft* or "family liability," which in the case of my own family entailed the arrest of everyone, old or young, male or female. "The family of Stauffenberg," Himmler raved on August third, to massed *Gauleiters* in Posen, "will be extinguished to the last member, root and branch." There was prolonged sycophantic applause. The mob stood. Then he went on. "This will be a warning, once and for all. July twentieth was the ultimate manifestation of a long-term trend in the officer corps, of incompetence and sabotage, especially among the intellectuals of the General Staff. It even goes back to the First World War, but it belongs nowhere at all. The army has now adopted the raised hand of our Party salute, and it will stay that way. The army belongs to the Party, and not the other way around. The army does not belong *even to itself.*" The applause resumed and lasted for a full three minutes, followed by ritual, percussive chanting of "*Sieg Heil! Sieg Heil!*"

Unbelievably, in view of all that Himmler ranted forth, and the Nazi decision to change my children's names to Meister and Nina's to Schank, the children went unsuffocated by thugs or beaten to pulp in some remote cowshed behind a chalet in the Riesengebirge Mountains (the evacuation site chosen by Kaltenbrunner), and Nina went unmolested during her imprisonment and got special rations because she was pregnant. There was always, thank God, a sympathetic friend who knew who the "Meister" children really were, and "Frau Schank," whose regal bearing suggested that she was a *von* Schank to say the least.

Only because Göring, for reasons of his own, wanted to thwart Himmler, did it happen that my stranded, amputated darlings did not end up, in Himmler's pretty locution, "spread . . . in the manure ditches," as Beck, Olbricht, Ali, Haeften, and I had been. Again I saw my children's names set out on a hymnal board sinking into slime, Berthold, the oldest, already under the surface, Heimeran with sealed lips already flush with it, Franz Ludwig with averted eyes willing the board to rise again, Valerie, only four years old, wondering how to float. The names had eyes and ears, mouths and, most wonderful and terrible of all, Meister-like hair: unruly flax in flames.

At four in the morning on July 23rd, the Gestapo came pounding on the doors at Lautlingen, yelling barbarously and plying their searchlights' big white blobs from door to window, from window to door, as if putting the house under a spell. Nux had little to say to them, but stood at attention, ready and waiting in a dark suit, his gaze fixed on something beyond the trucks, beyond the trees. Nina, locked into a glacial reserve, they allowed to look in for one last time on the sleeping children, but with an armed Gestapo thug right behind her. To each she mouthed a different silent kiss, and not one of them awoke. Then she gave concise orders to the governess: "Keep them together at all times. And *explain*." Then she told the Gestapo, "I am as much now at your disposal as I ever will be."

"We are waiting for your mother-in-law." One of them made a throat-cutting motion with his hand. Finally my mother came downstairs, a sleepwalker, a disdainful ghost. "Put up your swords," she said distractedly, "or the dew will rust them." Then she yawned and said, "God bless the children. Hitler is dead."

"Time to go, dam of traitors," the Gestapo officer growled. "We want everybody except the nurse and the kids. You stand here with us." They combed through the house again, waking the children, who called out for help, ran about in night clothes, indiscriminately shouting, "Goodbye," and, "I love you, come home soon, bring Daddy with you." At length they all gathered just inside the front door in the governess's wide caliperlike embrace, much calmer and uttering fractional allusive calls as the searchlights blazed.

"No toys, please, Mamma. I have enough."

"I'll say a special prayer."

The oldest, Berthold, managed a salute in his pajamas while Valerie said only the one word, "Doll, doll."

As if the idea had only just occurred to them, or had only just seemed good, the Gestapo rummaged through the entire house while Nux, Nina, my mother, and my aunt stood in the predawn chill like refugees, wanting to run back to the children in the doorway but unwilling to mend a break already half made. I had exposed them all to *this*. My three boys, who understood what the radio said, had had to be told the truth as soon as Nina had it, on July 21st.

"Your father tried to do something very hard and very dangerous, for which he paid with his life." Then she tried in a rather different idiom. "Think of him as being away on a long mission abroad, which gets longer and longer until there is no way, absolutely no way, of his ever being able to come home again. We shall have to be more than brave. Whatever you see or hear, remember he gave everything for Germany."

Then, unable to flee or hide, to disguise themselves or die, they waited and waited, as if already extinct, murmuring, reminiscing, playing leapfrog under the July sun in Lautlingen.

Now the Gestapo officer ran into the house in response to a shout, carving right through the children, and the guards moved closer to their prisoners with dawning ghoulish grins.

"Well, a few more for the bin, huh? It never ends, this shit. In the cellars now, in Prinz Albrecht Strasse, they have so many clients they can offer one client, when he seems exhausted, a cup of another's blood! They never drink it, though. But wouldn't *you*, if you were really thirsty? By God, I would, I'd drink his piss. How about you, Mutti? D'you swig anything these days? You wait and see."

My mother ignored them, stiffened her back, and tapped her stick in rebuke against the senior ghoul's boot. Her motion might have been an excerpt from a puppet show.

On they talked, less to frighten or sicken her than to titillate one another. "At Vercors, on July fourteenth," one began, "when the SS settled the hash of all those partisans, going in by glider with their flamethrowers blazing. Ja!"

"Tell us again, Sergeant!"

He rolled his eyes at my mother, who was murmuring irately to herself, and raised his voice. "You mean the stern hour of General Stundt! What a man. Well, boys, he had the balls cut off every peasant they captured alive, and the tits off the women. But that was nothing. You hearing me, grandmother? They strangled one old bitch with her own intestines, a slow and slimy job."

My mother looked into the blue vault of the sky and drymouthed a prayer, and then said another word again and again: "Vulgar, vulgar, vulgar . . ."

"That evening, my hearties, he took an early dinner in the nearest restaurant, with the town officials made to watch. Big white cloth of crispest linen. Silver candlestick. Waiters whitegloved. A little Mozart to sweeten the hour. Then they served him three boiled eggs which he crushed in his hands, rolled into a paste of shell and yolks, and plastered on the face and head of the local mayor. Then, yes, wait for it, *wait for it,* something pale and smooth, you might say, gently poached in white wine and sautéed with garlic and butter, like a small loaf of squid. They say the general's face as he savored the dish flew this way and that in twitches of uncontrolled delight."

My mother was still saying, "Vulgar, vulgar, vulgar," to her private God.

"Tell us, Sergeant. What was on the menu? Tell us again!"

Clearing his throat as if for an operatic tour de force, the sergeant launched a gob of slime in the rough direction of my mother's foot in its lace-up boot, and guffawed. "Baby's brain! *Imagine* that Stundt! They say he's cannibalized his way through the infants of five countries, and he has the best digestion in the whole SS, the finest complexion. It's enough to convert you. You know what they say. Herr Himmler, he feeds the SS trainees on porridge, like the boys in the best British schools. What pig swill! The SS make it in their own factory! But the payoff comes later, when they turn into gourmets right after combat. General Stundt has solved the supply problem in the occupied countries!" They all laughed uncontrollably.

It was General Stundt who had agonized facially in front of the van Gogh when Ebo and I talked in the Jeu de Paume on June 23rd. Even those who managed to wipe the S'grubers off the face of the earth would always have the Stundts to deal with, the cut-rate Satans ever willing to oblige, vice's flunkeys who'd always survive their chief. Why kill one if not all?

Then my mother launched those awful pleas at them, like roses under the treads of a tank.

"My son Claus's cello, please?" The plea overt.

"No music where *you're* going, sourpuss." They hooted.

"His signet ring and cross." The plea querulous.

They ignored her and began to bawl orders at someone in the distance when they saw the officer returning with two men who hefted a cardboard box.

"My son Berthold's Greek lexicon, then, the *duplicate*." She said this in milling tears, unsure what to ask for next: what she would not get. For a moment Nina and Nux enveloped her, before two of them hustled her off into the truck and drove away, churning black smoke, burning rubber, sounding the siren. It was the beginning of her solitary confinement, during which she recited entire plays, at least during the first weeks, thereafter going through the actors' motions in dumbshow, with an occasional line flung out—"Damnable, bricked-in, cabined hole!"—repeatedly when a full heart drove her lips and larynx into motion. Babbling otherwise a chain of her sons' names, she grew thin, hesitant, and remote, until the loud, overweight female warder gave her extra soup and black bread.

"Strength," growled this ogress. "Be lively now."

"What in me is strong," my mother said, "needs no Nazi slop, and what's weak I'll starve to death."

She stood by her candle as the door slammed, her white hair blond in the darkness, her eyes wet with so many tangled feelings, pride and tension and unutterable, cold, insect-ridden loneliness. Then she faced the one wall from which she felt a dead son's love might come and, with drooping face, palmed the dank stone, huskily beseeching, "Give him back. Send him back. *I want him back*. I have only two sons left."

Once, while she was nursing me back to health in Lautlingen, I had wandered into her bedroom and dressing room while she was in the garden with Nux, and I flipped open the door of her shoe cupboard, almost without thinking, perhaps to make sure that she hadn't changed her ways. It was also where she always kept an old-fashioned, big purse that held her birth certificate, her passport, and usually a bundle of money together with the smallest of her photograph albums.

I saw, as if for the last time, row upon neat row of her shoes, each pair touching but with a hand's breadth between the pairs themselves, and I felt overwhelmed by the sight of so much of her life without her, so fastidiously ordered, the toes all pointing outward into the world, the years of use apparent on most pairs, and her age blatant in the button-up boots she still kept but never wore. A cupboard full of empty shoes seemed like her death, and I thought my heart would split as the tears poured down my face and my throat heaved with the miserable inevitability of all partings; I cried at the tidy, meek stoicism with which she awaited the end of her days, and I wished I had only a fraction of her spry, doom-laden dignity. Nursing me again, she must have dreamed she was at the beginning of my life, doting on her third baby son, but it was not so, and a day would come when we would never meet again, as long as the universe endured.

Yet how cram eons of love into the short time left? That it was to be shorter than I'd guessed—I snatched from her before she from me, but severed nonetheless—I had no idea, and had some seer told me so I'd have turned to stone at that very place, in front of the opened cupboard, heaving with immediate and anticipated grief, unspeakably moved by all those paired open mouths of dead leather which thrust the finality of death even deeper into me and yet, in that instant, also brought home to me the beauty of a lifetime's wear. My mother had rubbed off into the leather: she, *she*, had made it unique, and that is why she had thrown none of her shoes or boots away, but kept her past life by her, for reference or completeness, until she would need them no more, any more than her mind her body.

I must have been there an hour, at first overcome, then vainly trying to regain a modicum of self-control, enough to go back down into the garden to Nux's crusty quips and my mother's passion to make me whole again. *Last things*, as they are called, had sunk into me with a taste of iron. "That eye," she said as soon as she saw me, "needs bathing. Doesn't it, Nux?" He grunted even as I began to answer, poking his thumb at a bee inside a tulip.

"Yes, mother. This eye wants a lot it can't have, and that's why it has to be bathed. I would love you to bathe it." Then I realized I had left the cupboard door open, but, when I went back in to cover my tracks, my hand froze, and I left the door as it was, that much afraid of closure, that little troubled by being found out; after all, I was only her child, and not expected to know better than to pry. Usually, by the time you amount to anything, those to whom it might mean something have gone. I would rather have amounted to nothing; and, in my ruinous way, perhaps I did, so perhaps it's better, before amounting to so lethal a zero, to wait until your loved ones are no more. The only paradox more grievous is that the thought of death makes you want to die, never to think it again. Thus death, which has us to begin with, wins us over too. The incurable's the only cure.

26

August Seventh, A.M.

◆

Following up on Himmler's fanfare of hate, S'gruber first of all made into civilians the fifty-odd officers he wanted to make an example of, beginning with twenty-two on August fourth: the insult preceding the injury, the so-called court of honor preceding the so-called People's Court, which got down to business on August seventh.

Successive pairs of policemen with faces of gnarled righteousness haled the eight unshaven accused up the long rectangular room containing busts of Frederick the Great and S'gruber, plus three long swastika banners. Because of the heat, the five tall windows along one wall were part open, admitting the fragrance of magnolia, strong and heavy, almost as if emanating from Freisler himself, clad in a voluminous wine-red robe like a doctor of death. Hard to believe, the room nonetheless contained eight bogus "defense" counsel got up in black gowns and seated immediately in front of the accused, also eight in number, separated from one another by two policemen on either side. Some two hundred spectators, of whom only perhaps half a dozen were overcome by disgust, shuddered at the faces of those police, some with enormous beak noses, some with peeling lips compressed into a line of mediocre rebuke aimed at the accused while he spoke. On the front of their helmets they wore an enormous eagle flying upward, which gave them a look of Inca priests, inhuman and mechanically gruesome. Walnut-faced men, these, case-hardened by non-stop contact with the doomed who had already been tortured to the brink, and utterly given over to their calling. The coarse grain of the functionary had never shown to more sickening effect.

Each accused came forward to be identified, escorted by his two policemen. When Witzleben heard his name, he made an automatic, almost plucking gesture with his right hand (minus its baton it floated about a bit), and Freisler homed in on him, tigerish and deafening.

"What right have YOU, a man in your position, to use the salute sacred to the very cause you have betrayed? WELL?"

The one thing Witzleben had not been intending was a Nazi salute; accumulated body tension had vented itself, that was all, but Freisler had given everyone a sample of how he was going to conduct things. It was not a courtroom but a bearpit. Or so it must have seemed until the bears appeared for sustained examination.

Poor hunchbacked Stieff came first, swiveling his head to take in the entire room and gently feeling the bristles on his throat and the sides of his neck. Like all of the prisoners, he wore—or rather was afloat in—shabby civilian clothes: no tie, of course, no belt, his hair plastered back with accumulated sweat. He seemed too small, too junior, to be tried for anything, but there he stood, part the erring schoolboy, part gargoyle. His Adam's apple seemed bigger than before, and his eyes were sunk deep into their sockets, as if in recoil from the scalding lamps that lit the room for the movie cameras.

"I wouldn't be exaggerating, would I," Freisler roared, "if I claimed that what you first told the police was all lies? Is that so?"

Without a trace of emotion, Stieff began to answer, his voice correct and formal as if he had long ago made up his mind what to say. "I have—"

"Yes or no?" Freisler's voice slammed throughout the room. "ANSWER *THAT!*"

"I failed to mention certain matters." Stieff seemed to adjust the focus of his eyes, looking first through and then right over Freisler, who was getting louder with each word, and now explosive.

"*Yes* or *no?* Let's have no hedging. Did you lie, or did you speak the whole truth? ARE YOU *AWAKE?*"

Unflustered, Stieff said simply, "I did speak the full truth subsequently." He seemed to inhale something lovely.

Freisler closed his eyes as if to bottle up his malevolence the better to pound it across the intervening space. "I asked you whether you spoke THE WHOLE TRUTH during your initial police interrogation."

"On that occasion," Stieff volunteered as if he had just been away, out of earshot, "I did not speak the full truth."

"Very well, then," Freisler growled, jutting his chin forward while hooding his eyes, "if you had any guts, you would have answered me right away: 'I told them a pack of lies.' Why *lie* about BEING A *LIAR?*"

Then Freisler questioned him about his dealings with Tresckow and Beck. "And is it true that, instead of knocking him down with a punch on the nose"—a bizarre image of Beck—"you merely asked for time to think it over?"

"Yes, that's right." Stieff had an almost dapper serenity; he wasn't so much being questioned as exposed, and Freisler took every opportunity to ridicule and insult the man whom everyone in the room knew firsthand or by repute as "Poison Dwarf."

"Is it true that when we made our offensive withdrawal from the Dnieper, round about October 1943, that murderous lout"—*Mordluder* was the actual word he bellowed as if to raise the dead: *MORD-LUDER!*—"Count von Stauffenberg urged you to join him, and that you did not refuse? WHY DON'T YOU STAND UP STRAIGHT?"

Stieff explained that I had indeed come to see him and that he did not refuse. ("How can you just *stand by?*" I'd said.)

Now Freisler resumed at only half volume: "Is it true that you didn't refuse because you wanted to *shove* your *fingers* into the *pie?*"

"Yes," Stieff told him with weary finality.

"That's what you told the police, and you damn well did *shove* your *fingers* into it, never mind your head! As well as your honor, which you have now lost forever. Do you realize *that?*" He flicked the bauble of honor off the nail of his middle finger, but Stieff didn't even look his way.

"I refer to the statement explaining my motives." Ice-hard.

"Did you take in what I said? You played *FINGER PIE!*"

"Yes, but I wish to refer to my statement."

"You can refer to it until you're blue in the face. What matters *here* is that you have broken faith, broken the oath of loyalty of a National Socialist—"

"I," Stieff said with crisp stateliness, "owe *my* loyalty to the *German nation*." Freisler blew up at that, would have tolerated the interruption only had it been an impetuous admission. Now he raved at Stieff's averted face, invoking the German nation and S'gruber as one and the same, and howling that Stieff was a jesuitical quibbler. Then he got back to the rehearsal of guilt.

"Did you or did you not know before July twentieth that Stauffenberg was going ahead with his murderous plot on that day?" Freisler for a moment seemed to ebb, to flag.

"I was told of it," Stieff said in a small parabola of tones, "by General Wagner on the evening of the nineteenth."

"So you already knew that evening that on the next day this horrible deed would be attempted, more horrible than any in German history! Tomorrow, while we were all fighting for the nation's life and liberty, our Leader would be assassinated. You knew even more. You knew that on the next day your companion in crime, Count Stauffenberg, would *murder our Führer* at the very time when he had been sent for *because the Führer trusted him*. You knew all that. Did you *report* it?" Then the key words came like a compressed-steam whistle cutting the room in half: "Because the FÜHRER *TRUSTED* HIM! DID YOU *REPORT* HIM?"

"*No*," Stieff said violently.

"Say that again, and say it louder."

"NO!" It was as if someone had switched off the current that so far had flowed through Stieff and kept him firm. He slumped and his hands, which he had kept behind his back, now came forward as if to grip something: the table (which he was short enough to reach without stooping), then the flaps of the pockets in his hunting-style jacket. Freisler pounded on, raucous and maniacal, now raging with invisible fangs, now slinking to the kill like the navanax that prowls along the ocean floor and engulfs its prey.

But he could be bland as well.

"What do you think our soldiers would have said when they switched on their radios and learned all of a sudden that from now on *Herr* von Witzleben and *Herr* Beck would be looking after things? Have you ever given a thought to *that?*"

"Of course. Over the past few days, I *have*."

Like the squad of baby-faced junior officers in the second row, there on orders for the good of their military souls, Stieff had nothing to lose, neither his hunch nor his officer status; the former was irrevocable and the latter had already been removed. All he had was his forfeit life, like clay he could mold this way or that to leave an image which no hand of his would touch again. He was one of the least cluttered, least obligated, least commonplace of the eight men in the room. He had the final platform. Would he make use of it? By no means all the officers in the public seating were inimical to our late conspiracy.

"Well," Freisler barked, driving on with eyes and mouth even more implacable, "and what *were* your thoughts?"

Stieff seemed abruptly to remember where he was. "I was preoccupied with the military situation."

Freisler: "Very well. So you tried to do what Badoglio did before you: to tell the soldiers that their passionate and heartfelt beliefs were all wrong and that, in future, they must merely fight for the implementation of Cabinet decisions. Of all the jaundiced filth—"

"No," Stieff shouted, "for *Germany!*" His cheeks flushed and faded as he interrupted, and now Freisler really began to rave, baiting and reviling, first with barbaric obscenities, then with sarcasm so caustic that certain observers began to take notes with disgruntled sighs. Abruptly terminating his litany, he dismissed Stieff as undeserving of further interrogation and called Stieff's assistant, Hagen, to the stand. What followed was classic music hall, a gallows farce that made consciousness ashamed to be its witness. Poor Hagen, the young newly arrived lieutenant with whom I'd had such sprightly although pessimistic conversations in North Africa, was far too young and too intellectual for the role of goat; he was sleepwalking on a faraway pink beach east of Gafsa, his eyes out of focus and his mouth convulsed in stately slow motion. Never had his charcoal-dark good looks seemed more boyish, or so sapped from within, like something two-dimensional drawn by Albrecht Dürer.

"Did you deliver the explosive to Stauffenberg?"

"Yes." His blistered lips peeled open along a ragged seam.

"And that was the end of it? So far as *you* were concerned . . . "

"No."

"Well? *WELL?*"

"I asked Stauffenberg, 'What do you want this stuff for?' He said it was to destroy the government. Or the Führer." Again he sealed his lips awry.

"And you don't remember exactly?"

"No, I don't remember the exact words."

"You don't *REMEMBER EXACTLY?* What sort of a *Lump*, or SHITHEAD, are you? Someone tells you he wants to blow up the Führer or the government, and you just don't *remember*."

"It seemed to amount to much the same thing, Herr President." Poor Hagen, awed by authority for once.

"You didn't know whether Stauffenberg meant business?"

"I considered it impossible."

"But you gave him the explosives nonetheless?"

"He already had them."

"Where did he keep them?"

"So far as I can remember, in a drawer of his desk or cupboard." Vague minds came to exact ends.

" 'So far as I can remember'! It doesn't seem to have made much of an impression on you! WELL, did you report it?"

"No, I didn't do that."

"You *didn't do that?* Well, in that case we needn't waste any more time on you, you sniveling mongrel of an amnesiac."

"I didn't consider them criminals, Herr President."

"You *didn't?* Tell me, how on earth did you manage to pass your law examinations? You *did* pass them satisfactorily, didn't you? Aha! How on earth did you manage *that?* So far, I've had you pegged as just a shady specimen. *Ein Charakterlump!* But what you just said makes you out a fool as well, even though you did manage to pass your examinations."

That was all for Hagen, and nobody called out to him, "Speak up, man, you're as good as dead. You stand on a platform where *anything* is permitted. Say your terminal piece and speak it well!"

Yet Stauffenberg, trying to accomplish a last, invincibly histrionic gesture, hadn't done much better. Hagen went his dumbfounded way with numb finesse, pliable as a skein of cobweb between a door and its frame, stretching and shrinking each time the door opened, but never breaking or falling: he was close to the hinge, where next to nothing happened, his face Pagliacci white.

Now Freisler brought out for an airing the only witness who wasn't an accused. Frau Else Bergenthal, formerly Beck's housekeeper, pursed her lips in a sycophantic tiny smile as Freisler, in pompous and bloated language, filled her in with platitudes about truth, honor, and perjury, all the time addressing her as *Volksgenossin,* a National-Socialese term meaning "citizenness" or "comrade." Once his baroque politeness had run its course, and the entire court had seen enough of this flower of German matronhood, he tucked her away for later use and called for Witzleben, who somehow had contrived to stick a corner of white handerchief in his top jacket pocket. Erect even while doddering, he seemed lost in trousers too big for him, which he tried to haul up, in slow spasms. Something austere and powdery in his face made the entire court gape, with relish or pity, it mattered little. Witzleben was "big stuff" and Freisler had warmed up for him. As he began the onslaught, a small commotion began among the newsreel cameramen: Freisler was shouting so loud that he ruined the sound. Witzleben gazed wanly into space, without his false teeth. His face went on echoing with the torture he had been through, but his old acidulous haughtiness kept him calm. The clothes he wore were dead already; he was there only to be reviled, degraded, but he answered as best he could, in a dry-throated imperious hack, the brassbound bellow of the German Robespierre, the heavy-lidded sadist Freisler, who asked, "Why are you fiddling with your clothes? Have you no buttons? NO *BUTTONS?*"

Nervously clutching the waistband of his trousers, Witzleben chose not to answer that one and merely shrugged. Then he coughed almost tenderly and said, "I . . . " but nothing else. There was something of my mother in his ruined face: where love had bloomed, golden in her, silver in him, there was now only its harmonics left, the shriveled and drooping core which nonetheless yearned on, wan as pumice, grand as God, wanting to care, to love even into the afterlife, to create worth through sheer affection, as if no other creative power in the universe mattered a damn.

"You said you once called on General Beck, at his home, during February of 1943, and that you discussed the situation, which you found extremely serious. You remarked to him that the Führer had made changes in personnel, and the people who impressed you as capable had been removed, to the detriment of our ability to pursue the war. Army leaders, in short. Did you think on that occasion about who might do it better?"

High-voiced, but with palpable snap, Witzleben said a composed "Yes."

"*Yes!* You *did* think about who could do it better! Then *who* could have done it better?" It was a verbal booby trap.

"Both!" cried Witzleben, bent it seemed on one-word answers to chide Freisler's antagonistic verbosity.

"Both! *Both* of you! So you said to each other, '*We* could do it better.' Why don't you *say* that so it can be heard?" Again the bullying half-invitation, the half-leer.

I should have been there, to parry, to slash back, denouncing Freisler to his face as a sadistic wolverine, a gnome of pus, a salivating wart on the human race, slamming him with my bad Latin—"*sordes, colluvies, squalor, foeditas!*—filth, filth, filth, filth!"—even as I wept with anger, and calling out to all the wives and children of the accused, as I'd called out at a distance to Frau Leber, I'll get them out, I'll set them free, I'll stop the pain and the loneliness and the not-knowing and the whole miserable circus of love incinerated and loyalty befouled; I'll make our hearts new again; the mutilated will walk home intact.

More loudly, Witzleben stuck to his one-word way. "Yes!" He seemed in acute pain, made worse by no teeth and the utter absence of any identifiable protocol for the occasion.

"Then I must certainly say," bellowed Freisler while the cameramen flinched, "this is unheard-of arrogance. A field marshal and a colonel general declaring they could do better than the man who is the *Leader of Us All*, the man who has extended the frontiers of the Reich to the ends of Europe, the man who has established the security of the Reich throughout the length and breadth of Europe. So you actually admit to having expressed this opinion?"

"Yes." Would he ever break down and use two?

"You will, I hope, pardon me if I use an expression like 'megalomania'? All right, you shrug your shoulders. No doubt that's a good enough answer too . . ." Freisler seemed mentally to back away, but only to lull Witzleben before he struck again hard. He was soon screaming, "You can register *that* patent in hell!" and, "What a *fiendish* crime, what a *fiendish* betrayal by a liegeman of his lord! By the soldier of his superior!" Witzleben seemed bemused by these antique terms, hardly aware, touching his wrists as if he couldn't believe the handcuffs were no longer there. Nose kept high, he didn't even change expression when Freisler changed tune and worked on him with lugubrious pity.

"You suffered from ulcers, didn't you? And, oh dear, *piles* as well! Were you *very* ill?"

"Yes." Witzleben's handkerchief had slipped, but he restored its point with a neat pluck of his right hand.

"Well," Freisler whispered with oily finesse, "I can't quite follow you in this. You see, I can understand a man being annoyed because, on account of illness, he can't *command* an *army*. But for such a man to say, 'I'm not *too* ill to *meddle* in this *conspiracy*.' Well, it doesn't seem to be quite *logical*, does it? But, of course, you could quite properly answer me, 'Herr President, *life* isn't always logical.' And you wouldn't be far wrong, either."

Witzleben said nothing, glad to keep his gums from view.

Low comedy followed as Freisler, much louder, quizzed him about his trips to and from his country estate.

"Or, rather, *Count von Lynar's* country house at Seesen?" Witzleben closed his eyelids in response. Something invisible in one corner of the chamber, high up, took his gaze, causing him to slant his face this way and that, as if looking beyond time while his mouth tightened in rough approximation to the geometry of the crude button-up collar at his neck.

"So you drove out again? Just like a *country squire?*"

"Yes, back to the country." Someone laughed at this flood of words, but ceased abruptly as Freisler went gloating on. "I say, don't we have petrol for the purpose of keeping our *tanks* on the move? You certainly did gad about with our petrol!"

Checking that handkerchief and smoothing out its point, Witzleben said haughtily, "My car does not use *petrol;* it runs on *gas.*" It sounded as if he had said, "My kind of person doesn't bandy words with the likes of you. We run on *honor.*"

All Freisler could say was "Well, surely even that could be economized?" They might have been conversing on a train, their newspapers on their laps.

"I had my *regular allowance,*" Witzleben announced.

"But not exactly for the purpose for which you *used* it! I hope I am quite clear."

Then, all of a sudden, the semi-civil fencing was over; Freisler had decided to sink his knife. As he lunged, his robe flamed in the kiln-white glare of the lights. "You were going to govern *against* the people! *You!* That's true, isn't it? *WELL?*"

Witzleben, icy-gentle: "What makes you think so?"

"You *were* going to govern against the German people!" It was that treacherous thing, the interrogative affirmation. Those present could hardly believe their ears. The interrogation was over; but Witzleben didn't know, and he even began responding with the kind of patrician bark he'd addressed to Beck, Olbricht, and me just before darkness fell on the twentieth.

"You *were—*"

"Certainly not," Witzleben snapped, the short lines round his eyes starting to flex and tremble.

On it went, *corrida* fashion.

"I need," Witzleben informed Freisler and the court, "to know where I stand. In the circumstances."

Freisler foamed with glee; Witzleben still had no idea what was going on. He backtracked a bit, asking, "So you didn't hear the Führer speak on the radio? You dashed off?"

"Yes," Witzleben sighed.

"Where to?" Very loud and very rude. "*WHERE TO?*"

"To see General Wagner." Wagner was two weeks dead already: self-shot.

"Did you tell Wagner all about it?"

Shaking his head at all this ponderous folderol, Witzleben answered, "Yes. He said, 'Let's go home.' Or something like that. I said to him, 'That notorious emetic, Corporal Hitler, is still alive and breathing. I've had enough.'"

"EMETIC? *EMETIC?* You swine, you dare . . . " Freisler was puce, but he couldn't cope with such infamy at all. He moved on. "So you went home, and that was that? Are you *DUMB?*"

Tired of this subject, Witzleben inhaled deeply and tried something else. "Will you finally inform me what you consider to be my part in the whole matter?" As if saying, cut out my liver, my heart, but at least tell me which. The field marshal had never been so plaintive, so much at anyone's mercy.

Freisler left him dangling on his own question. "That seems well enough established. You've told us all about it yourself. You stand *self-damned.*"

Witzleben hovered there, awaiting further attention, or even an answer, until the same two police lugged him off to his seat on the next to the back row of chairs, right in front of Paul von Hase, who stared straight ahead, the muscles of his jaw drawn tight. Yet Witzleben had been *seen*, and less as the humbled derelict clown, toothless and in pantaloons, than as someone stern and irascibly highhanded groomed into a new register of scornful calm. He dithered here and there, of course, just as he flashed and fumed; and yet he was so confident of himself, of what his actions had been, that he stood at the bar of justice and asked for an appraisal. Flanked again by the two policemen—the one's face a plaque of censorious gloom, the other's drawn upward into an ogreish squint—he had the look of a man honed by isolation, failure, and pain. He was sharp, with a cutting edge so keen it couldn't be felt.

27

August Seventh, P.M.

◆

'Next came the burly Hoepner, my old commander. Thinned-out now and eroded-looking, collarless, in breeches and an old cardigan, he might have come in straight from gardening: his eyes looked stained with dirt and he kept trying to muster an amiable face without an actual smile. Easy meat for Freisler, he had to endure the long, indeed the protracted, story of how he'd smuggled his uniform into the Bendlerstrasse on July twentieth.

"What a good thing you forgot to pack your Knight's Cross." Freisler sneered with histrionic solicitude. "After all, you were dismissed for *cowardice!*" He moved on at once, giving the dumbfounded Hoepner, dismissed for disobedience in 1941, and lucky a couple of weeks ago to miss the firing squad, no chance of answering back. Hoepner's face twitched, twice.

"A change at the Führer's headquarters? Why are you such a *coward*, man? Why don't you say what you mean?"

Hoepner tried in his unwieldy way. "Well, what we hoped

was that a number of generals would be able to influence him—the Führer—to bring some pressure to bear, to persuade him to give up the leadership."

With an ironclad bellow, Freisler pounced. "Pressure on *our Führer!* Well, that's enough for *us.*" But it was not; he took poor, bungling Hoepner right through the day's events at the Bendlerstrasse, ridiculing the passivity of what he called old and out-of-date officers and pointing to the muddle in which the younger ones had embroiled themselves.

"During interrogation," Freisler shouted with that awful stabbing, megaphonic voice, "you spoke of 'a trial of strength' between the National Socialist leadership and Beck's motley crew. *A trial of strength!* Right? *ARE YOU DEAF?*"

"In effect it was what I said." Hoepner shuffled with both feet, tightening his fists behind him. Had he been drugged? Certainly he seemed a soporific inferior of his usual self.

Then Freisler surprised him. "Very well, then. You can sit down. We now want the Volksgenossin Else Bergenthal. Perhaps she can give us a picture of what sort of man it was who wanted a trial of strength with our leader."

So they tried the dead Beck.

"You were a housekeeper? Where?"

"At Herr Colonel General Beck's." Her whiskery mouth shook.

"The then Colonel General Beck! Tell me, was he a strong personality who could have made an impression on the German nation?" Freisler was as soft as moss, as genial as a bribed interviewer.

"I don't know, sir. I wouldn't venture to have an opinion on that." Awed by her spurious importance at this graveyard conversation, she huffed and puffed.

"You think that's a difficult question to decide and none of my business. 'How should I, *a woman*' "—and Freisler actually muted his voice—" 'voice such an opinion?' Nevertheless, you know what kind of a man he was. Was he as firm as one would expect a soldier to be? Or was he a man given to worry and indecision?"

Still she hesitated on the brink of Beck's unknown grave, in potter's field or under a dungheap.

"I couldn't venture to say that, sir."

"Well," Freisler cooed with relish, as if surprised to have to turn the subject round, "perhaps it was possible for you to notice when you made his bed in the morning whether there were traces of *restlessness?*"

That last was the key word. "Oh yes."

"But *how?*"

"I was on holiday myself during that last fortnight, but Frau Kuster told me that he must have sweated a lot at night, and that he was very excited." Frau Kuster had told me too.

"Meaning that when he got out of bed in the morning, it was quite *wet? How disgusting.*" If only I'd been there to shout him down.

"Yes, sir." She almost curtseyed.

"That doesn't seem to indicate a particularly firm and well-disciplined man, now, does it?" He soon finished with her, informed her that she was not under oath. "We consider you an honest German woman and we accept your word, with or without an oath." Salt of the Nazi earth, she was the anti-rebel come to roost. Now Freisler brought Hoepner back in the spirit of one who keeps a prisoner warm by shoving his toes deep into the fire.

"Why did you not shoot yourself, like Beck, when you had the opportunity?" Again that death's-head leer.

"I was thinking of my family." Hoepner's gaze was dull. "Don't you understand? Salbach, my wife's furriers, had asked her to . . . try on a fur she'd, well, inherited from her mother. Firstly, that. Then I had to buy some cigars, yes, that was it. And then I had to see about a uniform, of course. I had so many things to think about. That's three. And then, fourth, I had to take my wife to Salbach's, to try on a fur."

"That was *firstly*," Freisler snapped, with a mobile leer at this meandering, muddled wreck who had been my commanding general in the Sudetenland and once a brilliant, dashing tank commander, but now couldn't connect thought with mind.

"THAT WAS FIRSTLY!" screamed Feisler in a reprise that made his lips froth. "The *Führer himself* forbade you to wear a uniform. Why should such scuttling nincompoops as you have cigars, or wives with furs? If I had a toy tank, *Herr* Hoepner, I'd stick its barrel up your nose and puncture your brain to let the poison out." Now he went back to his original question. "Why didn't you shoot yourself?"

Someone in the courtroom sighed while inhaling.

"Beck missed twice. *You* might have been a better shot. Things would not have looked so *messy*."

Hoepner drew himself up straight, presenting the full humiliation of his face to the newsreel lights. "I did not consider myself such a *Schweinehund* that I had to kill myself."

"You are not a *Schweinehund?*" The drastic bark told everyone that Freisler had yet another victim on the run. He sprawled back in his judge's chair, inhaled dramatically, then yelled, "Well, then, if you don't want to be a *Schweinehund*, tell us what zoological class you consider to be your *proper* category. Well, which one, you non-*Schweinehund?*"

Like some ponderous coxcomb, Hoepner paused as if he knew the answer already but wanted to make them wait for it. The sound camera ground away against the sounds of birds from the trees that remained. Still not a word. Freisler wooed the answer, half knowing what would come. (Had they drugged Hoepner with a script in hand?) A beam creaked. A pin fell.

"Well, what *are* you?"

"An ass."

Freisler nodded, like some long-frustrated zoologist clinching a long-fought hypothesis. Policemen took the square-head-

ed ass back to his seat and left him alone with the ghost of
Beck.

Peter Yorck came next, a man far wilier than Hoepner, with
no free gifts for sadists. At once Freisler taunted him, but Peter
Yorck wasn't really in court at all, he was at home, where he
belonged, either in his small house in the Hortensienstrasse, in
Lichterfelde, not that far from Beck, or in the big house in the
Great Park at Klein-Oels, which had a superb library of some
150,000 books, as well as a notable collection of woodcuts and
engravings. Liszt and Rubinstein had played there; Hegel and
Schelling had been family friends. It was as if there were no
past where the past had been, and all things were contributive-
ly present; indeed, he had six sisters and three brothers, in
whom the past had come to reassert itself, multiplied many
times over, lest there be losses. Dissenting elites, having always
had in the family enough crystal, never needed the psychopathic outlet of a *Kristallnacht*, but had to make doubly sure
of the odds. At home a genial, calm smiler with wide-spaced
big front teeth, he became chillier and even sardonic when in
other surroundings. His manner in that courtroom was a scal-
pel of honed ice.

"I do have your attention, *Count!*"

"No," said Peter curtly; he belonged elsewhere.

"For a few of your valuable moments, then?"

"Only if you ask politely."

Freisler held himself in check, but only just. *"Please!"*

"Well?"

"Are you attending?"

"Here I am." Peter gave a faintly shaded grin. "Say something interesting."

"I should compliment you on your truthfulness under interrogation. You didn't *hold much back*, did you?"

Yorck stared through him.

"You people don't lie much, except in little things. You tell
the truth to save yourselves, you lie to save the others." This

went on for some minutes until Freisler saw that Yorck did not rise to the bait. Then he fished in another way. "You never joined the Party?"

"No, I did not join the Party." A parallel like rock.

"Nor any of its subsidiaries?"

"No."

"Why on earth not?" Said with gloating geniality.

"Because, on principle, I didn't happen to be a National Socialist."

"Very well. That's clear enough." A new tone had come to the fore; if they bullied Peter Yorck, he would just recite the facts again and again.

". . . I did not approve," he told Freisler moments later.

"You didn't *approve!* You stated that you were against our policy of rooting out Jews and that you didn't approve of the National Socialist concept of right."

"What matters," Yorck told him as if giving a tutorial to some slow lout from a urinal reserved for Party syphilitics, "is the connecting link between all these questions—the state's totalitarian hold on the citizen, excluding the individual's religious and moral obligations before God."

Freisler's face rippled with fury: he was going to have to argue with this one, and he did, for some time holding forth on the "deep moral concept" of the Party line. Then he called Yorck an anarchist.

"I," Yorck said quietly, "wouldn't put it that way." Nor, he implied, would anyone with half an education, a quarter of a heart, one-fiftieth of a brain.

Now Freisler asked about his role on the twentieth. "Did you have some prior notification . . . ?"

"Yes." Although his hands rested on the back of the chair in front of him, Yorck seemed to be gaining strength; he stared before him with almost propulsive zeal.

"When?" Freisler seemed out of steam, perhaps because he operated at full blast only when there was scope for some loud-mouthed sadism.

"On eighteen July."

"From whom? Was it Schwerin von Schwanenfeld?"

"Yes."

There was some more quibbling, then: "What did he tell you? That Stauffenberg had landed at Rangsdorf?"

"Yes." Again Yorck drew strength from the fug and, half opening his mouth as he killed a yawn, exposed his big wide-spaced front teeth.

"And that the attempt had succeeded?"

"Yes, that was the first message. They all believed it."

Freisler could hardly contain his disgust. "How *utterly horrible!* Think how National Socialism has trusted these people! There we've got three men: Count von Stauffenberg, Count Yorck von Wartenburg, and Schwerin—who is also a count, I believe? *Three* slobbering pigdog aristocrats?"

Yorck didn't answer him, perhaps still pondering Freisler's lumbering attempt to expound the Nazi attitude to religion. "You believers can oil your souls all you want," said Freisler, "but keep away from *us* with your pious demands. . . . Your souls, after all, can do their fluttering around in *the other world.* Here on earth our *present* life counts." There was no answer to that, only perhaps a quick sigh in the air, a shrug timed to set off a curt, ironic bow. Having only half-heard, Yorck bowed.

Last of the day came Klausing, who had given himself up after getting right away, and Bernardis, who had been watching it all with clean, unimplicated-looking avidity, whereas Klausing, at least as a spectator, looked mostly down.

About seven, Lautz, the chief prosecutor, who had been silent up to now, denounced the defendants in formal terms as well as the army for shielding them. He then requested the death penalty whose mode, hanging, S'gruber had already decided with the executioner in their tête-à-tête.

Freisler had not finished, of course, so he ordered a recess until the following day. Back went the eight accused, in trucks, to their cells, for their last night; there was no doubt of that, the whole of Germany knew it, and the only thing in doubt was how to while the time away if left in peace. They had virtually nothing to say to one another. Their wooden clogs rasped on the cement floor of their cells. The rusted springs of their noxious broken mattresses gave out an occasional hoarse twang. Their bellies rumbled, their heads felt light, their eyelids grated with every blink. After their day in court, they had more in common than they didn't, certainly more in common than they began the day with; and each to the others sounded like a skeleton moving around. Their fates had fused.

In Bamberg, when on leave, with the boys and little Valerie intervening busily in everything I did (just to be close), I'd shift a log or check the sit of a fence, almost always managing to move my hand through an unseen cobweb, which then trailed faintly from my wrist until I brushed it off. In similar fashion, the Plötzensee eight had in the course of one day moved their entire bodies through as many cobwebs as you find in a lifetime, and so felt the invisible, faint tracery of death. It would take an entire other lifetime to tell how this tracery felt, and this they would not have. They could tell in smuggled letters: that was all.

28
August Eighth

◆

August 8, 1944, one of the foulest days in German history, brought Witzleben back to the stand after what had visibly been a wretched night. Men had been kinder to butterflies, lettuces, bits of quartz. Again Freisler went after him, turning each word into a harsh caricature of itself. His first question sounded like a series of orders on a parade ground: "Why—did—you—think—a *conspiracy*—could—succeed? *WAKE—UP!*"

"I thought that reliable units were available." Nothing was clearer now than the answer to Witzleben's fumbling inquiry of the day before. Where he stood was blatant as the scorching sun: he was the ringleader, or at least the only one left alive.

"You mean *reliable* in your own sense, as well as senior officers who might be induced to join?"

"Yes." Witzleben's trousers were drooping again, but he still had the point of handkerchief in his top pocket: a last flash of etiquette.

"And that, as you said, was a basic error?"

Again Witzleben agreed, a bedraggled aquiline man who wanted these proceedings done with, come what may.

"And this is your opinion at present?" Freisler was preparing the ground for some further denunciation, but Witzleben was a straightforward soldier, never one of the wily ones.

"Yes." He stared vacantly in front of him; he had not even had slop for breakfast.

"MEANING," bellowed Freisler as he warmed to the kill, "to use your own words when interrogated by the police, that you 'had been basically in error, having misjudged the National Socialist attitude of the officers'?"

"Yes." Spoken in a dull dark-brown undertone. Once again Freisler had proved, at least to his own satisfaction, that the conspiracy was the work of a tiny clique and in no way represented the sentiments of the army as a whole.

"*IN FACT,*" Freisler was unnecessarily proclaiming, in something between a boom and a yelp, "this clique of officers was in the pay of the Allies. They were Allied agents. But how the Allies would have sneered if the putsch had succeeded! Its very failure is honey to them. What do *they* care? All they have is a sweet tooth for German misery, whichever way things go."

Witzleben was bundled back to his seat and the former City Commandant, Paul von Hase, the only one so far not arraigned, now had to go over the same drab ground, which he did in clipped, brisk sentences, never once coming out from behind his mask of officerly stoicism. This was the man who, in ironic travesty of his role as commandant of the Berlin jails, had taken food and drink to his nephew, Dietrich Bonhoeffer in the Wehrmacht Interrogation Prison, Tegel, and had remained with him for over five hours, talking about all manner of things, from the death of his (Hase's) mother to how Gieseking played Beethoven, from a display of phosphorus bombs to Berlin beer and rambles in the Black Forest, from a little heirloom rosewood cupboard and Don Quixote and circumcision to hot countries versus cold ones, *Proverbs 24.11* ("Rescue those who are being taken away to death; hold back those who are stumbling to the slaughter"), and Dietrich's recollection of how it had felt to travel from icebound North America into the blooming vegetation of Cuba, where he had been asked to preach. "I almost succumbed to the sun cult," he said. "To me the sun's a living power, not an astronomical entity," which his uncle answered with a story of his own, about a wounded ensign who cried out on the field of battle, "I am wounded. Long live the King!" only to have General von Löwenfeld, also wounded, call out to him "Be quiet, ensign! We die here in silence."

The Hase who had drunk four bottles of *Sekt* with his nephew on June 30th, making a great display of how close to Dietrich he was, did not know how to waver. His fierce, old-fashioned autonomy declared itself in concise sentences trim as his mustache and sharp as the brushed uptwist (like an ear of black corn) in his right eyebrow.

"Yes," he told Freisler curtly, "I had heard from Olbricht that an attempt would be made on July 15th. Yes." Hase looked carved in ivory and coal.

"What did you say?"

"I couldn't say anything. I was too dumbfounded."

"But," Freisler stormed, "he had given you PRECISE OR-DERS and he surely expected a PRECISE *RESPONSE?* After all, any day, any moment, there could have been a report: 'Führer assassinated.' You couldn't just walk off with all this left in mid-air. And you *didn't!*"

Hase shrugged his mouth. What a beautiful stance the man had: erect, hands clasped behind his back, his eyes traveling through Freisler and beyond. *"No,"* he said, proud he could say it at all.

"But?" Freisler exploded, his face a sheen of wet as he wait-ed for the rest of Hase's statement.

"I said *Jawohl,* and then went out and got the written or-ders." Once more Freisler went over the events of July twenti-eth, as if schooling everyone for a history examination, and then it was over, apart from the trumped-up defense speeches: "a thankless task," the counsels protested to a man.

"You might ask," said Dr. Weissmann, there to "represent" Witzleben, " 'Why conduct a defense at all?' It is stipulated by the letter of the law, and, moreover, at a time such as this in our view it is part of the defense's task to help the court find a verdict." He smiled the face of black seaweed and broken bones. "Undoubtedly in some of the trials it will prove impossi-ble even for the best counsel to find *anything* to say in defense or mitigation of the accused. . . . One really has to try extreme-ly hard to come up with any word in their favor." On went the "defense," a long cold needle in each man's back. "Witzleben? An ulcerous hyena," said Weissmann.

Now each defendant was given a last chance to speak, to make a formal statement. Lautz had once again asked for the death penalty for all.

Blinking a lot, Witzleben said in a clear, high voice, "You can hand us over to the hangman. In three months the enraged and tormented people will call you to account, and will drag you alive through the muck in the gutter." Tugged away again, he almost reeled, weightless as a dehydrated bird, and his eyes bleached by fatigue. His stare had closed.

"I did it for Germany," Stieff said mechanically, his entire upper torso a fidget. "I ask to be shot. I was misled throughout the whole affair." Lying now to save someone else.

"Nothing to say," Yorck said resonantly, unperturbed and mentally going over a letter to his wife, Marion, which she would not receive until April 1945, when the ubiquitous SS General Stundt came prancing to see her with an out-of-the-blue offer: a state pension, which she refused, at the same time demanding the letter, which with a leer he gave her right away. "It seems that we are standing at the end of our beautiful and rich life together. . . . I hope my death will be accepted as an atonement for all my sins, and as an expiatory sacrifice."

"*Guilty,*" called Bernardis. "I have a bad heart, but I ask to be shot as befitting an officer and a gentleman." Peter Yorck was deep into a thought his letter spelled out at length.

"Guilty," said Klausing, which he had given himself up to be able to say. "Shooting, if you please."

"I did not act out of any motive of personal gain," Hoepner told them in his fumbling way. "I ask that my family be provided for."

Yorck was kindling the torch of life in the midst of a sea of incendiary bombs, rubbing his fingernails hard against his sleeve.

"I did not really know what the explosives were for," Hagen claimed, and left it at that.

Freisler now tapered things off with a detailed account of Beck's suicide and the executions after Fromm's kangaroo court. "Some have already paid for their *treason.* Yes, let us name it! A few bullets, and an irrelevant clique was wiped out. Germany was cleansed." On he raved, his master's voice. They adjourned for lunch, after which Freisler delivered himself of a fat summary, bloated with wooden maxims and endless recapitulations of everything said over the past few days. The de-

fendants looked half asleep, of all men the least concerned
with what he said all the way to four-thirty, when he sentenced them to death and they were rehandcuffed, dragged
out of the courtroom, and shoved with unnecessary force into
trucks.

On the way back to the jail, Stieff tried to smile at Witzleben, whose eyes had closed up dry. Peter Yorck's mind spun
the pure gold of the fatalist. Paul von Hase plucked sideways
at his badly trimmed mustache, aching to clip it for the final
act. The police guards looked grimmer than the condemned.
No one said a word inside that hollow in time.

Over at Plötzensee Prison everything was ready; the outcome had never been in doubt. The ghoulish place buzzed
with excitement and a new smell floated along its dank corridors: burned wood mixed with stale onion. By five-fifteen the
convicted eight had arrived and fifteen minutes later had been
fitted out with prison clothes and wooden clogs.

During a lull on that steamy evening, a grinning coarse-nos-
triled police sergeant taunted Stieff about his newly reassumed
prison garb: "Now you're wearing the *right* kind of general's
stripes!"

But he said no more when Stieff, with a demure little pucker of his cheeks, answered, "What do *you* know about what's
honorable on a day like this?"

So that the camermen could film the condemned in shackles
in their cells, the doors were opened wide and the cells flooded
with light. Elsewhere in the prison, as all other activity ceased
and officials began arriving in the company of Gestapo, a couple of "trusties" who served as prison librarians or clerks
shoved a table under their window and looked out. It was
about seven o'clock. Already the first of the condemned, Witzleben, was being led across the courtyard, filmed the whole
way, escorted by two warders: somnambulistically erect. The
rest followed, also filmed, with a column of officials bringing
up the rear.

"Away from the window!" a police sergeant yelled at the librarians as if rebuking errant boys, but, once he had gone, they rigged up a small mirror after the fashion of a periscope and saw that no priest had joined the procession. The last pair of wooden clogs tromped across the courtyard to the creeper-wreathed trellis just outside the execution shed and went in through the open iron gate.

Now the eight stood in a single row facing a black curtain while the public prosecutor, Kurt-Walter Hanssen, read the death sentence, adding the words "Defendants, you have been sentenced by the People's Court to death by hanging. Executioner, perform your function."

His natural sadism egged on by orders to protract and to feel free to humiliate the eight in whatever way he chose, S'gruber's appointed ghoul showed a victor's relish, knowing the odds of an executioner's surviving his victim were stupendous, and moved up and down the line, badgering those annulled souls with his notorious humor, guffawing about anything that came to mind.

"No chance of syphilis from the wife tonight, lads!" He winked and leered. "This is the best cure for constipation in Germany. Bunged up, General? We'll soon cure that." The same leer as before continued into this and subsequent remarks, although he could not sustain the wink. "Not had it up for months, duckie? We'll make it jump tonight. You'll go out with a splash, no fear!" At this point he seemed to wish to make a speech, a kind of professional's policy statement, but he failed to muster the pose at the right distance (the curtain was too close, so he was on top of the eight). All that came out was a ghastly reference to his prowess.

"Some thousand heads or necks—oh yes, *I*'ve not been idling the war away, gentlemen. I've had them all in here: Czechs, nuns, Poles, Frenchies, countesses, clergymen, cripples, beards, twins, dwarfs, gypsies, Jews, madmen, children, but I'll tell you this, you lucky lads, I've never yet done a nigger or a dog, I think the good Lord's got it in for me, he surely has. *Now,* if there's any noise, you'll get a towel in your mouth, so you might as well come quietly. Best rest easy, boys, you'll soon have a toad between your cheeks. I wonder who's got the biggest balls." His gaze fixed on Hoepner, whose gaze had embedded itself in the coarse but dense mesh of the curtain.

Not even the denatured language of emergency could answer such filth, and no one did. It was still light outside, with a few swallows cleaving the drained mauve of the sky and the first cicadas beginning to creak. From the other side of the curtain came a few clanks, then a tinnier scrape, followed by the sound of a table being grated into position. Still manacled, the eight kept their line straight, no longer having (as in court) a clock to ogle. They were so deep inside themselves that they would never come out again, neither to attend to Röttger the hangman nor even to die. Was that why he kept taunting them, to provoke a response, so as not to hang men already dead?

"Soon be taller for your next date," he said in a spit-thick whisper to the impassive Stieff, who had never looked taller in his life.

He tried them all and, by mistake, almost the public prosecutor, a man incapable of aversion and keenly aware that Röttger had orders from the on-high.

Bad breath, like rancid cabbage, into Klausing's bone-sharp face. "Don't worry, darling, you'll stick it in a hot one tonight. Sorry we can't offer a cigar."

Then, to Hase, "Any message for the church? Sorry we don't run to crosses. We could hang you real slow with a rosary, though, till you seemed the right color." Hase might have been reading a timetable of trains as he set off for a fishing holiday.

Bernardis received only "We'll blow your nose *in there,* whoever *you* are." Bernardis was in pain to begin with.

At Hagen he just laughed hysterically, incredulous that he should have to bother with such a tiro. "Do me a favor, sweetie, swallow your tongue." Hagen merely squinted at him.

"You'll take longest," he told the zinc-white Hoepner. "I

have orders. We mustn't lose *you* too soon, oh no. You should thank the Führer for taking such a personal interest in you."

Yorck he told, "You'd guillotine right nicely, milord. Got the neck for it, if you don't mind my saying so. But the machine's in disfavor, has been since 1942. Would you like to go away now and come back later? Ha. *Ha.* Special favor to a man of quality!" Yorck took a deep breath of aloof contempt, and that was all.

"Well, my lovebirds," he gobbled, eyes in ceaseless motion, his mouth assuming extraordinary shapes full of straight lines and obtuse angles, "we'd better make a start, hadn't we now? The wife says I'll get a cold supper if I'm not back on time. No sympathy with a master craftsman, eh?" He paused in front of Witzleben, who braced himself involuntarily and opened his eyes, at the same time trying to nudge off his arm the hand of the warder called Hoffmann.

"You first, Erwin, my lad. Now, none of your flatulence, if you please! There's decent gentlemen to follow within the hour, see?" He turned and pushed through the curtain, the split in which emitted blinding light from the reflectors set up in the execution chamber to ensure that S'gruber's ongoing movie would register all. He held the curtain as Hanssen went through to take up his position, and then bellowed as if the line of condemned men were several hundred meters away and refusing to budge, "Come on. Come on, let's have you now!" Then he beckoned at Witzleben, in whose head an empty igloo echoed where his mind had been. He'd found himself unable to think of his family, his nestlings, any more.

The warders holding Witzleben were too slow to respond. Out from the other room, through the head-wide gap in the curtain that revealed nothing save two barred windows, came the exacerbated roar: "I'll have *him* now! *Bring him here!*" They did, making up for having dawdled by bustling him at a speed greater than he could manage in clogs.

29

"Austrian Method"
(Octet)

◆

The monstrosity behind the curtain was a low room with whitewashed walls. Just under the ceiling ran a heavy girder on which slid eight hooks fetched from butchers in the neighborhood. In one corner was the movie camera and against one wall sat a small table with a bottle of cognac and glasses. Over in the corner was the guillotine, like something antique thrown out by a 24-hour laundry. Whereas the cells had been bad enough, with no toilet, no basin, no water, no mat, and no privacy, this terrible above-ground cellar, with its moldy walls, blood-smeared sloping floor, and slime-caked manhole lid, all cast in relief by the avalanche of light from the studio reflectors, was the image of a last place. It was where everything died, even the idea of death as a release. It had no more conscience than a churning star. It had haunted me for years.

That is what Witzleben saw as he tromped in on his clogs, ungainly as a marionette, perhaps not even hearing the dead clop of wood on the concrete floor. Shod thus, he trod on a dimension that had no give in it.

With a sadistic chuckling feint at the guillotine, they frogmarched him to the end of the room, all the time urging him to get a move on. Once there, he was obliged to make an about-face, his head held high. Off came his handcuffs, his shirt. Round his neck went a loop of thin hempen cord, the loop at the other end of which they put on the first hook after lifting him between them (Röttger slipped it over the hook's point). Then they eased him down, the noose tightened gradually, and Witzleben began to strangle even as they slid his pants off once the clogs had dropped. The camera missed none of this, although it could not smell the soiled pants from the last wearers, or what began pooling under him as he twisted, unable even to gasp. Face dark as liver. Froth. Penis like the iron crotch struts that jutted out, with metal foreskin flared, from the burning stakes of the Inquisition. Not a sound as they uplifted him, a thin calf—one holding him round the waist, the other under the arms—to his looped reward; and those behind the curtain, ears pitched for the slightest sound, heard only a small sigh as they heaved him up, the hollow knock as the clogs fell, and Röttger abusing him to the very end, in the low raucous voice of a disappointed parent. Witzleben's eyelids fluttered on.

They referred to this as the "Austrian method." Thus, so-called traitors died by foreign means borrowed from S'gruber's native land.

The two sound-cameramen were immobile behind the blazing lamps, with playing-card features, obliquely askance or front-on shallow: mere functionaries compared to the two assistants able to take life as if removing your hand from a banister. Blowing hard through taut lips to keep the cigarette smoke from their eyes, these gasped and perspired as the evening wore on, each of them with a wedding ring on the appropriate finger. Where did they find such men?

Now it was time to march Paul von Hase in through the gap in the curtain, but all he could see of Witzleben was a narrow body-length black drape, concealing the body's full width (the twisting had stopped). Giving them nothing to work with or exploit, he slapped them with his non-presence, and so occupied less of their time than Witzleben. He gave them his deadly aloof look and was raised.

Stieff, when his turn came, mustered a smile of sick jubilation, which he prolonged even as they gazed, first making his smile haughtier, then supercilious, then full of broken grandeur as if he were going to shout, "Alleluia," only to fix his lips at last in an irate gape that a dentist might have arranged with pads of cotton and wads of cardboard. Out of this, or from its midst, he actually laughed at them with defiant hoarseness, at which they seized him and put him up. I should have been with them, strangling and voiding, with my cousin Peter Yorck, and my sometime adjutant Klausing, and the others, even Hoepner, whom they kept for last to make him suffer most. Imagine, as they haled him in, seeing the seven bodies dangling behind blackout cloth at intervals along the girder, and Röttger smirking into the camera, at his Führer, with a half wink tightening his eye to a garlic clove.

But history lied. They did not use piano wire. Nor was the hook forced up into the head through the tender slot beneath the chin. Something beyond the five known senses kept them brave all the way to the hook, and then beyond, hurting, twirling, shuddering until the last thin line of consciousness went dead. I had made beeves of eight good men; and because of me scores more padded barefoot and naked in the corridors of the converted arts-and-crafts school at 8 Prinz Albrecht Strasse, headquarters of the Gestapo.

Unspeakable and unwatchable, the film of that evening's events, all the way from the pitiful eight squatting in shackles in their cells to the last agonized twist, went to S'gruber that very night for him to drool over. Goebbels hid his eyes, unable to look; but Gruppenführer Fegelein, the illiterate jockey married to Eva Braun's sister, and a survivor of my bomb, looked hard and long at the atrocities, wishing Stauffenberg had dangled from the girder too. Later on, at Wolf's Lair, the SS turned out for a special film show of their own, but not a single army officer showed up, and when the film was tried out on cadet audiences in Berlin the effect on morale was so awful that all copies were eventually destroyed on S'gruber's and Goebbels's express command. Anyone who watched such an obscenity, for whatever reason, had become a half-accomplice, and was already halfway to the flank of S'gruber himself, alone in his private stench, briefing the rotten Röttger, who then briefed his two aides. Never forget those three, the technicians of death, one an unmilitary fat youth with fair hair and a shiny metal plate mounted in his scalp. The other had a pumice-gray face and bloodshot almond eyes, a voice like a hoarse and antagonistic waiter. Röttger himself had olive-black eyes, a bad shave, and bee-stung maroon lips over a scooped-out cleft chin like the top of a wickless used candle. Three ghouls: the last thing seen by thousands. Three heads, like rotting balloons of hell, their three minds one long revolving fecal joke. *Consummatum est,* some pastor said when all the eight were dead; but it was not over, only likely not to go on forever.

The coda to this butcher's-window display was viler than anything. Off went the bodies to the Anatomical Institute of Berlin University, in little decrepit backfiring trucks that came and went twice a week; Berthold and I had been there ourselves, not long ago. The Institute's head, Dr. Stieve, knowing some of his own friends were among the dead, had the bodies cremated untouched and the urns, most of them, interred at Marzahne Cemetery, which was later bombed; but Thierack, the Minister of Justice, duped him, taking them with him, one or two at a time, whenever he drove off to his estate in the Teltow district for the weekend, and clandestinely burying them in this or that forest glade. Then a bottle of beer for relief when he was finished. We none of us knew where we were, just as none of our relatives knew either, but once in a while a mote of Beck, a flake of Peter Yorck, blew into what was left of me and a brief pulverized ditty began as the wind fondled our atoms thus, and ended as it dropped.

30

Two Lions, Two Doves

◆

Two days later Fritzi, draped in some abominable cast-off suit worn by several condemned men before him, raised high in the courtroom his bold, rugged face with its distorted nose and its saber slashes, and raked Freisler with his sarcasm, tightening his eye to hold a monocle long gone.

"Wait three months. The situation in which you will find yourself is precisely that from which we set out."

"Count Schulenburg—" Freisler began. At his oiliest.

"*Criminal* Schulenburg, if you please! Throughout these proceedings you have called me 'Criminal,' not 'Count,' not '*Graf*' but '*Straf*.' Kindly do not weaken at the last jump." They'd stomped his monocle to bits.

Freisler's face mutated—flushed and then wanned—as if a plague had marched through him. "Red Graf," as we used to call Fritzi, was at it again. Face of the scrupulous pugilist, mouth set in an Olympian sneer, hands clasped in front of him as if fondling a grenade. He *belonged* in an arena.

Brother Berthold went even less easily. During his interrogation he'd kept begging to be told if his brother was alive or dead: a prudent enough question, although he was not asking out of prudence, not he. In court, flanked by two policemen whose clothes and insignia seemed to be *wearing them* (one impassive, in glasses, but affable-mouthed, the other sunken-faced and daunted by so much pomp), he looked like some haggard tennis champion, with open-necked shirt and a passable sports jacket. His face wholly at attention, with Heidelberg, Jena, Berlin, Tübingen (hard universities) far behind him, he had already made his statement, to Maria, his wife: "We cannot succeed, and yet we have to do it." He even knew the exact dimensions of the bomb. Hounded by Freisler, he at times derisively talked Greek, non-answering with the dry clatter of Aristophanes' frogs: *"Brekeke-kex, koax, koax,"* which gave the cognoscenti in the courtroom a sickened laugh. But not Freisler. "What," he roared, "was *that?* If you want to vomit, you'll have to go outside."

"Brekeke-kex, koax, koax."

Now Freisler leaned to ask someone sitting beside him, "Did you catch it? What was that?" without getting an answer. So he asked elsewhere, only, in the middle of being told what Berthold was saying, to bawl with jutting head into the courtroom at large, "Do I hear giggling? I can assure you, and not the condemned only, this is no laughing matter. I mean the accused. Now," in a much lower voice, even as constrained laughing began again, "what the hell is he on about?" Told, he bawled right from his slouch at the straight-faced Berthold, "GREEK! You come in here and talk *Greek?* Isn't good honest German fit for your slobbering aristocratic trap? *Greek!* I'll give you Greek. You'll have a Greek neck before we're through with you, and you'll quote something a damned sight different then. Quote, will you? I'll teach you to quote, you navy bunny rabbit."

"I already know. *Brekeke-kex—*"

"Stop it now or I'll have you removed."

"I wouldn't mind," Berthold said trimly. "You don't like frogs, that's clear. Or sailors. Or rabbits. We're not going to get on. *Brekeke—*"

"*Frogs* is it? You Stauffenbergs amaze me. You get nothing right. You have no sense of occasion, no dignity, no respect for authority, law, Germany, the Party, the Führer, your own family, your children, your wives, your parents, your ancestors, your regiment, your birthplace, your name, your reputa-

tion, your *title*, even. You babble a piece of Greek at me and
expect me to bow the knee, is that it? I can see that the bene-
fits of a classical education belong under a manure heap. Now,
say that piece of claptrap Greek again, and we'll see where it
leads you within a few hours."

"Not when I'm *told* to," Berthold said silkily. "Greek is op-
tional, even here, and Latin isn't compulsory, especially when
the officers of the kangaroo court are just a bunch of jumped-
up illiterate psychopaths to whom a book's as foreign as original sin is to a cockroach in heat." Sniggers again.

"*Brek*—" Freisler foolishly began, in sweating, livid echola-
lia. "What was that twaddle you spouted?"

"Aristophanes, sir. Hardly what *you* used to read in school.
You'd never get past the alphabet."

"Don't try to provoke me. What did you say?"

"It was a chorus of frogs just frogging."

"So, then," Freisler yelled in the biggest, most insensate non
sequitur of his life, "you hate the Führer, you want him dead,
you and your damned frogs? Answer that!" flung at Berthold
with a leer of goggling triumph; but Berthold, like Odysseus,
whom he knew by heart, had seen men converted into swine,
and his face, with only hours to go, had taken its cue with a noble finality that rode easily on his jokes. Eyes widened so as to
miss nothing; chin thrust forward and down; mouth swollen,
not from being beaten (or not recently, anyway), but more
than ever shoved truculently outward. Unshaven. Used-look-
ing. No longer the chic naval lieutenant who gossiped with
Kranzfelder, he stared them down with his terrible matter-of-
fact gaze that held in perfect diapason both contempt and indifference, both shock and the preposterous half-giddy certainty that he was looking with eyes that would not see the
next day dawn. He held still, his hands in the too-long sleeves
gently crisscrossed before him in light composure. Only three
years later did his last message reach his children, written as

neatly as a handcuffed man can write. It delivered him up to them and away from the ghouls in Plötzensee and assigned him to a flawless futurity of heirs who could see him plain.

My beloved children, My dear Alfred, My dear Elisabeth,

Always think with pride of your father, who wanted the best for his country and people. Be pure and strong, great and true, and remember always that you must live nobly, true to your birth. From now on life for your mother will be very, very hard, and I beg you to do all you can to make her life as beautiful as possible and to give her a little joy and happiness. You, too, should try to be cheerful and enjoy yourselves, despite the heavy burden. That will give you strength and make your mother happy. How I long to see you once more and hold you in my arms. I kiss you, my Alfred, and you, my Elisabeth most affectionately.

Your father.

Berthold had the directness of the introvert. In court he told them that he and I were not so-called Catholic believers in the proper sense, that we didn't go to church very often, or to confession. "My brother and I believe," he told them, "that Christianity is unlikely to produce anything creative." In his very statement I lived on! What did they do to him in the Gestapo cellars when he said, "Nearly all the basic ideas of National Socialism were *completely reversed* by the regime"? They slapped him.

The Kaltenbrunner reports paid him tribute:

... one of the very few who remained utterly incorrigible and fanatic. His short evidence was the clearest and most important document indicting Hitler that may ever have been written and shown to him. It manifested a type of German manhood with deep religious, political and artistic principles, utterly divorced from Hitler and National Socialism.

All this in private, never quoted in the court lest he turn the tables on them and indict the accusers! The kings of latter-day

Sparta could have done no better. He and Fritzi made no attempt to defend themselves, but only to express how deeply they felt; after all, when death was certain, better a trumpet voluntary than an excuse.

So, then, only a few hours after Freisler made his final warty hurrumph at him, they went behind the curtain, Fritzi first. Two lions. Two doves. Two of *us*. Followed by our friend Kranzfelder.

After weeks on the run like the Wandering Jew, with knapsack and staff, Goerdeler took refuge in a country inn and ordered breakfast. He left before it came, though, and ran into the woods near the village of Konradswalde, where he was soon apprehended. The Luftwaffe Waf eying him from the table she shared with a couple of air force men had indeed known him, just as she had seemed familiar to him. For turning him in she got one million marks, personally presented by S'gruber himself. Yet it wasn't much of a chase.

"It was *Goerdeler!*" she whispered. "I swear it's him!"

"Where?" Goerdeler had gone, a decrepit ghost.

"That table there. The one like a tramp, with the white face and gray hair." The hunt began, for a man too tired to run. He gave up with a calm, pastoral smile. Breakfastless.

On the next day they started in on him with drugs, and he began to deluge the Gestapo with misinformation or non-information mixed in with useless but astonishingly precise matters of fact. They hardly knew how to cope with him, little realizing that his far-reaching statements embodied what he saw as the moral core of the opposition to S'gruber.

31

Schlabrendorff & Others

◆

Back on July 21st, after an order of the day extolled Tresckow as a model officer lamentably murdered by cutthroat partisans, Schlabrendorff went off with the body to Brandenburg, as ordered, and then returned to Ostrov to sit things out. Major Kuhn had already gone over to the Russian lines, and Schlabrendorff kept a pistol by his bed against emergencies, though more to soothe him than to use.

On August seventeenth, a hand grabbed him by the throat from a fitful sleep; but, although his pistol was within reach, for suicide or resistance, something prompted him to do nothing and trust his luck. For reasons he could not fathom, he was convinced that he would escape the Gestapo. On his way to Berlin, he was put in a house only the front of which had a guard while the back door opened onto a nearby woods. Yet he chose not to run. Nor did he run when he had another chance, when he could have melted into the crowd at the railroad terminal in Berlin, swarming with refugees. The moment came: the two sergeants were carrying his baggage, the officer was telephoning for a military car. There Schlabrendorff stood, virtually unguarded, a doomed man suddenly offered a reprieve as the mob heaved and split, then sealed up again, making him lurch this way and that in time with its pulsation. No, he decided, he would have no guarantee of food or shelter, without which an escape into Berlin was pointless. It could be said, then, that on a summer evening he *allowed* himself to be installed in the Gestapo prison in Prinz Albrecht Strasse, where the civility of his military escort gave way to the loutish knockabout of the criminal police.

After two days in solitary confinement, he was taken to the cellars for interrogation, and on the way down caught sight of Goerdeler and Canaris, both in floodlit open cells, and in a washroom, Fromm, a prisoner since July 21st. Schlabrendorff denied everything, even when confronted with false documents that seemed to incriminate him. Then they put him in chains and began to question him more boisterously, calling him names (compound words using "wife" or "mother" or "shit"), but only becoming, by his own standards as a criminal lawyer, clumsier and clumsier. Sometimes they would haul him from his cell, then just leave him alone in an anteroom without being interrogated at all. Sometimes they used a three-man team, one of whom reviled and threatened, one of whom pretended to soothe and might offer a cigarette, while the third prated of honor.

"Now then, shitlicker, tell us about these people or you'll be shot this evening, right through the groin."

"Calmly, sir. Collect yourself, we can't have you answering off the top of your head, can we now? Smoke? No, it's quite all right, go ahead. No? Very well. Do you mind if we resume?" The velvet lifebelt, sleek to save.

"Don't you think, as an officer and a gentleman, that you owe certain answers to the conscience of the nation?"

Divide and conquer, but Schlabrendorff was too canny; in courtrooms across Germany he had outwitted and demolished better inquisitors than these. The Gestapo soon lost their patience and Commissioner Habecker struck him in the face.

"Vile and illegal treatment," lawyer Schlabrendorff told them through the blood in his mouth. He got a cold-water douche.

Then they thrashed him with leather switches and bamboos. The commissioner, a Security Police sergeant, a civilian, and a girl about twenty got to work on him in four stages, first pinioning his hands behind him and forcing needles into his fingertips with a thumbscrew, then strapping him face down on a bedstead and forcing cylinders over his legs, after which they turned a screw, and nails inside the cylinders pierced the flesh. Now the bed became a rack on which they stretched him, gradually or in jerks, and finally they tied him in a ball and belabored him from behind with heavy clubs, each blow slapping him forward onto his face. After he passed out, they dragged him back to his cell, where the guards turned away in pity and disgust after laying him back on his cot in his blood-soaked underwear. On the following day he had a heart attack, and a token visit from a doctor. A few days later they began to torture him again, in the same fashion. The girl smacked him with relish and spat on him.

"What you have enjoyed so far," Habecker told him with wolfish hauteur, "is as nothing to the *horrible* things that will come." He smirked at the truculent, clammy girl, who pointed a sharpened pencil at Schlabrendorff's groin.

Schlabrendorff decided at once that he must ponder some way of killing himself; thus far he had revealed not a single name. Once he began to ponder, however, he hit on another way of saving himself and told his interrogators, "Tresckow told Oertzen he was planning to persuade the Führer to hand over the conduct of the war to one of the field marshals." At once they left him alone, warning him that they would return, but inexplicably leaving him in some kind of peace. His body felt as if it had exploded, but its pieces were coming back together, ill-matched and ragged, yet unmistakably his. Would he ever practice law again?

Without warning the Gestapo frog-marched him from his cell to a waiting car, and Schlabrendorff made up his mind: *This* was how it happened, not always with a bloodthirsty oaf roaring, "Come on, now, let's have you!" as the cell doors opened for the last time, or with a slow, polite ritual that ended with a bullet through the back of the neck. Sometimes you went to your end alone, chauffeured by clean-collared psychopaths, and riding through high summer at speed.

"Where is this?" Had he actually asked? Already he knew,
from the barbed wire and the watchtowers, the dogs and
guards, the reek of burning bone that reminded him of glue
made from fish. "Sachsenhausen," someone told him, and he
mentally added the dreadful suffix "concentration camp."
How his heart fluttered at that moment.

"Come." Half thinking he was going to be confined in the
camp, though for who knew how long, he soon saw a different
end right in front of him. Sandbags, a trench, sturdy posts
erected at regular intervals, and some distance away small concrete pads for the machine-gun crews.

They conducted him all the way to one of the posts and
stood staring at him with sulky loathing. No blindfold, no red
card to flutter over his heart in the faint breeze, and no machine guns either. He stared back at his guards in the same
state of reprieved disbelief as he had felt when his interrogators left him alone after he named the two dead men,
Tresckow and Oertzen.

"Now you know what is going to happen to *you*."

But no. It had not happened. They were pulling him away
from the shooting range to a low building, and all he could
think was the one word: *incineration*. The low building was
the crematorium. They had just promised him death by shooting, a supposedly honorable death at which it was traditional
to shout, "Long live the Führer!" And here they were, dragging him toward an oven. He could smell seaweed and see
white dust on the floor, the doors, the walls. But there was no
dust on the coffin in front of him. Shoved hard from behind,
he almost collided with its side, realizing he had seen this coffin before. Up came the lid to reveal half of Tresckow's head:
mottled, greener, and with the bone showing through like pale
good-quality cork. Months had passed. In Brandenburg the SS
had assembled the Tresckow family round the grave, reviling
them as the digging went on. And now, once again, here was
his old friend, whose body he had escorted home for burial

with full military honors. Shocked as he already was, he felt some unspeakable seam deep inside him open up as he peered in spite of himself at Tresckow's head, withered and rotting, though the body seemed more or less intact. He tried to cry, but could not. He heaved dryly, but managed not to throw up. He looked away, only to meet the eyes of the officer in charge of him, who with an odd, half-amused shyness, had promised him death on the ranges.

"You'd better confess. This man is dead. Give us the names of the living." It failed. Schlabrendorff, his mouth parched from mingled fear and nausea, said not a word, but stood there with head slightly bowed. There was a thump of gas igniting and Tresckow's body went into the flames. Instead of being shot, Schlabrendorff found himself being driven back to prison, where he decided to withdraw his admission about Tresckow's intentions; it had been extorted from him by torture, and this he was going to say, if he got a chance, at his trial. The evidence against him was trivial, so far at any rate, but for how long could he hold out if they began torturing him again? In fact they left him alone, although his torment was by no means over.

Again and again the Gestapo were amazed by the frankness with which members of the opposition spoke without being interrogated, even without being asked. The point was that they were accustomed to giving evidence to courts of honor selected from our peers, not to blabbing in the presence of police thugs with twisted mouths to match their lives. They went down like ninepins, but the rattle was a kind of music.

"I stand by my friends of July twentieth," Haeften's brother Hans Bernd announced in court with caustic finality. "I abhor murder because I am a Christian, but in Hitler I see the supreme embodiment of evil in world history." Off he went with Klamroth and Hayessen and Helldorf, the last of whom they forced to watch the other three being hanged, even pinching him to keep his eyelids open. It was Helldorf who, not long before, had shown Gisevius his chevalier's cross, newly received, stroked his handsome new uniform, and said, "The whole system is too damned shaky for them to dare to take the police chief of the country's capital to the gallows!" August fifteenth, they showed him otherwise with vile punctilio. Helldorf's ant was free.

Three days later the infamous Kluge, for once not dithering, set off by car eastward from Paris for the old battlefields of the previous war, just as Stülpnagel had. It was midday and the sun was stunning. West of Verdun, Kluge called a halt, had his simple lunch plus a bottle of champagne spread out on a rug laid beneath an oak tree, then asked for an envelope in which to put a letter for his brother.

"Get everything ready in about a quarter of an hour," he told his aide, "and then we'll go on." He soon snapped a phial of cyanide and swallowed the poison, dying a clever death only ten miles as the crow flies from where Stülpnagel had shot himself. Finding Kluge sprawled out by the remains of the lunch (he had actually taken a few bites and a drink), an orderly exploded in frantic shouts. Kluge's body lay in state for almost two weeks in the church at Böhme, where it was eventually placed in the family vault. A death by heart attack, it was supposed to have been; he *should* have died of shame. "No military honors," S'gruber rasped after the post-mortem; he was right.

Almost a week later, Carl Hans von Hardenberg, who had married Margarete von Oven, one of our secretaries-extraordinary, was sitting at dinner when the Gestapo broke in from the corridor and marched into the adjoining room, the door of which was open. He and the countess could see them, and they the two of them. He rose, bowed to Margarete, and advanced to meet the intruders. Shots followed. He sank to the rug, having wounded himself in the left chest, but also one of the Gestapo. Now they mounted guard over the couple, but Hardenberg managed to seize the paper scissors from his writing desk and shoved the point into the revolver wound. And still his heart beat on.

He came to in bed, with a doctor by him, whom he at once asked to leave him alone while he cut the veins in his wrist. The doctor agreed, Hardenberg lost a lot of blood, and was taken to jail for medical treatment. Weirdly enough, he survived to talk about it all, as good at suicide as some of us at Latin. Perhaps he was just too healthy, having been a big man for hunting in the marshes, the fields, or the forests.

Kurt von Plettenberg, an old friend, had taken up boxing in the early days. "My delicate constitution," he explained, "needs a little firming up." So he boxed, with funny helical motions of his arms as if intercepting moths; but when his day came, he went like a Spartan.

"Who else was in the conspiracy?" the Gestapo asked.

He refused to speak and was given twenty-four hours in which to reconsider; then he would be tortured as Schlabrendorff had been.

"I shall take my own life," he told Schlabrendorff, "before I reveal a single name." Toward noon that day, as he was being removed to a room on the fourth floor, he knocked down the official who had been questioning him and leaped through a window to his death on the pavement of the prison yard. Perhaps, as a former boxer, he had felled a guard as well. No one would install *him* in the Unter den Linden Museum as a classic of creeping paralysis.

32

"Peking Sky"

◆

At his trial, Adam Trott, as if at some in-between point in a lecture he was giving, had thrust his thumbs into his belt behind him, pushing his shoulders up and making his open jacket furl sideways like an academic robe. It was being handcuffed, though, that made him stand like that, as if inviting everyone present to take him on. They did. His giant brain hummed with it all, told the head prematurely to go bald. His face was puffy from merciless interrogation; but no Rhodes Scholar would be *exactly* prepared for such an outcome. Walking by moonlight in the quadrangle of Balliol College, Oxford, he recited poetry to himself, most of all Hölderlin. Goethe's he thought the greatest German life. Oxford found Trott richly attractive, but also elusive; not so the Gestapo, who did not relish his high mercurial flow that ran through all sides of all questions. His interrogators wanted him to turn his grays into blacks and whites, which struck him as intellectually boorish.

Then the long wait: "At today's meeting with SS Oberführer Panzinger the following emerged: (Von Trott zu Solz will be condemned to death at the next session of the People's Court, probably on Tuesday or Wednesday of next week." He was, on August fifteenth, only to have to wait again. "Since Trott has undoubtedly withheld a great deal, the death sentence pronounced by the People's Court has not been carried out so that Trott may be available for further clarification."

Phonograph records of children singing. Full volume.

Insult and injury, as to Schlabrendorff, after seeing the four other condemned hauled off in the Plötzensee truck for immediate execution. That honed aquiline glower of his, and the frown forcing the bridge of his nose into a furry welt, watched them out of sight until he made as if to lunge, but the affable-mouthed bespectacled policeman who had previously held on to Berthold tugged the handcuff. The policeman looked as if he might enjoy a bit of fishing when business was slack.

August 26th, they finally shrank Adam's IQ to zero with one of their standard double loops. They'd heard him out.

Had cord never snapped? Did they use the same one twice? Ever? No one had asked. Why should he care *what* they hanged him with? His black matted body hair bristled as he twirled. "Last meeting with the examiners!" he told someone who can no longer be found.

"A sower," he also said, "is reluctant to leave germinating seed for others to look after, for between sowing and harvest there are many storms." His eyes were violet, his long domed cliff of a forehead reminded me of the Droeshout portrait of Shakespeare. He was mortified when he took only second-class honors at Oxford, and he would never become a Fellow of All Souls, or again wave from the roof of an old medieval building called the "Barn" to invite a girl friend, ensconced on the roof of the Warden's Lodgings, New College, to go for a jaunt on the river. Adam had wolf-whistled the Prince of Wales in Beaumont Street, Oxford, in 1933, and had told his friend A. L. Rowse that Germans rejoiced in *Sturm und Drang*—all that hectic and poisonous emotionalism—because "unless we live that way, we feel we are nothing." At the Balliol Commem. Ball in the same year, he and Diana Hubback danced together until dawn.

"Why should I sleep," he asked in 1944, "when there's so much to do? Besides, *old* people don't need that much sleep anyway." I thought he was kidding, and I winked hard.

"But you're only thirty-five," I said in a milky, teasing voice, but he seemed to hear me only from afar, nodding at me.

"No, I've had this conversation before," he said with combative jaw. "I'm at least sixty, and I'll never be younger. I think I've done what I was supposed to do in my life, whatever was asked of me—and I'm ready to die."

"A dishonest and ambitious climber," Freisler called him, "who must be thrown back into the sewers from which he came." On the day they hanged him, he wrote to his wife, "There is a clear 'Peking sky' and the trees are rustling."

The day after August 29th, when he had achieved soldierly bearing on a cot at his ludicrous trial, admitting all with marmoreal candor, the blinded Stülpnagel was led by two ogres to his hook.

The hangman found him a novelty and held up the action, to taunt him, indeed to swig from the cognac meant for witnesses.

"Never fear, my lord, we'll soon have you away. There's many as wish they *couldn't* see. It's the last look as gets them going. But you, you could come in here, and a roomful of dangling corpses wouldn't be any bother at all. I wouldn't need the black curtain—wish I'd thought of that. Kind of forgotten you were coming, highness. My God, I must say I like the occasional blind one to polish off. Shot yourself, did you? I heard about that. Well, this is the way you *don't* prefer, then. You'd better shoot straight next time! Not that there'll be one. Elephants will walk up chickens' assholes before you get another shot. Right, let's have you now. Heave-ho. Upsadaisy! *Ready,* my lord? This was Karl Heinrich in his day, a real general. Let him go, lads, easy now. I'll bet he can see again. Look at him popping. I do declare, I think we've found the cure. Now, let's give him a chance to finish off. Only two more." The air roared with filth and pain as Stülpnagel gave up the ghost.

In fact, they paused five minutes to watch the blind man twirl, foam, and spurt. Another cognac.

In and up went Linstow, just as speechless with shock as he

was in Paris when the bad news came in. This time, no water to revive him, though.

Then my old friend Ebo Finckh, last seen in Paris. White hair, but a florid, youthful face; now he was the color of blood sausage. We would never tour a gallery again.

Next the change from rope to guillotine, in November. A man with undulating eyebrows, a face of jaunty sensitivity, and a heavy pointed jaw beneath which a hint of double chin led downward to prominent neck cords, General Lindemann, who was to have read our proclamation on the radio, found a Berlin family to take him in. Until September third he survived, then leapt from a third-floor window. Or tried to leap; the police shot him in the legs and stomach. The price on his head was half a million marks. For six weeks he had posed as a retired major and journalist named Exner. Now they operated on him to save him for the hangman-guillotiner, but he ripped off his dressings and died of his wounds on the 21st.

The Gloeden family received unspeakable interrogation. Some did. On November 27th, Freisler's court condemned Erich Gloeden, an architect, to death. All through, he had claimed that his wife, Lilo, and her mother had no idea who their houseguest was. A "General Lindemann"? Never.

"I knew from the outset," Lilo protested to the court. "I wish to die with my husband."

Then her mother, Mrs. Kusnitzky, spoke up: "I too knew. We were all in it. Life will have no further meaning for me after their death. I wish to join them in their fate."

National Socialism obliged three days later in Plötzensee, beheading them at two-minute intervals: man, wife, mother, in that order, not even allowed to huddle together on the way to the block, arms round one another, eyes full of love, the two younger hurrying the older one to the door before she can think of it: *Mamma, we're coming, we'll be together in a matter of moments, it's only a small transition*, and only willing to engage in such a fiendish maneuver because their own lives, no longer worth living either, were forfeit. Eyes closed against scalding tears. They wanted it to happen to them at the exact same time while they looked into one another's faces like three parachutists hovering in mid-air; but the guillotine was not thus designed, and the waiting mother heard its slamming hack twice before they hauled her through and strapped her in, right over the as yet uncoagulated smears, her mind and body a distant relay station full of hideous buzzing and a twitch so fast it rippled through her.

Röttger and his two assistants had a field day.

And then they received Fellgiebel, but not before he had given them a run for their money. Wavy hair, chalk-textured skin, with moles, and the just-so mouth backing up the scholarly look of his round spectacles. A master of whimsical scorn, he withstood three weeks of brutal torture before yielding up the first name, but was candid from the outset about his own role. "You'd better hurry up with the hangings," he told Freisler, "or you'll hang before we do." A man, he was being tried by a court one of whose deputy judges was a baker, another an engineer. When they hanged him, he was a mere remnant, a durable wraith, with no Hereafter to take him in.

"Did you," they asked him to the end, "have a direct wire to Switzerland to reveal the Führer's plans?"

"Only a regime of trash heads," he kept answering, "which itself had land lines to Athens and Lapland, would ask such a damned silly question as that. My only wire was to God, and it went dead long ago."

33

Slag

◆

Uncle Nux, he bore the entire thing with militant indifference, as if long ago in Hungary, where he was born in 1877, he had invented his own caustic against death. "The leaders of the present regime," he had told the Gestapo interrogators, "ought to be tried before a properly constituted court of law." He had nothing to lose by then.

"Give us the list of names, grandfather," they told him, "and you can go back home to your rocking chair."

"I am a soldier. I was involved heart and soul in the conspiracy. It was all I lived for. I wanted to kill *him* from the first. I would have killed any of you. I would do so now if only you'd provide me with a weapon." He coughed a little blood and foam. "I beg your pardon. A man's ultimate weapon is his life. My sister told me that. I have nothing to tell you. The only one I knew was my nephew Claus. I had two lists: one of whom to kill, the other of who would replace them. If you want a model for behavior, copy Claus. Otherwise you might as well pack up and settle on the island of your choice with the bitch of your preference, you'll get no more guidance from me. Above all, don't make me measly offers of my life. I'm proud to give it up." They beat him unconscious and let him be, a harmless but contaminated old crank whose presence in the world offended them out of all proportion to his deeds.

And, in the end, when they tired of him and his barbs, they wiped him out, a family in one man; and, if they could do that, lowering a cord past the feathery hair just above where his sideburns would have been had he had them, what of the others? The women? Alexander, our surviving brother, and Melitta, his wife?

Little dog woofs from Nux's mouth blotted thought out. He went fast, without goodbyes. He went among the gone, yet, in a weirdly sickening way, not half so *finally* as when, rousted out around 0400 hours on July 23rd, he had thundered briefly at the Gestapo who tugged him this way and that: "I need a map, dammit, and my good old binoculars. Where the hell am I going? Would *you* go out ball-naked into the dawn? With nothing to read, no aspirin, no umbrella, no toothbrush, nothing to write your impressions in, your favorite samovar, a box of mentholated pastilles for your nose and throat, a rug, a box of cig—"

"Can it, grandpa, you won't even need to shit."

"My bowels, you bilious young puppy, are my own affair. Let's keep it that way. When I need advice, I'll mail them to you in a shoebox. Now, do I have to fetch these things myself, at *my* age?" He did, and then he stood erect and dumb for half an hour, waiting to go.

They at last threw his suitcase after him into the van, where he sat like an infuriated squirrel, giving himself a high-speed shoulder-scratch, oblivious of everyone and muttering, "You won't get Claus, you *can't* get Claus, you've blundered there, and the next bomb will shift you all."

No, I had set off my bomb in the dead center of my own family, slaughtering and jeopardizing *them* in the interests of their own future. Thank God my father hadn't lived long enough for me to give him to the Gestapo too. An officer with a finer regard for life and death would have killed his loved ones off beforehand, just in case. Oh, Stauffenberg, the sitting ducks you left behind.

At one point, in Buchenwald, there were ten Stauffenbergs, eight Goerdelers, Hoepner's brother . . . A punitive anthology, almost too many to manage; the only place to keep them would have been a loving mind.

What were they doing to them, other than shunting them back and forth as the Reich got smaller and smaller between the two converging battlefronts? In cattle trucks. Some to Stutthof. Others to Lauenberg. Some to Buchenwald, Sachsenhausen, and Dachau. While their men lay bound hand and foot in brilliantly lit hovels, receiving the special dispensation that went "If more than twenty blows are to be administered, a doctor must be summoned."

"We have your wife, your children, your parents. How can you refuse to answer?" Amazing to relate, some did, either not believing it or making up a cold-stone policy that no longer counted the cost. How many died not as men but as homuncules of slag, blackmailed into an agonizing moral death? Refusing or giving in, it cost lives.

October ninth: Halem, hands shackled, managed to write a last-minute note to his mother. The Gestapo found it and read it operatically, with boisterous sadism, even as he walked his last steps. "I have now overcome the last little tremor that seizes the top of the tree before it falls." He heard their stammering laughs, their viscous braying. "And so I have attained the goal of humanity, for we can and ought to endure consciously what the plants undergo without consciousness.

"Farewell, I am being fetched. A thousand kisses. Your son." They screwed it up, threw it down.

At least it wasn't one of those they folded up into a crude paper airplane, or a dart, and sailed up and down the corridor between the two rows of death cells. Crying in uncouth blurts, "It flies no higher than he will! He's airworthy today, and no parachute either!" And it cannot have been one of those read with jeers, then rubbed to and fro until its fibers were bent or broken enough to serve in the lavatory. Whence came that awful quotation "I wiped my ass today on some asshole's last words"? From Plötzensee? Why not. It wasn't the only death sink in the country, but it worked non-stop.

On October fourteenth Generals Burgdorf and Maisel took

poison to Rommel, who told his wife, "In a quarter of an hour
I shall be dead." Off he went in the small green car with the SS
driver. On the way to Ulm, Maisel got out with the driver.
Then the oafish Burgdorf, who strode up and down, slogging
the bushes with his stick. When they got back in, Rommel was
slumped forward and sobbing, with his cap off; but the SS
master sergeant driver set him upright again, good as dead or
not, and put the cap back on.

"Give him a heart injection at once," Burgdorf yelled on arriving at Ulm hospital. "He's had an embolism!" Such was the
cover story for the general public: "natural causes."

"An autopsy, you mean," said the chief physician.

As a matter of fact, a large wreath had already arrived in
Ulm by train that morning, and a study group had already
been considering the finer points of something entitled "Se-
quence for a State Funeral (R.)."

Rommel's relatives were struck by the expression of colossal
contempt on his face, such as they had never seen while he
lived. As if he were holding his breath. Stülpnagel in his delirium had uttered Rommel's name. To lay a false trail, as well as
to make himself seem grand, my cousin Hofacker had used it
repeatedly; and so had Speidel, Rommel's chief of staff, for
reasons of his own. I knew, but who else? that in 1906 Rommel
and a school friend had built a glider that looked like a collapsed windmill, and it actually flew, but no great distance.
His military career, for the greater glory of S'gruber, had tak-
en him into posterity as a gallant pinup. In 1915, on the western front, he kept a fox as a pet. In the desert, his lips cracked,
as did my own. He hated piano music. But in the end who
cared?

Hofacker next, just before Christmas. They found him an
extraordinary man. "I," he told his interrogators, "acted with
the same justification on July twentieth as Hitler had when he
fired his pistol into the beer-cellar ceiling in Munich, November 9, 1923, and proclaimed the national revolution!"

He was thinner, but his eyes burned still in their puffy sockets.

On he went, loud and civil. "I myself assume full blame for the events in Paris, and I am only sorry that I myself was not chosen to carry out the attempt on Hitler—in which case it would not have been a failure."

How could he have been so wise and known so much and not become famous? No Hofackerstrasse; but no Rommelstrasse either.

"I several times offered myself to Stauffenberg for just that purpose." He paused, but noticed that Gestapo had come in from more boring cellars to hear him out.

"You," one interrogator jeered, "a man with a wife and five children: how could you do such a thing? You—"

"Stauffenberg had four. We both could count."

In the conspiracy's shadow cabinet, Hofacker was to have been Ambassador to France, so no wonder his gestures weren't small. "I know," he'd said, "my life is forfeit."

Now he had a real audience of goons, thugs, intellectualist sadists, most of them in short sleeves; the work in the cellars was taxing. Hofacker was in full cry.

"Besides, what do *I* care about wife and children when Germany is at stake?" He streamed with undabbed sweat.

Vigny's "Suffer and die speechlessly" was not his final style; Caesar was Caesar to the end, except when, under unspeakable torture with fire and dental tools, he told of the part played by Rommel, Kluge (precious little), and Speidel, who was lucky enough to survive to be interrogated postwar by a young American assistant-professor-of-history-to-be.

Caesar received a pre-obituary from the interrogators: "the most dangerous internal enemy we have found in Paris." Then from SS General Oberg, who called him "a dangerous enemy of the state, *but what a man!*" They hanged him in Plötzensee five days before Christmas, removed his children from their mother, split up the daughters from the son, Alfred, and told them they would all be boarded out separately with various SS families, to be properly brought up, renamed.

"Your mother is dead." A lie.

Christa wound up in Munich, sharing a room with a young contemporary of famous name, Utha von Tresckow, and allowed now and then to telephone the nine-year-old Alfred. They were in so-called children's homes, with no photographs of anyone.

"They have taken away all my money," thirteen-year-old Christa told Utha. "Even Daddy's and Mommy's pictures." She knew her parents had been imprisoned, but nothing more. As the year wore on, some of the children died of this or that illness (scarlet fever was rampant) and the survivors spent much of their time sheltering underground from non-stop air raids. Some shelters were not deep enough; more children died.

"What is your *name?*" demanded a nurse in heavy tweed kilt and a blouse with a linen front. "*What?*" It was a voice of aggressive rectitude, stopping just short of the vocal prelude to a smack. A mode of speech learned in zoos.

"Hof—"

"*Never!*" Too absolute to be addressed to a child.

"Christa, then." A bit of Caesar's effusive truculence.

"Say the other name. You are not to use the one you were going to say. You must be grateful for your new name: *Franke.* You are fortunate to be alive." The linen breastplate heaved.

"What about my parents?" Christa had her father's pluck without, so far, his passion for the starring role.

"There is no news. You had best forget." Her tone echoed it.

Utha had known for months that her father was no more, but the fact didn't help her to forget. Nor would knowing that he blew off his head with a grenade. Next thing, the two girls were separated and there came into Christa's room, in front of a nurse dinosauric in starch and brogues, a darkish-brown-haired, quite tall little girl with a concise, almost grave face.

"Valerie Meister," said the nurse, turning on her heel with a linoleum squeak. "She does not know air raid drill. Children walk on the *shadow* side of the street. Tell her now."

The two were alone, staring at each other as if they knew each other; but they had never met in person.

"Not *Meist'*," said the four-year-old. "My name is *Stauffenberg*. My daddy killed the Führer." She sighed.

"*Hitler* is still—alive," Christa told her with a ravenous hug. "That's why you are here. Don't worry, I'll take care of you. I'm big enough for that." A motherly kiss.

"My daddy, then?" She already had his obstinate pout.

"Don't you know?" Christa's eyes opened and froze.

Valerie shook her head, having failed to assimilate the rumors and counterrumors of the last few months. She knew some people, her parents included, were missing, but not why, and she converted me into a hero I never was. Instead of a bungler. I caught my own child in *his* net.

"Nobody knows yet," said Christa, hastily improvising. "The one thing is, we don't want to get blown up by a bomb. So when you hear ... " Air raid instructions followed, but diluted and made into a beguiling game. There stood Valerie, a four-year-old hostage, whom I risked in order to do something that just might not expose her to the chance of being a victim. History's boomerang had never been more cruel.

It was almost Christmas, but not even S'gruber celebrated.

Through some fluke, the guillotine was dry. It would be ten days before they despatched my dear friend Julius Leber, whom the Gestapo arrested ages ago on July fifth. I had never got him out, as I'd promised; I never saw him again. His name came up time and again in Kaltenbrunner's interrogation reports to S'gruber, but never anything he'd *said*, even under the obscenest torture. Six months of taciturnity while his body exploded with pain (his mind too, since the Gestapo had seized his wife and children too, she straight from hospital).

At his trial, back in October, he'd flayed Freisler with invin-

cible scorn, his scarred hands tugging the lapels of his shabby
coat, and the heels of his worn-down shoes moving slightly up
and down, answering one tirade with a mild observation delivered from as far away as Andromeda: "That is an error. In re-
ality it *was* so." Was that not just how Hofacker used to talk in
Paris, his back against some balcony or other, theorizing lucid-
ly and implacably? "What are our chances, Caesar?"

"Ten per cent," said with sibylline hauteur.

Leber, an abrasive and incisive hawk, loomed over Freisler
with his pummeled jaw and transformed him into a bungling,
cross forensic ham.

Christmas 1944 was a tired farce in a grim land at the end
of the worst year: green leaves and red berries, green for inex-
perience and red for bloodshed. The condemned kept themselves busy by rubbing the dirt off their skins into little black,
dank balls rolled together to make a pea-sized one, which they
then revolved between finger and thumb until it fell.

34
1945

♦

The cannonade of gruesome things extended into 1945, befouling yet another digit. In a tiny cellar, by candlelight, a few of
Leber's surviving friends heard his last message, written with
only minutes remaining to him. The one who read aloud un-
rolled the slip of paper as he read, tilting its curvature to the
light of the flame. The words came in clusters, from an unbro-
ken man, whom I failed to rescue.

"One's own life is a proper"—he twisted the little scroll a bit
as the flame guttered—"stake for so good . . . and just a cause."

He passed it to one of the others. "We have done what lay in . . . our power. It is not our fault"—a gentle triple knock on the cellar door—"that things turned out like this, and not otherwise." He put the tiny roll of paper in his mouth, and the cellar flooded briefly with light as the door opened. Someone had a hurricane lamp. Frau Leber stood on the threshold nodding with militant grief. "Is it true . . . ?"

"Is it true?" Her voice was moss-soft, incredulous, bereaved. Nods in the heaving gloom.

"The . . . thing is over?"

Turning her face away from them all, she said simply, "They had no chance to get him out. Claus would've. Now they are together. There's a peace of sorts in that. It's as if they've managed to do the thing together. It's more than nothing. Their honor's final now."

It was January fifth, but it seemed a day deprived of month or year, a capsule of black filth in which Leber's caliber of mind and contour of face took on an eternal dimension while the act that ended him faded away from unthinkable, into vulgar, into myth.

January 23 they made away with Kaiser, the enigmatic diarist, and Planck, son of the renowned physicist: two men who held books close to their eyes. And with refocused gaze they read, even as their heads fell.

Just over a week later, the day after they dragged Goerdeler from his condemned cell while he shouted, "Let me write a few last words, for the love of God!" Schlabrendorff went back to Freisler's court. Air raid sirens wailed. Waves of Allied bombers flew right over the building. The court broke up as everyone ran, but police guards refettered Schlabrendorff in order to take him downstairs. There he was, staring across the dim, dusty cellar at his accuser, who was just an ordinary crude-faced, lascivious-looking curmudgeon of a man, his mind not on the case at all, but on the bombs, with utterly no rights over them. Then one came through the roof and hit the cellar ceiling, collapsing a beam right across Freisler where he stood, still clutching Schlabrendorff's folder: not the end that thousands would have chosen for him, but *an end* to him, his blood lust, his hooting vilifications, his mediocre leers. Although he did not actually die until in hospital, the top of his head, as Schlabrendorff saw it through the dust and smoke, seemed to lift free as if tapped away by a breakfaster's spoon, whereas some would have trepanned him with a potato peeler over several weeks.

"Freisler's *gone*," Schlabrendorff whispered, electric with news, to Admiral Canaris on his return to jail. "He's *dead*. He must be."

"How? Shot?" Loud flushing sounds from an overhead cistern. Canaris, the master spy, doted on stealthy marksmanship.

"A bomb, a beam." Schlabrendorff mouthed it, and Canaris's face shivered around the axis of his nervous eyes.

"How can he be dead? *Freisler* dead?" Canaris was almost shouting with exhilaration.

"He is," Schlabrendorff said confidently. "We'll never hear from him again. He's pulp." He limped away.

The news made its ragged progress through the cells, provoking stunned giggles, prayers of thanks, and, in a few, a freezing rage because now he'd never hang from one of the short thin cords he'd meted out to hundreds with such bullying aplomb.

The ways of God are marvelous, Schlabrendorff kept thinking. I was the accused, and he was the judge. Now he's dead and I'm alive. He's judged and condemned and disposed of and I'm going to survive. A lawyer turned army ordnance officer never knows his luck, by God. With God. At the hands of God. All along, I've known, I've just *known*; they can't kill everybody, after all, can they? Only one in a thousand. Am I that one? Are the odds a thousand to one against or just fifty-fifty? Who's the best mathematician in here? My hunches aren't those of a lawyer, yet it's by *them* I live on.

Between then and March sixteenth, the date of Schlabrendorff's postponed trial, "Goliath" Fromm got his reward in Brandenburg Prison. As they shot him he cried, "Long live the Führer!" the standard last phrase for those granted the "clemency" of death by rifle fire (restricted to those still enamored of his name). Initially accused of breaking court-martial regulations on July twentieth, but in the end condemned for cowardice, Fromm never quite believed in his fatty heart of hearts that they'd do it to *him*, never recovered from his shock at being lumped with the five plotters *he'd* had shot. Now he knew how it felt to be in the minority and to have the body's pump smashed to bits with invisible hot lead. Was he, in the end, parodying me?—I who cried, "Long live holy Germany!" He wasn't thinking any such thing; he was merely uttering the only thing left him to hold on to. He knew they could not miss his vast tank of a chest, or even the round hole in the center of his tubby chin.

Now, after five postponements, Schlabrendorff's trial finally began in a city without water, electricity, or food. A raw potato was manna. Conducting his own defense, attorney Schlabrendorff took on the vice president of the People's Court, who knew nothing of him whatsoever.

"More than two hundred years ago," he told the court, "Frederick the Great abolished torture in Prussia, but it has been used on me." All the details followed: the spikes and the racking and the beatings and the cold-water douches and the abuse, followed by the heart attack. Schlabrendorff wept openly and no one spoke for a full minute. Then, with composure renewed, he completed his case, arguing that Habecker, the commissioner of police, should be brought to trial for using illegal methods. "He should be charged forthwith."

Questioned out of court, Habecker had not denied using torture. The public prosecutor moved for Schlabrendorff's acquittal. What else could he do, with a jurist after him?

"Without, however, being released." Insult to injury.

The Gestapo didn't need a court case to inform it about its doings; only recently the ancient torture chamber in the Burg at Nuremberg had been re-equipped with devilish modern appliances. He returned to prison in the same green car.

And they taught him the meaning of words he thought he understood. "Sign here, Schlabrendorff. It says that, since you have been acquitted, we will shoot you instead of hanging you. We wish to close our file. This is a Gestapo concession. Accept it now. Your acquittal was an error, but we'll let it stand." In a numb dream he signed, a few days later hearing Habecker tell the guards, "Keep a close eye on that one. We have something in store for *him*."

Now the green car ferried him to the extermination camp at Flossenbürg, in the Upper Palatinate Forest, where the Nazis murdered those whom the court had acquitted or whom it had never taken the risk of judging publicly. Again he was in chains, but this time the chain was attached to one wrist only and he could move around in a half-circle. By climbing on a stool he saw out through the tiny window near the ceiling, but the only sight was that of prisoners carrying bodies in the early morning downhill to the funeral pyre because the crematorium had broken down.

He could hear, though: British prisoners singing "Land of Hope and Glory" and "Roll Out the Barrel." At five or six in the morning, when the executions began with loud voices and incessantly barking guard dogs, he heard the condemned being awakened with the cry "Out you come!" and then a slap-pad of bare feet along the stone-flagged corridor, followed by the order "Get undressed!" from the area of the bath cubicle near the guardroom. At his window again, he saw the blaze of light from the arc lamps in the execution yard and, sometimes, through a crack in the door, pale naked bodies reeling past, their shorn heads drooped forward; but he did not see the wooden roof projecting from the west-end wall, or the hooks and nooses fastened to the supporting beams, or the little step-

ladders beneath. He could imagine. Compared with this raucous arena of horrors, Sachsenhausen had been quite genial,
and he wondered if he were going insane to think something
so outrageous.

A guard burst into his cell, machine gun raised. "Your
name? Quick, your name, slowpoke!"

Mumbling the name, "Schlabrendorff, Schlabrendorff," to
memorize it, the guard went away, only to come storming
back. "Liar. *You* are Bonhoeffer, the clergyman."

"I am not, I am *not. Is he here?*" Again the guard went.
Schlabrendorff had come to know Dietrich Bonhoeffer in the
Gestapo prison, where they had exchanged a few words in the
shower or through the cracks of the door hinges when their adjoining cells were opened up. Cigars, apples, bread, sent weekly to Bonhoeffer, had become part of Schlabrendorff's fare, as
had Bonhoeffer's even-tempered quips.

On one occasion they got more time than usual, and Bonhoeffer had an apple for him, offered with ironic affability.
"Take it, Schlabrendorff. I have connections, I'm afraid. I get
extras. I'm even allowed a walk outside, which I'm afraid I will
not let you have! I've even seen Admiral Canaris, strolling
about in a suit and tie. He has connections too, as you might
expect with the former Chief of Intelligence, in disgrace or
not."

"Good God, *I* saw him at the sink in the washroom, holding
on for dear life, as if he were going to faint, naked and scared
to death." Years ago, Canaris had advised Schlabrendorff never to deal with the British secret service: "They do not pay particularly well, believe me, and they'll betray you in a flash."

"God," Bonhoeffer was whispering, "is not a demonstrable
entity. The Admiral is. His life in here is a mixture straight
from hell. He's quite unfitted for it, whereas the cabarets and
cafés of Madrid and Estoril. . . . Ah, that's different. You know,
what bothers *me* most, apart from the brutality here, is that I
have no calendar; I try to go by the Church's holidays, but I

never really know when even they occur. My niece baked me some of those S-shaped Christmas biscuits, but they ended up at another communion than mine! Never mind, there'll be other years."

"One or two, less a few. Sorry: lawyers are more sceptical than theologians, Pastor. The brutality bothers me so much that nothing else does. I've no faith in their good will, if you see."

"Faith to you, I suppose, is just another of the ways of not knowing?" Bonhoeffer sighed slowly and amply.

"It's more than that. It's the *best* way of not knowing."

"As you say. Here they come. Hard to believe it, but that awful noise is a warder's voice, a human throat."

"Good night, Pastor. Don't you loathe doors?"

"Our Lord's tomb had a stone in its mouth."

"It had no number on it, though, did it? Rest well."

"In God's hands, Schlabrendorff, wherever we are."

Exchanges like these had taken place only a few months ago, but had ended abruptly with his arrival at Flossenbürg, and now the same SS guard who had accused him of being Bonhoeffer flung in some bread and jam like a bloodknot on a slab of oak, laughing with sadistic zeal.

"We had a good time this morning, Schlabrendorff. We hanged some men of the counter-intelligence. There was a court-martial in the camp laundry last night, see. We gave some of them a good drubbing too. Traitors and scum, they deserved worse." He motioned at Schlabrendorff to eat the bread and jam; the gesture befitted a small boy refusing a crust.

"Who?" asked Schlabrendorff, beginning to quiver.

"Judge Thorbeck had to bicycle all the way from Weiden to here! Standartenführer Huppenkothen did the rest." More guffaws.

"Who, then?"

"Canaris, Oster, Sack, Bonhoeffer, and some others. Feeling lonely now, prisoner Schlabrendorff? They found old Canaris's private diaries, see, and the Führer said he'd been too lenient. Sent special instructions about Canaris too. We made him watch the whole show, then hanged him six times and revived him five. Once for each of them, see. Up, down, up, down. It took forever to do, but it showed him how the Führer felt. We just patted his cheeks a bit to bring him around, let the breath come back and his color go normal, then strung him up again. *He* won't trouble the Führer any more!" The image of Canaris blotted even Bonhoeffer out, as if they were all hanged in the one man, and, for one last time, Schlabrendorff saw the little white-haired admiral: lisping and nattily frail, forever popping pills, sleeping a dozen hours, phoning from enormous distances to check on the bowel movements of his dogs. Canaris had been famous, and now a gross death had replaced his picturesque, hedonistic life.

They threw Bonhoeffer's Bible and a volume of Goethe into the camp guardroom along with a few rings, a pencil, a pair of spectacles. His connections had finally failed him.

Now Schlabrendorff heard the distant bang of American guns and the quite different explosions when the shells landed. A guard appeared. "Get ready to go." Off came his chain.

"Get *what* ready?" He had only blue prison clothing and canvas sneakers. Off to Dachau. In the camp courtyard for a head count, surrounded by SS with yelping, vicious dogs. His name was missing from the roll, for which the SS abused him vilely, while he thought, I am alive only because of a last-minute oversight. I was never meant to leave Flossenbürg at all.

Now, chainless for the first time, he shared with, of all people, the Bishop of Clermont-Ferrand the SS guards' former recreational room, its filthy walls daubed with giant vulvas, broom-long penises, toilet scenes that only Helldorf could have savored to the full. It was a sordid little Pompeii. Next thing, Schlabrendorff sauntered out in quest of a razor, which he borrowed from another prisoner. There were few guards. The bishop shivered with terror while Schlabrendorff shaved.

Then the trek to Innsbruck camp, where the column acquired a new prisoner: General von Falkenhausen. "This war is almost over," he said. "Believe me. Believe the map." He showed them all how the Allied armies had advanced.

Next through Austria, into Tyrol, picking up more and more prisoners all the time, including the circus clown Wilhelm Visintainer, Goerdelers, Hofackers, and Stauffenbergs, and Molotov's nephew, former French President Léon Blum, and some Greek generals. Virtually free to come and go, they wandered around, introducing themselves with nervous, oblique formality.

"How do you do," uttered with chaste reserve, and in no way interrogative.

"*Enchanté.*" An air of festivity, for all their rags.

"Aren't *you* . . . ? Of course you are. Such a pleasure."

And then a whole series of impetuous interactions: "So-and-so is here. You'll really have to meet. I have the honor to present. . ."

Some German soldiers attached themselves, their rifles pointed submissively down on slings. Would they shoot the SS guards or vice versa? Would Italian partisans kill them all, the prisoners too? The prisoners had to wait in the rain in Niedernhausen City Hall, where some stood guard lest the whole column be wiped out while it slept.

Next morning, in came the foul-mouthed SS master sergeant in charge of them. They braced themselves for the death sentence and its immediate execution. He grinned.

"I wish the arrested gentlemen," said the bully after removing his cap, "a good morning." Everyone was stunned except von Falkenhausen, who observed in a voice commandingly loud: "*Now* Hitler *has* lost his war!" No one disputed it.

"We treated you well," said the master sergeant. "Will you now please write it down—certificate of good behavior?"

No one would. The SS disappeared to be shot and dismembered by the partisans. The British prisoners took charge, saying, "We've won, *we*'ve won. Half this lot's Germans after all." The non-British milled about weeping and applauding, embracing and praying. The bishop blessed, the clown juggled, the Greek generals danced a step or two, and General Franz Halder, my old idol, amazed but grateful to be among this motley crew, removed his monocle and polished it long and slow in the morning sun. The frail, white-maned banker Thyssen clapped his hands against opposite bicepses after folding his arms—an odd, contorted gesture of relief—and Léon Blum tried to make a speech but couldn't unstick his lips. On the fringe of this group stood a young-faced, uncannily self-possessed clergyman, smoking a pipe: Pastor Niemöller, in whose Dahlem church I had gone to pray on the evening of July nineteenth.

On May fourth, an American general addressed them in cautious, sanitized English, having come freshly from his tailor. He gleamed in his knife edges and immaculately fitted collar and tie.

To Verona by jeep, three ex-prisoners to one driver. To Naples by plane, where in a former hotel Schlabrendorff ate and smoked his fill. The few Russians vanished as discreetly as the SS. The remaining prisoners now went to the Hotel Paradiso on Capri, where they received generous and civil treatment, but were not allowed to leave the grounds.

In June, Schlabrendorff acquired an American car in Wiesbaden and drove to his mother's home in upper Franconia, a region of evenly rolling and melancholy plateaux, where his wife and children had taken refuge after leaving Pomerania ahead of the Red Army. He passed through Würzburg and Bamberg, a deformed piece of itinerant meat, his bones cold enough to be full of snow, his heart a snoozing strawberry.

A woman was approaching him on a bicycle. He stopped the car, got out. His wife rode unhurryingly up to him, dismounted, leaned the bicycle carefully against the car, and stood there looking at him in the act of looking at her through his thick lenses and with his mouth a sagging slash, his hair much thinner, the whole of him years older for the ten months of his arrest. Their weeping was voiceless.

There was no Stauffenbergian equivalent of this, nor of Schlabrendorff's visit in August to the rubble of the Gestapo prison in Berlin, where he picked his way to the stairwell that led down to the cellars and cell 25, murmuring other numbers and other names as if irrevocable hell, like some film reversed, would rise up again and, this time, in a blur of sulfur and roasted skin, engulf him too, even if only, as the Gestapo told him, "to close his file."

VII

35

Aunt Lassli

♦

It was six months since Nina, sitting in front of my mother's house on the last day of my life, had in unstated amazement heard a passing official yell, "An attempt on the Führer's life!" It was teatime, and they went on sipping tea, while my mother mused on fate as a dragon and Nina's heart began to beat upward as if to unseat her brain.

Next day, Nina heard I'd been shot, and she and my mother clung to each other, stunned in their tears, alone with that gross finality. On July 23rd, the Gestapo picked up the whole family. Had Nina stayed in Bamberg and not made the trip we had discussed by telephone ("I'm sorry, but the bags are already packed and loaded"), the Gestapo would have had her on the 21st, when she was not ready. While the governess tried to keep the children together, Nina went into solitary confinement in the Alexanderplatz, Berlin: five months in disgrace, after which they transferred her to a cellblock in Ravensbrück, where life was raucous and stark. To have our baby, however, she was taken to a maternity home in Frankfurt an der Oder, where she had a private room, freedom to turn her own lights on and off, and something even rarer: a handle on the inside of her door, a little sop to privacy. The door locked from the outside anyway. Once each week she was allowed a bath.

To be alive but awaiting trial and execution, imagining my beloved giving birth in a pauper's room provided by the Third Reich, would have been a humbling agony. I had never quite accepted the helpless stewardship of women as, century after century, the race seeped and bulged inside them, then blasted a way through them into the air. Legs forked wide, with their most private organ swollen beyond mucous flower into a delivery hatch for heads, they heaved away at the world in the most durable form of bittersweet known in history, while we the sperm bearers waited in the margin, anxious and trivial. We made war, I thought, only because that fruitful violence of giving birth was denied us; what our loins put forth was tiddlers, and then we had to find something else, in that banana republic of the flesh we males embodied, to keep us busy. Never did we have that bloody avalanche of the future from within our guts; and when we reached down, easing the sit in our underwear of an awkward tube and a prune bag stuffed with two silvery beans, we felt more important than we were, whereas, when women eased themselves, they found a helix of oysters which nonetheless was a miraculous human manger, elastic and coral and moist, a law beyond laws.

So Nina once again, for the fifth time, did that down-bearing shunt, a widow and alone, almost as if her man were coming back to life, slithering through her pain on a sheet the color of skin. A heave. A writhe. A chunk of gristle battling into the air. A scream of triumph when the butting head, propelled from above by her galvanic belly, came free, and she softly bayed, "Claus, Claus, *Claus*," as if an accommodating heaven had sent me back to *be me* again, while overhead the bombers droned and defecated death.

My three boys were born in summer, my two girls in winter. Now there were five, still subject to the ice-pick mercies of Himmler and his black-suited sadists. This new one had a taut and sneezing face; born into an historical volcano, she had every right to cry and cough.

After Constanze was born, on January 27, Nina had only a week's peace before being shipped off to the St. Joseph's Hospital in Potsdam as "Frau Schank," a name that fooled no one, least of all her doctor, who'd been sympathetic to our cause and still was, even though the thing seemed lost. "*Frau Schank*," he said with a bow, "I have never been so honored. Your true name is in your face, and in my heart."

And in mine too, through some unspeakable knack of post-mortem possession: hoarding, caching, secreting, a last bit of my flesh that mouthed on against time and decay, begging forgiveness from and return to the Nina who knitted and dusted, who stayed home among the bombs when there were no letters coming through, who soared on a wave of aromas into and out of the radiant consummation of our Italian honeymoon; Nina of the wild strawberries, Nina of the enfolding arms that held me firm as a kernel in a shell, Nina who dabbed my eye, Nina who steered me with her tact, Nina who made no bones about a mutilated man whose mind, even as she hugged him, heard out a howling germ that kept on saying Kill, Kill, Kill, kiss away but don't forget to kill; Nina, as Dido, with a willow wand in her grasp, trying to bring her true love home again and refusing to remember him (as he her) as a simple sum of syrup and shudder in a bush of hair, not a function but a mystery, not a namesake but an entity more complex than even the race's evolution from blue-green algae all the way to Pablo Casals, and not a heart carved on a tree trunk but a heart cut deep into a human one, whose possessor says, "Is my heart still there, inside, though shot to bits?" only to have her reach inside and lift it out, murmuring, "Dear one, this is *mine*, with its bird-flutter beat, whereas yours is here, held so hard, so deep inside me, its pieces have begun to beat together again as one. *There is no end.* Now I give it back again to make you warm, whose knees and nose were always cold, we never knew why. You never were that strong when young, you never were that old. You warmed at me."

Back in the autumn of 1943, before Stauffenbergs became notorious, with his plump paw Hermann Göring had enveloped the dainty hand of a woman in flying coveralls whose goggles sat atop her leather helmet. She had just received a medal for services to the Reich. My sister-in-law Melitta, my brother Alexander's wife, unstuck her hand and went away, caught between a giggle and disgust.

A year later, heavily rouged, clad in a tunic of duck-egg blue, and wearing on his head the stag emblem of Saint Hubertus with a swastika of pearls flashing between the antlers, Göring rattled a handful of uncut gems in cupped hands above the sheen of his outsize desk, and said his piece with heavy emphasis into his chest. "Very well, Countess, you are no longer under arrest or even open arrest. Your duties will be special and secret. You will go to the Air War Training College at Gatow to train night-fighter pilots in the use of your night-landing device. There have been far too many crashes. You can still be of use, but we would prefer that you use your maiden name, Schiller."

Melitta von Stauffenberg suppressed a sneer. "What about Alexander, my husband? He knew no more about the plot than I." This was true, but Göring had no power, no excuse, and no desire to free him from the arrest he'd been under since July 24. "Live for your work, Frau Schiller!" His unstated *otherwise* made her tremble.

So she began to fly about the country again, taking messages from one sequestered family to another, and not only the Stauffenbergs. She managed to "drop in" at airfields in the vicinity, always under cover of darkness, for the best national reasons, bringing news and gifts. She did this all autumn, through Christmas, well into the new year, an angel of largesse in heavy leathers.

My mother had been back at home in Lautlingen, under Gestapo surveillance, since the autumn of 1944, and Uncle Nux's widow was with her, fidgeting to know where all the children were. Melitta flew in, reported the children were in Bad Sachsa. She used my mother's nickname, "Does."

"Forbidden to use *their* real names," she said with one fist clenched. "I am told the original plan was to kill off the parents and the older children and then farm out the little ones to SS foster parents or to SS-run schools. They have changed their minds on this. Claus and Nina have a little girl, another little girl, born in the Gestapo prison on January the twenty-seventh. Her name is Constanze." On she went, the sound of her voice seeming underwater, reporting that Nina was well, being treated humanely (even some extra rations!), that Goerdeler's grandchildren arrived without warning.

"Rainer, who is four, was crying, and he told Christa Hofacker he wanted to go home—told her in Swabian, at that. The other, Karl, is only nine months old. There is a rumor that the children are destined for Buchenwald, by train from Nordhausen Station. Fortunately the station has been bombed and no trains are leaving. Yet the situation is dangerous. The SS seem in no hurry, but they won't dawdle forever, I'm sure."

The two other women stared at each other in voiceless horror. "What can be done?" my mother asked.

"The war *will* end," Aunt Alexandrine said. "The war is ending. The Americans will help us." One of our old jokes about her was that, like the verse line she evoked, she had one foot too many; but there was nothing ungainly about her now. "Or the Red Cross. *Somebody* will see to it. Somebody will care."

"I am not certain," my mother droned as if gnawing on something, "they will care to bother themselves with *German* children. Weren't we recently at war? Who were those vulgar men in black who took us away? Were they the enemy?"

"Somebody," Aunt Alexandrine told her, "is bound to do something about them. Children are children, the world over."

On April eighth, not having slept properly for several days, Melitta took off in daylight with a pocketful of contraband toys—a car made of lead, a scout's knife, a frail bakelite telescope the size of a baby's hand, some balloons with bear and fox faces, a stick of plasticine—and, humming the refrain of an old drinking song against the engine's chatter, quite failed to see an Allied Typhoon fighter-bomber line up behind her and take aim. Shot down over Straubing, her plane fell into the Danube, and our one line of communication was gone.

On April eighth too, a field gendarme motorcycled Nina in his sidecar some 250 kilometers southward as far as Hof, where she gave him a note relieving him of responsibility for her and her baby. Off he went northward while she trudged in search of relatives in the area, arriving like a gypsy in charge of a piece of the Holy Grail, a picaresque matron with plump arms and a breast full of milk, babbling to everyone about scarlet fever and an overdue operation on the middle ear of our youngest boy, Franz Ludwig. Weirdly, the Nazis had treated her with meticulous care, no doubt in some last perverse fling of chivalry: a jackboot kneeflexed harshly down which made no stamp, no thud.

Also, on April twelfth, the Americans occupied Bad Sachsa, but they had no vehicles for German children. Nor had the Red Cross. The answer was at home in Lautlingen. The French arrived and, by incalculable good luck, the local commander had been a prisoner of war there and treated well.

"I must go," the resilient, persuasive Alexandrine told him. "This family has endured and lost enough. The children have no guarantee from the Russians." She hesitated.

Wet-eyed, he assigned a military vehicle to her, and off she went all the way up Germany to bring the children home, going northward on a line parallel to Nina's journey southward, with about 125 kilometers in between. On May fourth, the new burgomaster of Bad Sachsa made a speech, telling them, "Now you can use your real names again. You have no need to be ashamed of them or your fathers. They were heroes." But he still couldn't procure transportation. After an appalling journey through a landscape of craters and debris, roadblocks and military traffic jams, Alexandrine arrived in Nordhausen on June sixth, collected the children, and left with them in her truck on the seventh, the day the Russians were to move in. The war had been over for one month. Alexandrine's long drive was the earthbound version of Melitta's flights. Aunt "Lassli," as we used to babble her name, won the peace in her uniform of a Red Cross hospital matron. Singlehandedly she beat back what might have been the next installment of death, cruelty, grief, waste, and shame.

All of a sudden, through the Pied Piper magic worked by the indefatigable Aunt Lassli, Nina once more found herself enveloped in fast-growing children, mixing the quietly murmured benison "We are alive, we are together, it truly happened" with stern-faced pursuit of furniture scattered by the SS, who had taken over the family homes.

"They have taken Claus's desk," she complained. "Where is his desk? And the Mehnert bust?" In fact she got them back, put them in their place again as if rededicating a pagan altar, beside which to stand in a homemade peasant dress in the style of 1820, her face raked and tweaked by anxiety, her hands at a curious descended peace below the frills of the sleeves, her expression one of assimilated shock as she looked into the sun, saying over and over, "I am conservative. There can be a future only when the past isn't blotted out."

Claus could have come back and written his memoirs at a desk rescued from a bonfire and, when his thoughts wandered, stared himself out in front of his bronze replica like an angular angel whose wounds had blurred in the sculptor's final pour. None of my dear ones floated dissected in a vat of slop. God was good again.

But only to a point. From time to time, at home on leave in Lautlingen or Bamberg (with my mother and Nux in the one place, with Nina's mother and the children in the other), I'd noticed how an outside light, switched on briefly during the blackout, sometimes imposed the room's interior on the outside scene, table upon tree, painting upon sundial. All that was needed was a big window and enough light. I'd stand inside and watch the two worlds blend on the glass, little knowing I'd found the perfect image for the pressure on the living of the dead. I didn't know my heart would have no chance to break, or that so much emotion saved up for after July twentieth would simply have nowhere to go: no use, no time, no vent. Little Valerie, alive in that time of hell, would die of leukemia at twenty-six, while Constanze, the newest of the new, still in the womb when I was shot, survived and flowered. Did, even then, before July twentieth, the images of those soon to die glide against the images of the living, but invisibly? Was I already, without knowing it, mouthing future pain against the glass? Was my brain's heart babbling, *"Mutti, Mutti,* for something vague I got you shoved into a stinking cell, and Nux and Berthold hanged, their breath actually sealed off, and Nina and the children orphaned, trucked into camps, buried away under aliases like felons"?

And on, and on: "My friends and colleagues tortured, befouled, reviled, dragged shuddering to the block or the scaffold—all for something vague in which vanity played a part, oh yes. Wasn't that why, time and again, I longed for a seaplane to touch down on the Grosser Wannsee and fly all of us away to Brazil, until the red-hot lava of our homeland cooled? My own poorest hours—of glory and of fame, of disgrace and pain—belonged to others, whose lives I stole and brutally cut off. The thousands of the dead had millions of hours to come, all of which, like some butchering pawnbroker, I made miserably cheap. Why didn't *I*, like the wallpaper hanger whom I failed to kill, have an occasional screaming delirium? A Hitlerian fit? How, gambling with so many lives, of those near and dear as well as of those I'd never even met, did I keep so straight a face, a heart so correct, a mind so trim? Perhaps I didn't; I was as limp as moss, as blurred as cloud. I faltered, I dithered, I bungled, I queried, I dawdled, I hung back, I ducked, I hovered, I blathered, I wondered, I asked, I always had a second thought, a Hamlet of the abattoir, *when I should have given my life*—flung it away, but on target, like so much bloodstained newspaper—*in order to wipe out his.*"

Were we fit even to run a nursery or a lettuce garden? We wanted the future all ways. We wanted to clean house, but without soiling our hands. We wanted to kill, but without jeopardizing our careers. We wanted to run the country, but without the faintest idea how to take over and use a radio station or, much more grievous, how to place a bomb. The lethal distinction that never occurred to me was that between an assassin who succeeds by losing his own life in the very act of murder and an assassin whose failure the firing squad makes plain. With S'gruber dead, my fellow conspirators might have done much better with the coup, in practice, than I in theory thought I would. Was Stauffenberg essential back at the Bendlerstrasse on that dreadful terminal day? Only to fan the embers of a failed takeover, inasmuch as only I could insist on trying to wring a miracle out of a mess, whereas Fritzi or Ali, Beck or Schlabrendorff, would have run the coup smoothly even if only to honor my death—a death earlier by only a dozen hours.

Hindsight, conjectured out-of-time, could not affect me then, or point the way to the richest hour of all; not a shoddy, bungled symbolic act, a last-ditch gesture to the Allies and the family of Gneisenau, but an authentic final stitch in time, when Adolf Schicklgruber breathed his last.

England's fault, said Adam von Trott zu Solz, whose name, they said at Oxford, was too long. No, we should have arrested Goebbels, using a few men with revolvers, and offered him a chance to use his suicide pills. And we should have used *both* bombs. And our heads: the trouble with new brooms is that they have bristles for brains. If we had only watched the squirrels more, whose antics round and about the lawns always reminded me of the primitive hunter-gatherers we had been, when we had tails and used the trees, and made no wars on anyone.

Did some prophetic part of me already know what in the end would become of my Russian volunteers? When your life had to be truncated, did it reach past deathpoint for an illicit glimpse of what was going to be? Whether volunteers or conscripts (later in the war, nobody bothered to *ask* them), these wretches were captured by the western Allies in 1944 and 1945, most of them, anyway. The Americans then handed them over to the Russians, who insisted on having them back in order to hang them from the trees on the Russian side of the border. The forests bloomed with men and rope. The British, however, were kinder, describing such Soviet prisoners as "Poles," who then eked out the remainder of their lives deep in the alien British countryside, as lost and dumb as if they had been exiled to the moon.

In my big fresco on the window glass, time had no width, but it hurt, and to peer too close into the source of pain wiped out everything with living breath.

36

Pass

◆

I would always be thirty-six years and four months, yearning for one last ride on Jagd, I stiff-lipped and taut-backed in the crisp swill of winter air, and Jagd gasping and coughing as her perspiration cooled. Then a game of tag with the children, and a ball thrown, a paper glider sharply folded, a small girl tickled with a three-fingered hand. After which, a late dinner for two by candlelight on an old ill-repaired terrace, next to a magnolia bush in bloom: "I love you, I love loving you, I can feel it growing inside me like a diligent pain. I walk about so full I seem to have a meniscus; I might even spill."

I would always be the copper flange in the flashlight, aching for the current to flow through it again, for there to be light. "Arm both bombs, Werner; I'll wait them out this time."

I would always have the same boyhood dream, the cause of many a reverie, wrong in detail but right in shape: An orchard. A clearing. Bees. Vapor of rain. The trunk of an elm. Two patches of bullet holes at head height and heart's. Meat flies asleep in the holes. Blossom. The quiet. Then trucks. Gravediggers. Medical officer. Guards. Chaplain. A coffin of rough wood. The condemned's clean burly jaw. His roaming eyes. His white silk shirt. Manacles. The white card over his heart. The butterfly hovering about his face. The blindfold refused. The crucifix accepted. The sentence read aloud. The orders. The ragged salvo. The cluster of punctures in the white card. The slow clean-up. The permanence of the thing just done. The weird sense that they *all liked* it, even the one shot to death. It would all have been so different if I'd entered history as the man who killed Hitler: the one man, the only.

The old Bendlerstrasse courtyard, an ugly compound reeking of exhaust fumes, echoes with the dispersed and oddly elongated voices of tourists:

"His driver said he lost the first and middle fingers of the left hand." A buxom, oratorical nun.

"The surgeon said he lost *three* fingers."

"Fifth and fourth only." Nina's voice.

"Lost his right hand as well." Schweizer (whose logbook led so many to the gallows).

"Right *arm*." Sauerbruch.

"Right *hand*." Nina.

"Bullet in the head that entered through the eye." Sauerbruch again.

"No." Nina, who knew.

"His first name was Werner." No. Students in sunglasses,

with notepads and cameras, invade the courtyard, eyeing the
plaque which commemorates those shot here soon after midnight on July twentieth. I had a lovely office here, with French
windows and a parquet floor. Now the High Command of the
Armed Forces has its headquarters elsewhere and the Bendler
block houses a cosmetics firm, but you enter the courtyard
from a street renamed the "Stauffenbergstrasse." There is even
a "July Plot" game played with dice, in which Himmler, as in
history, makes his getaway wearing an eyepatch, but which
omits General Stundt, the cannibal, sneaking away to Scandi-
navia and South America, with his mauve pajamas, a pair of
mated matching hairbrushes, and enough gold to feed him till
he dies.

Out go the students, disappointed, into the street I haunt.
"He was only in his forties," babbles one, having read something somewhere. I was not even thirty-seven. Away they go.
These too are among the deaths a hero dies. There is nothing
to *see*, whereas over at Plötzensee the death shed stands, a
shrine, near which the bereaved gather once a year on simple
chairs to dream the heroic agony anew.

We were all shot together. No. Friedrich first. Then I. No,
Werner threw himself in front of me. No. Ali did. No. Was I
shot at all? Or only in a boyish dream? If not, why did I cry
out, "Long live holy Germany"? No, I cried, "Long live *sacred*
Germany!" And Werner cried it too. No, Werner cried, "Long
live *freedom!*" No. I cried, "*Holy* Germany!" No, it was "Long
live *our* sacred Germany!" Nobody knows any more. Two
cried out, Werner and I. The others were silent. Friedrich did
not see which of the other two leaped in front of me. Perhaps
we both leaped upward, crying out in unison, whether shot together or one by one. The zero hour was blurred, and all we
had were names.

There is always something better to go back to, even if only
the statue of "The Rider" in Bamberg Cathedral, whom I little

resembled. Inhale the chill of that Gothic pile. Relish the fluted, ribbed, or squared columns. Honor the medieval prince who rides a stone horse. It is not my face at all. Then look beneath the horse's feet at the acanthus-leaf mask carved on the console. That broad, coarse foliate head, pocked with holes in the shapes of leaves, belongs to the devil himself, and the demented eyes tip sideways into hell. This is not my face either, except for the tincture of blood behind the leaves, like a red berry behind holly: something sacred that goes on, and on, despite the universal feast of death it flowers in.

Appendix A. Names and Places

◆

"Ali" (Mertz von Quirnheim, Colonel Albrecht Ritter)

"Aunt Lassli" (Üxküll-Gyllenband, Countess Alexandrine von)

Bamberg, home of Countess Nina von Stauffenberg; also location of 17th Cavalry

Beck, Colonel General Ludwig, Chief of Army General Staff until resigned in 1938; Head of State designate after coup d'état

Bendlerstrasse, location (11–13) of High Command of Armed Forces; street name used as synonym for the building; later renamed Stauffenbergstrasse

Berghof, Hitler's mountain retreat at Obersalzberg, overlooking Salzburg and Berchtesgaden

Bernardis, Lieutenant Colonel Robert (General Staff); transferred because of illness to General Army Office in 1942

Bonhoeffer, Dietrich, Protestant theologian, scholar, and teacher, member of German Intelligence (Abwehr)

Bormann, Reichsleiter Martin, secretary to Hitler

Brandt, Colonel Heinz (General Staff), assistant to General Heusinger

Canaris, Admiral Wilhelm, Chief of German Intelligence (Abwehr) 1935–44

Cords, Captain Helmuth, in charge of security at Bendlerstrasse on July 20, 1944; a survivor

"Ebo" (Finckh, Colonel Eberhard)

Fahrner, Professor Rudolf, member of Stefan George circle; taught at Heidelberg University, also in Spain, Greece, Turkey; born in Austria; a survivor

Fegelein, SS Gruppenführer Hermann, Himmler's personal representative at Hitler's HQ; married Gretl, sister of Eva Braun; April 27, 1945, in Hitler's Bunker, degraded in rank for desertion and, April 28/29, executed for supposed involvement in Himmler treachery

Fellgiebel, General Erich, Chief of Signals, Wehrmacht, Mauerwald; broadly educated in both natural sciences and the classics

Finckh, Colonel Eberhard (General Staff), old friend of Stauffenberg from Staff College days; Quartermaster with Army Group South at Stalingrad; June 1944 transferred to Paris, on staff of C in C West

Freisler, Roland, Nazi lawyer and politician; President of People's Court in Berlin 1942–44

Fromm, Colonel General Friedrich (Fritz), C in C Reserve Army, Bendlerstrasse; Stauffenberg became his chief of staff in June 1944

George, Stefan, (1868–1933), poet; cosmopolitan and oracular, with perhaps more influence on the politics of his day than on its poets; according to Sir Maurice Bowra, "began as an admiring pupil of Mallarmé and ended as a national prophet." Stauffenberg told wife he had had the greatest poet of his age as his master, and George himself, when asked what was his most important work, would sometimes answer, "My friends," who included the three Stauffenberg brothers and, among others, Rudolf Fahrner and the elder brother of Albert Speer

Gerstenmaier, Dr. Eugen, former lecturer in systematic theology, Berlin University; also worked in industry and, during war, looked after interests of foreign workers in Reich; sentenced to death by People's Court, but got off with seven years; survived to become President of the German Bundestag

Gisevius, Hans Bernd; formerly in Gestapo; worked for Canaris's Abwehr from Swiss base; survived to write biased memoirs of the German Resistance

Gneisenau, Field Marshal Count August Neithardt von; one of the heroes of the war of liberation against Napoleon and cofounder, with General Scharnhorst, of the Prussian General Staff; Stauffenberg's great-grandfather on his mother's side

Goebbels, Josef, Minister of Propaganda from 1933; suicide May 1, 1945

Goerdeler, Carl Friedrich, Lord Mayor of Leipzig 1930–37; from 1937 the main advocate of resistance among the older generation

Göring, Hermann, C in C Luftwaffe; sentenced to death at Nuremberg; suicide October 15, 1946

Haeften, Hans Bernd von, former exchange student at Cambridge; in Foreign Office during war; brother of Werner

Haeften, Lieutenant Werner von, Stauffenberg's adjutant; formerly a legal consultant; joined Olbricht's office in November 1943; brother of Hans Bernd

Hagen, Lieutenant Albrecht von, legal adviser to a bank prewar; served with Stauffenberg in North Africa in 10th Armored Division; with Klamroth procured explosives

Halder, Colonel General Franz, Chief of General Staff 1938–42, when Hitler dismissed him; Stauffenberg close to him from 1940 as subordinate and friend

Halem, Nikolaus von; in early years of war worked in Reich Office for Industry, Berlin; an independent plotter against Hitler and an early advocate of assassination

Hansen, Colonel Georg; succeeded Canaris as Head of Abwehr in 1944; often at Stauffenberg's apartment in Wannsee June–July 1944

Hardenberg, Count Carl Hans von, landowner, associate of Tresckow; married to Margarete von Oven; a survivor

Hase, Lieutenant General Paul von, Commandant of Berlin; uncle of Dietrich Bonhoeffer

Hayessen, Major Egbert, City Commandant Hase's aide on July 20; one of the coup's liaison officers

Helldorf, Count Wolf Heinrich von, President of Police in Berlin; his deputy was Fritzi von der Schulenburg

Himmler, Heinrich, founder of SS, Chief of Gestapo 1936; Minister of Interior 1943; suicide May 23, 1945

Hoepner, Colonel General Erich, commander of armored forces; dismissed by Hitler in December 1941 for disobeying instructions on Russian front; to replace Fromm as commander of the Reserve Army; until November 1938 commander of 1st Light Division, Wuppertal, which Stauffenberg joined in summer of that year

Hofacker, Lieutenant Colonel Caesar von, Luftwaffe officer serving on Stülpnagel's staff in France; a cousin of Stauffenberg's initiated into conspiracy October 25, 1943, when he visited Berlin for a family wedding

Kaltenbrunner, SS Obergruppenführer Ernst, head of Reich Security; responsible for the so-called Kaltenbrunner Reports to Bormann and Hitler about the assassination attempt (published Stuttgart 1961)

Keitel, Field Marshal Wilhelm, Chief of High Command of German Armed Forces (OKW); Hitler's closest military adviser; executed October 15, 1946

Klamroth, Lieutenant Colonel Bernhard (General Staff); with Hagen procured explosives (German-made) which proved unsuitable because the fuse hissed

Klausing, Captain Friedrich Karl; seriously wounded on eastern front, transferred to General Army Office in 1944; accompanied Stauffenberg to Hitler's HQ on July 11 and 15, since Werner von Haeften was ill; Klausing won over to conspiracy by Fritzi von der Schulenburg

Kluge, Field Marshal Günther von, Army Group Commander in France; reluctant to join conspiracy; refused his support on July 20, but dismissed by Hitler anyway

Kranzfelder, Lieutenant Commander Alfred, liaison officer between Naval High Command and the Foreign Office; joined Stauffenberg as soon as latter came to Berlin to join Olbricht's staff; close friend of Berthold von Stauffenberg

Lancken, Lieutenant Colonel Fritz von der, Olbricht's aide-de-camp; prewar head of a country boarding school; kept at his home in Potsdam the explosive used in July 1944

La Roche-Guyon, France, HQ of Army Group B; a château in which the famous Hall of Ancestors became the staff's table-tennis room; the French owners left the original furnishings in place for Rommel and his staff to use

Lautlingen, the Stauffenberg family estate

Leber, Julius, German Socialist leader; spent four years in concentration camps; was to have been Minister of Interior after the coup

Lerche, Anni, Olbricht's secretary at Bendlerstrasse

Lerchenfeld, Baron Gustav von, Stauffenberg's father-in-law and co-owner of the horse Jagd

Lindemann, General Fritz, Artillery Ordnance Officer, High Command, whose main job was to put out feelers to Corps HQ's whose commanding generals or chiefs of staff were old colleagues of his; a friend of Stieff's

Linstow, Colonel Hans Ottfried von (General Staff), Chief of Staff to Stülpnagel

Manstein, Field Marshal Erich von; refused to involve himself in the conspiracy; sentenced by British court in 1949 to eighteen years' imprisonment; later released on medical parole

Mauerwald, High Command of German Army's camp in East Prussia, near Wolf's Lair

Meichssner, Lieutenant Colonel Joachim (General Staff); with Stauffenberg at Staff College, was devoted to him; at first in Organization Section, OKW Ops staff, with some access to Hitler; then posted to OKW Ops in Potsdam-Eiche, but still with access to Jodl or Keitel

Mertz von Quirnheim, Colonel Albrecht Ritter ("Ali") (General Staff), Staff College friend of Stauffenberg's; succeeded him as chief of staff to Olbricht in June 1944; wife, Hilde, diarist

Müller, SS Obergruppenführer Heinrich, head of Gestapo; known as "Gestapo" Müller

Mumm, von Schwartzenstein, Dr. Herbert, former diplomat; collaborator with Halem

Nina (Nina Schenk Countess von Stauffenberg, née Freiin von Lerchenfeld)

"Nux" (Üxküll-Gyllenband, Nikolaus Graf von), Stauffenberg's uncle

Oertzen, Major Hans Ulrich von (General Staff), a career officer in signals; close friend of Tresckow's; excelled at racing horses and cars

OKH (Oberkommando des Heeres), the High Command of the German Army

OKW (Oberkommando der Wehrmacht), the High Command of the Armed Forces (Hitler's staff as Supreme Commander)

Olbricht, Colonel General Friedrich, head of Supply Section, Reserve Army, then Commander of General Army Office, OKH

Oven, Margarete von, secretary to Stauffenberg and Tresckow; later Countess von Hardenberg

Plötzensee Prison, execution prison in Berlin

Rastenburg, site of Hitler's East Prussian HQ: Wolf's Lair

Remer, Major Otto Ernst, commanding Berlin Guards Battalion of the Grossdeutschland Division, at first obeyed orders of the conspirators, then helped squelch coup on Hitler's direct command

Ribbentrop, Joachim von, Ambassador in London 1936; Foreign Minister 1938; executed October 15, 1946

Rilke, Rainer Maria (1875–1926), poet with vast influence on German poetry; corresponded with Stauffenberg's mother

Rommel, Field Marshal Erwin, Commander of the Afrika Korps and later of Army Group B in France; opposed to the assassination, and involved in the Resistance only belatedly and peripherally; forced to commit suicide for disloyalty in 1944

Sander, Lieutenant Colonel Ludolf Gerhard, Wehrmacht signals officer at Wolf's Lair HQ

Sauerbruch, Professor Ferdinand, surgeon at whose home Stauffenberg met with senior conspirators, and whose son Peter, a colonel, he knew well

Schlabrendorff, Major Fabian von, staff officer working with Tresckow on eastern front, and liaison officer between Tresckow and Berlin; author of an important memoir

Schulenburg, Count Friedrich Dietlof von der, Deputy President of Berlin Police under Helldorf; born in London

Schweizer, Corporal Karl, Stauffenberg's driver; a fellow Swabian; unimplicated in the plot

Schwerin von Schwanenfeld, Count Ulrich Wilhelm, a captain at the Quartermaster General's office (Wagner); acted as go-between for the senior conspirators; born in Stockholm

Skorzeny, SS Hauptsturmführer Otto, abducted Mussolini from the Gran Sasso in 1943

Speer, Albert, Minister for Armaments and Munitions; planned an assassination of his own recalled in his memoirs

Speidel, Lieutenant General Dr. Hans, chief of staff to Rommel at Army Group B, La Roche-Guyon

Stauffenberg, Count Alexander von, Claus's elder brother, twin of Berthold, not involved in the conspiracy; husband of Melitta von Stauffenberg, the airwoman

Stauffenberg, Count Alfred Schenk von, Claus's father

Stauffenberg, Dr. Berthold Schenk von, Claus's elder brother, to whom he was very close

Stauffenberg, Count Berthold Cajetan Maria Schenk von, Claus's first son, born July 3, 1934

Stauffenberg, Countess Caroline Schenk von, *née* Countess von Üxküll-Gyllenband, Claus's mother

Stauffenberg, Constanze' Schenk Countess von, Claus's second daughter, born January 27, 1945

Stauffenberg, Franz Ludwig Schenk Count von, Claus's third son, born May 4, 1938

Stauffenberg, Hans Christoph Schenk Freiherr von, a cousin of Claus's

Stauffenberg, Heimeran Schenk Count von, Claus's second son, born July 9, 1936

Stauffenberg, Maria Schenk Countess von, *née* Classen, wife of Claus's brother Berthold

Stauffenberg, Melitta Schenk Countess von, airwoman, wife of Alexander

Stauffenberg, Nina Schenk Countess von, *née* Freiin von Lerchenfeld, Claus's wife

Stauffenberg, Valerie Schenk Countess von, Claus's first daughter, born November 15, 1940; died 1966 (Valerie von L'Estocq)

Stieff, Major General Helmuth, chief of the Organization Branch at OKH, Mauerwald; in 1944 the youngest general; a friend of Lindemann's

Strasser, Otto, brother of Gregor, Hitler's former rival for Party leadership

Stülpnagel, Colonel General Karl Heinrich von, Military Governor in France 1942–44; prime instigator of the coup in France

Stundt, SS Obergruppenführer Rolf, formation commander in Waffen SS until removed from military action on medical grounds and given high-level assignments in Germany; disappeared in 1945; rumored to have been in Brazil and Paraguay

Thiele, Lieutenant General Fritz Walter, senior signals officer at OKH

Bendlerstrasse; recruited for the plot by Fellgiebel, with whom he went
to the gallows

Tresckow, Major General Henning von, chief of staff in Central Army
Group on eastern front; a prime mover in the resistance and deviser of
the Valkyrie plan for takeover (wife, Erika, secretary to Stauffenberg
and her husband in Berlin)

Tristanstrasse, number 8, Stauffenberg's Wannsee address

Trott zu Solz, Adam von, official in the Foreign Office and Abwehr; former
Rhodes Scholar at Oxford; met Stauffenberg in November 1943

Üxküll-Gyllenband, Countess Alexandrine von ("Aunt Lassli"), aunt to the
Stauffenberg brothers; author of a memoir published in Stuttgart 1956

Üxküll-Gyllenband, Count Nikolaus Graf von ("Uncle Nux"), a retired colonel; born in Hungary; uncle to Caesar von Hofacker

"Valkyrie," code name for assembly of units and soldiers present in Germany in the event of domestic emergency—i.e., mobilization of the
"Home Army"; this plan the conspirators incorporated into their own
scheme

Wagner, General Eduard, Quartermaster General at OKH, Zossen; in daily
touch with Fromm's and Olbricht's departments; shot himself in Zossen
at 1241 hours on July 23

Wannsee, southwestern suburb of Berlin where Stauffenberg had an apartment he shared with Berthold and others

Witzleben, Field Marshal Erwin von, C in C West from March 1941 to February 1942; one of the older conspirators; nominated to be C in C of
German Army after coup

Wolf's Lair, Hitler's Rastenburg HQ

Yorck von Wartenburg, Count Peter, with the Eastern Department of the
Military Economics Office; previously served as a tank officer in Polish
campaign; a cousin of Stauffenberg's

Zeitzler, Colonel General Kurt, Chief of the General Staff of the Army, who
posted Stauffenberg to North Africa; successor to Halder

Ziegler, Delia, secretary to Olbricht and Stauffenberg in Bendlerstrasse

"Zollerndorff," Stauffenberg's code name

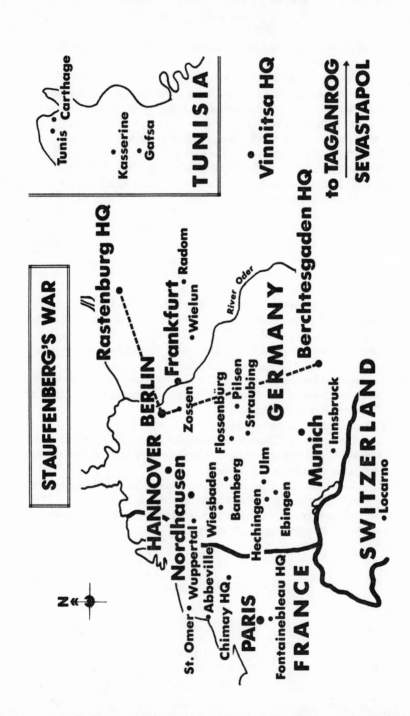

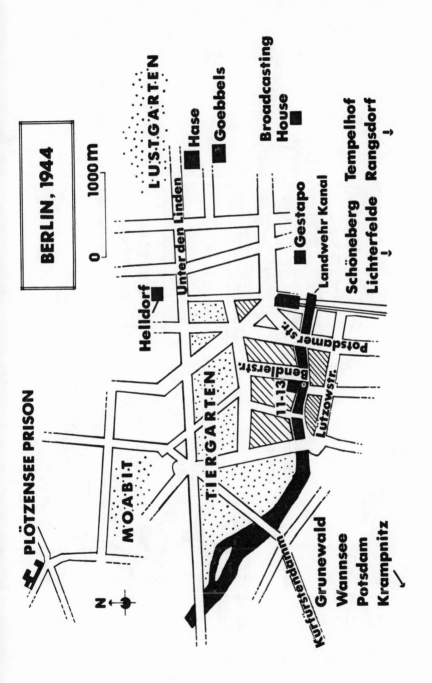

BERLIN, 1944

PLÖTZENSEE PRISON

N

0   1000m

LUSTGARTEN

Helldorf

Unter den Linden

Hase

Goebbels

Broadcasting House

MOABIT

TIERGARTEN

11-13

Bendlerstr.

Lützowstr.

Potsdamer str.

Gestapo

Landwehr Kanal

Schöneberg
Tempelhof
Lichterfelde
Rangsdorf

Kurfürstendamm
Grunewald
Wannsee
Potsdam
Krampnitz

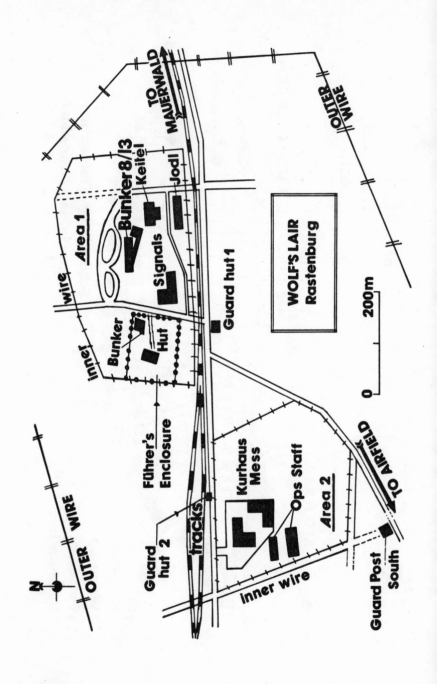

N

OUTER WIRE

TO MAUERWALD

OUTER WIRE

Bunker 8/13 Keitel

Jodl

Area 1

inner wire

Signals

Bunker

Hut

Guard hut 1

WOLF'S LAIR
Rastenburg

Führer's Enclosure

Guard hut 2

tracks

Kurhaus Mess

Ops Staff

Area 2

inner wire

Guard Post South

TO AIRFIELD

0   200m